Innuendo

Also by
R.D. Zimmerman

Outburst

Hostage

Tribe

Closet

Red Trance

Blood Trance

Death Trance

Deadfall in Berlin

Mindscream

Blood Russian

The Red Encounter

The Cross and the Sickle

Innuendo

R.D. Zimmerman

DELACORTE PRESS

PUBLISHED BY
DELACORTE PRESS
Random House, Inc.
1540 Broadway
New York, New York 10036

Book design by Donna Sinisgalli

Delacorte Press® is a registered trademark of Random House, Inc., and the colophon is a trademark of Random House, Inc.

Library of Congress Cataloging in Publication Data

Zimmerman, R.D. (Robert Dingwall)
Innuendo / by R.D. Zimmerman.
p.   cm.
ISBN 0-385-32377-8
I. Title.
PS3576.I511815 1999
813'.54—dc21   99-31966
CIP

Manufactured in the United States of America
Published simultaneously in Canada

November 1999

1   3   5   7   9   10   8   6   4   2

*For Leslie Schnur, for making
this series possible*

Acknowledgments

Many thanks to the usual suspects, including investigative reporter Gail Plewacki, producer Cara King, Sergeant Rob Allen, Dr. Don Houge, Gail and Betsy Leondar-Wright, Ellen Hart, Katie, and Lars. Special thanks as well to Rick Nelson for the inspiration and to Tom Spain for the green light.

Prologue

In the last minutes of his young life, Andrew had never known such bliss.

His eyes covered with a thin black blindfold, he blindly kissed his lover just when they were at their peak. Right there, right at the height of their pleasure, the very one the two men had been humping and groping toward for close to forty minutes, Andrew's mouth locked onto the other man's, sucking, biting, doing everything and anything but letting go. With his eyes covered from the very start, Andrew had no idea what his carnal partner actually looked like, yet he clung to the gorgeous body as if his life depended upon it.

But soon, of course, it was over. They spent themselves within seconds of each other, and then as Andrew lay there reveling in the dreamy afterglow, he wondered if this mysterious guy was it, his Mr. Wonderful. Unable to bear the curiosity, he broke the one cardinal rule, pushing the blindfold up on his forehead and staring right into the eyes of the stunning man who'd just taken him to the stars and back.

"Oh, my God," muttered Andrew in total shock.

"You dumb little shit," snapped the other. "You shouldn't have done that, you really shouldn't have."

Chapter 1

Well, thought Todd, looking down at the mass of newspaper clippings and articles spread on his dining room table, what if it was true? What if one of the biggest stars in America, one of the most famous actors in the world, was really gay? And what if Todd, an investigative reporter for WLAK, actually got an interview with Tim Chase, who was in Minneapolis shooting a film? How would Todd approach it, what angle would he take?

Raising his head, Todd stared out the balcony doors of his condo. An interview with Tim Chase was, to put it mildly, a long shot, but if by chance Todd got it, he'd have to handle it with the utmost care. After all, it was only a year or so ago that Chase had sued one of the supermarket tabloids over a headline that read "Mean Queen Chase Denies 7 Year Gay Romance & Buries Boyfriend in Poverty." And he'd won too. Big-time. While the tabloid had sold completely out of that issue, the story had eventually cost the journal $8.5 million, a sum that Tim Chase's spokesperson said, ". . . clearly vindicated Chase's sexuality." Todd still shuddered at the homophobia permeating that quote.

A shrill ring broke his thoughts, and he quickly reached for the cordless phone lying atop the glass table.

As if it weren't late evening and he weren't at home but still at work, he said, "Todd Mills."

"It's me."

"Hey, you."

Todd glanced at his watch, saw that it was just after nine, which meant that Steve Rawlins, Todd's lover, had less than ninety minutes to go on middle watch. With any luck, Minneapolis would remain murder-free at least until ten-thirty, when Rawlins's shift on Car 1110, which was manned twenty-four hours a day by homicide investigators, was over.

"I wish you'd come home so I'd stop working," said Todd.

"Well," began Rawlins in that deep, buttery voice, "that's why I'm calling. Something just came up."

"Don't say that."

"Unfortunately, it's all over the police bands. You haven't heard anything yet, huh?"

"No."

But Todd was sure he would any minute. If it was all over the police bands, the tip callers—any variety of nerdy informants who sat by their radios—would be calling WLAK and every other station in town with the hot information. Which meant that it would not only be a late night for Rawlins, who would automatically be assigned the case, but for Todd as well. No doubt about it, Todd was going to have to scramble like hell just to keep up with the competition.

"I'm guessing I won't be home until very late, if at all," Rawlins said.

"That doesn't sound good—what happened?"

"Foster and I are on our way there now—I'm calling from his car. All I know is that some kid's gone and got his throat slit."

"Oh, God," replied Todd. "Where?"

"Twenty-fifth and Bryant."

"Got a name?"

"Todd . . ." muttered Rawlins, clearly irritated.

"Well, you know damn well I'm going to find out sooner or later."

Rawlins hesitated before saying, "No, I don't have a name yet. All I know is that it's a young white male."

Todd grabbed a pen and jotted down the address and bit of information, knowing that no matter how hard he tried he wouldn't get anything more out of Rawlins, for the collision of their careers was one of the two most contentious issues between them. The second, which had only recently come up, was whether they should continue to have a monogamous relationship or perhaps agree to an open one.

"I guess I'll be seeing you in a few minutes," said Todd.

"I guess."

They chatted a bit more, and then Todd hung up. As was his habit, he glanced again out the balcony doors at the dark sky over Lake Calhoun and made a mental list of whom he had to call and what he had to do. Next he went into full speed.

Some fifteen minutes later Todd was racing north on Lyndale, thinking that, no, this wasn't like being an ambulance chaser, it *was* being an ambulance chaser, this push, this desperate rush not simply to be the best, but the first. And not simply the Johnny-on-the-spot, but the one with the most dramatic, the most real and gruesome of shots.

Glancing at his watch, Todd saw that it was twenty-five minutes until the ten P.M. Yes, it could still happen. Before leaving his condo, Todd had called WLAK and requested an ENG truck, one of those boxy vehicles equipped with tape decks, video monitors, and a microwave mast. He'd then phoned Bradley, his photographer, at home, interrupting him and his wife in the middle of their favorite show. And with any luck, Todd, Bradley, and the ENG technician would converge at the scene of the crime, get all set up, and start broadcasting live right at the top of the late news, WLAK's *10@10*. If things went perfectly, too, Bradley would still be able to get some tape of that all-important shot, the one of the body as it was rolled away. Then again, who knew just when they'd be taking the body away. The scene was sure to be a madhouse, swarming with cops, the Bureau of Investigation team, and the guys from homicide, namely Rawlins and his partner, Neal Foster, who'd been on duty on Car 1110 since three that afternoon. So it could be hours, perhaps as long as two, even three, before the medical examiner rolled out the victim.

Driving his new Jeep Grand Cherokee, his old one having been smashed in a tornado that past summer, Todd took a deep breath.

Brace yourself, he told himself. Who knew if this would be a great story, but it definitely would be a late night.

In his early forties, Todd Mills was almost too old to be chasing around like this, at least by television standards. He was still in great shape, no doubt about it, and his face, which was almost rugged but definitely handsome with a small mouth and chin and eyes that were much too soft, still attracted attention. He had a full head of medium brown hair, too, the importance of which could never be overlooked in television. But this was a young person's job, and at some point in the not so distant future he was either going to have to make the leap to an anchor position, in which case he'd be one of only two or three openly gay anchors in the country, or he'd have to retreat, per se, to the position of a producer. And if he stayed in the area, Todd was betting on the latter. As liberal and open-minded as Minnesota liked to believe it was, there was only so far, Todd had come to feel, things could be pushed. In other words, he was highly skeptical that viewers would knowingly tolerate a homosexual every night in their homes, let alone see an openly gay anchor as a pillar of honesty and trust. And if even a handful of viewers objected to a gay anchor, that would be one too many for management, which could only be described as skittish.

His truck hit a pothole, of which there were so many these days, particularly on Lyndale, an old street pocked with time, and the entire vehicle rattled. His fingers tightened on the wheel, and his mind skipped back to the official request he'd submitted to Tim Chase's publicity people just last week. What he wanted to find out, of course, was if what he'd heard about Chase was really true. He couldn't deny he'd been all but obsessed since he'd heard the story several months ago and particularly now that Chase was in town. Todd had heard lots of gossip about famous people from friends of friends who knew someone whose uncle was in the movie business, but this was as direct as he would ever get. Marcia, an old college pal, had called Todd up not even two hours after she'd heard it directly from John Vox.

"Oh, my God, Todd, you're not going to believe this!" she'd exclaimed.

While Marcia had appeared in a couple of commercials, she'd never made it literally beyond the role of a Skippy mom, and so she'd gone back to school and gotten a degree in accounting. However, John Vox, one of her instructors from Northwestern, had eventually left the university and been "discovered," becoming not one of the big stars, but establishing himself as a quality actor known for his wide range. Now in his mid-fifties, his blond hair gone gray, his cherubic face interestingly lined with time, he was in recent years becoming America's favorite bad guy, playing every part from conniving con man to corrupt congressman. And just a few months ago when he was in Chicago playing some loan shark in a film based on an Elmore Leonard book, Marcia and he had had lunch at the Ambassador Hotel's Pump Room. They talked about it all, Marcia's life in the corporate world, her divorce, and eventually John's films, including one that he'd done a couple of years ago playing an evil traitor opposite none other than America's favorite, Tim Chase.

"You know, John, I'm sorry, but I gotta ask you this," said Marcia, leaning across the table. "I mean, I know he's married to Gwen Owens, and, my God, she's *sooo* beautiful and such a talented actress. And I know they have a little boy. But I've heard this rumor—and of course there was that big lawsuit when he sued some magazine or something—so you gotta tell me, is Tim Chase gay or isn't he?"

The way Marcia told the story, John Vox covered his mouth with his fine white napkin, leaned back his head, and roared with laughter.

"Well," demanded Marcia, unable to bear it, "is he or isn't he?"

"Let me tell you," Vox finally said, his face all red, "Tim is a great guy. And a real pro, too. I mean, he's one of the finest actors around because he wants to do it right, get it right. He's very smart—always picks good scripts. And his wife, Gwen Owens, was a wonder—she brought their son and spent a week on the set. And make no bones about it, they are devoted parents."

"So, get to the dirt, already, alright!"

"Well . . ."

"Well?!"

"Tim had a lover, a very nice guy, very handsome, who lived with him right in his trailer."

"You're kidding!"

"No. And everyone knew it, from the gaffer on up."

"But what about . . . what about Gwen Owens? Did she know?"

"Actually, things did get a little messy. I can't quite remember the sequence of events, whether she flew over and then Tim and this guy, Rob, had a huge fight, or . . . or they had the fight first and then Gwen came. I don't know. But Rob was there, all over Tim, for about two-thirds of the time we were shooting in Europe."

All of that was whisked out of mind when Todd turned a corner and saw an orchard of cherry lights throbbing in the late-September night. Parked this way and that, cop cars and an ambulance filled the narrow street, a déjà vu image of autumnal pandemonium that conjured up the darkest time of his own life.

Quickly scanning the area, Todd noted a boxy electronic news-gathering vehicle off to the side, which unfortunately wasn't theirs but WTCN's. Great. That meant not only that the competition had beat him to the scene, but that his former coworker Cindy Wilson was probably lurking somewhere. Looking farther ahead, he saw a photographer with a WTCN camera hurry across the street, and beyond him a crowd of gawkers. Cindy, he guessed, was already worming her way to the body, going for some grisly shot.

Driving at a crawl, Todd pulled in front of a thick old elm, parked, and got out. The night air was chilly and damp from a slight, early evening rain, and Todd caught the gentle but distinct smell of smoke. Yes, he thought, as he made his way across a mat of sodden elm leaves, the lucky ones were home in front of the first fire of the season.

Wearing black jeans and a maroon shirt, black leather boots and a black leather coat, Todd crossed the street and zeroed in on the vortex of tonight's attention, a dark brick apartment building. Three stories tall, the structure was rectangular and squat, the kind that had been built in this neighborhood, the Wedge, in the teens and twenties. Studying the flurry surrounding the building, Todd noted the cops slipping on latex gloves as they rushed through the front door, and saw the dozens of people held at bay by a band of yellow police tape. Spying a knoll in the park across the street, he thought that, yes, that might be a good place to do the shoot. It wouldn't be the tightest angle, but they'd get the apartment building, the flurry of flashing lights, the cops darting around, and, of course, the tantalized crowd. A great background indeed.

"Todd!"

He looked over, saw Bradley pushing through the crowd, his camera, a large Betacam, held awkwardly under his arm. A tall thin man with skin as dark as the night, he had a small face, short hair, and now wore khaki pants and a blue nylon jacket.

"What's up? What happened?" asked the photographer.

"I don't know anything more—I just got here too."

"Any sign of the ENG?"

"Not yet. It'll probably be another five minutes or so. I think they sent Jeff," said Todd, referring to the technician who'd been assigned. "Listen, I gotta try and find Rawlins, see what he can tell me."

"Sure."

"Why don't you get some footage—let's say fifteen seconds of cops, ten of real estate. And ten of the crowd out here."

"Sounds like a plan."

The band of yellow police tape had been set up at the sidewalk's edge, and fifteen or twenty people stood crowded around, trying to see what was going on. Todd peered through them all, but Rawlins was not among the cops out front. Undoubtedly he was inside along with the B of I guys, who were surely already going at it, documenting anything and everything.

Coming up next to a guy with a shaved head and a pierced nose, Todd asked, "What happened?"

"This guy got himself fuckin' killed."

"Really? Who?"

"Our new caretaker, that's who."

"You live here?"

"Yeah. And this guy—he just started a month ago, moved into the basement apartment behind the laundry room. Young guy too. A kid."

"That's awful."

"No shit."

"What was it, drugs?"

He stared at Todd with angry eyes. "How the fuck would I know?"

Todd shrugged. "What was his name?"

"Fred Flintstone," he said, turning away.

It was a start, anyway, but if Todd was going to do a live story in a few minutes, he was going to have to dig up a hell of a lot more information. Glancing to the side, he saw a small woman with big blond hair, who was laughing and smiling and batting her eyes at a young cop who looked like he'd eat right out of her hand. It was Cindy Wilson. Some things never changed.

Someone in plainclothes emerged from the building and ducked to the side. If there'd ever been such a thing as a press badge, Todd wished he had it now. Equipped with nothing more than a business card, however, he knew there was no way he'd get past the police barrier, and so he shouted out.

"Rawlins!"

Without lifting his head, Rawlins circled a birch tree and headed to the distant end of the police tape. Todd scooted out of the crowd and around, staring the entire time at the other man. Seeing Rawlins raise one hand to his eyes, a tremor of worry rippled through Todd.

Hurrying up to him, Todd said, "What's going on?"

They stood with the yellow tape slowly rising and falling between them, and at first Rawlins shrugged and said nothing. Todd, however, could see that the other man's eyes were red, which was odd because Rawlins was more than used to this kind of thing. Sure, Todd had held this shorter, stockier guy as he sobbed over the death of a friend from AIDS or when Rawlins, himself, had discovered that he was HIV-positive, but he'd never seen him teary, not over murder. This was business, his business, and when it came to that, Rawlins was as butch as the next investigator.

"What's up? What's wrong?"

Rawlins bit his lip and looked away, obviously eager that the other cops didn't see him. More cute than he was handsome, he had dark hair and a short dark mustache, not to mention those dark brown eyes, all of which were usually lightened by a smile, broad and quick. Long ago he'd decided what he lacked in height he'd make up in beef, and so he was broad-shouldered and stocky, a borderline muscle queen to be sure. Tonight he wore blue jeans and a brown cotton jacket.

Finally he muttered, "Oh, fuck."

Todd reached across the tape, touched him gently on the elbow. Jesus, what had happened in there? How horrible was it, and just how had the purported young white male met his end?

He asked, "You been in?"

"Yeah."

"And?"

Rawlins wiped his eyes, said, "He . . . he was just a kid."

"Who?"

"Wait a minute," said Rawlins, catching himself and remembering who was who and just why they were both there. "We haven't notified the family yet, so this isn't for public consumption, okay?"

"Sure."

"I'm serious—you can't go on the air with this."

"Of course I won't."

"Well, then . . . oh, shit. I can't believe this. I mean, he—"

"Who?"

"Andrew—he was just seventeen."

At first the name rattled without an echo, but then Todd began to remember that wonderfully charming grin, the toothy one.

"My God, you don't mean that kid down at the DQ, do you?"

"Yeah."

"Oh, shit."

The Domain of Queers, or the DQ, was the official youth center for, as Todd called it, the corporation of queers: gay, lesbian, bisexual, transgender, and the sexually questioning. One of the few such centers in the country, it was located in an old ballroom above a drugstore on Franklin Avenue, and it operated both as a haven for runaways as well as a center for fostering pride. Todd and Rawlins had spoken there twice, talking about the closet, which Todd knew far too well, and about finding and developing a healthy relationship, which the two of them were inching toward. Getting still more involved, Rawlins had joined the mentoring program.

"When I was a kid," Rawlins had ranted not long ago, "we didn't have any heroes. There was no one to look up to, no one to show that you could be gay and happy. And, you know what, it did zip for my sense of self-worth. I don't want to be invisible too."

Yes, Andrew was Rawlins's first mentee. Todd remembered the cute kid and that engaging smile, a young man whose folks had kicked him off the family farm when they found out he was gay. Over the course of the last two months Rawlins had taken the younger man out to lunch a few times and had even given him a tour of the police department.

"Oh, my God, I can't believe it," Rawlins now said, his eyes beading with tears as he looked back at the entrance of the building. "He was a smart kid too. Really capable."

"I'm sorry."

"I . . . I was trying to help him see that being out and being gay didn't mean limiting what you could do. He was even talking about going to law school."

"You were good to him, Rawlins. You were already making a difference in his life."

"Evidently not enough."

"Don't start thinking like that," Todd softly said. "There was nothing you could have done."

"He was really proud of himself, proud of getting his own apartment and everything."

"Someone out here said he was the caretaker."

"Yeah, he took care of a couple of buildings around here." He took a deep breath. "Oh, my God. Why?"

Why would anyone want to murder a nice, energetic kid who had a productive, robust life ahead of him?

Todd said, "I don't know."

But he was wise enough to know that this would be a well of obsession from which they would both drink for weeks if not months. He just hoped it wasn't a bottomless one, for the search for the truth was a compulsion to them both, to Todd the investigative reporter as well as to Rawlins the homicide investigator. Just as a number of gay people had become psychologists in an attempt to understand what made them different, just as a number had become artists to explore their individuality, so had Todd and Rawlins chosen fields where truth was paramount. That was what they had in common most of all. No, actually it was what they had in common more and more, because initially for Todd his career had been all about image first, substance second.

Todd hated to ask. Fearing the answer, fearing that it wasn't a simple robbery or argument gone bad, he took a deep breath.

"What happened?"

"I haven't heard too much yet, but he's lying in bed with his throat slit. Chances are he picked up some guy and . . . and . . ."

Oh, shit, thought Todd, he didn't want to have to go on the air with this. "And they had sex?"

"Yep."

He knew what that meant. And he knew how, in the greater scheme of things, the reportage of this crime was doomed to go. It wouldn't be seen as an argument between friends gone horribly wrong. Nor would it be looked upon as someone killed by a lover. No, by and large this would be treated as it had been treated historically, an incident between two deviants, who by their very nature were so twisted that of course they couldn't help but kill.

"That means we have a gay murder on our hands."

Rawlins opened his mouth to confirm, then caught himself, remembering the thin line that divided them, and said, "Is that what the media's going to say?"

Chapter 2

Clutching the green plastic bag in his right hand, the unseen man crept through the dark and pushed through the thick lilac bushes. He trotted lightly over the first of the fall leaves as he made his way right up to the wrought iron fence and peered through the bars. On the other side and across the lush green lawn stood the yellow brick house, an enormous dwelling built in the 1890s for a lumber king who'd made a fortune hacking down the northern woods and floating the timber down the Mississippi. Searching the property, he turned slowly, his eyes following the front walk all the way to the gate that opened onto Mount Curve Avenue, a twisting street lined with any number of old robber baron mansions. He couldn't be sure, but when he'd driven slowly up Mount Curve, he thought he saw someone waiting in a car. Whether it was a fan, a stalker, or a photographer hoping for a shot, he couldn't tell, but he most certainly had to be careful.

Even though it wasn't that cool, he wore gloves, lightweight brown ones, and he tightened his grasp on the dark green plastic bag. He surveyed the house and its grounds one last time, then confident that he couldn't be seen, reached out with his left hand and took hold of one of the thick iron bars. Not wasting a moment, he put his right foot on a crossbar at the bottom, then started pushing and pulling himself up. In one quick swoop he was atop the iron fence, then jumping down on the other side. Landing on the soft ground, he hurried forward and sank behind an hydrangea bush. No, there was no way anyone had seen him. No way anyone would even suspect.

The house itself was one enormous rectangular box constructed of brick and covered with a slate roof, a structure built like a palace and meant to last the centuries. The place was dotted with any number of windows, all of which had their curtains pulled shut for privacy and many of which now glowed with light. The large piece of property, covered with a glen of oaks that swayed like exotic dancers in the light breeze, sloped downward from the street. At the rear of the house a basement-level room opened onto a terrace, and next to that stood the garage, built sometime in the teens or twenties and, with the Minnesota climate in mind, politely attached to the house. He just had to get there, just that far, just to the garage, and everything would be fine.

From his hidden spot, he checked the street one last time and tried to ascertain if they were up there, any of the dreaded paparazzi. He didn't doubt it, for they were always lurking around, hoping for that one photo that would make them rich. After the death of Princess Di things had quieted down, but now they were back, hungrier and worse than ever. A picture of Tim Chase and Gwen Owens kissing and holding hands wasn't even worth five grand, but a picture, say, of them fighting might bring upward of twenty thousand. And a shot of any star in the nude or perhaps kissing someone other than his or her spouse would bring dramatically more. With prices like those it was no wonder the photographers were as aggressive as they were. Just two months ago Gwen Owens herself had been nearly forced off a mountain road by three swarming photographers on motorcycles.

Like the best of spies, he crouched over and darted across the lawn, racing across the open space and right up to the edge of the house itself. Reaching several towering old arborvitaes, he paused behind their evergreen branches. Yes, so far so good. He was, he knew, just outside the living room window, and he listened but couldn't hear any voices from inside. That, however, didn't mean much because the six or seven people living here could be anywhere in the huge place. The kid was probably upstairs with either Gwen or the nanny, the personal trainer was perhaps either working out in the basement or was up in his room, while the cook was, as usual at this hour, probably watching the food network in perpetual search of new creations.

Moving along, he crept through the bushes planted along the foundation of the house. He passed beneath a series of high windows, then came to the rear corner of the house. Peering around the edge, he saw the lawn fall away and then, below, caught sight of the old patio, which was now submerged in darkness. Not far beyond stood the garage. From here, even in the faint light, he could see the side door.

More eager than ever to be rid of it, he clutched the plastic bag and felt the long, menacing blade of the hunting knife within. Yes, he thought, you've almost made it. You've nearly done it.

Chapter 3

Knowing what he did about Andrew, knowing without question that he'd most definitely been gay, Todd also knew that he had information no one else did. Which, in fact, was the ideal situation for any reporter to find himself in. Unfortunately, Todd was none the happier for it.

Once Rawlins had pulled himself together and returned to the small apartment in the basement of the building, Todd studied his competition, this circus of media activity zeroing in on the meat of their business. Cindy Wilson and her WTCN crew were claiming turf, setting up equipment so that the apartment building door would be right behind her. Another ENG truck had arrived, this one from WMDW-TV, the third of the local affiliates. And off to the side, Todd took note of a reporter, a tall thin guy from Minnesota Public Radio, who was speaking into a small digital cassette recorder slung from his shoulder.

So in the space of about fifteen seconds, Todd realized that if he broadcast live from here his coverage would be just like all the others. And that just wouldn't do when he possessed the opportunity to do something different, which of course was the name of the game.

Much to his relief, he finally saw WLAK's big white ENG truck pulling up and parking on 25th. He then pulled his cell phone from his black leather jacket and dialed the station, getting immediately through to the assignment editor.

"Steve, it's me, Todd. I'm here at this murder scene—along with every other reporter in town. It's kind of a zoo, but I think I've got a way to come at this thing that's entirely different."

His was a deep voice that was no-nonsense, no-shit, just-get-to-the-point. "So what do you want from me?"

"Another photographer—right away."

"Oh, come on, Todd, give me a break. Do you know how short-staffed we are tonight? Besides, you've already got Bradley, and he's the best. Plus you got the ENG van. That's more than plenty."

It was all about resources and the limit thereof, Todd knew that only too well. To get what he wanted, therefore, he knew he was going to have to come at this one hard. And big.

Keeping his voice low, he said, "Steve, like I said, this is a very hot scene—and this is potentially a big, big story."

"Yeah, yeah, yeah."

"Listen, I knew the guy who was murdered. I met him a few times. He was only seventeen." He paused not only for effect, but to make sure no one else could overhear. "And he was gay, which is why I want to do the report from another scene."

There was only an instant of silence. "Let me check this with Craig."

Todd was parked on hold while Steve went to confer with the ten o'clock producer. It took all of five seconds.

"Okay, I'm sending Mark," said Steve. "He's already on his way out the door."

"Great."

"Just don't leave until he gets there."

"Of course not."

That was one thing you never did, leave a site like this unattended, not at least until it was cleared. It might be hours and hours before the police left, but who knew what might happen during that time, and so you sure as hell didn't want to miss any shots. Or worse, leave something for one of the other stations to get.

"So where are you going?" asked Steve.

"I knew where this kid used to hang out. I want to get some footage from over there."

"Okay, so what do you want to do, a VOSOT?"

No, thought Todd. A voice-over-sound-on-tape would require that at least part of the sound—say, an interview—would be married to the videotape. But Todd couldn't guarantee that, not with so little time. All that he could hope for was a simple voice-over.

"No, let's just do a VO."

"Sure."

Todd hung up, then searched the crowd for Bradley, finally spying him, camera on his shoulder, as he photographed the crowd. Todd wasted no time in working his way over there.

"You got it all laid down?" he asked.

"Yep, and then some," replied Bradley, who was sure to have gotten extra footage. "The cops, the crowd, the real estate—all just like you asked."

"Great. Let me take the tape over to the truck. You stay here." In a low voice, he added, "We got another photographer on the way. As soon as he gets here, we're leaving."

"Just say when."

"Cover the front door in the meantime."

"You bet," replied Bradley, handing Todd the tape then loading another.

Todd wound his way through the crowd, a growing group of gawkers who were simultaneously stretching their necks and gossiping in whispers. As he neared the street, he saw that the ENG truck's mast, a towering pole with a microwave dish atop, was already fully raised. Even though they weren't all that terribly far from the Golden Valley station, everything would have to be bounced off their downtown antennae.

Todd came to the rear of the truck and knocked once. Jeff, the technician, immediately opened the door. A young guy with short red hair and a pasty complexion, he had a mountain of energy, which was usually what it took to get into this business. And last more than a few months.

"Hey, Todd."

"I want you to feed this back to the station right away. We're going to do a VO, so they're going to have to edit it. I want fifteen of cops, ten of real estate, and ten of the crowd."

"Sure, thirty-five seconds in all."

"Right, and as soon as you've sent that, I want you to pack up and go to this address," said Todd, taking out a pen and paper and writing it down. "Park across the street so we get full angle. And don't make any big deal about getting out of here either. Just do it as quickly as you can. We'll shoot live from there."

"Yep."

Todd turned back to the crowd, studied the scene, tried to get the story rolling in his head. Seeing a clump of neighbors gossiping, he thought he should drift over there, see what they were talking about, glean what they might know.

"Hey, Todd."

He turned to see an attractive woman with big blond hair and a big fake smile. She wore a puffy olive parka that made her slim body look all the trimmer, gray pants, and black shoes. Todd bristled immediately.

"Hi, Cindy."

Not so very long ago, during his days at WTCN, she'd worked for him. For a while they'd attempted to be a team and even pretended to be friendly. But then, of course, Todd had been accused of murder and she'd feasted on the story, hoping that Todd's demise would propel her rise. She had far less talent than she did ambition, though, and she was still groping for that career-making story.

"What do you hear about this?" she asked with a coaxing grin.

Todd shrugged. "A young guy was killed, not much more."

"That cop over there—see the cute one with the light hair and mustache?—he says they're already calling it a *homo*cide. That true? Was he gay?"

Yes. Yes, of course it was. Some poor gay kid whose family kicked him out because he was queer has ended up in some dump of a basement with his throat slit. But who in the hell had leaked that? Never mind, he thought just as quickly, for Cindy was a pro at using that smile and that figure. If she knew or even suspected, however, did that mean it was going to be all over her report? And would she press the issue, using Andrew's sexuality to paint him the deviant?

"That's news to me."

"Really?" she said, studying his face, searching for the truth. "Say, I've been meaning to call you. Arsenio Hall's coming to town next month, and I'm going to do a piece on him. Is he gay? A friend of mine said he was, said there were all these gay comedians—Louie Anderson, Paula Poundstone. In fact, my friend says all the men on *Frasier* are gay except for Frasier himself. What do you think, that true too?"

The names of supposedly gay celebrities were continually flying—John Travolta, Richard Gere, Tom Selleck, James Spader, Kevin Spacey, Mark Harmon, Ellen DeGeneres, Rosie O'Donnell, Jodie Foster, Lily Tomlin—some of them true, some of them not. But as always, the media, which had left in the closet such greats as Rock Hudson, Barbara Stanwyck, Errol Flynn, Tab Hunter, Cary Grant, and Malcolm Forbes, was shy of such things.

"Cindy, you're walking through land mine territory, you know. You say stuff like that on the air and you're liable to get your ass sued, which actually would be just fine with me."

"Well, I just thought—"

"That they were guilty of something?"

"God, Todd, you're so touchy."

He didn't know why he said it, except of course that he remembered she was a huge fan of his, and it just came blurting out: "You know what, I heard that Tim Chase is definitely gay."

"Him?" she said as if she'd been slapped. "Dream on, Todd. That guy's so gorgeous—don't be ridiculous."

Behind him Todd heard the familiar sound of an electric motor humming away. He glanced over, saw the mast on their ENG truck begin to lower. Nope, he couldn't let her see that they were packing it in. No way in hell.

He turned back toward the apartment building, and said, "Hey, is that the medical examiner? Is he here already?"

"Where?"

"Up there. I think he just came out of the building."

She was gone in a second, determined to miss nothing.

Relieved, Todd wandered over to a group of three or four people who he assumed were neighbors, because, as if they had just dashed outside, none of them wore jackets. Without trying to be too obvious, he slipped alongside them, tried to hear what they were saying. His eyes, of course, were elsewhere, on the building, on the cops gathered off to one side.

And it was then that his gaze fell upon someone in particular, a tall, thin young man.

Todd noticed him at first because he just stood there crying, his eyes puffed and raw as tears came streaming unabashedly down his cheeks. Crushing the yellow police tape in both hands, he stared at the front of the door, his young, pale face transfixed with shock. He had very long light brown hair that he flicked back with a shake of his head, and it was that movement, that toss of his silky mane, that made Todd realize something. Surely this kid wasn't even twenty, but somehow Todd knew him, somewhere they'd met once or twice. But when and where?

Instinctively Todd started toward him, but just at that moment the kid lifted the yellow tape and lunged toward the building. The very next moment a couple of cops shouted out and came running over. Still the young man didn't stop, hurrying forward one long step after another, until the cops caught him and took him by the arms and pulled him back, shoving him once again beneath and behind the police tape. And as they herded him back, the kid said nothing, did nothing to protest. He only stared with sodden eyes at the building.

Of course, realized Todd. That's one of Andrew's friends.

Todd beefed it up, hurrying around one clump of gawkers, another. He ducked around a tree, saw the kid just standing there looking as if he'd never move again. But then the next instant the young guy was gone. Immediately Todd started both running and scanning, checking the side of the building, the scattered clumps of people, and the various media. He looked toward the park, down the street, back toward the building, but there was no lanky figure with fine, long hair hurrying away. Todd ran right to the spot where the kid had been standing and crushing the police tape in his hand, turned from side to side.

Wait.

There he was, scurrying across the street, into the park. Todd burst forward. And then someone caught him by the arm.

"Hey, Todd. I'm here. I made it."

It was Mark, the second photographer. Todd glanced at him, then took one last look across the street as the kid disappeared into the park and the night. Next Todd checked his watch.

Running one hand through his hair, Todd said, "We don't have much time, do we?"

"No shit," laughed Mark.

The people on the technical side of things were always pretty macho, in part because they were mostly guys who were proud of the heavy equipment they lugged around. Mark, holding his Betacam beneath his arm like a large football, was no exception. With a sort of stocky, square body, he had hair that was cut into short bangs, while the back was long, almost shoulder length. It was the perfect Minnesota hockey haircut, and Mark stood there chewing gum and grinning, ready to play any game. This was going to be close, and he loved it.

Todd said, "Just keep this place covered until we get back."

"You got it."

"Where the hell's Bradley?"

"Right over there."

Todd saw him and darted through the crowd. He grabbed Bradley by the arm, and the two of them made their way out of the crowd, around a few cop cars, and toward his Jeep.

"Think we're going to make it?" asked Bradley, a twinkle in his eye.

"Five bucks says we will."

"You're on."

They had less than three minutes, and Todd wondered if there was a chance in hell.

Chapter 4

Once inside the huge house, he stood there barely breathing. But there was nothing, no one, not as far as he could discern.

Carrying nothing, he proceeded up a half-dozen steps, entered a back hall, then froze. Just up ahead he heard running water, followed by the dull but steady sound of something striking wood. Following that, he came to a doorway and peered into a huge kitchen. Scanning the room, he saw countertops of rare blue marble, an eight-burner range, a separate high-powered wok, an enormous Sub-Zero refrigerator, and, standing at a copper sink, a lone woman. Wearing a baggy T-shirt and blue jeans and with her light hair put up in a loose bun, she was chopping vegetables on a cutting board.

He cleared his throat, and said, "Hi, Amy."

She gasped and spun around, her left hand on her chest, her right clutching a small paring knife.

"Tim, oh, my God, it's you." She took a deep breath. "You scared me."

"Sorry," said Tim Chase, one of Hollywood's top stars. "Sometimes I feel like I'm sneaking around my own house. I mean, there's not one but two photographers out front."

"It's awful."

"Yeah." He nodded toward the pile of vegetables next to the sink. "What are you making?"

"Oh," she said, turning back to her work and collecting her thoughts. "Just finishing up some broth for tomorrow. I'm going to

poach some fish—that Hawaiian fisherman I use is Fed-Exing me
some onaga and ahi he caught this afternoon. Isn't the world a wonder? He caught it at four this afternoon and it'll be here in fly-over
land by ten tomorrow morning."

"I'm sure it'll be great."

"Are you hungry? Can I get you anything to eat?"

"Nope, I'm all set, thanks." He glanced at the wall clock, saw that
it was just about ten. "Where is everyone?"

"I'm not sure where Vic is—I think he just went up to his room.
Charlie's downstairs watching a movie."

Vic was Tim's main bodyguard, a skilled professional who traveled
with him and who organized security whenever Tim appeared publicly.
Charlie was the number two guy, not only Tim's personal trainer, but
also in charge of household security; he was hired a year ago after
Gwen and Tim started having trouble with a stalker.

"I think Maggie and Gwen are upstairs."

"Thanks." He grabbed an apple from a bowl on the counter and
started out. "If you see Vic, tell him I need to talk to him."

"Sure." A moment later she called, "Breakfast at five again tomorrow?"

"Yep. Gotta be on the set at six."

He passed through the pantry, a long room with shelves of dishes
and two dishwashers, then entered the dining room with its tall ceiling and mahogany paneling. Next he stepped into the entry hall, an
enormous space nearly twenty feet wide and some thirty feet long. It
was ridiculously big, this place, much more than they needed, with an
indoor pool and ten bedrooms, but the producers had just wanted to
make sure Tim and his entourage were happy. And the owner, the top
saleswoman for a cosmetics company who'd totally rehabed the place
just several years ago and who was now off in the Aegean, had been
only too eager to lease it for fifty thousand for ten weeks.

Tim just hoped to hell it wasn't a mistake coming to the Midwest
and doing this film.

With a face that was too often described as all-American, rich brown hair, a lean, hard body, and a smile that could light up any room, not to mention any screen, Tim Chase was everyone's heart-throb. By everyone's count, he was one of a few truly bankable stars whose name alone—like Harrison Ford, Julia Roberts, Tom Cruise, and Mel Gibson—could open a movie. But his successful fare had always been action heroes—an underdog soccer player in one film, a DEA agent in another, a diplomat in one of his latest. Yet here he was in Minneapolis shooting *The Good Heart,* the story of a gay man who watches not only his lover die from AIDS but his conservative, judgmental father, from whom he has been estranged for over ten years. It was the riskiest of roles for him, there was no doubt about it, and his agent and manager had deeply questioned whether he should play the role of a gay man.

"Fuck it," he had told them all. "This is an Oscar-winning role if I've ever seen one. Besides, it's a story that should be told."

"But, Tim," whined Jed, his agent, "you know I'm as queer as a three dollar bill, and I'm not sure this is good for you. What about all your fans, what about your sex appeal? You're one of the four or five most valuable franchises in Hollywood. This is not good, this is not wise. All those girls in middle America are not going to be cool with this."

"I'm married, Jed. I have a kid. Everyone knows that."

"Yeah, but, Tim, you do this and the rumors are going to start flying again. Trust me, the tabloids are going to have a heyday."

"Don't you see, Jed? My fans aren't going to think I'm gay because I'm playing a gay part. If anything, this is going to make them think I'm straight . . . and kind of gutsy. And when they're bawling their eyes out at the end of the film, they're going to love, love, love me all the more."

"It's your career, pal."

"Hey, don't forget how great Tom Hanks was in a role like this—*Philadelphia* was a terrific flick."

"Yeah, but . . ."

But maybe he was right, Tim now thought. Maybe it wasn't going to work. Maybe America couldn't handle Tim Chase in anything but the role of the charming hunk next door. Over the years and with the advice of many, from his mother to his agent to numerous studios, heads to the most expensive public relations firm in the country, Tim Chase's career had been carefully carved and molded. And the secret of his appeal was no secret, but simply its breadth. Guys loved him for his virility, while women of every age loved him for his blatantly charming and sweet sex appeal. Tim knew and knew well that it was a numbers game, that his superstar success was due, of course, to his mass appeal.

But don't worry, he told himself as he reached the imposing staircase. It's going to be okay. Everything's going well—great script, great director, great cast.

Grabbing onto the carved newel post, he bounded up, taking the steps two at a time. As he neared the top, he heard the large and unmistakable voice of Jack, who wasn't quite three, piercing the quiet of the house. Of course the kid shouldn't be up this late, but Tim smiled anyway. Gwen and Jack, along with Maggie, officially the nanny, had arrived just yesterday, and Tim was more than glad for it. This house had been much too big, much too quiet without them.

Stepping into the middle bedroom, the one at the front of the house and over the front door, he found them all, mother, nanny, and child, sitting on the floor, a veritable riot of multicolored Duplos scattered all around them.

With a big smile, Tim asked, "Hey, is this a party or what?"

"Daddy!" shouted the kid, jumping to his feet and running over.

Tim scooped him up, taking the tiny kid with the angelic face into his arms and kissing him on the cheek. His son, Tim swore, was not only the best thing that had ever happened to him, but was the most gorgeous child in the universe. Blue eyes radiated from his round face, and his dark hair was thick and rich. Nothing, absolutely nothing, gave Tim Chase the same thrill—not Academy Award, not rave review, not legions of adoring fans—as did this boy.

"Oh, I'm so glad you're here now," said Tim, snuggling Jack and kissing him. "It was so lonely without you. But what are you still doing up, Jack? Don't you know that all the other little boys in the world are already asleep? Don't you know how late it is?"

He put a finger to his mouth and shook his head. "Noon?"

"Noon? Noon? You think it's that early?"

"Yeah, it's noon!"

Gwen, wearing a long cotton nightgown with a floral print, pushed herself up from the floor. "What he thinks is that it's two hours earlier than it really is. In other words, the little charmer's not quite used to the time change yet."

"Ohhhh." Tim kissed his son again. "Listen, Jack, you know you're my favorite son, don't you?"

He nodded quickly, having heard that line any number of times.

"Then I want you to do exactly what I tell you, okay?"

"Hmmm, okay."

"I'm going to bed now because I have to get up very, very early to work. And I want you to go to bed now too."

"But . . . but I want to play! I want to—"

"Nope, it's time for bed, Mister Twister."

"But—"

Maggie rose from the floor, saying, "How about I read you a story, Jack?"

"Great idea," said Tim.

She came over then, eternally patient and beautiful Maggie with the slender waist and bobbed dark hair. She wore jeans and a loose striped top, and the truth was that she'd spent more time with Tim and Gwen's son than either of them had. She'd been there right from the day he was born, caring for the child as if he were hers, and she now lifted him from Tim's arms and carried him to the bed against the far wall.

Gwen brushed back a bit of hair, and called, "I'll be back to give you a kiss, sweetheart."

"Love you, Jack!"

"Love you, Daddy."

With a small, but warm smile, Tim stepped into the hall, followed by his wife. God, he'd hated being away from them. And, dear God, he was glad they were here now.

"I missed you," he said, taking his wife's hand.

"Me too," she said, pulling the door shut with her free hand.

She was beautiful, he thought. Several inches shorter than him, Gwen was one of the most regal young actresses around, her chinalike skin offset by soft brown hair. She had a small mouth, lips that were full and always plush with color, and long legs. Although her father was American, she claimed her mother's homeland, England, as her own, and in fact she had lived almost half her life there. Though she could convincingly play any kind of American, she was a natural for English roles, and just last year she'd been nominated for an Oscar for her part in a Jane Austen adaptation.

Standing there in the hallway, Tim reached out, took her into his arms, and kissed her. "Hi."

She came into his arms without a wisp of resistance. "We worked everything out this afternoon—we'll be able to stay for the rest of your shoot."

His lips touched her forehead. "That's great."

"Are you okay? Is something the matter?"

"No, I just need to talk to Vic, that's all."

"Where'd you go earlier?"

He shrugged and grinned. "Out."

Eyeing him suspiciously, she said, "Tim?"

"It was my first time off, the first time I could get away since I got here. I just wanted to escape . . . so I did. I just drove around, that's all."

She rolled her eyes knowingly and shook her head. "I just hope to hell you were careful."

"Aren't I always?"

"Yes, but . . ."

"But what?"

"This is a new city. The people are different here." She shrugged. "Did you take Vic with you?"

"No, I didn't need to."

"Oh, Tim. I don't know. Anything could happen. I just worry about you so, that's all, particularly since that creep started stalking us."

"Don't worry, we're in the Midwest now and there's nothing to be afraid of. You just have to trust me, Gwenny. Believe me, I love you, I love our son, I love our life together. I'm not going to screw that up."

She took a deep breath, ran her slender fingers through his hair. "Okay, then, my hero." She kissed him. "Good night."

"I love you."

"I love you too."

"Will I see you for breakfast?"

"I think I need to sleep. How about Maggie, Jack, and I drop by the set sometime late morning?"

As he headed off, knowing he had to find Vic before going to bed, Tim Chase said, "Sounds great."

Chapter 5

A good reporter was never afraid and never excited, just prepared.

So as Bradley drove Todd's Cherokee to the live shot, Todd sat in the passenger seat scribbling away in his reporter's notebook, one of those elongated pads. He was writing it all down in detail, exactly what he'd say in those thirty-five seconds of voice-over, though of course he knew from experience that he wouldn't end up reading it word for word. Somehow it just never turned out that way, somehow he always ended up punting. After all, as they said whenever there was a screwup, why do you think they call it live TV?

But how was he going to come at this thing? In many ways Todd had the perfect situation, the best of both worlds. Not only did he have the crime scene footage, which viewers always wanted to see, but he was going to be shooting live from this other location. In other words, he would have something no one else would, not to mention an entirely different angle. But he was going to have to be careful. On the one hand the police hadn't officially released details of Andrew's sexuality, yet on the other Cindy Wilson already knew. And whatever was in her head would come out her mouth, of that Todd was sure.

Fortunately it was only a matter of eight blocks to the live shot, straight out to Lyndale, then directly north to Franklin, and finally a left. Two blocks down, on the same corner where it had stood for nearly sixty years, was Oak Drugs. And above that neighborhood fixture of medications and Hallmark cards was the neighborhood newcomer, the Domain of Queers, which had moved there just over a year ago. To the surprise of many, there had been no resistance to a gay youth center opening in the neighborhood, and the DQ now included a small handful of meeting rooms, a coffee bar, and a large, old ball-room used for Friday night queer teen dances. It was here that Todd and Rawlins had first spoken to a group of young gay people, and it was here that they had first met Andrew.

As Bradley pulled up, Todd looked at the second floor windows draped with rainbow flags, saw the big pink neon triangle framing the initials DQ. Yes, it would provide a great backdrop. And their ENG truck, the mast raised high, the microwave dish aimed toward down-town, was parked exactly opposite the building, just as Todd wanted.

"Perfect," said Todd as the truck came to an abrupt stop.

"Looks like I lost," said Bradley with a laugh. "We've got all of about fifty seconds."

Todd liked to have anywhere from eight minutes to a minimum of thirty seconds, although the latter was cutting it rather tight. And now leaping out of the Cherokee, Todd and Bradley went into armylike ac-tion, charging across the street, and then, with the help of Jeff, who emerged from the ENG, setting up. Cables were dragged out from the rear of the truck. Cords were attached. A single light stand thrown up. And then seconds later Todd was standing in front of Bradley's cam-era, which was now poised atop a tripod. As Jeff hopped back into the ENG and started to adjust the transmission levels, as Bradley placed a small monitor at the base of the tripod, Todd simultaneously grabbed a stick microphone and an earpiece, which he slipped into place. No sooner had he gotten the small plastic thing in his ear than the news director called out.

"Voice check, please."

Todd lifted up the mike, said, "Good evening, this is Todd Mills reporting live from—"

"Got it."

The line producer came on next, saying, "What's your roll cue, Todd?"

He glanced at his pad. "Ah . . . 'Night of darkness and mystery.' "

"Check: 'Night of darkness and mystery.' " A moment later he advised, "Ten to the top."

Todd rolled his neck from side to side, gave it a small crack. Just as he couldn't reveal Andrew's name until the authorities released it, nor could he come right out and say Andrew was gay, at least not at this point. Yet while he didn't know if Andrew's sexuality would ever prove to be relevant to his murder, he couldn't ignore it tonight, not simply because he had to give viewers a reason to watch him, Todd Mills, but because Cindy Wilson and WTCN were already clued in. Which left Todd precious little room in which to maneuver. Therefore, it would be best, not to mention safest from a legal standpoint, to speak from his personal contact with Andrew.

Via IFB transmission, Todd heard the line producer give his final count, "Five to the top."

Todd adjusted his black leather coat, then glanced down at the monitor that was aimed up at him from the base of the tripod. The screen flashed from an herbicide commercial—after all, this was the Midwest and this was the late news, when every farmer tuned in if not for the news, then certainly the weather—to the *10@10* logo. Next filling the screen was the face of WLAK's star anchor, an indisputably handsome man with a long face, dark hair gone quite salt and pepper, and an unwieldy ego that was, fortunately for WLAK, invisible on television. Gaining stature as the most valued and watched anchor in the Twin Cities, he'd recently demanded and gotten a new contract paying him just over a million bucks a year. Such was the value of those white teeth, the even cadence of his speech, and the trust that he could, with cool professionalism, turn on in a second.

"Good evening and welcome to *Ten at Ten*. I'm Tom Rivers, and we have a number of stories tonight, from a problem with the Teacher's Pension Fund to a cancer-fighting enzyme recently discovered at the University of Minnesota. We begin tonight's coverage, however, on a very serious note, that of the murder of a young white male in south Minneapolis. Just over an hour ago Minneapolis police received a call reporting the crime. Here with a live report of this

still-developing story is our investigative reporter, Todd Mills."
Tossing it, he said, "Todd?"

Holding the stick microphone in a tight grasp, Todd stared
straight into Bradley's camera. Yes, that's how these things went.
Anchor toss, reporter in full-on camera, VO, reporter tag, ad lib. All of
it back-timed to the second.

Todd forced every thought out of his head, and then let it flow
back, evenly and precisely. All you have to do, he told himself, is walk
your viewers through this, one steady step at a time.

"Tom, this story is still evolving, very much so, and the police have
been reticent to release what little information they may have. What
is known at this point, however, is that a young white male, whose
name is being withheld pending notification of family, has been murdered in his basement apartment in a building at 25th and Bryant
Avenue South. I've been told by residents of the building that the victim was recently employed there as a caretaker. And I do believe that
that job represented the first major step for a young man embarking
on a dream. Unfortunately, it was a dream that has now dissolved into
a night of darkness and mystery," said Todd, giving the roll cue.

The video, which had been edited down from Bradley's footage to
precisely thirty-five seconds, began to roll, and Todd's eyes fell to the
monitor. Nine times out of ten, he helped edit such things, and, of
course, wrote the script for them, marrying video and sound into a single prerecorded package. Tonight, however, he was simply going to
have to watch the monitor, try to read what he had prepared, or, more
likely, simply talk to the pictures.

Seeing footage of marked units, flashing lights, and cops in their
blues, Todd looked at his notes and said, "After receiving a frantic call
from a building resident a little over an hour ago, the Minneapolis police were quick to arrive at a small apartment building at Twenty-fifth
and Bryant Avenue South. As you can see, there are a number of police at the scene, along with homicide investigators and the team from
the Bureau of Investigation. Both the front and rear entrances to this
building have been sealed off, and a barricade has been set up to keep

the crowd at a distance. The authorities are now going over the apartment, searching for any evidence that may be relevant, and the medical examiner has yet to remove the body."

The video cut to an image of the rectangular, redbrick structure, and Todd said, "I'm told that the victim only recently moved into this building, a two-and-a-half story walk-up located in a neighborhood known as the Wedge, and that he lived in a small basement apartment at the rear of the building. He was employed here as a caretaker for this and several other apartment buildings on the block."

His eyes flicking between the monitor and his notes, Todd now saw a crowd of neighbors milling around, gawking and gossiping. Most of them, he knew, were as horrified as they were entertained.

"As you can see, Tom, quite a crowd has gathered here, primarily neighbors who are both upset and worried by the crime. The Wedge has a very strong and active neighborhood organization, and they've spent a considerable amount of time and effort in maintaining the safety of—"

The news director, via the earpiece, said, "Three seconds."

"—their neighborhood. Naturally, this comes as quite a shock."

Todd looked up, staring into Bradley's camera, which was now live on him. "As I said, Tom, little information has been released on the victim, but he was known to frequently visit the Domain of Queers, which is a center for gay, lesbian, bisexual, and transgender teens. I'm currently standing just across the street from this center, which you can see is located on the second floor of that building, just above Oak Drugs. It moved to this location just over a year ago, and has been very successful, serving not only local teens, but a number of runaways as well."

Tom Rivers cut in, his voice deep and luxuriant, and said, "Todd, was the victim simply employed at this center as well, perhaps as a caretaker or janitor, or was he there as a teenager to use and enjoy the facilities?"

Todd knew damn well, of course. When Rawlins and he had spoken at the DQ, Andrew had not only been in the front row, he'd been sitting there holding hands with some other guy. With a bright, eager grin, he'd asked lots of questions, laughed, and gotten a veritable debate going regarding—what was it?—the feasibility of a gay relationship. Right. And later on, of course, he'd met with Rawlins.

"I do believe, Tom, that the victim came here for the center's services. As a matter of fact, I first encountered the victim two months ago when I was here giving a talk to gay youth."

"Does that mean for a fact he was gay?"

Rawlins was going to give him shit for this, but Todd had no choice, and he said, "Well, the Domain of Queers, or the DQ as it's commonly called, is a center to serve gay teens. Whether the victim was indeed gay and/or possibly a runaway will soon, I'm sure, be officially known."

Even though Todd always tried to focus every bit of his energy and attention on the camera, out of the corner of his eye he saw a tall figure come hurrying around the corner. It was a young man, his head bent, his long, silky hair bouncing with each of his long, awkward strides, and Todd recognized him immediately. And the kid, seeing the camera and the lights, looked up, his eyes red, his cheeks still wet with tears, and froze in surprise. An odd, almost fearful look washed over him, and then he turned and quickly hurried off.

Into the earpiece lodged in Todd's right ear, Tom Rivers said, "Thank you very much, Todd, and we look forward to any other information you might have on this sad story. In other news . . ."

Todd glanced down, saw the image of Tom Rivers fill the monitor. Then he looked up, saw Bradley still hunched behind the camera. The next second, Bradley raised his head.

"Clear."

Ripping away the earpiece and stuffing that and the stick mike into Bradley's hands, Todd said, "I'll be right back!"

Spinning around, he saw the kid scurrying across the street not toward Oak Drugs of course, but toward the DQ. Sure, scared and upset, horrified and confused, he'd walked here from the murder scene and was now fleeing to the one safe isle he'd ever found, that

refuge of his peers. Which is exactly where Todd had seen him before.
He didn't know the kid's name, but Todd was sure of it, this young
man with the long, silky hair was a friend of Andrew. Or was he more?
Had he been the one sitting there holding hands with Andrew during
Todd and Rawlins's talk? If so, what did that imply, that they'd simply
been queer friends, or that they'd perhaps been sweethearts?

A boxy truck with a smiling cow on the side rolled past, next a
blue van and two cars, and then Todd darted into the road. His eyes
fixed on the tall young man, he watched as the kid hurried up the sidewalk and reached the double doors that led to the Domain of Queers.

"Hey!" called Todd from the middle of the street.

Spinning around, the kid brushed his hair back and glanced toward Todd, his eyes now smoldering with what, anger? Recognition?
The young guy hesitated for a second, then lunged for the glass door
and swung it open.

Every bit of his reporterly instincts was piqued, and Todd wasted
no time, breaking into a quick jog, charging up the sidewalk and past
the display windows of Oak Drugs that were already filled with
Halloween costumes. This kid, Todd was sure, wasn't just upset, he
knew something. Throwing open the door and hurrying into the building, Todd looked up the broad staircase that was easily six feet wide
and lit by row after row of fluorescent lights. The walls were painted
a bland white, and Todd saw him just past the mid-point landing,
climbing two steps at a time.

"Wait a minute!" When the kid didn't stop, Todd called, "I need to
talk to you, just wait a—"

Without turning around, without stopping, he screamed, "Fuck
off!"

More than a little surprised by this opening salvo, Todd hesitated, even slowed. Okay, what was going on here? Was Todd merely
being an asshole of a reporter by treading into tender territory? Or
was Todd right in chasing after this kid, sensing he might know
something about Andrew's tragic end? There was, for sure, only one
way to find out.

Todd didn't remember the rules, couldn't remember if uninvited adults were even allowed in the DQ, particularly at this time of night, but he plunged on, unable to stop himself. Grabbing the railing, he started up the wide stairs. He was about to call out again when the kid reached the top and disappeared from sight.

Todd continued up, and when he reached the top, huffing for air, he was immediately greeted by a young African-American girl, perhaps no more than sixteen or seventeen and wearing a plain white T-shirt and blue jean overalls. Her face round and cute, she wore glasses and had her hair pulled back in pigtails.

"Can I help you?" she said, from behind a reception desk.

"I'm looking for the guy who just came in here. I need to talk to him."

"Well, I'm afraid you can't. I mean, adults can't come in unless they're invited to speak or do something official. Anyway, from the looks of it, Jordy doesn't want to talk to you or anyone else, for that matter." She pushed up her glasses and glanced down a hall. "What happened, anyway? He's awfully upset." She looked Todd up and down. "You're not his dad, are you?"

Gee, thanks, thought Todd with a scowl. But it was true. He was easily old enough. Todd's own son was, in fact, even older than this kid. And, yes, that was his name. Jordan. He'd been the one sitting there, holding hands with Andrew. Todd was sure of it now.

Trying not to sound like a bullying adult, Todd said, "No, I'm not family. My name's Todd Mills, and I'm a television reporter from—"

"Oh, yeah, I remember now," she said with a bright smile. "You're the gay guy on TV. Didn't you and your lover come in here and speak or something?"

"Right. That was a couple of months ago. But we've got a problem tonight, and I need to speak to Jordy."

"You know, I really don't think he—"

"I'm sorry, but either I talk to him or I call the police."

"Wait, wait, wait, wait, wait, wait," she said, holding up both hands, palms out. "Come on, we don't need any shit like that.

Particularly not on my shift, okay? I mean, I'm just supposed to be monitoring the place. I'm just volunteering."

"I mean it."

"Oh, man." She bent her head, rubbed her forehead with one hand, and then, without looking up, pointed down the hall and said, "He's down there, first room on the right. Leave the door open. If I hear him shout or anything, you're gonna have to leave. Clear?"

"Thanks."

Todd took a deep breath, held it a second, then blasted it out between pursed lips. Feeling oddly like the enemy, he proceeded past the monitoring desk and down a hall with fresh beige carpeting and newly painted walls.

Originally the DQ had been in a dump of a storefront on Lake Street, an idea born of a dream and that functioned on a shoestring. And it had worked, not only proving to be a much-needed haven, but garnering a lot of media attention, gay and straight. The dollars had followed, both from the queer community as well as, surprisingly, the corporate, and the organization had expanded and grown and moved here.

Todd stopped at the first door and looked into a room that was furnished with two couches, a coffee table, and a couple of standing lamps, one of which now dimly burned. A counseling or conference room, Todd assumed. Jordy was in there, slumped on one of the couches, his long hair swept forward, his body trembling and shaking as he sobbed. He wore old black and white high-top tennis shoes, baggy jeans, and a ratty, old wool coat that he'd either gotten from his grandfather or the Goodwill, probably the latter.

Todd glanced down the hall, saw the girl at the front desk staring after him, then knocked twice on the doorjamb and said, "Can I come in?"

Jordy looked up, and though he'd perhaps reached his full height, his face was still that of a boy, the skin smooth and pure, untouched by either acne or, for that matter, much of a beard. His face was long and thin, his chin narrow, and his eyes—those red, red eyes—were small, etched on top with two heavy eyebrows, the most manly of his features. A kid, that was all he was, frightened and scared to hell. And now witnessing Jordy's grief, the raw pain that was flowing unrestricted out of his soul, Todd knew what this was all about. Not some little tale of intrigue, but the death of a friend. The loss of a loved one.

Todd spotted a box of Kleenex on the coffee table, picked it up, and placed it on the couch next to Jordy. He then sat down opposite him.

"I'm sorry."

Jordy caught himself, wiped his wet nose with the back of his hand, then tossed his hair back. "Is . . . is it really . . . really true? Did someone kill him? Kill Andrew?"

"I'm afraid so."

"Oh, God!" He grabbed some tissues, blew his nose, started crying all over again. "Andrew wanted me to come over a couple of hours ago. I should've gone. I should've been there. Maybe he'd be okay. Maybe . . ."

"It's not your fault."

"But . . ." He slammed a fist down on his knee. "Fuck!"

Todd was at a loss. What was he supposed to do? Sit there at a distance and let this kid fall on his own, or take him into his arms and catch him? In a moment of panic, Todd realized he didn't know what to do, how to handle this, in large part because he'd never learned anything like this from his father, who'd been so physically reticent.

Jordy shook his head, buried his face in his hands. "Andrew was just trying to get away from his family, just trying to start his own life, that's all! He just wanted to be himself, nothing more." He stopped breathing for a minute, then blurted, "I hate this! I hate being fucking gay! Why? Why the fuck was I born queer? I didn't ask for this, I didn't!"

He dissolved into a fresh round of tears, and Todd felt something in his heart begin to break. A young man tonight had been murdered, the truth of which might never be learned. It was a tragedy, no doubt, but it was the sight of a kid beating himself up with self-hatred that crushed Todd. Perhaps it was because this was simply too familiar, that Todd had been there, berated himself time and time again, and had for so long hated himself for his sexuality. It had taken almost all of his adult life to get past it, and even then just barely, and so seeing it now, seeing it so fresh in someone so young, was almost more than he could take. It was as if he was watching a movie of his own emotions. Was there nothing he could do, no way he could protect this kid, make him see the truth?

He got up and crossed the room, sitting down next to Jordy and wrapping one arm over Jordy's shoulders. Just as quickly, Jordy elbowed Todd in the ribs and shoved him away.

"Get away from me, you fucking queen! Get your fucking hands off me!" he shouted. "You guys—all you think about is sex! You're nothing but a bunch of old trolls!"

It was like someone had slammed a board into Todd's gut. The color rapidly falling from his face, he jerked away his arm, pushed himself up, and quickly moved back across the room.

"Jordy, that's not what—"

"Shut up!"

How the hell could he convince him that he hadn't come here to lurk?

A head poked in, and, through a nervous smile, the girl from up front said, "Everything okay in here, guys?"

Todd nodded curtly. "Fine."

"Jordy?" When he didn't reply, she said, "Well, I'm just down the hall. Holler if you need me, okay?"

Oh, Christ, thought Todd, sinking back in the couch and folding his arms. Sitting there in tepid silence, he watched as Jordy grabbed some Kleenex and blew his nose. Now what?

"When's . . . when's it going to get easier?" Jordy mumbled.

"Trust me, it does. It will."

"Trust you?" said Jordy, looking at Todd as if he were crazy. "Why? Why the fuck should I trust you of all people?"

Something else was going on here, that much was clear. And Todd didn't like it, not one bit. He felt Jordy's accusative eyes glaring at him, and Todd, for some inexplicable reason, became suddenly afraid. Shit, what did Jordy know that he didn't?

Spitting hate as he spoke, Jordy demanded, "You've come for me too, haven't you? That's why you're here, isn't it?"

"Jordy, I don't know what you're talking about. I was just doing a report out front when I saw you. I just wanted to talk about what happened tonight, I just wanted to see if you might be able to help."

"Bullshit!"

"Jordy, I—"

"Awhile back you came in here, you and that boyfriend of yours, and told us how happy you were, how lucky you were to have found each other. You came in here and told us how much you loved each other, but—"

"What the hell are you talking about, Jordy?"

"—but it was nothing but a bunch of fucking lies! You know what, I hate you! And I hate fags! I hate 'em, because they just turn into old trolls like you that feed off kids like us!"

Through a haze of confusion, Todd began to see a glimmer of what might be going on in Jordy's head. Was that what this was all about, vulnerable boys with perfect bodies and powerful men with bulging wallets? Had Andrew, the runaway, found a way to make a buck not by cleaning hallways but giving blow jobs? And if so, did Jordy know who Andrew had been with earlier this evening?

"Jordy, was Andrew hustling?"

"How can you say that?" he said, staring at Todd with utter shock. "What do you think I am, just some sort of dumb-ass kid?"

"I'm sorry, I'm just trying to understand."

"Understand? *Understand?!*" He bit his lip, reached down, and started pulling at a button on his old wool coat. "Well, understand this: I loved Andrew. I mean, I really loved him. I wanted him and me to live together forever, you know. I wanted to get married to him so I'd never lose him. I wanted the two of us to be happy, just like you two fuckers said you were when you came in here prancing around like the beautiful couple, all happy and everything. But then he came and took him away. He had everything too. Everything I didn't. He was so butch and muscley and hairy—it drove Andrew crazy. He fell in love with him right away. He had a car and money and—"

"Who, Andrew? Who?"

"Why are you doing this to me? Why?" he cried in a shrill voice as he pulled at his long, gorgeous hair. "Just stop it! Stop fucking with my head like this!"

"You're telling me Andrew was having sex with some older guy?"

"Of . . . of course I am." He wrapped his arms around himself and started shaking. "You mean, you really don't know?"

"No," said Todd quietly, as something akin to fear swept through him. "Why should I?"

Suddenly he knew. Or feared he did. And his entire insides wrenched. The answer was right there, too horrible to be thought, let alone spoken.

Still, he had to know, it had to be said, and in a deep, slow voice, Todd demanded, "Jordy, who was Andrew sleeping with?"

"Are you going to hurt me if I tell you?"

"No, absolutely not," replied Todd, his voice shaking.

Andrew sat there for a second, wiped his nose with the back of his hand, then stared at the floor and said, "It was him, your . . . your boyfriend, Rawlins. That's who did it, who took Andrew away from me."

Chapter 6

It took more willpower, more self-control, than Rawlins thought he had.

He stepped through the front door of the apartment building, continued down the half-flight to the basement, and then just stopped and stood there. Leaning against the cool wall with one hand, he put the other to his head. *You've got to get yourself under control. You can't let anyone see. You can't let anyone know.*

He took a deep breath, then lowered his right hand and studied it. Seeing it violently tremble, he grabbed it with his left and clutched it. *Just stop it! That little shit's dead and there's nothing you can do!*

Jesus Christ, he thought. Todd hadn't guessed, had he? He couldn't possibly suspect anything, could he? Already Todd knew him better than almost anyone, not simply through the actual time they'd spent together, but through their long hours of conversation, during which Rawlins had divulged more about himself than he ever had to anyone else. It seemed as if he'd told Todd every secret, every fear, every hope, and every lust. Every lust, of course, but one. So had Todd just caught a glimpse of that through Rawlins's tears? Had he sensed the truth in Rawlins's panic?

Oh, shit.

Just be cool. This was going to be the worst. If he could get through tonight, even the next fifteen or twenty minutes, then he was sure he'd be able to handle it. He'd nearly vomited when he'd first gone in and seen Andrew lying there, his eyes covered with that black mask, his naked body half concealed by the sheet, and the river of blood that had flowed from his neck onto the bed and floor.

"Sergeant?"

Rawlins turned to see a young officer before him, her wiry brown hair cut short beneath her hat, her face sincere and plain. She was just about Rawlins's height, and she wore a gun belt with ease, but Rawlins had never seen her before. That didn't mean much, however, since the force had in the past few years expanded from slightly over seven hundred to just under a thousand officers. There were tons of younger cops like this one—seventy percent of the force had less than two years' experience—and Rawlins wondered how long this woman had been at it. She was obviously into what was going on here tonight, there was no doubt about that, but that could simply stem from the fact that she'd been the first one on the scene. She'd been on patrol nearby, and dispatch had sent her over. Finding the victim DOA, she'd sealed the scene, called her supervisor, who in turn had called Cars 1110 and 21. All exactly according to the book.

Right, thought Rawlins. Just follow procedure. You know how these things are supposed to go. Just do it.

Rawlins wiped his mouth, cleared his throat, and said, "Yeah?"

"I've checked with several different people in the building, and as far as anyone knows, the victim was the only one residing in the apartment."

Rawlins knew that of course, but he asked, "How about the mailbox in the lobby?"

"Only one name on it."

"Good."

"Anything else for now?"

Rawlins looked down the hallway, saw his partner, Neal Foster, stepping out of the apartment, and said, "Yeah, get two other officers and canvas the building. I want a complete list of the residents' names. And I want to know everyone's schedule—who was here this afternoon and when, who was at work and when they returned. Be sure

and see if anyone heard anything or noticed anything—including anyone unusual in the past few days."

"Yes, sir."

His gut cinched tight, Rawlins proceeded down the stark hall.
Overhead ran a series of pipes and wires, and he continued past a
door labeled BOILER ROOM and met Foster halfway. Rawlins immediately felt the older man's eyes studying him, and Rawlins stopped,
scratched his chin, and leaned against a wall. Just be cool.

"You okay?" asked Foster.

Just a year short of retirement, Foster had gray hair, a chubby
body, a round face, and a smile that was reticent, reflecting of course
the years and years of gore he'd seen as a homicide investigator. It was
Foster who had plucked Rawlins out of the juvenile division and
brought him into homicide after they'd successfully worked a bridge
case, that of a teenage murder. Foster was also the first person
Rawlins had come out to as a gay man, and perhaps he'd also be the
first person on the force Rawlins would come out to as being HIV-
positive.

Rawlins replied, "Yeah."

When he'd first walked into that room down there, it was almost
more than he could take. Speechless, Rawlins had struggled not to
hurry to Andrew's side and cry out. Foster, who knew him so very well,
had sensed something like that, and of course he'd seen Rawlins's
eyes redden and swell as he turned and darted out of the room.

Feeling a need to explain, Rawlins now said, "I met him a few
times—down at this gay center for teens. Todd and I gave a talk there.
He was a good kid. He was interested in law enforcement, and I . . .
I was helping him try to figure out some career stuff. It's just such a
shock, that's all."

"Sure." Foster, a sweet but gruff kind of guy, ran a hand over his
mouth and looked judgmentally at Rawlins. "You gonna be able to
handle this one? It's not gonna be a problem, is it?"

It wasn't that unusual for a cop to know a murder victim. Over the course of his police career Rawlins himself had known roughly ten men and women—mostly drug dealers, but others who'd been abused or been involved in previous crimes—who'd ended up dead one way or the other. So it wasn't a problem for a cop to investigate the death of someone he knew unless, of course, there was a relationship, either platonic or romantic. And that's what Foster was asking here, that's what he wanted to know: Was this going to be a conflict of interest for Rawlins?

Rawlins looked down at the floor and simply said, "No."

"Good. Come on, I got the girl who found him."

Relieved that he'd gotten over that hump—and certain that Foster would never bring it up again—Rawlins followed his partner through the first door on the right and into the laundry room. Like everywhere down here, the concrete floors were painted a glossy battleship gray and the walls an old, dull white. The room itself was a large space, holding only an old table and chair, two deep sinks, two mustard-colored coin-operated washers, and two coin-operated dryers. On the outside wall were three high, narrow windows that peeked onto a walk alongside the building.

Near one of the washing machines stood one tall cop, and next to him sat one distraught young woman.

The officer, a big guy with a dark goatee and a rather severe look on his face, had obviously been grabbed from the perimeter and now stood nearly motionless. The girl, somewhere in her twenties, sat on a ratty orange chair, her dark brown hair tumbling down and around her round face. Wearing ragged jeans, a baggy Carleton College sweatshirt, and only socks, she fiercely clutched a wad of tissues and stared down at the floor in shock.

"Rawlins," began Foster in a soft voice, trying to sound sensitive, "this is Kathy Diedrich. She lives in the building and she's the one who found the body. Ms. Diedrich, this is my partner, Sergeant Steve Rawlins. Together we'll be investigating what happened here tonight. Thanks for talking to us."

She slowly looked up at Rawlins, her red but dry eyes studying him for an odd moment. A flash of panic zipped through Rawlins. Did she recognize him? Had she seen him here in this very building?

Her gaze then falling slowly to the floor, she said, "I've never seen a dead body before—never."

Rawlins managed to say, "I'm sure it was a shock."

"My grandfather died last year, but . . . but I didn't see anything." Her bottom lip started to quiver. "It was a closed casket, you know."

It flashed through Rawlins's head: Girl, do you have any idea how lucky you are? Do you know how many I've seen? Then he took note again of her sweatshirt. A Carleton grad. Okay, so she was probably smart. Probably from an upper-middle class family. Relatively sheltered. This was probably her first apartment, her first time living in the city. And her first real taste of tragedy.

"Can you tell us," asked Foster, "why you came down to the apartment and what you found?"

She looked at him, shrugged, and in a small voice said, "My sink backed up. I didn't have a plunger, so . . . so I came down to ask Andrew for one. I mean, he was the caretaker and everything so . . . so . . ."

"About what time was this?" asked Rawlins.

"Eight-twenty."

"You're sure?"

She nodded. "My favorite show was on at eight-thirty and I didn't want to miss it, so I glanced at my clock just before I came down."

Rawlins continued, saying, "So you came down the front steps?"

"Uh-uh. The back ones."

"Did you see anyone else?"

"No."

"Notice anything strange?"

"Uh, I don't think so."

Foster cut in, keeping his gravelly voice soft. "And then?"

"Then . . . then I came down here. His door was open."

"You mean, unlocked?"

"No, I mean open. You know, cracked open about three or four inches. I called out to him and knocked and just sort of stuck my head in." She put a hand to her mouth and started softly crying. "He . . . he was there on the bed and . . . and there was all that blood."

Rawlins said, "Did you go in?"

"No, I screamed. I screamed and I ran back upstairs. I was scared that whoever did it was still in there . . . or somewhere else in the basement."

"But you didn't see anyone, right?"

"No, not at all."

"And then?"

"Then I ran straight up to my apartment and called nine-one-one."

Rawlins looked over at Foster, and they both intuitively knew it. This was as much as they were going to get out of her here and now. Neal Foster raised his brow in silent question, and Rawlins replied with a nod. On to the next phase.

Posing it as a request when actually it was a necessity, Foster asked, "Ms. Diedrich, would you mind coming downtown to the police station? We'd like to get a full statement from you."

Her eyebrows pinching together in an anxious roof shape, she said, "But . . . but I don't know anything else."

"It's just a technicality, that's all."

"Well . . ."

"It would help us very much."

"Okay, sure." She wiped her nose. "But I don't need, like, a lawyer or anything, do I? I mean, I didn't do anything. I'm not in trouble, am I?"

"No, it's just standard procedure to get a statement from all witnesses."

"Oh, yeah," she mumbled, as if she remembered seeing something like that on television. "But can I go up to my apartment? I need to, like, get my shoes. And . . . and can I call my boyfriend and tell him where I'll be?"

"Of course." Foster motioned to the tall cop, who had stood quietly this entire time. "You go upstairs and make your call and get your stuff, and then Officer Sandvik here will take you downtown in his squad car."

She nodded, wiped her nose, and then pushed herself to her feet. Rawlins caught Sandvik's eye and gave him a nod, and the officer followed the young woman out. Once they'd disappeared, Rawlins crossed the room and leaned against one of the beat-up washing machines.

"She doesn't seem to know much."

"Nope, but we'll just have to see what we can jog loose." Foster shrugged. "She didn't mention the mask."

"Maybe she didn't notice it. Maybe she just saw all the blood and . . ."

"Yeah, probably." Foster thought for a moment, then said, "Let's not release that to the media—you know, that his eyes were covered."

"Good idea," replied Rawlins, hoping to God there wouldn't be any copycat murders.

"From the looks of it—I mean from the way the blood is still pretty wet—I'd say this happened pretty recently, maybe within the last two or three hours. Of course, we won't know for sure until the ME has his say."

"Now what?"

"The B of I guys are in there goin' full tilt."

Right, thought Rawlins, scratching his chin. Technically, at this point the B of I team and Foster and he were the only ones who were supposed to have access to the crime scene itself. Once all the forensic evidence had been gathered, once Rawlins and Foster had completely gone over the scene, then they'd call the medical examiner, who'd remove the body for autopsy.

Rawlins said, "It looks like the kid lived alone."

"Well, you never know," replied Foster. "We still need to get a search warrant. I mean, we don't want to lose anything."

If they didn't and there was something in there that belonged to someone else—say, to a kid who had crashed there for a few days— that evidence would become inadmissible, no matter how valuable. Something like that had happened a year ago on a murder case when a rookie cop had discovered a gun in a closet and taken it without a warrant. It had turned out, in fact, to be the murder weapon, but because it belonged to the victim's sister, who also lived in the house, it was thrown out of court. And the sister, who had become the prime suspect, went free.

"You want to write up the warrant?" said Rawlins, wondering how in the hell he was going to get back in there.

With a shrug, Foster replied, "Sure. I got my computer out in the car, all I gotta do is find a printer. You want to go downtown and take her statement?"

"Actually . . . actually, can't we get someone from the dog watch to do that? We're going to have a shift carry over in a few minutes," he said, meaning that the next Car 1110 rotation was about to begin, "and I really don't want to leave here yet, not while this is so fresh."

"Sure."

An empty silence fell between them. They both knew what had to be done next. And they both knew it was the worst.

Foster said, "What about the family? You want to do it? I looked in his wallet and got his home address."

"Listen . . ."

"Okay, okay, I'll do it but you're gonna owe me, big-time too." Foster pushed himself to his feet. "You know what the best part about retirement's gonna be? Not having to make these shitty calls, that's what. Not having to call up some mother or father or wife or husband in the middle of the night and say, guess what, your worst nightmare has just begun."

"Thanks. I'll do the next call, I swear. And I'll take care of all the other ones tonight."

Among other things, of course, he'd have to call dispatch and see if they had a record of any recent calls from this address. Then he'd have to run a CAPRS check and see if the Computer Assisted Police Reporting System indicated the victim had any felonies or arrests.

"I want a beer and a burger out of this one," said Foster.

"You got it."

They left the laundry room, Foster heading to his Crown Vic, parked somewhere in the mayhem outside, and Rawlins starting down the hall toward Andrew Lyman's apartment.

Rawlins figured he had an hour, plus or minus. It would take Foster that long to write up a warrant on his laptop, swing by one of the precinct stations—probably the fifth—to print it up, then stop by an on-call judge, who'd read and sign it. And that, Rawlins was sure, would give him more than enough time. Technically, of course, he shouldn't look through anything, but a search warrant in a murder case was a foregone conclusion—no judge in his right mind would deny it—and who was going to quibble with a bit of time this way or that?

You just gotta do it. You just gotta go back in there.

Right. He simply had to get some distance. And then he had to walk back into that single room basement apartment and not see some kid who was lost and looking, not some gorgeous farm boy whose young, firm body had pressed against his. No, he had to go back and look at a corpse. Andrew was gone. All that was left was the shell. This was work, and in the scope of things Rawlins had seen much worse, from decapitations to vivisections.

Forcing himself down the hall, he took a deep breath, then turned into the room.

This was the door, he told himself, that Kathy Diedrich had found ajar. She'd come down, found it cracked open, knocked once or twice. And perhaps the door had swung open. Looking into the room just as she must have done, Rawlins saw the body, the blood. But not the mask. No, Andrew's head was tilted back slightly, so she easily could have missed the thin black material covering Andrew's eyes.

Ignoring the two people from the Bureau of Investigation coolly going about the room doing their work, Rawlins focused on the double mattress on the floor. The sheets were kicked this way and that. And the beautiful naked body, trim and muscular, once so active, now lay forever still. It was a perfect body, Rawlins saw that now more than ever. The chest was big and broad, the nipples erect with just a trace of youthful blondish hair around them. And that perfect waist was smooth and lean, again with just a hint of hair leading up to and surrounding the navel. The arms were big, too, not pumped up, not overblown, but firm and naturally muscular. Exactly, Andrew was no gym queen, vainly working biceps or triceps over and over again. There was no one muscle that had been overworked and swollen to the point of deformity. No, this boy's body was perfect, naturally so, because he'd grown up on a farm, hauling bales of hay, shoveling seed, driving fence posts. And in that regard, Andrew had died at his physical peak.

But the neck . . .

Once lean and powerful, now destroyed by a single powerful slash that cut deep into muscle and vein. And, yes, blood. A great river of it that had burst from the body and spilled onto the bed as if onto a floodplain.

Oh, Christ, thought Rawlins. What a handsome kid. He saw those small, firm lips, the very ones that had kissed his neck, and Rawlins felt his stomach swell and shrink. Just keep it professional, he told himself. Just pull back. Just look at the scene. What's going on here?

There's one very dead young man lying in the middle of this room and, besides himself, there were two B of I guys circling the body; only they weren't both guys like they usually were. One was a heavy man in gray polyester pants and a striped shirt, his hair gray, his face wrinkled. The other was a woman wearing dark slacks and a blue sweater, her long, thick hair just barely streaked with gray. He was putting a new filter into a small, handheld vacuum cleaner, and she was holding a small video camera to her eye and obsessively taping every inch of that beautiful body, every fold of the sheet, and every drop of death.

Slipping into professional mode, Rawlins stepped farther into the room, crossed to their work kit, and grabbed a thin pair of latex gloves from a small cardboard box. He pulled them on and went to work.

The acrid smell of death filled the room, both from the drying blood that was growing more thick and syrupy by the minute as well as from the body's bowels, which had discharged. Rawlins stepped closer, saw that the apricot-colored sheets were darkened with a foul stain. The top sheet was pushed halfway between the navel and the crotch, and Rawlins lifted it up and peered in. Ignoring the fresh gust of fecal matter, he saw light brown pubic hair and a shrunken, lifeless circumcised penis. He also saw exactly what he expected, a dried milkish dab of semen on the tip of the penis and a glycerinlike shine on the shaft. As if to confirm it, Rawlins dropped the sheet and glanced to the left of the bed and saw a plastic bottle of lubrication and a crumpled white towel that had surely been used for cleanup. Could the perfect DNA samples be simply and easily found in those soft folds?

Turning his attention to the slashed neck, he saw that the deepest part was in the center and then continued to the left, a thick cut that indicated the perpetrator was right-handed. The blood spilled down the neck and to the left as well, then onto the mattress, some of it soaking in and a great lot of it flowing over and onto the floor in a puddle that was undisturbed by footprints or the slightest of smears. That alone indicated that the body hadn't been moved and that the victim had been killed not simply in this apartment, but right here in this bed. Rawlins surmised there had been no struggle, that the attack had come as a total surprise.

But why the mask?

Turning his full attention to Andrew's face, Rawlins studied the thin black mask covering the eyes and held in place by an elastic band around the back of the head. A narrow thing, it resembled the infamous mask of Zorro, except of course this one had no slits cut for the eyes. So it wasn't really a mask, but a blindfold. But why? The obvious reason was to prevent Andrew from seeing someone, and that someone was most surely either the last person he'd had sex with or the person who had killed him. More likely than not, it was one and the same, but perhaps not. In any case, the mask indicated why there'd been no struggle—Andrew literally hadn't seen what was coming.

Oh, God, the poor kid. Shaking his head, Rawlins turned away and rose to his feet.

Andrew, Rawlins knew, had taken the job as caretaker to this and two neighboring apartment buildings not because of the pay, which was nearly negligible, but because it included this cold, one-room apartment. Actually, caretaker was a glorified title. Andrew's job wasn't to screen tenants and lease apartments, for that was done by the owner, who lived in a big ranch house in the suburb of Richfield. Rather, Andrew's job was to vacuum the hallways, empty the trash in common areas such as the laundry rooms, rake the leaves outside, and shovel the walks front and back. All of which he gladly did in exchange for his own place, his first apartment, which was furnished with the abandoned goods of former residents—this lumpy mattress, the beat-up white dresser, the sagging couch, that broken coffee table.

Where would Andrew have put it?

Standing up, Rawlins looked around. There was this room, a closet in the corner, and an alcove that held a small kitchen with a built-in dinette table. Rawlins turned and headed straight to the dresser.

As the B of I guy started vacuuming around the bed, sucking up any fiber, any hair that he could into the small brown, high-filter machine, Rawlins scanned the top of the dresser. Some change, a movie stub, a mostly burned candle. Keys. A beat-up old nylon wallet, dark green with worn-out black stitching on the edges. No, realized Rawlins, Andrew wouldn't have kept it in the open, not just sitting right out here for anyone to see.

Looking carefully over his left shoulder, he saw that the woman—what was her name? Glass? Marcia Glass?—had put down the video camera and picked up a 35mm camera. Focusing her complete attention on the body, she was now shooting picture after picture of the slash on the victim's throat, a close-up from this angle, a broader shot from the right. Good, thought Rawlins, relieved not to be in the camera's view, for he couldn't by any means have this documented.

There were three drawers to the old dresser, the top one narrower than the bottom two. Obviously the piece of furniture had been painted a number of times, the latest coat being white, and he had to tug at the top drawer to get it open. As it revealed its contents, Rawlins's eyes were immediately caught by a photograph of a naked body, a muscular guy posed on a beach, his cock fully erect. Reaching in, Rawlins did a quick check, guessed there were, what, three, maybe four porno magazines. Tugging the drawer a little farther, he saw a small stash of sex toys, including a handful of condoms, a chrome cock ring, and a pinkish latex butt plug. Ignoring the paraphernalia, Rawlins saw a handful of pencils and pens on the other side of the drawer, some paper clips, a rubber band, a checkbook, and a small spiral notebook with a red cover.

A rush of relief surging through him, Rawlins reached for the notebook, then just as quickly caught himself. Glancing back, he ascertained that neither Glass nor the guy was either watching or photographing him, but were both still focused on the corpse and its immediate environs. Knowing that he'd never have another chance, Rawlins lowered his hand into the drawer, cracked the small notebook, and saw the small, neat handwriting, page after page.

Oh, Christ, it was all in here, wasn't it, just like he'd said it was.

And without another moment's hesitation, Rawlins shut Andrew's diary, carefully lifted it from the drawer, and slipped it into his coat pocket.

Chapter 7

It was their nightly ritual.

While the water power of the mighty Mississippi had once made Minneapolis the milling capital of the world, the title, due to the advent of the gasoline-powered engine, had been lost decades earlier. A substantial share of the world's grain was still grown in the upper Midwest, of course, and the most important thing to the people who farmed the land even today was simply and absolutely one thing: the weather.

So as they did every night just before ten, John and Martha Lyman sat down in their living room and turned on the television. They lived in a white three-bedroom rambler that John's father had built some thirty years ago when he'd torn down the old farmhouse that had stood for almost seventy years. They'd wanted something new. Something modern. A few of the conveniences, because, after all, they did live almost one hundred miles west of The Cities and the land did stretch boringly flat for as far as the eye could see and the mind could imagine.

And while what happened in Minneapolis and St. Paul was of little concern to those who lived out here on the plains, the weather forecast was critical. Particularly now. It was mid-September, and things would start changing fast. The first snows could come anytime, really, though usually nothing stuck until after Halloween. After that, pretty much anything went. Two years ago the summertime high had been one hundred and five above, while the wintertime low had been forty-four below.

"Don't forget tomorrow night's the parent-teacher conference," said Martha, sipping some strawberry herbal tea as she sat down on the couch, a plaid thing done in orange and green.

She was a trim, reasonably handsome woman, with shoulder-length blond hair that she usually pulled back into a ponytail. She wore a wool sweater and, as she did most days, blue jeans. A busy woman, her days were filled with two things, the farm and their children, two of whom still lived at home.

"You're not going to be late again tomorrow, are you?" she asked.

Relaxing in the brown imitation leather recliner to her right, her husband replied, "Nope."

He'd been gone all day until just a little while ago. Off doing some business, he told her. It was something about a loan for a new piece of equipment, though she didn't much like the idea of that. It had been John's grandfather's farm, and while they owed no money on the land, trying to keep this place going was more than a challenge. For over five years now they'd been trapped in a cycle of horribly low prices, grisly weather, plant diseases, not to mention a bad dip in the export market. In the last two years alone six nearby families had gone bankrupt.

Glancing at her husband, she saw a big man, his skin weathered, his shoulders thick, and his jaw square. He'd put on weight, no doubt about that. And too much of it, for sure. She still saw it in him, though, the cute high school guy she'd fallen in love with. And they were still in love and they were going to make it, right? Right?

Actually, she thought, sadly staring into her tea, she was no longer sure. With each year it seemed John had grown more distant, more preoccupied, so much so that Martha sometimes wondered if she really knew him anymore, if they weren't together just as a matter of habit. She tried to tell herself that it was the farm, that John was simply overwhelmed with financial worries, but sometimes she couldn't help it, couldn't help but worry that he didn't find her attractive anymore, that perhaps he had someone else. To top it off, of all their years, of all the troubles they'd been through, this last had been the hardest to come their way. Drought and debt, blizzard and isolation, the near death of Annie, their youngest—Martha had thought they'd been through it all. But they hadn't, not until this past year.

Just one day at a time, she told herself. Isn't that how you were supposed to get through these things? The kids were already in bed, and her day would last just a few minutes longer, until about 10:17, when the weather segment concluded.

Hearing the all-too familiar music, she blew on her hot tea, then looked at the TV screen and saw the *10@10* logo.

And then that wonderfully familiar man said, "Good evening, and welcome to *Ten at Ten*. I'm Tom Rivers, and we have a number of stories tonight, from a problem with the Teacher's Pension Fund to a cancer-fighting enzyme recently discovered at the University of Minnesota. We begin tonight's coverage, however, on a very serious note, that of the murder of a young white male in south Minneapolis."

"Oh, God," she muttered.

It struck her immediately, of course, just the way such things had since he'd disappeared in the dark. Practically every moment of every day since then she'd wondered what had happened to him, just as she'd wondered how the news would finally come back. Would he call? Would he write? Would he simply come walking up the drive, his boots kicking up the dirt the way they always did, that playful grin lighting up his face?

And as she did every single time she heard any horror story, she now silently prayed. Don't let this be about him. Not about my baby. Not about Andy. She was planning on getting up enough money to hire a private investigator, though she didn't actually know how to go about finding such a person. She was, however, almost positive he was there, somewhere in The Cities, and ever since that horrible, horrible night she was afraid of something like this. Afraid that one of these times she'd pick up the newspaper or turn on the television and the news was going to be about her boy.

"Just over an hour ago," continued Rivers, "Minneapolis police received a call reporting the crime. Here with a live report of this still-developing story is our investigative reporter, Todd Mills. Todd?"

Her husband immediately sat forward and started groping around for the remote control.

She quickly said, "Leave it, John!"

"Oh, come on. We don't need this crap," he snapped back, zapping the off button.

In an instant the television screen went blank and melted into blackness. She sat forward, her hands clutching her mug of tea, and fear clutching her heart. There'd been no word from Andy, not since John had dragged him kicking and screaming into the barn. For his seventeenth birthday three months ago she'd wanted so very much to send him a birthday card, a present, money, something, but where? Where in God's name was he?

"But what if . . ." she protested, "what if it's something about Andy? What if something's happened to him?"

"Then he'll have gotten exactly what he deserved, just like I said!"

"Jesus Lord in heaven, how can you say that about your own son, John Lyman?!"

"Because he's no son of mine no more, that's how. If you had seen what I saw, Martha, you'd still be sick to your stomach, just like I am. That kid's not natural, and he's no son of mine! It's time you forgot about him. We got two kids now—two beautiful girls, that's what we got."

The tears just burst out of her, and she dropped her entire mug, its handle cracking off as it hit the floor, the hot tea streaming onto the beige carpeting. Stumbling to her feet, she burst into a run and charged into the kitchen. She hated what had become of her son, she was disgusted by the very thought of it, but now she was beginning to hate her husband too. Would they never, she thought, dropping herself on a chair at the Formica breakfast table by the back window, get past this?

"Jesus Christ," cursed John, tromping into the kitchen after her and throwing the mug into the garbage beneath the sink, "you went and broke my favorite mug. Plus you got tea all over everything, and that shit stains, you know. It stains real bad."

One hand over her mouth, she stared out the window at the old silo and the two white metal pole barns they'd put up some years back. In the pale farmyard light, she saw his blue Ford pickup, her old Chevy.

And that night came whirling back.

They'd dropped the younger ones at her mother's for the night, left Andy at home with a friend, Jordy Weaver, and gone to town to see a movie. It was the first time they'd been out in months, but rather than stopping for a drink after the show they'd come straight home. John was exhausted, and they'd come home over an hour earlier than they'd told Andy. She'd gone to the barn to see how that litter of new kittens was doing, and John had come in, gone straight to their own bedroom, and what did he find in their queen-sized bed but the two of them, Andy and that Weaver kid from the other high school, both of them buck naked. John had knocked out two of Weaver's teeth, then dragged Andy naked and kicking and screaming into the barn, where he threw him up against a wall, stripped off his own belt, and screamed, "You little shit, I'm gonna kill you!"

Oh, God. She'd thought she'd known her husband. She thought she'd seen every one of his dark corners. But she hadn't. Not until that night. He would've killed Andy, too, would've beat him to death, unless she'd come out there with the twelve-gauge.

"Stop it!" she'd screamed, firing a shot straight through the metal roof.

"Do you know what ungodly things they were doing? And in *our* bed for Christ's sake!" John had countered, his face flush with disgust. *"In our very own bed!"*

"Just stop it!"

Then, while she'd held the shotgun on her husband, she told her oldest child to run. And run he had, charging into the house for some clothes, next down the dark road and into the night. He'd never returned, and the only thing they'd heard from him since was a phone call three days later, apologizing and saying he wouldn't be back.

So whose fault was it? Hers? His? Theirs? Was it something they'd done? Something they didn't do?

Starting to cry all over again just when she thought it wasn't possible to shed another tear, she bent her head forward. And that's when it happened.

The phone rang.

Martha spun around on the first ring, stared right into her husband's eyes, her husband who still stood at the sink. And they both silently thought it: Who in the world would be calling this late?

Clutching her stomach with her left hand, clasping her mouth with her right, she knew in her heart that this was it, the one call she'd been fearing all these months.

And the tears started sliding from her eyes even as her husband picked up the phone and in a weak voice said, "Hello?"

Chapter 8

In the City of Lakes water was never far away.

Clutching the dark green plastic bag, the bald man stood on the edge of Lake Harriet, the cool fall water nipping at the soles of his heavy black leather boots. Like the other lakes in the city, this one wasn't so large, just an oval body of water some three miles around. And like the others, it, too, was surrounded by a parkway of road and paths, both bicycle and pedestrian, as well as huge old homes in a riot of styles, from French Normandy to Prairie School and Italianate. There was a band shell on this lake, though, and a rose garden and a heavily wooded bird sanctuary too. Beautiful in a way, he thought, peering across the dark waters and at the lights on the far side, yet so quiet, so utterly calm. Exactly. Which was why he had left here so long ago. Much too dull.

Though he wasn't a towering man, he was good-sized, with broad, muscular shoulders and massive arms. The first thing that people noticed about him was not his high cheekbones or quick eyes, but his smooth head, which actually wasn't bald, but shaved. In college at the University of Minnesota he'd been a star football player until he'd been kicked out for selling pot, and then he'd somehow ended up in Los Angeles. There'd been trouble and then some with the law out there, but then, of course, some twelve years ago his life had dramatically changed. Until then he hadn't had a career, yet now he was a professional whose work took him around the world, including back to Minnesota, his home state. Never in his life would he have predicted it, that he'd voluntarily return, if only for a few months.

His jeans and leather coat were black like his boots, and he would have blended perfectly into the dark Minneapolis night except for his head, which glowed like a moon. Wondering if anyone had noticed him, he glanced over his shoulder. On one path a woman with a nylon pack mounted on her back went riding quickly by on a bicycle. And there, farther down, he saw a guy walking his dog. Yes, he had to be careful. He remembered from his childhood that there was always someone down by these lakes, and that was still the case now. He remembered, too, how surprisingly deep this particular lake was, and he was counting on that. It was the only reason he was here.

He twisted his feet so that his black leather boots sank slightly into the sand, then, clutching the bag in his left hand, bent over and grabbed a rock with his right. So how did you do this? He hadn't done it in years, not since he'd left the Midwest, but he did it now, bent low and to the side, brought his arm back, and heaved. The rock shot out over the water but then abruptly sank with a distinct plunk. Not sure what he'd done wrong, he bent over and fumbled around until he found another one. Holding the rock carefully, he brought his arm back a second time, launched the rock, and watched as it hit the water's surface and dove under without a single skip.

Was anyone watching his failed attempts?

He looked around, saw no one. And then he reached into the plastic bag and pulled out the long metal object. Not wasting a moment, he bent slightly to the side and threw the heavy knife as hard as he could, watching it whirl far out over the water until it, too, sliced through the surface and disappeared.

Satisfied, he bent to the water and rinsed his hand with a couple of quick swirls. He then reached for one last rock, took it, and hurled it out over the lake. Success was not his.

He crumpled the green plastic bag and walked slowly away from the lake, stretching once and yawning. He crossed the pedestrian path, stuffed the bag into a metal garbage can, and continued on past the bicycle path to his car, which was stopped along the parkway next to a stand of trees and the bird sanctuary. He sat for a few minutes in the white Saab as if he were relaxing, but in truth watching to see if anyone—anyone who might have seen him—came along.

But there was no one.

Pleased, the large man with the shaved head started up the car and was just about to drive away when his cellular phone started to ring. He immediately knew who it was.

Picking it up from the passenger seat, he flicked on the phone and said, "Good evening, this is Vic."

"It's me. Did you get it all taken care of?"

"Absolutely. Don't worry, it's all under control."

"Great," said the voice with an audible sigh. "Thanks a million."

"No problem, that's what I'm here for."

Standing in the woods of the bird sanctuary, the attractive man with the light hair watched as the white Saab pulled away from the curb and sped off into the night. Wearing a rust-colored cotton coat and clutching a camera, he peered suspiciously around a thick oak, saw the red taillights shooting away, and he said to himself, Okay, remember this. Remember this because something important just happened. Did that guy just throw what you think he did into the lake?

He'd been there the entire time, hidden by the trees and wondering just what in the hell that other guy, the bald one, was up to. In the faint light from the streetlights he'd taken note of the large, muscular man in the shiny black leather coat. And at first he'd presumed the other had come down here to cruise these woods, like the handful of other men lurking among these trees tonight. But, no, the bald man had instead crossed the road and gone straight down to the small beach. And then . . .

Behind him he now heard the snap of a twig, which sounded so jarring in the night shadows. He turned, saw a bush, a tree. And finally eyes. They burned out of the darkness, focused straight on him. The light-haired man stared back, and a moment later a man emerged out of the pool of blackness. The other was of medium build, not trim but not fat either, and he wore a dark suit, white shirt, and tie. Nice-enough-looking, too, with thick eyebrows and chestnut brown hair and what looked like a heavy beard. His mouth was pinched tight, his face taut, even tense, and he looked almost angry, but of course he was merely hungry, his body famished with lust. The younger one had seen him earlier, their eyes had caught when he'd first made his way in here. He'd seen the wedding ring too. Some exec, he presumed, who'd probably told his wife he'd be working late tonight. Probably made a couple of hundred thou', had two kids, a dog. And while the wife might one day suspect her husband of screwing his secretary, she'd probably never imagine that he was instead down here screwing the boys.

Shit, he thought, feeling his heart suddenly tighten. He's just my type. But, no, not tonight.

Diverting his eyes, he slipped his camera inside his coat and turned away, abandoning any pretext of interest. Carefully and purposefully not looking back so as not to encourage the other, the young man moved out of the woods in two quick steps, then dashed to the left and hurried off to his car.

Chapter 9

Was the idea of a gay relationship ludicrous? Impossible?

Immediately after speaking with Jordy, Todd bypassed the station and returned to his apartment, a two-bedroom condo on the fifteenth floor of a high-rise with killer views of Lake Calhoun. Usually hesitant to drink alone because of the alcoholism that had run so freely in his family, he poured himself a large glass of cabernet just moments after he walked in the door. He was desperate for something to slow his thoughts, if not his heart, and he stood at the sliding glass balcony door, peering into the night and thinking only: What the fuck was Jordy talking about?

Not long ago Todd had seen something on CNN about sexuality and the sexes, and it now came back to haunt him with the thought that a relationship between two men could never work. According to the report, which was done to explain the sundry interests of none other than the President, a man's evolutionary duty was to spread his seed far and wide, while a woman's was to guard her future, i.e., the offspring. In scientific terms that made sense, he thought, but how did it apply to two gay men? And did it mean that by their very nature they were doubly destined to sleep around?

Todd took a long, deep swallow of red wine, then turned and wandered over to the black leather couch that was the main fixture of the living room. He dropped himself into the deep cushions and thought how the heterosexual role model that his parents had provided him as a kid was certainly nothing to rave about. In fact, it was all but a lie.

His father had been a drinker, verbally abusive to both his wife and sons. His mother had been sweet on the outside, but torn with anguish within, coming to life only after her husband had drunk himself to death. In retrospect, Todd thought they should have divorced, for neither parent had been happy. It was, looking back on it, a pathetic waste of two lives.

Yes, Todd had grown up with that archetype and had for a good while mimicked it nearly to a T. He'd married Karen, and they'd looked the beautiful Chicago couple, he a dashing reporter, she a successful physician. They'd been popular and well-off, the quintessential yuppie couple all about the Windy City. The entire time, however, Todd's truth, his sexuality, had been eating at him, and eventually he did the best thing he ever did for his wife, he divorced her.

So he didn't want either the type of relationship he'd seen while growing up, or the type he'd lived before coming out. Yet for all intents and purposes, his relationship with Rawlins had fallen into that marital model and that monogamous expectation, at least until recently.

"I love you and I want to spend the rest of my life with you, I really do," Rawlins had said over dinner last month. "But I'm not sure a monogamous relationship can really work, that it's really practical for two guys. Do we want to be that confined? That restricted? I mean, if by chance I end up having a quickie with someone, I don't want to have to end up lying to you just to save our relationship."

Totally unprepared, Todd asked what immediately came to mind. "What . . . what are you saying? Are you trying to tell me you've already had sex with someone else?"

"No, I'm just trying to be realistic, that's all. And I'm not just talking about gay people either—just look at all the straight people screwing around and lying about it. They always end up splitting up because of some stupid expectation. I want us to be better than that and . . . and I don't want us to break up. That's why I've never been in a monogamous relationship before."

"Well, maybe that's why none of your other relationships has lasted more than a year."

"Todd, come on, be serious."

"I am. It's fine for other people, but an open relationship is not what I want. I just don't think it can work, at least not for me. I don't have that kind of energy."

No, either he didn't have that kind of emotional and mental energy to be continually processing who was seeing whom and doing what with whom. Or he simply wasn't secure enough. It was, he thought, surely a combination of the two, but the latter, if he was completely honest to himself, was probably the far greater of the reasons. No, he didn't give a rip what anyone else did or wanted or how they defined their happiness, but in this restless world he wanted one rock that he could claim and rely upon as his and his alone.

It was the beginning of an ongoing conversation, one that didn't leave Todd with any warm, fuzzy feelings, either.

"I don't want to be confining and restrictive, I really don't. The last thing I want to do is try to crush someone," Todd had recently said. "But, I'm sorry, I just can't handle the thought of me staying at home watching TV while you're off screwing someone else."

"But what about this: You're out of town doing a story, you have too much to drink, and a gorgeous waiter seduces you. It could easily happen, you know."

"Yeah, but, Rawlins . . ."

"Yeah, but what? If it happens you'd rather lie about it?"

"No, I . . . I . . ."

The closest they'd come to a compromise was to agree upon total trust and total honesty. In other words, they wouldn't go looking for it, but if something happened, if one of them strayed outside the relationship, the first to find out would be the other. And then it would be no big deal, end of story.

Todd's black cat, Girlfriend, came sauntering into the room, her tail swishing from side to side in that seductive kitty way. She jumped onto the couch, then made her way into his lap, and he stroked her, running his hand down the length of her spine and all the way to the tip of her tail. She had belonged to Curt, who'd died of AIDS and who'd been so terribly worried about what would happen to the simplest, most innocent thing in his life, this creature. Todd gently pulled her closer, nuzzling her until she broke into a motor of a purr.

Oh, shit, thought Todd as he took another sip of wine, the fucking problem with a gay relationship was that it was like trying to reinvent the wheel. First of all, there was no one sanctioned way to establish a same-sex relationship, particularly not legally, which certainly didn't help. After all, how could you encourage a union with someone without the support of the community, the culture, and the legal system? And how could you support your rights to happiness and prosperity when you had no legal rights to look after your spouse's well-being, health, or financial needs?

On the other hand . . .

Perhaps it was good that everything was open to discussion and negotiation, particularly if the archetypal model, the heterosexual one, had its flaws. And perhaps it was better if things didn't work between two people that they simply split and went their own ways.

But where could you turn for a model of a gay relationship that worked? And what, for that matter, did work?

Trust. Honesty.

Once again, when it came right down to it, that was all Todd wanted: the knowledge that no matter what happened in this wonderful, shitty world, there was one person he could count on for his integrity, for his word. And that was why his heart now ached, not so much because Rawlins might not have kept his dick zipped up in a chastity belt of morality, but because it looked like Rawlins had already broken their recent agreement by not saying anything. Had the entire discussion been futile? Had Rawlins merely been trying to justify something he'd already done?

Or had there been nothing?

Of course that was a possibility, but if something had happened it was now infinitely more complicated. Andrew was seventeen, just a kid. Rawlins was a cop, someone in a position of authority. If something sexual had happened between them, not only did Todd find it reprehensible, but it also opened an insidious can of trouble. Major league trouble. Todd didn't know the exact Minnesota statutes, but there was no doubt in his mind that sex between someone that young and someone that much older constituted criminal sexual conduct.

And now Andrew was dead and Rawlins would be investigating his murder.

"Oh, shit," mumbled Todd to himself.

This was not good. If Rawlins had screwed Andrew, things couldn't be worse, both in terms of the law and in terms of Todd and Rawlins's relationship. And, Jesus Christ, what if . . . what if Rawlins knew something relevant to the murder case itself? Would he withhold it, just as it seemed he had been withholding information from Todd?

It was almost more than Todd could stomach, and he downed the rest of the wine, then sat there in the dim light, slowly stroking the cat over and over. His eyes wide and tired, he looked straight ahead but saw nothing. Some fifteen or twenty minutes later Girlfriend, unable to bear the monotonous, nearly compulsive attention, scurried off, bounding behind a chair and out of Todd's reach. Seeing that it was well after midnight, Todd got up, took his wineglass into the kitchen, where he set it on the white counter, then sauntered down the narrow hall to the bedroom.

Dear God, what was he going to say, what was he going to do, when Rawlins came home, whenever that might be?

He washed, brushed his teeth, and stripped, then went to bed and lay just like that, awake and naked, for well over an hour. He fully knew how these things went, that the first hours of any murder investigation were the most critical, and that if Rawlins came home at all it wouldn't be until very late. Very, very late. In fact, he might just work through the night. And although with each wakeful moment Todd seemed increasingly confident that he himself would never fall asleep, somehow he did just that.

But then he heard the click of keys in the front door.

Rolling over, he glanced at his digital clock and saw that it was 4:09. Lying as still as the dead, his ears traced Rawlins's every movement. He heard the zipper of his jacket, the closet door. Then came the soft padding of steps down the carpeted hallway, through the bedroom, and into the bathroom. A door was shut, the fan went on, a spray of water charged to life. Just as he so often did after a long, tense day of work, Rawlins took a brief shower, washing away the grime of his job and, undoubtedly tonight, the odor of Andrew's death, which was sure to have permeated so very much.

Tense with fear and worry and still without the faintest idea of how he was going to handle this, Todd continued to lie motionless until Rawlins finally came out. With all his attention, he discerned Rawlins coming around the foot of the bed, then sensed, of course, the comforter pulled back. Next the mattress sank as Rawlins climbed in and scooted across, and a second later he was spooning Todd from behind. Todd bit his lip, forced himself not to move, not to say anything, as he felt that thick hairy chest press against his back, as the muscular arm wrapped around his stomach. And it was more than he could bear when he felt Rawlins kissing him on the back of the neck.

Finally, in a faint voice Todd said, "Hi."

Right off the bat Rawlins said, "I love you."

It was far more than he could resist, and he turned his head so that his mouth could find Rawlins's.

"I love you too," he said, and then kissed him.

Never had Todd meant it more. And never had Todd wanted him more, both physically and emotionally. In one quick swoop he twisted fully around, and then they were in each other's arms, kissing and groping, pulling and tugging.

I want you, thought Todd. I need you. Don't go. You're the best, the most wonderful thing that's ever happened to me.

In an instant he was ready. His hand shot down, surfed the fur on Rawlins's stomach, then plunged into Rawlins's coarser pubic hair and found him just as he wanted, rigid and erect. Todd stroked him, and Rawlins shook and clung to Todd, his strong fingers digging into Todd's shoulders.

And then Rawlins, his voice deep yet weak, said, "Are . . . are you alright?"

"Not really."

Right then Todd realized that no matter how desperate he was to know, he wasn't going to ask, not about young Andrew. No, if this relationship was going to work Rawlins was going to have to come to Todd and tell him.

"How about you?" asked Todd, realizing that he had just given Rawlins rope and then some with which to hang himself.

"I'm . . . wiped out."

Todd clung to him, kissing him pathetically on the cheek, the ear, the neck, and realizing finally what was going on here. This was a test. A test Rawlins didn't even know he was taking, but one that he was, at this point, most certainly failing.

Chapter 10

It was just after seven when Todd sensed Rawlins forcing himself out of bed, then back into the shower and eventually back into his clothes. Through a haze of sleep Todd wondered why Rawlins had bothered coming home at all, but of course it wasn't that unusual. When a murder investigation was just cranking up, Rawlins grabbed sleep whenever and however he could.

With each moment Todd woke up more and more, quite quickly so, but he didn't call out to Rawlins, nor did he even flinch. Rather he just lay there completely still until he was absolutely positive that Rawlins was out the door. He didn't get up because he didn't want to talk to Rawlins. And he didn't want to talk to him because he simply didn't know what to say: I love you, I hate you.

Once he heard the front door open and shut, Todd was pulled out of bed by the rich smell of coffee, the lure of which he could rarely resist. He slipped on his dark maroon terry-cloth bathrobe and headed down the hall to the kitchen, where he saw not only the red light of the coffeemaker still burning, but his favorite mug, a tall, thin black and white one with a large handle, which Rawlins had set out for Todd. For Todd's perusal, Rawlins had also left today's issue of the *Star Tribune* on the middle of the counter. And he'd fed the cat. Yes, thought Todd as he surveyed the scene of seemingly domestic bliss, it certainly looked like just another day.

"Good morning, Girlfriend," said Todd, when the cat looked up from her kibbles.

As he poured himself his first cup of coffee he realized that he felt, well, numb, his insides heavy and his limbs weak. He wasn't much interested in the idea of breakfast. Actually, the thought of going back to bed sounded best of all. Okay, Todd, he told himself, face it: You're depressed.

Carrying his coffee, he slowly made his way back down the hall, through the bedroom, and into the bathroom. He reached into the shower stall, turned on the water, then slipped off his robe. Mug in hand, he stepped into the shower and just stood there as the hot water pounded on his back. Shit, he wondered, taking a sip of coffee, what was this all about? And what the hell was going to become of them, Rawlins and him? This couldn't be the beginning of the end, could it?

Unfortunately, the only thing he was sure of was that he couldn't lose control of the story of Andrew Lyman's murder. Which meant that he couldn't stay in the shower as long as he was tempted. Nor could he mope around the apartment or lounge on the balcony and stare out at the lake. Or crawl back into bed and doze away the morning. He simply didn't dare. It was approaching eight o'clock and WLAK's daily editorial meeting started in just over forty minutes, with last night's murder surely at the top of the agenda. Forcing himself to move, he grabbed the pile of articles on Tim Chase from the dining room table, stuffed them into his briefcase, and was out the front door, his second cup of coffee in hand.

Rarely did it take more than twenty minutes to get anywhere in the Twin Cities. This morning it took him just over fifteen to traverse the ribbon of freeways and flat landscape to reach suburban Golden Valley and WLAK, a squat, mostly concrete structure that looked more like a war bunker than a successful television station. Immediately to the rear of the building were a dozen or so satellite dishes, and a parking lot filled with a fleet of trucks and vans and ENG vehicles, all emblazoned with WLAK's logo.

Using his ID card to enter the rear glass doors, Todd bypassed the crowded and busy newsroom to his right, headed down a wide, dimly lit corridor lined with awards and photographs, and turned into a large conference room. Their yellow legal pads and morning coffee before them, a dozen people sat around a dark wooden table in the middle of the room.

It began this way every day at WLAK.

At eight-thirty every morning the news director, the five P.M. and six P.M. producers, the executive producer, a scattering of reporters, and the crew from the assignment desk, including the manager, the editor, and a couple of assistants, all filed into this room. First on the agenda would be feedback from the previous few days' stories. Then those who had been up since the crack of dawn reading any and all newspapers, studying the wire services, and taking as many calls as came in would present a slew of story ideas. Next the general tug would begin as they hashed out what would be reported as the day's most compelling news, who was to handle it, and exactly how it would be covered. If you didn't get ownership of a story right here, Todd knew only too well, there was no telling which way an idea would go. That was exactly why Todd was here: some of the things these people came up with were absolutely nuts, particularly when it came to homosexuals and murders.

Rather than taking a place at the table, Todd leaned against one wall, ready to pounce on the Andrew Lyman story, determined to claim it as his own. He stood silent, half-listening as the news director, Tom Busch, opened the meeting and covered the usual items. As they discussed the ongoing saga of whether the omnipotent MnDot—the Minnesota Department of Transportation—was going to persevere in building a huge bridge over the St. Croix River, Todd decided on the angle he was going to take for his own story and just how he'd pitch it.

"The federal judge assigned to this bridge thing will be announcing her decision just after lunch," said Busch, a burly guy with brownish hair and big round shoulders. "Any of you reporters want to pick it up?"

Carol Wyman's hand immediately shot up. "Yep. I'll take it. My parents have a cabin on the St. Croix, so I'm quite interested in this."

"Fine, it's yours. Just remember, I want equal coverage of the issue. 'MinnDOT's' all worried about traffic congestion, and the Department of Natural Resources is concerned about the quality of a national scenic waterway."

"I'd like to get something in there about the bridge encouraging urban sprawl, which it certainly would do," said the attractive, slim reporter, her brunette hair clipped short. "I mean, if they build a four lane bridge from Minnesota to Wisconsin you can bet the subdivisions are going to sprout like weeds over there."

The executive producer, Bill Summers, a lawyerly looking type with silver hair, looked up and coolly said, "Just keep it even."

"So what are we talking here?" asked Steve Carlson, the assignment editor, who figured prominently in all these meetings. "A sixty second package?"

"No, we covered this one pretty extensively about two months ago," said Busch. "I think a thirty second live report just about the judge's decision would be enough."

"How about I do it from Stillwater?" suggested Carol. "We can get a downstream shot of the river."

"Fine."

"Okay, it's a go," said Carlson, writing it down. "A thirty second live shot from Stillwater. We're talking for both the five and six, right?"

"Right." Looking up at Todd, Tom Busch said, "Now, what about this kid who was killed last night? What's the story there, was or wasn't he gay?"

Todd, who had correctly assumed the story would come up on the early side of the meeting, stepped away from the wall, and said, "I couldn't report on it any more directly last night because the police haven't released it, but Andrew Lyman, the kid who was killed, was most definitely gay."

"That a factor in the murder?"

"I'm pretty sure it was. He was found in bed at eight-thirty in the evening with his throat slit. From what I was told by one of the homicide investigators, chances are he'd just had sex with someone," said Todd, knowing that this was it, his pitch to obtain complete control of the story. "Andrew was a runaway, and he grew up on a farm some-where outstate. I think it was in western Minnesota, actually. From what I understand, his parents found out he was gay and kicked him out. I met him at the Domain of Queers, the gay/lesbian youth center where I gave a talk."

"Did you know him well?" asked Summers, scrutinizing him.

He was asking, Todd knew, if it was going to be a conflict—which of course it would be for a host of different reasons.

"No," replied Todd. "I met him just a couple of times. But that's enough, of course, for me to be able to put a personal angle on this thing."

Busch said, "So we got a gay murder on our hands? Is that how you want to come at it?"

"Absolutely not. First of all, I think just about every other station is going to use that tack. Second, I want to give the story more depth, if for no other reason than it raises some very complex questions. I want to start out by talking about a young, healthy kid who happened to be gay. I want to talk about a kid who was lost and looking, a kid whose parents threw him out because of his sexuality. And I want to work this in with the Domain of Queers and how they're trying to provide a sense of place and direction for kids with poor self-esteem and nowhere to go."

Carlson, always wanting to keep things focused on who was doing what and when, asked, "What are you thinking? A package at five?"

No, Todd wanted the big one. He wanted the six P.M. All of this, though, was simply a matter of negotiation.

"No, I'm not sure I can be ready by then. I want to get as much from the police as possible, and I want to try and dig up something on the parents too. The more time I have the better."

"Then how about a VOSOT at five?"

Perfect, he thought. He could easily do one for the five o'clock, which would in turn give him exposure on both evening shows.

"Sure," he replied. "Then I can front a package at six."

"Okay," said Tom Busch, looking around the room, "then let's make this our lead story on both the five and six. Do we agree?"

"Sure," replied Carlson.

Bill Summers nodded, which prompted a few more heads to go up and down. And then it was all set. Todd's work for the day was cast in stone.

As they launched into a discussion about the proposed merger of two area banks and how it should be covered, Todd grabbed his briefcase and ducked out. In the hallway he passed several reporters just now heading into the meeting, and then he turned into the newsroom. It was a large space filled with cubicles and dominated by the assignment desk, which was elevated and looked out over everything, functioning much like flight control. Only a handful of producers were at their desks, some hammering away at keyboards, a couple yammering on the phone, as producers, of course, were wont to do.

Todd passed a dark hallway of glass edit booths, wound his way around, and turned into his glass-walled office. As always, the first thing he did was hit a couple of keys on his computer and check his e-mail. There was not much of significance—notification of a joint birthday party for four coworkers at five this afternoon, a message from one of the producers that she'd submitted one of Todd's pieces for an Emmy, and a staff-wide notice about vacation procedure. He then picked up his phone and listened to his voice mail, finding that three tip callers had phoned in last night to tell him about the murder, then someone else had phoned this morning from one of the local gay organizations wondering if Todd had any more information. The last call was from a man asking if Todd knew anything about a recall on blue cheese. There was nothing from Rawlins, which Todd didn't know how to take.

While he worked almost exclusively with Bradley, whom he considered to be their best photographer, not to mention the easiest and most flexible, Todd didn't have his own researcher/producer. Last month the news director, Tom Busch, had told him he could have such a person, but Todd had been and still was reticent. Perhaps he was being both foolish and selfish, but he didn't want to be tied down, just as he didn't want to be responsible for filling another person's day.

In the past when he'd needed either research assistance or a producer he'd always simply commandeered someone. It was times like now, however, that were making him reconsider. Not only would it be good to have someone to bounce ideas off of, there were a myriad of questions that had to be answered today. Exactly how old was Andrew? Was he previously in any kind of trouble? What were the names of his parents and what was their phone number? Exactly who was Andrew working for here in town? And, of course, had the runaway with no assets except his body ever hustled?

Todd was just reaching into his desk when the phone rang. Hoping it wasn't someone else calling about a blue cheese recall, he picked it up.

"WLAK, this is Todd Mills."

A bright female voice said, "Hi, Todd, how are you?"

"Ah . . . fine."

"I hope I'm not calling too early."

Uncomfortable with her personal tone, he hesitated, then said, "No."

"Oh, good. Listen, I just wanted to check in. Do you have a couple of minutes?"

She was young-sounding and definitely energetic, but who the hell was she? Another crackpot caller? Her voice didn't sound the least bit familiar.

He asked, "I'm sorry, but who is this?"

"Oh, how stupid of me. It's me, Melissa. And I'm just calling regarding your request."

"My request?"

"Yes, it was faxed to me last week. Sorry it's taken me so long to get back to you."

Todd stretched his mind this way and that, but he couldn't quite get a handle on it. Just as he didn't know her voice or her name, nor did he know what in the hell she was talking about.

Melissa said, "So do you have a couple of minutes to visit with me?"

This wasn't making any sense, and he said, "I'm sorry I'm not tracking you here. You're calling regarding a fax?"

She laughed in an almost too familiar way. "No, no, Todd. I'm calling you regarding the interview with Tim Chase. They faxed me your request from Hollywood. I'm Mr. Chase's publicist."

Suddenly Melissa, who was obviously not Minnesotan at all but oh-so-casual Californian, had Todd's complete attention. He sat forward in his chair and cleared his throat. Just sound cool. Just sound collected. And intelligent.

She continued, saying, "Didn't anyone from L.A. call to let you know I'd be in contact?"

"Actually, no."

"Oh, I'm sorry! And here I'm calling out of the blue and babbling on and on."

"That's okay. I'm just pleased someone's calling me back. Thank you very much."

"Of course. It's my job, after all. Actually I'm calling you this morning because I saw you on TV last night, you know, at ten o'clock. Nice work."

"Thanks," replied Todd.

"It's so sad, though. Was he really just a kid?"

"Yeah, just seventeen."

"Do his parents know yet?"

"That's a good question. Actually, I don't know." Trying to get control of the conversation, Todd said, "But if you saw me on TV last night that means you must be here in town."

"Yeah, I am. I flew in with Tim ten days ago." In a light way and with a slight giggle, she added, "I travel just about everywhere with him."

Which meant, of course, she had power. Big power. Todd had no idea if she worked for Chase or if something like a studio had in fact hired her to keep an eye out for one of their biggest investments. Regardless, she was obviously the gatekeeper—a purposely sweet, cheery one at that—to one of the most powerful Hollywood stars. So

what was this call? The nice letdown? Was she calling to tell Todd
that, no, he didn't get the interview? Perhaps. And perhaps he was getting this call simply because he was part of the media and Tim
Chase's keepers certainly didn't want to piss off anyone who could
make ripples, however small.

"So," Melissa continued, keeping the spotlight on Todd, "what are
you going to do? I mean, is there anything new on the case?"

"Not really. Not yet."

"So was the kid gay?"

"Well, the police haven't confirmed it yet, but, yes, he was,"
replied Todd, finding it odd that she was taking such an interest. "He
was a teenager and he was gay and he was a runaway."

"Wow. How sad. And now he's dead. What are you going to do
next? I mean, do you have another report to do?"

"Oh, yeah. One at five and then a larger one at six."

"I see. So do you have to talk to the police again?"

"I've got to talk to everyone—the police, people in the apartment
building where he lived, his friends, and hopefully his parents."

This, he thought, even as he spoke, was weird. Publicists didn't
keep you on the phone for seemingly no reason. They had better
things to do, like press releases to write, influentials to schmooze, not
to mention about a million phone calls to make. So what was going on
here? As friendly and as sweet sounding as she might pretend, Todd
definitely found himself squirming. What kind of game was this? He
had a distinct feeling that she'd done her homework and that she
knew a good deal about him. So could it be that instead of a thanks-
but-no-thanks call she was actually feeling him out? In other words,
was this an interview? It was, wasn't it? Shit, realized Todd, could he
be that close to Tim Chase?

Wanting to sound as real and intelligent as possible, he quickly
thought of a tack, saying, "I'm sure most if not all the other stations
will be exploiting the victim's sexuality, but I think that's too cheap. I
want to keep it as personal and real as possible. From what little I do
know at this point, I doubt this kid was killed simply because he was

gay. Rather, I'm going to try to show how a family broke down over one particular issue and what that eventually led to."

"You mean, like the permanent destruction of the family?"

"Exactly."

"Cool," replied Melissa with such an accent that it sounded as if she was saying *kewl*. "You know, that almost sounds like the theme to Tim's movie. You know, *The Good Heart,* the one he's filming here."

"Perhaps."

"Listen, Todd, getting to the point of why I called, Tim only likes to do one television interview per town. It just gets too competitive otherwise—you know, who's going to run the first interview, who's going to come up with the snappiest angle, the juiciest gossip. Let me tell you, it's a recipe for disaster."

"Sure, sure."

"So we have to be really careful about who we choose. And that means we kind of have a different process for doing these things." She paused, and in a kind of bright but fake way, she asked, "Am I making any sense?"

Todd sat there, the phone pressed firmly to his ear. What the hell was she saying? Did he or didn't he have the interview?

Todd said, "I think I'm following."

"Well, let me put it this way. Tim wants to meet you before we agree to anything."

"I see," he replied, hoping his tone didn't belie his surprise.

"Good. How about tonight? Tim was wondering if you could come over about nine for a glass of wine. How's that sound? Tonight okay?"

"Nine tonight sounds great."

"Fantastic. Here, let me give you the address."

Chapter 11

Wanting to see if anything new had come in, Rawlins and Neal Foster met the guys on dog watch, Meyers and Erickson, not long after they came off their shift. They gathered at a booth at Perkins on Lake Street, where each of them drank coffee like water and ate breakfasts that were massive enough for two or even three. Discussing the murder of Andrew Lyman took all of about ten minutes, for there was nothing new, at least not in the few hours that Rawlins and Foster had crept away to sleep. Even Kathy Diedrich's formal statement, which Meyers and Erickson had taken at the beginning of their shift, had revealed nothing significant about the way in which she'd discovered the body.

Immediately afterward, Foster headed over to the medical examiner's to take another look at the body, and Rawlins went to the downtown station in City Hall. Rawlins parked his silver Taurus alongside the huge red granite structure, the walls of which were as thick as a castle, then passed through the arched entrance on 4th Street. Entering the dimly lit lobby, he made his way past the large marble statue of Neptune and the small bust of Brian Coyle, the city councilman who had died of AIDS. Proceeding up the massive marble staircase worn smooth with age, Rawlins headed to the second floor, where a receptionist behind a bulletproof window buzzed him into the Criminal Investigation Division.

Everything here had been recently renovated, and the only hint that this was a turn-of-the-century building was the soaring ceilings and the huge windows, which were now covered with copper-colored miniblinds. While the Homicide Division used to be a true Bull Room, with a bunch of old desks in one large space and everyone shouting and moving about, it now more resembled a corporate office at the Pillsbury Company. The mauve carpet with its square pattern ran throughout, the cubicles, designed for two investigators each, were lined up in neat rows along the windows, and the modern desk chairs were not only ergonomic, but their mauve fabric matched the carpeting. Rawlins kind of hated it, particularly since there was no privacy. It didn't matter whether you were calling a suspect or a lover, everyone could hear everything—it was that tranquil, that professional-looking. The only indication of what went on here was a hanging clipboard that was packed full of arrest bulletins and the occasional gun belt draped over the back of a chair, neither of which you'd ever find at the Doughboy's.

Rawlins went directly to his cubicle, a long, rectangular space with two desks and one computer, which he shared with Foster. Without taking off his brown leather jacket, Rawlins sat down at the outer desk, then leaned forward and let out a distinct huff of air. No doubt about it, he thought, as he bent forward and bowed his head into his hands, this was all fucked up. That Andrew was dead was unbelievable. What was worse was that now he himself could be linked.

Leaning back, Rawlins glanced around the corner of the cubicle and saw no one. He then reached into the pocket of his jacket and pulled out the small spiral notebook. Opening the diary, he glanced at the first few pages, each one filled with Andrew's tight, precise handwriting, and each paragraph filled with details of his exploits. Seeing nothing of particular concern, Rawlins thumbed on, learning more than he actually cared to about someone else's life. Flipping toward the end, Rawlins saw his own name. Shit. He read a couple of more pages, which described everything, then pulled open his file drawer, found a file marked for receipts, and dropped the small notebook in the back.

Jesus Christ, how the hell had he gotten into this mess? Just what the hell had he been thinking?

He shook his head and forced himself to press on, for quite simply he had massive amounts of work to do. While last night he'd gone home to catch a few hours' sleep, more often than not on a new case Rawlins simply stayed up, working through the night, looking at every angle, examining each and every piece of evidence. Every homicide investigator worth shit knew it and knew it well: if a suspect didn't surface in the first twenty-four hours, your chances of identifying one began to plummet as fast as a boulder dropped in a lake.

As it was, Rawlins had stayed at the scene of Andrew Lyman's murder for over five hours. He'd been in the apartment until the Bureau of Investigation team filmed every square inch and sucked up every single fiber and hair, and then he'd watched in near shock as the medical examiner loaded Andrew's beautiful young body into a vinyl bag, zipped him up, and rolled him away. He'd then checked with CAPRS and the local police station, neither of which had any logged complaints against Andrew Lyman or record of disturbance for this particular address. Moving on, Rawlins had interviewed several other residents, searched unsuccessfully for any additional witnesses, then finally taken the license plate numbers for eight cars parked in the rear of the building. As a matter of fact, he now thought, the registration checks on those vehicles should already be complete.

So where was he going to start today? First, of course, he wanted to read through the statement of the young woman who had found Andrew's body. Then he'd contact forensics, see if there were any early results, perhaps any hair samples. And when, he wondered, was the autopsy scheduled? He doubted that they'd learn anything new on the manner of death—Andrew had obviously been killed by a large, sharp object slashed across his neck, and Rawlins was ninety percent positive that it had happened right there in Andrew's own bed—but he was curious to see if there were any drugs in Andrew's blood. That was the one thing he didn't know about Andrew, whether or not he did any kind of dope. And, of course, he had to find out who Andrew had been hanging out with at the Domain of Queers.

A list. Right, he thought, opening his top drawer and pulling out

a half-used pad. Just do what you always do: make a list and go down
it nice and methodically.

He was just taking out a pen when his phone rang. He yawned as
he reached for the receiver. Could it be Todd?

"Homicide, this is Sergeant Rawlins."

"Hi," said a hesitant male voice. "I'm trying to find the detective
in charge of the murder of that kid. Someone put me through to you.
Have . . . have I reached the right person?"

Rawlins was immediately awake. A tip call?

"Yes," he replied. "That's my case. Who's calling?"

"You know, I don't think that's really important. I mean, I'd rather
not say. I just can't get involved."

Okay, maybe he'd get the name later. The important thing was not
losing him, whoever he was.

In as even a voice as he could, Rawlins asked, "Is there something
you'd like to tell me? Do you have any information that might be helpful to us?"

"That's just the thing. I'm not really sure. You see, I was down at
Lake Harriet last night and . . . and I saw something kind of strange.
It didn't really click until I read the paper this morning. You know,
when I read about that kid getting killed."

"What did you see?"

"Well, there was this guy—he threw something in the lake. I
couldn't see what it was, but it looked like a piece of metal. I mean, I
don't even know if it was a gun or a tin can, but it was just kind of
weird."

"Where exactly was this?"

"You know where the Rose Gardens are? I was near there in some
woods. I mean, this guy, he couldn't see me."

Was Rawlins understanding correctly? The woods just to the west
of the Rose Gardens was a known cruising area. So had this guy been
in there, hunting for anonymous sex, and seen something? Quite possibly. Rawlins thought for a quick moment. How in the hell was he
going to get it out of him? Was his best chance being as direct as pos-

sible? Perhaps, but then again maybe not. If he was down in those woods he could easily be a closet case. And chances were that if Rawlins came right out and asked him if he was cruising, he'd hang up. A little information this guy didn't mind giving, but outing himself was, as they said in Russian, an entirely different opera. So how could he do this in the least threatening way?

"About what time was this?" asked Rawlins.

"Um, a little after eleven."

"And you were down in the woods by the Rose Gardens?"

"Ah . . . yeah. I was down there with my camera."

"And this guy, he was where? Down by the lake?"

"Exactly. There's a small beach. He was standing down there."

"I see. You know, this might be very helpful to us. I appreciate your calling." Okay, thought Rawlins, he'd just simply lay out his own cards. "I'm gay, which is why I'm particularly interested in this case. You see, the young man who was murdered was also gay."

"He . . . he was?"

"Yes, most definitely."

"Oh, God."

Rawlins could hear it, the trepidation quivering in this guy's voice. Which meant what?

"Listen," began Rawlins, "I don't want to get into anything too personal, but—"

"I'm sorry, but I can't tell you my name."

"No, of course not. Of course you don't have to."

"And if you're trying to trace this call, it won't work," he said matter-of-factly. "I'm not at home."

"Please, you don't have anything to worry about."

"I just wanted to tell you about something that might be important."

"And we appreciate—"

"I was down there," said the tip caller quickly, "and I saw this guy who was completely bald throw something in the lake. Then he turned around and stuffed something in a garbage can. And . . . and

then he got in his car—a white Saab convertible with a black roof—
and took off. That's all."

"That's wonderful, we really do appreciate it. I—"

"Listen, I gotta go."

"Wait, don't hang up!"

"You don't understand."

"Wait!"

Oh, shit, thought Rawlins, hearing the click on the other end.
He'd lost him. Shit, shit, shit.

He held the receiver to his ear for a long moment, then slowly put
it down, cursing himself for having come on too strongly. He'd been
out of the closet for so long that he'd forgotten how frightened, how
threatened, people could be by their own sexuality. Or how dangerous
it could be for someone. Perhaps the tip caller was married and had
kids. Or perhaps he was worried about work. Or maybe he was in the
military. But Rawlins was quite sure of one thing: that guy hadn't been
down in the woods taking pictures of birds or the moon. For Christ's
sake, it had been going on midnight and it was a cloudy night. No,
surely the caller had been tricking, surely he'd gone down there for
what he couldn't or dared not get elsewhere, sexual contact with another man. Maybe he'd had sex with this bald guy. Maybe not.
Regardless, he'd witnessed something he wasn't supposed to have.

Angry at himself for having lost the tipster, Rawlins sat there shaking his head, yet knowing what he had to do next. It might be nothing, but he certainly couldn't ignore it.

Right, time to go fishing.

Chapter 12

Todd stared at the piece of paper and couldn't help but grin. This was none other than Tim Chase's address here in Minneapolis. And none other than Tim Chase himself, one of Hollywood's biggest stars, had invited Todd over for a glass of wine. About nine tonight. Unbelievable.

Unable to wipe the stupid smile off his face, he rolled back his chair and stepped out of his office. Still shocked, he stopped dead, stared down at the paper, read it over again. No, he wasn't delusional. Yes, this might actually happen. And as the thrill of it all started pumping through his body, he cut through the newsroom, out the side door, down the corridor, and proceeded directly toward the conference room, where this morning's meeting was still in progress. Holy shit, he couldn't wait to tell them. Were they going to love this or what? Management would wet their collective pants.

Turning into the room, he saw them all sitting there, a stuffy hodgepodge of decision makers who were deciding what was news and what wasn't. A couple of heads turned his way, including the steely white hair of Bill Summers, the executive producer, who all but glared at him. That guy, thought Todd, didn't know shit about what it was like to go in front of a camera, to have your work judged every time you appeared on TV not in terms of quality but in terms of clothing and the way you smiled. He didn't know a thing about hunting for a story, finding a source, or digging out the truth. All that jerk cared about was what brought in the viewers. All he wanted were good numbers, big numbers.

And damned if Todd was now going to bring in news of his possible interview with Tim Chase.

For one thing, it was still just that, a possibility. After all, tonight was just a preliminary meeting, a chance to talk over a glass of wine. There were to be no cameras, no tape recorders. In other words, it was a test in faint disguise. Only if Todd passed—i.e., only if Tim Chase, Inc., thought Todd would and could deliver the right kind of image that would enhance his fame and fortune—would he get the chance to do the real interview. And if Todd flunked, then that was it, bye-bye. And if the latter came true, if Todd didn't get the interview, he sure as hell didn't want to walk back in here and say, Oops, sorry, I lost Tim Chase.

Second, Todd was sure of it, certain that Bill Summers hated him. The glare was that strong. The judgmental casting of the eyes that bitter. Did Summers simply dislike gays or had Todd done something specific that had pissed off this particularly powerful person? Whichever it was, nearly every time Todd saw Summers he wondered why the hell he'd been hired in the first place and if it had been against Summers's strong objection. Regardless, Todd didn't want to give him any reason whatsoever to add a black star to Todd's scorecard. Which meant he'd come back to them only when the interview was a sure thing.

Sobered, Todd turned away and started back down the dimly lit hall. So how was he going to do this, all the things that needed to be covered today? He needed to get a VOSOT ready for the five P.M. and a package for the six. But what about the late news, *10@10?* Who knew what they were deciding back in that meeting, whether or not they wanted a piece for then. If they did, there was no way it could be live. No, they could always run a tape of the story, because Todd for sure wasn't going to be around, he was going to be having his wine with Tim Chase. And if there were any problems he'd work it out with Tom Busch, the news director. Sure, Todd could confide in him, tell him what he was nurturing.

There was no doubt about it, the Andrew Lyman story was going to take up the vast majority of the day. Once Bradley arrived they'd have to dig in, Bradley working on the photography, Todd on both the concept and the text. Glancing at his watch, however, Todd realized the photographer wouldn't be in for another hour, perhaps two. Which left Todd a bit of time to prepare for tonight's meeting with Chase.

No, he thought, trying to imagine what a glass of wine with a Hollywood star actually meant, he wouldn't have to come with a host of prepared questions. Nor would he have to be ready to conduct the perfect interview. Todd just had to be sharp. Alert. And on guard. Right, he had to think in opposite terms, for the truth of it was that Todd himself was the person scheduled to be checked out and in essence interviewed tonight.

His pace definitely slower, he returned to the newsroom, which was slowly filling with associate producers and reporters, then circled the elevated assignment desk and went to the rear of the room, where he grabbed a coffee mug. Turning to one of the large stainless-steel urns, he poured himself a cup, glanced at the gathering of newspapers, including *The New York Times, USA Today, The Wall Street Journal,* and *Los Angeles Times*—all of them there to keep the staff abreast of world developments—then headed back to his office.

As he passed between the cubicles and toward the glass walls of his narrow office, Todd found himself wondering what the real Tim Chase was like, then realized he would obviously soon find out, more or less, anyway. Which was weird. While Todd had met a few famous people in his life, from politicians to newspeople, he'd never met one who was truly larger-than-life, one whose image had captured both the imaginations and hearts of so many millions. So who would be there tonight, just Tim? Tim and his publicist? Tim and his wife? Or would Tim merely make a token appearance and disappear? That, Todd thought, was a very real possibility. Tim might just come in, shake Todd's hand, smile that charming grin, perhaps proffer a wink, and then his publicist and someone like his agent might hammer out how Todd would conduct an interview *if,* they would probably say, hanging out the big carrot, Todd were so lucky to get an interview with superstar Tim Chase. Recalling an interview he'd done with conservative Congressman Johnny Clariton—an interview that of course had ended in total mayhem—Todd remembered all the restrictions and conditions his people had tried to get in place.

Damn, thought Todd. He should have asked Melissa more questions. He should have inquired as to who would be there tonight, what they wanted to know about him, what he might expect. Keeping Todd in the dark, however, was probably exactly what Melissa had wanted.

He suddenly felt the fool. Although he'd always been fascinated by the endless rumors of who was gay and who wasn't in Hollywood, he'd never been much of a star fucker. In other words, he'd never been driven to the point of obsession, to the point of sexual desires and fantasies. Or had he? After all, just why the hell had he pursued an interview with Tim Chase? Exactly what had gotten him this far? It was, of course, that stupid story Marcia had told him about Tim Chase having a same-sex lover. So what did Todd want to do? What was his goal? Out one of the biggest stars? Prove that Tim Chase was no god, but someone just like Todd? Did Todd need that kind of assurance, that kind of validation?

Well, you idiot, you need to go in for that glass of wine with a lot better reason than that. You need a real, solid angle, a specific idea of where you'd take an interview with Tim Chase, or you're going to be chewed up and spit out. Exactly. You sure as hell better get your head screwed on for this one, he told himself as he went into his office and sat down. Make no doubt about it, tonight wasn't going to be some nice little social call. Tim Chase wasn't just some cute guy. He was a multimillion-dollar industry, and Chase and his keepers sure as hell weren't going to let some shit from fly-over land do even the slightest bit of damage to a golden egg that was all about one thing and one thing only: money.

He took a deep breath, cleared his head. Throughout his career, Todd had faith in only one method, preparation. It was, he had come to realize, the lone rule that had saved him over and over again, not simply that he should go into an interview armed with a number of facts, but that he should search for a profound knowledge and understanding of the subject at hand. Like pulling a rabbit out of a hat, he'd gotten out of countless binds right in the middle of an interview by recalling a certain item he'd read somewhere. Better yet, being well prepared let him be flexible and creative, sparking new angles mid-conversation. Simply, Todd was well aware that the more he knew going into a story, the better the end result.

This would be no different.

Lifting his briefcase onto his lap, he found the inch-thick file he'd started months ago. It was all about Tim Chase, every piece of paper therein, and from the top Todd took a copy of his original request for an interview. No doubt about it, he realized as he now reread the letter, he'd been a tad cavalier, for in all actuality he had expected to be declined. Yes, Todd had played the gay card right off the bat. Using the "g" word right there in the first paragraph, he told them he was a gay reporter, said he was interested in how Tim Chase would portray a gay man, and wondered, too, how Tim Chase's fictional family in the film would deal with AIDS. That alone, Todd remembered thinking, probably would scare them away, for there was nothing that sent a publicist—particularly a Hollywood publicist—running faster and farther than those subjects. Oddly, however, that instead seemed to be what had caught their interest, or so Todd was guessing.

Tossing the letter onto his desk, Todd came to the real meat, a stack of articles he'd pulled from the Internet as well as Lexis-Nexis, the news service that had available in its memory just about everything printed. There were, of course, a number of bios, many so saccharine and banal that they were probably done for a legion of teen fans. Not the least bit critical or even questioning, they'd surely been written by a publicist or someone at a public relations firm who had probably never met Tim Chase, nor would even get close to him. In fact, they seemed obviously written to fuel the frenzy, to further the stardom of Tim Chase, to give him allure and magic that he very well might not, in all actuality, possess in real life.

Most of the bios began with Tim Chase's reportedly difficult childhood, which had, they claimed, been the source of his profound inner strength and resolve. His father, a traveling salesman for a lubricants firm in central Ohio, had been on the road constantly, but then was killed on his way home for the Fourth of July when his Oldsmobile was struck by a semi-truck. Tim had been eleven, his kid brother seven, and from there it had all been downhill. His beautiful mother, once the perfect housewife, had fallen apart, washing away her sorrow with gin-and-tonics and handfuls of valium. By the time Tim was thirteen, his mother's alcoholism was so severe that the county took steps to place little Tim and his brother, Greg, in foster care. However, Tim, the man of the house now, would have none of that, and somehow found a wealthy sponsor, once a lush herself, to pay for his mother's treatment and also to pay for summer camp for the little boys. Eight weeks later, with the mom just released and the boys just returned from the woods of northern Michigan, the slow, difficult task of rebuilding a family began. Tim took a job at a car wash, his mom took a job at a shoe store, young Greg concentrated on school. Tim soon took a second job, then a third, all in a desperate attempt to earn enough money to keep the family together. And somehow he did. His beautiful mother stayed dry but depressed, his little brother flourished in his studies and eventually became a doctor, a dermatologist to be precise. Tim, however, paid a price, for his school grades were nothing less than awful. While many thought him dumb, he was simply exhausted from working so many jobs, and barely finished high school. He made a brief stab at a junior college, then did the only spontaneous thing he'd purportedly ever done, he hitchhiked west with a buddy of his. A month later he found himself in Los Angeles without enough money to pay for a meal, let alone a place to stay or a bus ticket home. Desperate, he auditioned for a commercial. And a star was born. Only in Hollywood. Only in America.

Looking up for a moment, Todd wondered about it all, how much of this was fact and how much was myth. Todd didn't doubt that Tim Chase's childhood was a mess, for that of course was the case with many, many actors, but Todd couldn't help but look at a number of the purported facts with an air of skepticism. Had his father really been speeding home to be with his boys for the Fourth, or had he simply been returning from an arduous week on the road? And what about the mother, was she a drinker before her husband's death and was that what kept him away? How long did she work in the shoe store, a week? A year? And Tim's grades, why were they so poor? Sure, he easily could have been exhausted from working so much, but he could also simply have been tormented by same-sex feelings. Perhaps he was sleeping around with every boy in the neighborhood.

Homosexuality. Who knew if you were born bent, if you were made, or if it was a cocktail of the two, but Todd could definitely see a queer thread running through even these light biographies. There was the struggle over his parents, one who failed him by dying, the other who overshadowed his life simply by abdicating her parental role. Then there was Tim's overwhelming sense of responsibility, if that was actually true, which Todd tended not to doubt. Yes, and several of the bios told of Tim's poor sense of self-worth, that it had been and always would be his Achilles' heel. And what about that trip to Los Angeles? Who was that friend? A fuck buddy? Quite easily, Todd thought, Tim Chase could have thrown his cares to the wind for the first time in his life and followed the first big love of his life, some guy, to California.

Or was Todd wrong about that? He definitely saw something familiar there, something that Tim Chase and he both had in common, and realized it could just as easily be alcoholism in the family as well as homosexuality. Todd's own father, who'd emigrated from Poland just after World War II, had never found his place in America—except in vodka. For Todd it had meant that at a very early age he was more responsible than his father. He'd known, just by the glint of moisture in the corner of his father's eyes, when he'd had his first drink of the day. He'd known when not to argue, because, of course, it was futile as well as dangerous, for his father would whip him with his belt at the slightest of provocations. And he'd known when the old man had drunk too much and it wasn't safe to drive with him.

Todd had never known, however, how to earn his father's approval. No matter how hard Todd had tried, no matter how polite, nor how good his grades, he'd never won his father's praise. Todd assumed it was he, the son, who was doing something wrong, and that, naturally, that something was his sexuality. As long as his father was alive, Todd had lived in fear that his father would find out his boy was gay, and Todd had done everything and anything possible, including getting married, to prevent that from happening. In an odd but real way Todd came to believe that if he was good enough his father would stop drinking, but that never happened, of course, because Todd did the one thing good little boys never did, he had sex with other little boys.

Projecting his own needs and fears on Tim Chase, Todd was surprised to feel something he hadn't previously felt for the superstar—sympathy. Earlier, when Tim Chase was more abstract than simply tonight's date, Todd had been obsessed with the Marcia story. But, now, well . . . Shit, what was he going to say to Marcia when they next talked? Oh, say, Marcia, I almost forgot to tell you—I had a glass of wine with Tim Chase. Oh, he's cute. But, oops, sorry, I forgot to ask him who he slept with.

Reading on, there were several pieces about Tim's deep interest in horses, his recent purchase of a Montana ranch, and how he was often sighted at rodeos sporting cowboy boots and hat. Next came a slew of articles analyzing Chase's films, or more to the point, his acting ability. Many slammed him for his one-note acting, known more for its intensity than its finesse, the fury in his voice that brought attention rather than art onto the screen. Many others sighted his all-American good looks—that dazzling smile, the quick laugh, those charming eyes—as the overriding and perhaps singular reason for his success. That he was gorgeous no one denied. Nor did anyone deny that that was what had launched his career.

His films were many, particularly for someone so young, and they had earned fabulous sums of money, ranking as some of the largest-grossing movies in history. There was the hit he'd done about a hunk baseball player, another box office smash where he'd played opposite Robert Redford. Then he'd costarred with Tom Cruise in a Civil War epic. Next a popular comedy opposite Julia Roberts. That was fol-

lowed by another sports flick, which had done only so-so. Todd read
all the reviews, right up to the spy thriller that Chase had starred in
with John Vox, the very guy who'd started Todd's snooping by blabbing
to Marcia about the Tim Chase boyfriend.

So did it all seem possible? Could Tim Chase really be gay? In a
way, no, at least not the way his propaganda machine had construed
his life. But in another way, absolutely so. Todd could see the hints,
the subtle shading. And what reason, after all, would John Vox have to
lie about his friend Tim Chase?

Coming to the supermarket tabloid story, Todd read it all over again.
He'd gotten this copy from Lexis-Nexis, which was reproduced in simple text, so it didn't have all the flair of headlines and photos. It was all
there, however, beginning with the ball-buster headline, "Mean Queen
Chase Denies 7 Year Gay Romance & Buries Boyfriend in Poverty." The
story went on to tell about how Tim Chase met Rob Scott, a handsome
blond, at a bar in L.A. The two had quickly become passionate lovers,
the tabloid claimed, with Chase buying a condo and just about everything else for Scott. More important, they were the toast of parties all
over Hollywood, wined and dined by the likes of David Geffen, who was
gay, and Michael Eisner, who was straight. The affair continued even as
Chase married the beautiful actress Gwen Owens, and the two had a
child. But then there was a horrible spat, and Chase kicked Rob Scott
out of his life, more specifically out of the condo and onto the street
without so much as a dime. Furthermore, the writer claimed there was
a vast conspiracy of silence, proven by the fact that no actors or Los
Angeles journalists, who knew the truth of this story, would comment.
Almost immediately Tim Chase, Inc., went on the offensive, claiming
that *The National Times*, which had a huge national circulation, had paid
Rob Scott, who was destitute, $100,000 for a story that was completely
fictitious. A lawsuit against the tabloid soon followed, which Tim Chase
eventually won to the tune of $8.5 million and which his extraordinar-
ily powerful people claimed "clearly vindicated Chase's sexuality."

His head spinning with innuendo and information, Todd flipped through the last of the articles in the file. Most recently Tim Chase had been on the cover of *Newsweek* complaining about the lack of privacy suffered by stars. More to the point, they each had harrowing tales of the paparazzi, those nasty little photographers who were hiding everywhere to snap the juiciest of pictures. Todd didn't doubt it in the least, but was Chase just irritated, finding the photographers a mettlesome intrusion, or was he living in terror that one day they'd catch him with a guy?

Todd gathered the articles, laid them back in the manila file, and sat there. Nine tonight, huh? Unable to imagine what it would be like, he was sure of only one thing: at least the wine would be good.

Chapter 13

It was almost ten by the time Rawlins was able to get away from his desk. He wasn't totally convinced, of course, that he needed to go, at least today, for more than likely the tip wouldn't pan out. That was what this job was all about, however, going down every little path and checking around every single corner. Ninety percent of his job was monotonous footwork, most of which proved to be worthless, but it was the small details that he discovered here and there that eventually added up. And that's how you built a case, piece by piece by piece. More than once he'd staked out a suspect's house and sat there for hour after hour, day after day, only to discover something of critical importance just as he was about to give up.

So exactly what had the anonymous caller seen last night down at Lake Harriet? A man perhaps discarding some token of love after a fight with his girlfriend? Or a killer hurling a murder weapon into the dark waters?

Heading south on the freeway from downtown, Rawlins took 46th Street over to the lake, then skirted the eastern shore of the round body of water. Passing the huge houses, each one larger than the last and perched on the ridge overlooking it all, he followed the parkway, which eventually led down to the water on his left and, of course, the Rose Gardens on his right. He glanced at the expansive gardens, a large, rectangular space with a broad path down the middle, and knew that all the fragile plants therein would soon be buried beneath a couple of feet of straw and leaves to protect them from the winter freeze that was destined to come this way. No, Minnesota was not kind to roses.

Looking farther ahead he saw the large stand of woods that bled into the trees of the bird sanctuary. Of course that was the place. And of course he knew what went on there. Hidden by the depth of the night and the density of the trees and bushes, men met with men to get what they could get no other place, a touch, a kiss, a blow job, a hand job. And sometimes more, all with no strings attached. Rawlins had always believed that an inordinate share of men who frequented places like these—the banks of the Mississippi, the second floor men's room in the department store downtown, the basement men's room out at one of the malls—were simply closet cases. While a great many of these men were openly gay guys who liked sex—and a lot of it—an equal amount were either married men or others who masqueraded as straight.

Rawlins drove just past the Rose Gardens, parked, and got out, thinking how odd straight people were, or more specifically how odd it was that they confided so much of their sex lives to their gay friends. Did straights assume that gays thought about nothing but sex and would therefore be only too glad to hear of their endless sexploits? Or were straight people that uptight, that repressed, that they couldn't talk about sex among themselves? For whatever reason, more straight people than he could ever have imagined, men as well as women, had told Rawlins how often they had sex, if they'd ever had a homosexual experience, what position they liked best, with whom they'd had an affair, their penis size, what made them come, and so on. Usually once straight people got going, it just came flowing out of them, frequently punctuated by comments like "God, I've never told anyone this before" or "I can't believe I'm blurting all this out" and always "Please, don't you dare tell anyone, but . . ."

All this came rushing to Rawlins's mind, of course, because of Joe Younger, an old high school pal who had three kids, one boy and two identical girls. And these woods across from the Rose Gardens were Joe's. Once a month, perhaps more, he came down here to cruise. Joe had spilled the beans a couple of years ago, calling Rawlins out of the blue and inviting him out for a beer. And what Rawlins had expected to be an evening of awkward conversation—they really didn't have much in common—somehow turned out to be a night of Joe's confession. He loved his wife. He loved sex with her. But they only had sex once every month or two. He couldn't take it, needed it more. And here in these woods he had found it aplenty. Rawlins listened to it all, how Joe said he wasn't attracted to any women besides his wife, how he thought he had too much testosterone coursing through his veins, and wondered with a laugh if he shouldn't just get his nuts chopped off.

"I mean, I've tried, but I just can't stop coming down here," Joe had blurted over his beer.

None of this, of course, Joe had even hinted to his devoted wife, who, by the by, happened to be a workaholic. Hearing that, Rawlins surmised that Joe's purposely busy wife not only sensed her husband was a closet queen, but was in as much denial as he. And Rawlins felt nothing but an overwhelming sense of pity for this family, a wife who was being used for the socially accepted facade she provided and maintained, and a man whose integrity was as abject as it was bankrupt.

So, Joe, were you down here last night as well?

Rawlins looked in the woods, saw a few paths beaten down, and supposed that if worse came to worst he could try giving Joe a call. Maybe, if by chance he'd been down here just last night, he'd seen something as well. If he hadn't then perhaps he knew someone who had, although whether or not he knew anyone by name was one question, and whether he'd release such guarded information was altogether another. Getting someone to talk would be even still more complicated.

Studying the large trees at the edge of the woods, Rawlins guessed that the tip caller had been standing right in that area. And actually, Rawlins thought, as he rotated slightly, the bald man the tipster had spied had probably parked his Saab, the white one with the black convertible top, over there, just about in the same place where Rawlins's silver Taurus was now parked. Perhaps the tipster had seen the other man pull over, then watched him get out, hoping he was headed for these illicit woods. And then the tipster, hidden by a tree, had watched the bald one cross to the lake, stand there, and heave something shiny far out into the waters. Yes, and right there by the pedestrian path was the garbage can the caller had referred to as well.

Surely, thought Rawlins, now crossing the street, it must have gone something like that. That is, unless, of course, the tip caller was not calling to report something he'd actually seen, but done himself. And that was a very real possibility. It was not uncommon for the killers themselves to call in with the best tips of where to find the bodies, just as it was not uncommon for a killer to get the game afoot: Go on, you idiots, catch me if you can.

Studying everything about the scene—the trees, the parking area alongside the parkway, the spot where the bald man supposedly stood down by the water, the garbage can, that bush—Rawlins first of all tried to ascertain if it could have happened as the tipster had claimed. He checked the angles, the sight lines, and, yes, adding it all up, Rawlins realized it could have. The distance between the two was perhaps fifty feet, so the specifics might be a tad difficult, but even if it was a dark night, as it was last night, the lampposts would have provided a fair amount of light. Yes, there was no doubt, it was physically possible that someone could have stood hidden in those woods and watched as someone came down to the lake and heaved something out into the water.

But what about anyone else?

Minneapolis's saving grace—and perhaps the main reason it had not become the Los Angeles of the Midwest—was its extensive park system. More than a dozen small lakes dotted the city, all of them linked by fifty-plus miles of paths that led from lake to lake to Minnehaha Creek and the Mississippi River. Beautiful and safe, the parks were heavily used, day and night, winter and summer, which meant there were people out here all the time. Rawlins himself had jogged around Lake Calhoun at five on a dark winter morning, and he'd strolled around the very same body of water with Todd at midnight on a hot summer eve. So if one person had seen something suspicious, could there be a second out there somewhere, someone who might not have been lurking in the woods?

First things first, he told himself as he crossed the bike path. First you've got to find out if your tip caller really saw anything at all.

He spotted the green garbage can, an oil barrel of sorts with a small, spring-loaded trapdoor on the lid, the kind dotting all the parks. Crossing directly to it, Rawlins thought, okay, the bald man had reportedly stood by the lake, thrown something into the water, then come up here and thrown something away. But what? Lifting open the trapdoor of the receptacle, Rawlins looked in, but was immediately slapped with the most egregious of odors, something akin to a rancid melody of both food and excrement. Which, thought Rawlins, was probably exactly right. He dropped the small trapdoor, then pulled off the whole lid and let it fall to the ground. Peering in, he saw a small riot of garbage, from square Styrofoam containers dribbling refried rice to pieces of plastic wrap holding small crusts of bread smeared with sandy peanut butter. There was a running shoe, old and ripped. A healthy representation of just about every kind of pop can, the remains of their syrupy insides spilling over everything like a sticky waterfall. Entire newspapers. And a variety of plastic bags from clear to blue that held, of course, fermenting dog shit. Yes, by law and by nature, Minnesotans were tidy.

Rawlins spotted a small stick a few feet away, reached for it, then used it as a crude spoon with which to poke this stew of discard. Squinting as if the odor were burning his eyes, Rawlins poked about, thinking how things would be much simpler if he only knew what the hell he was looking for. He flipped back a newspaper, moved a dark green plastic shopping bag, lifted the shoe—had it given way midjog?—then dropped it. And suddenly saw that the end of the stick was covered with a dark red sticky substance. Was that what he thought it was?

A voice behind him said, "Are you looking for something, sir?"

Holding the stick high in one hand, he turned around to see a black woman in the blue uniform of the Minneapolis park police. So, he thought as he reached into his jacket for his badge, just whose jurisdiction was this going to come under?

Holding up his badge, he said, "I'm Sergeant Rawlins, homicide, Minneapolis police, and I think we need to cordon off this area."

It proved, of course, to be blood.

That was the first thing the Bureau of Investigation team from Car 21 did, study the stick and in turn the dark green plastic bag, the inside of which was smeared with the dark red substance. They then sprayed it with Luminol, held a black light to it, and the substance fluoresced with a real attitude, indicating a massive presence of certain proteins found only in human blood. After that, everything kicked into gear, quickly.

While they waited for the diving team to arrive, this team of B of I guys—two former cops, both around sixty, who'd burned out on street work and were waiting for retirement—practically combed the grass. They collected some pocket change, a couple of cigarette butts, and a pen, all of which they dropped into small plastic evidence bags even though it all looked as if it had been lying around in the park much longer than twenty hours or so. Rawlins, operating on little more than a guess, next had them search one particular area of the thin beach, hoping they'd be able to pick up something, ideally a footprint of some sort. But what the lake's small waves hadn't washed away since last night, a dog, running up and down the shore, had recently trashed. There was, in short, nothing to be gathered, save for a few pieces of junk Rawlins was sure were not relevant.

Just about an hour after Rawlins had made his first call, a team of divers arrived from the Hennepin County Sheriff's Office, which had jurisdiction over all the lakes and rivers, both above and below the surface. Launching their small aluminum boat by the band shell, they motored over, the sputter of an engine a rare sound on any city lake. By the time they dropped anchor and two divers in black wet suits plunged into the chilly fall water, the crowd of gawkers was none too shabby. Held back by a thin strip of yellow police tape, there was a gathering of thirty or forty people who'd stopped mid-walk and mid–bike ride to see what was going on. Turning slowly and looking about as casually as he could, Rawlins attempted to study them all, wondering if the tip caller was in the crowd and if he hadn't been a simple witness but in fact Andrew Lyman's murderer. There were three older men, perhaps retired, and a handful of older women out for their daily constitution. Some kids with skateboards. And any number of youngish people who seemed to be just out enjoying the day. When Rawlins saw some guy pulling out his cell phone, perhaps to report to someone what was going on, Rawlins knew there was a call of his own that he should make as well.

Staring out over the water as the divers slowly bobbed up and down, Rawlins took out his own phone, dialed a number he knew so well, and of course reached a recorded message. This, however, was too important, so he hung up and dialed a number based on WLAK's call letters and reached the front desk.

"Good afternoon, WLAK-TV, how may I direct your call?"

"This is Sergeant Rawlins from the Minneapolis police, and this is an urgent message for Todd Mills," he told the receptionist.

"Just a minute, I'll try his—"

"Wait, I just tried his office. Would you please just tell him to get down to Lake Harriet with a photographer right away?"

"You don't care to hold, sir?"

"No, just get him that message. Or give it to one of the producers or something. It's regarding the murder story he covered last night."

"I'll take care of it right away," she said as coolly as a 911 operator.

As he hung up and slipped the phone back into his pocket,

Rawlins saw Neal Foster ducking beneath the yellow tape and heading his way. His eyes lined with heavy circles, Foster had been down at the lab for the last several hours.

Mustering a small grin, Rawlins said, "Do I look as shitty as you?"

"Worse."

"Anything new down at the lab?"

Foster shrugged. "Just like you thought, that towel they found by Lyman's bed has a large semen stain on it. It's way too early, of course, to tell if it's Lyman's, but they're guessing that it is, and they're guessing that there's only one person's semen on there."

"Really?" said Rawlins, unable to hide his disappointment.

"But . . ."

"But?"

"Well, did you see any of that Kleenex they found in the wastebasket not too far from the bed?"

Of course he had, and he clearly remembered the B of I team emptying the contents of the cracked white plastic basket into a large evidence bag. By and large it had all been tissue, crumpled into tight, messy wads. And from the amount of tissue Rawlins had assumed that someone had either had a cold or used the tissue for cleaning up after a sexual encounter.

Rawlins said, "Let me guess, more semen?"

"Yep."

"Excellent."

"Again, it's too early, but let's hope we get lucky there. Otherwise, I spoke with the ME and he said so far they hadn't found any semen in the kid's mouth. None in his rectum either, but they have found evidence of a lubricant on his anus."

"Tell me it's from a condom."

"It is. At this point they think it's a Trojan."

"So . . . since we didn't find any condoms at the scene, it's safe to say that whoever last had sex with Andrew—let's just presume that it was the killer—either flushed the condom or took it with him."

"Something like that, anyway."

The phone in Rawlins's pocket began to ring, and he pulled it out, and said, "Sergeant Rawlins."

"Hey, it's me," said Todd. "The receptionist just paged me and gave me your message. What's going on?"

Wanting to talk to him about this and so much more, Rawlins hesitated a split second, then pushed into business, saying, "Well, I'm down here at Lake Harriet, by the Rose Gardens, and . . ."

Rawlins looked out over the small waves, which were moving across the surface at a soft but steady pace. He saw a man in the boat staring at the water. And he saw one of the two divers, his head sheathed in the black wet suit and his eyes covered with goggles, surface and swim to the boat. The diver raised one hand and gave a thumbs-up sign, and then a second diver appeared from beneath the water.

"Listen, Todd," said Rawlins into the receiver, "things are happening pretty fast. I think you better get down here."

He'd been almost positive of what he'd seen last night. He'd been lurking in those woods right over there and he'd seen that guy hurl something into the lake and then drive away in that Saab. And when he'd read this morning's newspaper, he knew he had no choice but to call the police.

Yes, thought the man with the light hair, standing deep in the crowd of gawkers on the end of Lake Harriet. There was no doubt about it, he'd done the right thing. He'd wondered how they would handle it, if they'd actually take him seriously since he hadn't identified himself to the detective this morning. But he just couldn't tell him who he was. Hell, no. There was no way he could have given his name, no way he could let anyone know he was down in these woods last night.

About a half hour ago he'd driven down here just to see if the police had followed up on his call. Surprised that they had already done so and that the area was now cordoned off, he'd turned past the Rose

Gardens and parked. And now, his large camera hanging by a strap around his neck, he surveyed the scene, looking for any good shots. There were a bunch of cops in uniforms and he wondered if one of them was him, that detective he'd spoken to. Or could he be that guy in the middle, the one in plainclothes with the dark hair and mustache? Or was he the old guy who'd just arrived?

Everyone's attention now seemed focused on the divers who had just resurfaced and were swimming back to the boat. What did that mean? That they'd given up?

"Look," said an older woman wearing a lavender nylon jogging suit and sun visor, even though she'd surely never broken into a sweat in her life, "the divers are getting back in the boat."

"What's that?" asked her friend, who wore a similar outfit but in peach, with fingernails painted a matching shade.

"What's what?"

"That thing. Doesn't one of 'em, one of the diver guys, have something in his hand?"

"Oh, God, Marge," said the lavender one with a sardonic chuckle. "The eyes—they're going!"

A nearby younger man, his large German shepherd leashed and sitting by his side, squinted and said, "Yeah, looks like the second guy's got something in his hand. Something like a knife."

"A knife?" gasped Marge, the one in peach.

"Heavens, I wonder what this is all about," said her walking pal, clucking her tongue and shaking her head in matronly disapproval.

So, thought the man as he stood listening, he'd been exactly right in what he'd witnessed last night. It was just as he thought. That big bald guy had snuck down here and disposed of a knife in Lake Harriet. Which meant what? That the police would be able to tie it to the murder of that kid? Maybe, maybe not. Maybe a night soaking in Lake Harriet would have washed away any definitive evidence.

Shit, he thought, raising his camera and peering through the telephoto lens at the divers, what the hell was he supposed to do now? Even if they were able to confirm it was the murder weapon, then what? How in the hell were they going to find the bald guy and then link it? After all, even if they somehow managed to find a few suspects for a lineup, he sure as hell wasn't going to come forward to identify the guy he'd seen down here.

Okay, he thought, you gave the police some information and led them this far. Now it was time to give them a little more.

Chapter 14

You're supposed to be a rich boy. A rich gay boy. Your family is supposed to have a huge house overlooking Lake Minnetonka, some twelve miles due west of downtown Minneapolis, and this is supposed to be the big homecoming scene. Big, big homecoming scene. After all it's been eleven long, painful years. Your sister's gotten married, has two kids, and Mom's gone totally gray and Dad's lost sixty pounds because it's eating him, this thing he himself once cursed as the gay disease. Just as you said to yourself when you drove out of the driveway and off to California over a decade ago, nothing would ever be the same again.

Get it? Dad's loaded, you're a fag, and now you're coming home not because you have the dreaded thing, but because he does. Think, thought Tim Chase as he sat in his trailer prepping for his next scene, big irony. He kicks you out because he thinks fags are vile and disgusting, as exemplified by AIDS . . . yet now he's the one that's got it. You want to say it out loud: Serves you right, you old bastard. But you can't. You can't even think that because those were his words the last time you saw him. He stood there at the big white front door with the shiny brass knocker, screaming, shouting, saying one thing that stuck like nothing else: *It'll serve you right if you get AIDS!* And for eleven years your very own father's curse has echoed in your head as you've watched friends and strangers in San Francisco succumb to the dreadful plague, and you've thought one thing over and over again: *No one deserves this, no one but someone like your own dad.*

And now he's got it. And you're sick with guilt as if you yourself somehow wished it upon him, as if you yourself somehow had been in that operating room and personally selected the two pints of tainted blood that were pumped into his body. So that's why you've come home, to untangle the love, hate, and guilt so tightly braided in your heart. And—

There was a light but distinct knock on the aluminum door of his trailer, and a woman's voice said, "Tim? Tim, are you in there? It's me, Melissa. I need to talk to you. Do you have a moment?"

Looking up from the script, he muttered to himself, "Oh, crap."

He should have left instructions that he didn't want to be disturbed. Not only did he have too many lines to learn, but every time someone asked a question, particularly regarding business, it pulled him out of the mind-set of the story. Hadn't he always been clear on that? Didn't everyone know that business came either at the beginning or the end of the day, but not in the middle, not during shooting?

Wearing a navy blue sweater, a freshly pressed blue shirt, and khaki pants—the costume his character would be wearing when the taxi drove from the airport and into the drive of his family's home—he remained seated on the couch, and called, "Yeah?"

The knob turned, and an attractive young woman entered. Rather short and small-framed, she had a gorgeous face with dark eyes and a bright white smile. Her long, curly brown hair was put up in a haphazard bun, and she wore a baggy gray sweater and tights that hugged her slim hips. Everybody loved her, not simply because she was beautiful, but because she had a knack for getting people to gab and, of course, eventually say more than they ever wanted to. Both of which were why Tim had hired her in the first place. More often than not, she was the first real image the media folk saw of Tim Chase, Inc., and he needed her not only for the positive first impressions she so easily made, but also for the information she could so successfully glean from the outer world.

"Hey," said Melissa, stepping inside. "Sorry to bother you. This will only take a minute."

"What's up?" he said, managing a smile, albeit a small one.

It was a typical trailer, with goldish-tan carpeting, one couch, a couple of chairs, and a tiny kitchen filled with a stainless-steel sink and some fake wood cabinets. In the back was a single bedroom Tim used for napping. Melissa, a thick file in hand, crossed to one of the chairs and sat down opposite Tim.

She said, "Okay, so this is all the stuff I have on him, this Todd Mills guy from WLAK."

"Oh, right, the guy I saw on TV last night."

He watched as she opened the manila file folder, which was stuffed, and pulled out a sheaf of papers. Taking them, Tim quickly thumbed through the printouts of articles and stories. All he saw were words, words, words and an occasional highlighted sentence.

"Jesus Christ, Melissa, the fucking CIA couldn't do a better job." He looked up at her with a grin. "Where did you get all this shit?"

"Mostly the Net. Some I had to have faxed from the California office. They pulled it off a news service we subscribe to."

"And?"

"And you're right, he is gay."

"Yes, I knew that," said Tim.

"He's got a good reputation too. He's won a couple of Emmys, a bunch of other awards, and he's very, very out. From what I read, he didn't used to be, but then he was implicated in some sort of murder case and was outed. Something like that, anyway. It looks like he used to work for one of the other stations in town, so he's been around here for a while."

"Perfect."

He glanced out the small window and down the hill toward the house and Lake Minnetonka, where they were setting up the cameras for the day's shoot. The house they'd leased for the film was long and white, a sort of French Colonial thing, a story and a half with a big cedar shingled roof. It had commanding views of the huge lake, a perfectly manicured lawn that spread down to the water's edge, massive oaks and maples that were just beginning to turn into perfect Martha Stewart shades of fall, and, of course, a large white dock. It reeked executive. Stunk of old money. Had WASP written all over it. In other words, it was perfect for this movie.

Late last night Tim had watched the local news. And as soon as he saw Mills covering the murder, he had that sense about him, that gut feeling. Right then and there he'd known that, yes, they needed him.

"But, Tim," pressed Melissa, "are you sure? Isn't giving him an exclusive opening a can of worms that you really don't want to have opened? You're paying me for my opinion and direction on these things, and frankly I don't think it's such a great idea. You know it's going to come up, the rumors and all, not to mention the lawsuit."

She didn't get it, he thought, looking at her. She didn't understand. But then again, why should she?

"Don't worry, Melissa. I know this is the guy we want. I know he's the one we want on my side. Besides, one meeting with him can't hurt."

"Well . . . okay." She paused, then said, "I just spoke with him and—"

"What's he like?"

"Nice enough. Rather direct, kind of smart. I think he was surprised I called."

"I bet."

"I wanted to see what he was really like, so I just started blathering away without introducing myself. Then I lied, told him someone from L.A. was supposed to have already called to let him know I'd be in touch. He was a little impatient, but then very, very nice once he found out I was your publicist."

"So he'll be there?"

"Oh, yes. Nine o'clock tonight, your place. I already gave him the address and all the specifics. Namely, I told him this was just sort of a preliminary thing to see how things go. No notebook, no recorders, no cameras. And no one else. Just a chance to talk a bit." Melissa added, "But I want you to think about it, Tim, I really do. If you change your mind, just let me know. I can always cancel, I can always tell him that you're going to be late on the set or something."

Tim cracked one of his famous smiles, bright and kind of sassy. "Don't worry, I know exactly what I'm doing."

"Okay, you're the boss, but I should be there too. Actually, you don't even have to—"

"Melissa, Melissa, there's no need to worry. Since when haven't I been able to handle myself with a reporter, huh? Trust me, there's no need for you to waste your evening. I can take care of this guy."

"But—"

"But what?" he said, the smile still coming, naturally so. "Everyone knows about the rumors. And everyone knows about the lawsuit, which, thank you very much, I won big-time. And I'm married—maybe I'll have Gwen swoop in for a minute or two—and I have a son. Yes, I'm doing a film where I play a gay man, but why? Because I work in Hollywood, because I've seen a lot of people die from AIDS, because this is a story that not only needs to be told, but transcends all sexuality. It's about family. It's about love and hate in a family searching for something good, and how, maybe, they might just find something great."

She folded the file shut and looked up at him with a small grin, and said, "You know, you are good. I mean, *very, very* good."

"I know," he replied. "How else would I have gotten so far in an industry as fucked up as this?"

Chapter 15

There was no doubt in her mind that it was Andy, that her firstborn was dead and gone. Martha Lyman felt it in her heart, felt the pain digging so deep that she could barely move. But still she had to do this. She had to go into that next room and identify her baby. The authorities here in Minneapolis already said they had positive identification—someone who had known Andy—but she wanted to make sure, absolutely sure. And, yes, she wanted to see him, Andy, her oldest child, just one more time. She wanted to look at him, touch him, kiss him, and cradle her beautiful boy in her arms just once again.

Oh, God, she thought as she sat on a short vinyl couch in some basement room of the Hennepin County Medical Center complex. It wasn't supposed to happen like this. Her family wasn't supposed to be torn apart. And none of her children was supposed to die before her. Nothing, nothing whatsoever, had prepared her for this kind of pain, this unimaginable horror. Even though she'd never said it, she'd always thought John would die first, that he'd keep gaining weight and that one day, perhaps during harvest season, his heart would give out and he'd peacefully collapse in the fields or in the barn. Then Andy, who would have a wonderful wife and lots of kids, would take over the farm. And when it was her time, she was supposed to fade away, watching lots of grandkids play in the yard and witnessing the miraculous cycle start all over again. That was how it was supposed to happen, how she had envisaged the closure of her life until the last year.

Instead . . .

She stared downward, her eyes wide and red, and saw nothing, particularly not the bland linoleum floor with its ripples of beige running through it. Her blond hair hung limply, and her blue dress lay wrinkled, particularly after the long drive here. How had she done it? How had she gotten to The Cities all by herself? She wasn't really sure, everything had been such a fog since the police had phoned last night, but somehow this morning she'd gotten in the car and driven a hundred miles. And now she sat alone in the waiting room of the Minneapolis morgue.

Yes, alone. While one part of her was collapsing under the weight of her grief, another part was seething with anger.

"I'm sorry, Martha," her husband, John, had said to her early this morning, "I just can't."

"You . . . you can't what?"

"I can't do it. I can't go with you."

"What are you saying?"

"I don't want to look at that body."

"Wh-what? What in God's name are you saying?" she had begged through her tears as she stood at the kitchen counter. "You can't be serious?"

"I swore that night that I never wanted to see him again. And I meant it."

"But . . . but he's your boy! Your own flesh and blood!"

"No, my boy, Andy, was someone else. Someone who died that night, someone who's long gone. Besides, Lord knows I've got work to do around here."

Everything came to an immediate rush of a boil—her grief, her frustration, her fury—and Martha had taken two steps across the kitchen floor, brought back her right hand, and slapped John as hard as she could. He took it without a flinch, standing there, his eyes shrinking, viperlike, his face flushing red. And then Martha had turned away, charging through the living room where her two daughters sat huddled in tears and confusion. She changed into the blue dress, made a feeble attempt at brushing her hair, then grabbed her purse and stormed out the kitchen door.

Over the past months she'd tried to forgive her husband for that night when he'd dragged Andy into the barn and threatened him so horribly. She'd told herself that, yes, what her boy had been doing was disgusting and ungodly and that her husband had been justified in losing his temper. But how in the name of the Lord could she forgive him this, for rejecting their boy even in death? It was too much, far, far too much, this double-edged sword of grief. Here she'd lost her boy, and now she felt as if she were clearly seeing the distance and difference between John and her for the first time. And hating him. Was he really so repulsive a human being?

"Mrs. Lyman?"

She looked up, saw a man with silvery hair and a kind face.

He said, "I'm Sergeant Neal Foster. I'm the one who called you last night. Thank you for coming."

Her voice barely audible, she replied, "Oh . . . yes."

"As I said on the phone, someone who knew your son has already provided positive identification. Are you sure you want to do this?"

Biting her lip, she nodded.

"Okay, then. It's this way."

She pushed herself to her feet, then felt him by her side as they walked toward a door, which he held open for her. Suddenly her heart started pounding, both horrified and fearful of what she was soon to see—Andy, really dead, the life truly drained from him? Suddenly she wanted nothing more than to run, to turn and charge away, but she couldn't, not by any means. As if by instinct Martha was drawn forward, her body operating on its own, her legs taking one step after another. She was aware of him, the policeman, close by her side. She felt his hand on her elbow as they left the waiting room and crossed a wide hall.

She heard him mumble something, and then, ". . . Through these doors."

She saw two wide stainless-steel doors, one of which he pushed open. Immediately she breathed it in, the strangest of odors, at once medicinal yet also repulsively foul. And immediately she recognized it even though she'd never sensed anything like it before: the smell of death. Suddenly she found it difficult to breathe. Suddenly the strength ebbed from her legs. Dear God, could she really, truly go through with this? Was she going to make it?

Straight in front of her was a woman in a clean white jacket, a woman who smiled but didn't smile and who said something else. Martha glanced to her left, saw a wall of stainless steel with row after row of small square doors, some fifteen doors long and four high. Yes, she knew what that was, a cold beehive of the dead.

With a gentle nudge on her arm, the policeman drew her to a stop and there it was, a long bed, a gurney to be exact, with a sheet-covered figure reposed like a white shadow. Her eyes ran up and down the outline of a body, realized the head was up there, the feet down at the other end. Andy? Oh, please, sweetheart, don't let it be you. I love you, you know I do. You know I never stopped. Please let this all be a mistake. Please come back. I've missed you, I really have.

And then she felt Foster's grip tighten on her arm.

He said, "Okay."

As neatly as if she were turning down a bed in the finest of hotels, the woman in the white doctor's coat pulled down the crisp sheet. First to emerge was the gorgeous hair, which in his childhood had been as white as cotton but was now in his adolescence the rich color of straw. Then came the forehead, John's forehead, wide and proud, with the slight scar right in the middle from when he'd fallen out of the hayloft. Next his eyebrows, flowing and golden. And then his eyes, once as blue as the sky, now closed and forever dark.

"Oh, God!" she sobbed as the world fell away.

Chapter 16

Rawlins hadn't been back from Lake Harriet for more than ten minutes when he looked out of his cubicle and saw Foster leading a woman with shattered eyes into the Homicide Division. He looked at Foster, then at her, the blond woman whose face bled with pain, and Rawlins was sure all over again that this was the worst, that interviewing a parent after the murder of his or her child was the toughest part of his job. Closing a file on his desk, Rawlins rolled back his chair and pushed himself to his feet. This wasn't going to be fun. Having to confront a parent and ask some of the toughest, most frank questions about their kid never was, particularly in a case like this.

Rawlins grabbed a microcassette recorder from a shelf above his desk, then started after Foster and the woman. Some ten steps behind, he followed them around a corner and to the second door on the left, entering the small room just as Foster was helping Mrs. Lyman into one of the four chrome-and-plastic chairs gathered around a table. It was a small, claustrophobic chamber with horribly bland beige vinyl wallpaper, an overhead fluorescent light bright enough for an operating room, and a vent in one wall that concealed a video camera.

"Hi, Neal," said Rawlins as he came in and headed for one of the chairs.

His face grave with compassion, Foster looked up briefly, then turned to the woman on his right and said, "Mrs. Lyman, this is Sergeant Steve Rawlins. He's my partner and he's actively involved in this case as well."

Without raising her eyes to his, she nodded.

"I knew your son," began Rawlins, his voice low, as he took a seat on her right. "I met him at a youth center here in town, and he was a very fine young man. My sincere condolences to you, Mrs. Lyman. Andrew's death was a big shock to me and has been very upsetting. You can be assured that Neal and I are going to do everything we can to find out what happened."

She nodded again, this time a bit more forcefully, then stared at the grill on the wall vent. Following her gaze, Rawlins was about to say, no, don't worry, we're not going to videotape this, but then she bowed her head and rubbed her eyes with her left hand. She looked too stunned to cry.

"To fill you in," said Foster to Rawlins, "we've just been to view the body. Mrs. Lyman came by herself, and she's headed back to her family farm this afternoon. She's kindly agreed to talk to us before leaving."

"Thank you very much, Mrs. Lyman. We need as much information as possible, and anything you can tell us will be helpful, I'm sure."

"Martha," she said, mustering the smallest of voices through her grief. "Please call me Martha."

"Of course."

Lifting the tiny cassette recorder onto the tabletop, Rawlins asked, "Would you mind if I recorded this conversation?"

"No. No . . . not at all."

He pushed a couple of buttons, placed the recorder on the table, and speaking into it, said, "This is Sergeant Steve Rawlins and I'm here with Sergeant Neal Foster and Martha Lyman, mother of Andrew Lyman. We're in a conference room at the Criminal Investigation Division in downtown Minneapolis. Is that correct?"

She nodded as she faintly replied, "Yes."

"And, Mrs. Lyman, you understand English and you're speaking of your own free will?"

"Yes. Yes, that's right."

Rawlins paused, rubbed his hands together. "I'm sorry to sound so formal, but the procedures for an interview are fairly rigid."

"We just want to ask you a few questions about your son, Andrew Lyman," said Foster, his voice buffed to gentle.

A handsome, stoic-looking woman, she nodded.

"How old was he?" continued Foster.

"Seventeen. Andrew turned seventeen just a few months ago."

"And where was he raised?"

"On our farm a hundred miles east of here."

"Was he the oldest? Youngest?"

"Oldest. We have two girls, both of them younger."

"When did you last talk to Andy?"

"This past . . ." She wiped her eyes. "This past fall. Almost exactly a year ago."

"Not at all since then?"

"No."

"Do you remember approximately when and where your last conversation was?"

"Yes."

"Could you tell us, please?"

"It was last October." She took a deep breath, then hesitated before continuing. "October the tenth, to be precise. It was at our farm."

Knowing the vague circumstances but nothing specific, Rawlins cut in, asking, "Can you tell us what that conversation was about?"

She nodded, started to speak, then stopped, and tried again. "We . . . we found out Andy was . . ."

When she failed to say anything, Rawlins interjected, "Gay?"

"Yes, exactly. That was when we found out our son was gay."

"Which was, what, a shock? No surprise?"

"The first. It was a shock. A big shock." She shook her head slightly and helplessly shrugged her shoulders. "I never even imagined."

"And what happened?" pressed Rawlins.

"He left."

"Left?"

"Our farm. Our home. He left that very night." Taking a deep breath, she let the air come out in one long, pained exhale. "It was very difficult, very awful. Trust me, it's not something any of us is proud of. We all said things we shouldn't have, and . . . and Andy left."

There was, Rawlins knew for a fact, far more to it. Over the course of his brief friendship with Andrew, Rawlins had gleaned some of the details, all of them ugly, all of them painful, and he could now see all of that and more etched in the fine lines of Martha Lyman's face. Rawlins couldn't imagine what it must have been like for young Andrew, tumbling out of the closet and landing at his parents' feet and at their mercy.

"I . . . I thought they were going to kill me," Andrew had confided in Rawlins. "I really did. But I guess it's my fault. I guess I deserved it."

As he told at least part of what happened, Andrew had been close to tears. And Rawlins hadn't doubted him one bit, for sex between boys in rural Minnesota was anathema to farm and family and church.

And now, sitting in the small room in City Hall, Rawlins, Foster, and Martha Lyman were going to have to revisit that night, searching the memory thereof for any details that might be relevant to the present nightmare.

He asked, "What do you mean he left?"

"Andy . . ." She wiped her eyes. "Andy ran away."

"Did he go to a friend's? To an aunt's? An uncle's?"

"I don't know."

"What do you mean?"

She shrugged. "Andy just walked down the drive and . . . disappeared."

"So you had no idea where he went?"

"None. I called everywhere I could think of. And I drove around too. I thought he'd be back the next morning, or even within the next day or two. A few days later he called and apologized, but he didn't come back. Eventually I assumed he came here, to The Cities, but I never knew for sure. I never heard a word. Not until last night when you," she said, nodding her head slightly to Foster, "called."

"Not a letter or anything?"

"No. Nothing."

Foster cut in, asking, "How about the local police—did you contact them?"

"At first no. My husband, John, didn't want me to. He said it was none of their business. He said it was a family thing." Martha Lyman slowly shook her head. "I don't know. I think we did it all wrong, made every single mistake possible. Actually, I think—no, I know that my husband didn't want to have to tell the police what the fight was about, and—"

"What do you mean he didn't want to have to tell them? Was he embarrassed? Ashamed? Angry?"

"All of that, actually. John just didn't . . . didn't approve. I mean, he still doesn't."

"Of what?"

"That life."

"Homosexuality?"

"Yes, and . . . and," she said, as if she were quickly changing the subject, "like I said, I thought Andy would come home in a day or two. When he didn't turn up after a week, I went to the police myself."

"You mean alone?"

"Yes."

"Why didn't your husband go with you?"

"Because . . . because . . ."

At first Rawlins thought she was going to say because he was harvesting the corn. Or tilling the field. Instead she looked right at him and told him what could only be the flat-out truth.

"He didn't come with me then for the same reason he didn't come with me today—he never wanted to see Andy again. And frankly, I'll bet he's—"

She cut herself off, then just sat there in silence. Rawlins studied every little flinch of her face. He's what? Glad that his boy is dead?

Rawlins waited and waited, and when she said nothing, he asked, "So what did the police say when you went to them?"

"Not much. I guess there wasn't much they could do. I told them Andy ran away—I didn't say why—and they filed a report, checked around some, but . . ."

Rawlins asked, "Has this been a difficult thing for your family, Andy's coming out as gay and then running away? What has the last year been like in your family?"

"You have no idea," she said, shaking her head as she stared at the plain laminate surface of the table. "It's . . . it's been awful. Just awful. I haven't stopped thinking of Andy, I haven't stopped worrying about him, not for one single minute. It's . . . it's . . ."

"What?"

"Well," she said, perhaps voicing the truth for the first time, "it has destroyed my family."

Rawlins wanted to come back to that, the night the Lyman family exploded. He wanted to know specifically what had happened. And he wanted to know exactly what had been said. But not yet. He didn't want to seem too antagonistic, too adversarial. In other words, he wanted to postpone her shutting down, which they always did at some point.

Rawlins glanced at Foster and nodded.

"Martha," said Foster, "could you describe Andrew for us? What kind of young man was he? Was he kind of a happy guy? Sad? Did he have many friends? Was he very social?"

"Andy was . . . sweet. He was just always kind. And gentle. That's why I can't understand . . . understand . . . how . . ." Her bottom lip started to quiver, and she pressed her right hand to her mouth as if to stuff back the pain. "I don't understand why anyone would have wanted to hurt him."

"He never got into any fights at school?"

"Andy? Never."

"So he didn't have any problems with other kids that you knew of? No, I guess you might say, rivalries? No enemies?"

"Everyone loved Andy. The girls and the boys. I mean, there was always a girl who had a crush on him because . . . well, he was cute.

And he was always popular with the guys because he was the best quarterback at school. You know, on the football team. Frankly, the team wasn't any good, but he was their star."

"How about his grades?" asked Rawlins.

"They were okay. B's and C's mainly, every now and then an A."

"What year was he in?"

"Last year he was a junior." She shook her head. "I wanted so much for him to graduate, to get his high school diploma. I wanted him to be the first of our people to go to college."

"What about drugs?" asked Foster. "Is there much of that where you come from? Was he ever involved in anything?"

"No, not my Andy. I'm sure of that. Oh, he might have had a few beers with his pals, but no drugs. I know that for a fact."

Did she? But how could she, Rawlins wondered, be so sure of it? After all, she hadn't suspected her son's sexual orientation.

"What about any kids?" continued Foster. "Did he keep in touch with any of them once he left home?"

She leaned forward, bowing her head into her hands. "Yes. I mean, I don't know for sure, but . . . but the other boy ran away from home a couple of days after Andy did."

Rawlins asked, "Other boy?"

She nodded.

"What other boy?"

"The . . . the Weaver boy. Oh, God, I just wish they'd never met. I don't think any of this would have happened."

"What are you saying?"

"This boy, the Weaver boy—Jordy Weaver, that's his name. Jordy Weaver. For something like six or seven months before all this happened, you know, before Andy ran away, Jordy was always calling up Andy, always hanging around him. It was like he was obsessed with Andy. He just never left my son alone. And . . . and . . . " She wiped her left eye. "And that's who Andy was with that night, with him, with Jordy Weaver."

Tripping over the name, Rawlins sat there speechless. He'd had no idea, not a clue. They were from the same town in western Minnesota? They hadn't met here in Minneapolis?

"Are you saying that these two boys, Andrew Lyman and Jordy Weaver, ran away together? That they came here to Minneapolis?"

"I never knew for sure because . . . because I never knew where Andy went, but that's what I always assumed. Like I said, Jordy was obsessed with my boy. He wouldn't let him go."

Chapter 17

Todd's day was like a moving sidewalk that he got on and couldn't get off. There was the call he'd received from Tim Chase's publicist to set up this evening's meeting, the numerous developments in the story of Andrew Lyman's murder, and then, of course, there was Rawlins.

Rawlins.

It was the one thing that Todd kept coming back to, compulsively so: was there any truth to what Jordy had said about Andrew and Rawlins being involved? All afternoon as Bradley and he dashed around town putting together tonight's story, Todd silently sorted through the past couple of months trying to ascertain if and when and how the two of them could have been carrying on an affair. A Saturday afternoon? That Monday morning? Wednesday nights? Was it even logistically possible? And if it had really happened, what did it mean, if anything?

No, he now thought, as Bradley and he stood on the shore of Lake Harriet waiting for the six o'clock, that wasn't right. It did mean something. It meant the world about Rawlins. It said everything about his ability to stick to their agreement. And it said everything about his integrity, for Andy was barely seventeen, a kid who by all means was still learning to cope and establish his own boundaries. If Rawlins had taken advantage of his position as a mentor, what in the hell did that say about him?

Oh, shit, Todd thought.

He wore a blue shirt with a blue and yellow tie, black pants, and his black leather jacket. In the field he never wore a coat and

tie, especially not a suit, because while he wanted to look professional, he wanted to look like what he was, an active investigative
reporter.

They'd arrived a little over an hour ago, with Bradley and he setting up the camera by the water's edge and the ENG truck pulling up
on the curb and stretching its microwave mast as high as it would go.
For the five o'clock Todd had done a VOSOT, where he'd talked live
to the recorded pictures for some thirty-five seconds. As VOSOTs
tended to be, it was also a little rougher, more immediate, and after a
sound byte from the police chief, the video had come back out to Todd
and he'd done a quick tag.

As they now approached the six o'clock, Todd once again ran the
IFB wire up the inside of his jacket, pulled it through the back of his
collar, and placed the earpiece snugly in his right ear. Not more than
two seconds later, the quiet, distant voice of the news director, speaking from Golden Valley, said, "Voice check, please."

Todd raised his stick mike, and said, "Good evening, this is Todd
Mills reporting live from—"

"That's perfect, Todd."

The six P.M. line producer cut in, saying, "We're two minutes away."

In front of him Bradley was peering into his Betacam, which
rested on a large aluminum tripod. From the camera a thick snake of
a cable stretched across the ground, then awkwardly across the pedestrian and bicycle paths to the ENG truck. Per usual, a crowd had gathered, this group numbering around fifteen and growing.

"Is my tie all the way up, Bradley?"

"Your tie is perfect."

He turned, glanced briefly over the lake, where a gentle wind was
sending an endless army of ripples across the surface. With that, the
small hill on the opposite shore, and the sunset, it would be the perfect
backdrop. In his mind he reviewed all that he had learned today, from the
specifics of Andrew's bloody demise, to a better picture of his home life,
to, of course, the most important item, the object the police divers had

pulled from this lake. Yes, whatever a reporter learned most recently was always the first information, the thing you gave right off the top. From the inside of his jacket he then pulled his notebook and read through his notes once, twice. The producer, who had these things back-timed to the second, had told Todd that he couldn't afford more than a ten-second intro to precede the one minute fifteen-second package.

"We're ten from the top," said the line producer as coolly as a flight controller.

Yes, everything was perfectly timed, had to be. A second of dead air on TV was more like an hour, a disaster to be avoided at any cost. And, at least on the computer line up, this was how this thing was scheduled to transpire: anchor toss, Todd intro, package, tag, ad lib.

"Five from the top."

Todd glanced at the base of the tripod, saw the small monitor aimed up toward him. A second later a color bar appeared. Moments after that, the end of the national news came on. As soon as that concluded, WLAK's star anchor, Tom Rivers, appeared, always dapper and now in a navy blue suit with an off-white shirt—a truly white one was much too stark, too contrasty under the lights—and a tasteful tie with ribbons of blue and red. That full head of hair, those big white teeth, the perfect cadence of his voice—every time he was on camera it was obvious why he was worth millions, particularly in the Twin Cities, which had one of the three highest production values in the country.

"Good evening, this is the WLAK evening news, and I'm Tom Rivers. Our stories tonight include the latest on the plans to put a freeway bridge over the scenic St. Croix River, the latest on the upcoming gubernatorial race, and our lead story, an important development in the murder of a teenager in south Minneapolis." He turned to stare into another camera, and, reading the TelePrompTer, said, "As we reported last night, shortly after nine P.M. yesterday evening police were summoned to an apartment building just off Twenty-fifth and Bryant Avenue South, where they discovered the body of a young man, Andrew Lyman, who was—"

A throaty, secret agent–like voice in Todd's earpiece said, "Ten to you."

"—killed by an apparent knife wound to the throat. For the very latest developments, we now join our investigative reporter, Todd Mills, at Lake Harriet."

"Five to you."

Tossing it to Todd, Tom Rivers said, "Todd, I understand some important evidence has been discovered. What can you tell us about it?"

"Well, Tom," said Todd, looking straight into the lens because he was full on camera, "following up on a tip, the police came here to Lake Harriet shortly after noon today." Offering his roll cue, Todd said, "And what they discovered beneath these waters may very well prove to be the weapon used to kill Andrew Lyman."

Todd held his position as they cut to the package that Bradley and he had earlier put together. They began, of course, with the few shots Bradley had been able to catch of the police boats on the lake, and then the camera panned the crowd of gawkers, men and women, walkers and bikers, kids and dogs. The clip showed two women with a stroller, a couple of women in nylon jogging suits, a few men, including one guy with sunglasses and a shaved head. As the images went by, Todd went into detail how a hunting knife had been found in about twenty feet of water. It was still too early to tell if they could get any fingerprints from the weapon, but early testing by the police indicated that the blade had been recently exposed to blood. At this point the police were not inclined to speculate, but many thought it might in fact be linked to the murder.

His eyes on the monitor beneath Bradley's camera, Todd now loosely watched as the package, with his recorded voice-over married to the tape, played on. There was a bit of last night's real estate and the crowd gathered around the apartment building, as well as the all-but-required shots of the bagged body being carted out. The package continued with some personal information on Andrew Lyman, including his athletic abilities and his popularity, both of which Todd had garnered from one of Andrew's former teachers, then cut briefly to a shot of the Domain of Queers. The piece then wrapped with the shot of the police chief and his sound byte asking anyone with any information to please come forward.

The line producer cued Todd, and then Todd lifted his mike. The package concluded exactly according to schedule, and they came back out to Todd for a live, on-camera tag.

"Tom, I find this story especially sad," began Todd, "because several months ago I personally met Andrew Lyman, and found him a bright, energetic, and handsome young man, eager to complete his high school requirements. Instead, a young man is now dead in what police are describing as a very brutal crime."

Beginning the ad lib, which was essentially just a Q & A, Rivers said, "Can you tell us where you met the victim?"

Oh, brother, thought Todd when he heard the question through his earpiece. What did Rivers think, that they'd met in a sauna? Under the bushes? Or was Rivers just trying to do it, make Todd say all over again that he was gay? Shit, didn't the entire world already know?

"Certainly. I met him when I gave a talk at the Domain of Queers, which is a center for gay, lesbian, bisexual, and transgender youth."

"My understanding is that there are a number of runaways there. Is that correct? Had Andrew Lyman run away from home?"

Even though Todd knew that Andrew's split from his family had been most acrimonious, WLAK lawyers had advised against broadcasting that information not out of good taste, but out of fear of offending the family and tempting legal fate. Evidently, though, Rivers hadn't gotten that information. Or had spaced it, which would have surprised no one at WLAK.

With no choice, Todd walked around the issue as gingerly as he could, saying, "Tom, I've been told only that Andrew had not been in contact with his family and that news of his death came as a total shock to his parents."

"I'm sure it did. You mentioned that the police went down to Lake Harriet to follow up on a tip. Can you tell me anything more about that?"

"My understanding is that they received an anonymous tip call from someone who'd been down at the lake and seen something rather mysterious. The police aren't saying anything more, but evidently that is what's behind the police chief's request for anyone with information to come forward. In the hope of learning more, they want the tip caller to come forward and identify him or herself."

"I see. And thank you, Todd, for a most interesting report." Rivers paused, turned back toward the first camera, and said, "In other news today—"

As Todd stood quite still, he heard the slight snap as the audio transmission was broken, then looked down and saw the image on the monitor disappear.

Raising his head from behind the camera, Bradley said, "You're clear, Todd."

Todd lowered the mike, rocked his head from side to side until his neck cracked, and then carefully lifted the earpiece from his right ear. Okay, he thought, that was done, now on to the next, a quick dinner with Rawlins. And then wine with one of the most popular stars in the world.

Chapter 18

They met at D'Amico & Sons, an upscale Italian deli on Hennepin Avenue South with a tall ceiling, open kitchen, dark woodwork, and a faint resemblance to things Tuscan. When Todd saw Rawlins push through the double glass doors he saw not the familiar man he was attracted to, but a near stranger who looked preoccupied and distant.

And the first thing that Rawlins uttered was, "You look tired, Todd."

Todd wanted to say, no, I'm just stressed. Stressed about you. About us. About where we're going.

"Yeah, I am exhausted," he replied instead. "You look it too."

"Tell me about it."

They knew the routine, and they moved silently to the large arching glass display case and studied the very nineties array of salads, sandwiches, salamis, and olives. For a long indecisive moment Todd looked at them all, the roasted vegetables, the couscous salad, the chicken and feta rotelle, and realized he just didn't care.

"Do you know what you'd like?" asked a server, a tall, young woman with a body like a boy's and cropped blond hair tucked beneath a black baseball cap emblazoned with D'AMICO & SONS.

"Ah . . ."

In the end, Todd asked for the chicken penne, a small Caesar, and black coffee, and the woman, leaning on the counter, wrote it all down. Rawlins ordered the pizza of the day, a concoction of artichoke hearts and feta cheese, and a glass of the house red. Todd let Rawlins pay;

they were almost to the joint checking account stage of their relationship, but not yet. And as he watched Rawlins write a check—which were accepted just about everywhere in the Twin Cities, more often than not without identification—Todd wondered if the two of them were now going to make it to the banking phase of their relationship.

"What are you getting coffee for?" asked Rawlins as they sat down and waited for their food to arrive. "Are you on at ten again?"

"Actually, I was going to be," replied Todd, taking off his coat and hanging it on the back of his chair, "but I'm not."

"What do you mean?"

Todd had held out when they'd talked briefly earlier today; he hadn't mentioned Tim Chase, and he wasn't going to, at least not yet. If Rawlins was going to start a game of poker, then Todd wasn't going to take the high road. Hell, no, he'd play right along too.

He volunteered simply, "I have a meeting at nine."

"Oh? With whom?"

Right, this was poker, and Todd decided he wasn't going to do it, he wasn't going to play his lucky card, the one that would dominate the conversation, just yet. No, he thought, looking across the small table, he wasn't going to tell Rawlins if for no other reason than he didn't want to sidetrack things. He had to keep things focused. Focused on Andrew Lyman. And Rawlins.

"It's not important."

Never a fool, Rawlins studied him for a long moment. "What's the matter? Everything okay?"

"It's been a long day, that's all."

As he unfolded his napkin in a manner that was much too deliberate, Todd realized that the test hadn't concluded last night. No, Rawlins was still taking it. This was part two, otherwise known as the second chance. And if he failed this part? Oh, shit, thought Todd, he already didn't know how to handle this.

He leapt right in with the acid question, "So, anything else new regarding Andrew Lyman? Anything turn up?"

The issues of Andrew Lyman and infidelity lay there, oddly, horribly, like a loaded gun waiting for someone to trip over it. Rawlins raised his eyes and, Todd was sure, looked at Todd with more than a little suspicion. And Todd sat there thinking, Yes, you fool, I know!

Rawlins said, "Aside from the knife, not really."

"But you still think it was the murder weapon?"

"It fluoresced blood when they sprayed it with Luminol, but I don't think they'll be able to get a blood sample off it. After all, it was sitting in water at least overnight. With any luck we'll be able to get some prints, but I don't hold up much hope for anything else."

"And the mom?"

"Like I said, she came to town alone, which was strange. I mean, where was her husband? Why wasn't he here?"

"I don't know. Why?"

"Beats me."

Todd looked at him with a cocked eye. "Divorced?"

"No, not that I know of anyway. But there's something strange, and I bet you dollars to donuts that it started when they found out Andrew was gay."

"Ah, homosexuality—the ruin of many a family."

Todd felt Rawlins's eyes upon him, felt Rawlins studying him. Okay, so what of it, so Todd was being pissy.

Rawlins leaned forward, cupping one hand over Todd's, and with those deep, warm eyes that had hooked him right from the start, said, "Man, you have had a long day, haven't you?"

Todd withdrew his hand, cast his eyes to the side. No, he didn't want to be pulled out of this. Rawlins had a gift for that, using those wondrous eyes or the subtle grin to lighten Todd's mood, and Todd was determined not to let Rawlins charm him tonight. Just tell me whatever happened, he wanted to say, because I don't care. I just can't stand silence. Do you get it? It's silence that makes me crazy. And I love you, and I need to know about Andrew and you right now. No, actually I need to know if there's only one of you and if that person is all mine. Or are there two, one guy who loves me and a second who loves many others?

"Well," continued Rawlins as he fiddled with a fork, "there is one other thing, something I don't think I told you. Do you remember another kid Andrew was with? Sort of tall, long hair."

Of course Todd knew who he was talking about, the very kid who'd leaked the news, but he said, "No, not really."

"He's maybe a year or so older than Andrew. Nice-enough-looking. I think he was at the meeting we spoke at."

"And?"

"And it turns out that he's from the same town as Andrew. His name's Jordy Weaver, and I think they had something going even back then. They were either little lovers or fuck buddies, I don't know."

"Really?"

"Yeah, and it looks like the two of them ran away together, came all the way here."

"Well . . ." Todd didn't know what to say, everything or nothing, and instead the snottiest came out. "So what do you think, was our little Andrew the whore about town? Is that what happened the other night? Do you think the two of them, Andrew and this Jordy—"

"Jesus Christ, Todd," snapped Rawlins, glaring at him. "Even if they were doing tricks, which I don't think they were, it doesn't mean Andrew deserved to have his throat slit."

Todd looked out the window and stared at a plain yellow car. "I'm sorry. No. No, of course not."

They sat there in silence. A moment later Todd looked over, saw Rawlins eyeing some other guy, some young stud with a bubble butt. Okay, great. Maybe this wasn't the big romance of Todd's life. Maybe they were already through it, maybe they were already finished with the best that they could be together. And maybe tonight Todd was just trying to make that perfectly clear, maybe he was merely trying to drive Rawlins screaming from the table.

With a cloud of savory steam, their food descended in front of them. Todd took one look at the beautiful nuggets of chicken, the glistening tubes of pasta, and realized this wasn't at all what he wanted.

Not some nice meal. Not some pleasant place. Fuck, he wasn't even hungry. He glanced out the large glass window, saw the same yellow car sitting there. Yes, the traffic on Hennepin was building to a forceful crawl. And, yes, little by little the Twin Cities were growing up, each year becoming less and less toy towns.

Again, Rawlins leaned forward and in the gentlest of voices said, "Todd, what's the matter?"

Some bullshit came to the tip of Todd's lips. He was going to say something about the station manager, something about running around all day, but then he tripped over his own insurmountable need to know. He speared some pasta with a javelinlike pitch of his fork.

And said, "You haven't been holding out on me, have you?"

Balancing a slice of pizza in hand, Rawlins clearly flinched. "What?"

"Let me be as blunt as possible."

"So what else is new?" asked Rawlins with a nervous smile, having been on the receiving end more than once.

"Is there more? Is there something about Andrew Lyman that you haven't told me?"

Todd watched him, studied his every facial tic, the cock of his head, the way his hand quivered ever so slightly as he put the uneaten slice of pizza back down on his plate. Oh, shit, realized Todd, he'd backed Rawlins into a corner from which there was no escape. And this was it, the final acid test. As Todd knew only too well from cornering a politician or a developer or a murderer, you learned more about a person by what he didn't say than what he actually did. Yes, that was the horrible truth.

"Actually . . . actually there is something," confessed Rawlins.

Todd's gut flooded with relief. "Yes?"

"Oh, shit . . ."

Rawlins wiped his mouth even though Todd didn't think he'd taken a single bite. Sure, in this long pause, Rawlins was weighing something: the consequences. And Todd's heart began to pound.

"Todd, it always comes down to this, doesn't it? It always comes down to our jobs. You know, that's the one thing that really scares me about us and our relationship. Our careers. It's the one thing that we keep coming up against, that we keep butting heads about."

"What?" replied Todd, afraid that he was in fact understanding.

"There is something else about Andrew Lyman, something that I haven't mentioned, but . . . but as a cop—"

"Oh, fuck, Rawlins, don't do this to me. Don't fuck around. I just want a simple answer to a simple question."

"And I'm just telling you—"

"I don't believe this."

"—what we both know. That as a cop there are certain things I can't say to you, Todd Mills, star reporter."

"Shit. Shit, shit, shit."

If they'd been at home Todd would have gone completely tilt. He would have started yelling, started stomping around and waving his hands and cursing at the top of his lungs. Because instead they were in a public place, he somehow mastered control of his fury. Every one of Todd's muscles tightened rock hard as he somehow perfectly folded his napkin and laid it down on the table, put his fork quietly down on the plate, then reached behind and lifted his coat from the back of the chair.

"Todd, what the—"

"I've got to go."

"What?"

"There's something I haven't told you, either. That meeting? It's actually, well, a date."

"What?"

"You heard me, a date. I've decided maybe I do want an open relationship after all." Todd was glad for the instant pain he saw burning on Rawlins's forehead. "I'll see you later. Like much later."

"Wait," pleaded Rawlins in a hushed voice that was pathetically weak. "Todd, don't do this! Don't go when you're so upset. Please, sit back down, let's—"

"Sorry." He pushed himself to his feet. "I just want you to think about this: I know."

A wildfire of shock whipped across Rawlins's face, and then Todd turned and started for the door, wondering just what in the hell he was walking out on, a plate of pasta or the greatest thing in his life.

Chapter 19

With a knot wrenched so tight in his stomach that he felt he might vomit, Todd headed home. Driving through a neighborhood that was dominated by clapboard houses with big Midwesternly front porches, he eventually came to Lake of the Isles, which in truth wasn't much of a lake but more of a sprawling pond long ago dredged to Victorian scenic standards. He followed the single lane parkway around the gently curving lake, past the Malt-O-Meal mansion, a Dayton dwelling or two, then three mansions built at the turn of the century for the Cream of Wheat clan. Oblivious of the couples strolling along in the cool air, and not so much as glancing at the tranquil waters, Todd eventually came to Cedar Lake Parkway, where he turned. Operating on automatic, he followed that and still another meandering parkway all the way to his condo. As he headed into the private drive that led up to the building's garage, he glanced at his watch and figured that he had about an hour and a half before he had to leave to meet with movie star Tim Chase. And about an hour and a half to get his shit together. Was he really going to be able to put on a happy face?

Coming out of the closet had had one remarkable and undeniable effect on Todd—he no longer felt obligated to any kind of guy stereotype. When he'd been in the closet he'd held back so very much, far more than just his sexuality. Preventing family and friends from discovering his "horrible" truth had meant he had also prevented them from learning just about all his inner hopes and desires. And once he'd finally admitted to himself that he was gay he'd liberated a great deal more than just his sexual orientation. Absolutely. Once he'd broken the dam so very much more than just his love of men had come bursting forward. Like a good chunk of his personality, not to mention his soul. And perhaps for that very reason he now felt totally flooded with emotion. Yes, and he was drowning in confusion. If he were a crier he'd be bawling right now, but he'd never been very good at that, expressing his pain in tears. For him being queer didn't automatically bring that benefit. So what in the name of God was he supposed to do? Beat his head against the wall?

The answer came bouncing back: honesty, you fool. That was all he'd been asking of Rawlins, and yet that wasn't at all what he himself had been dishing in return. No, he'd been making Rawlins feast on a bitter diet of Todd's own ruse, and as a consequence the both of them were getting more than a little queasy. Todd saw it now quite clearly, that after a certain point he'd been just as deceptive as Rawlins. And there was no quicker way to poison any kind of relationship, gay or straight, business or platonic, than that, the withholding of information.

Upon entering his two-bedroom apartment, Todd passed the kitchen on his right, entered the living room, and crossed right to the balcony. He pulled aside the door, then stepped out into a day that was dying beautifully, the sky fading from blue to red to midnight blue. A cool wind, fresh from the plains of Canada, whirled around him, and he breathed it in, relishing it as a chilly aperitif of what was soon to come these ways.

The great things in life were, if not impossible, then truly difficult to find. And yet he had found someone again. First there was Karen, then Michael, and now there was Rawlins. Somehow he had gotten that lucky. Lucky enough to have found someone like both his ex-wife, Karen, and Michael, who had loved Todd even though he'd been in the closet, and now lucky enough to have found someone like Rawlins, who loved him out. At this point in his life Todd was too humble to think he was so great that love was destined to tumble his way, but he didn't know how he'd gotten so lucky either. He wasn't particularly religious, but having found these people was the one thing that really made him believe in a higher power, because God only knew he didn't deserve it. Or was Rawlins not a gift? Was he a trick or a curse, something that was now beginning to come unraveled?

Leaning on the balcony railing, he fell into that hole—gift or curse?—and stood there for the longest time pondering a question that had no answer, at least not yet. Eventually Girlfriend came sauntering out, rubbing against the railing, then peering not out at the dark night waters, but straight down at the traffic below. When the black cat poked her head through the railing, followed by one paw and then another, Todd's stomach began to roll. No, those cars hundreds of feet down were not little ants scurrying around. And, no, this towering honeycomb of condos was not like a tree you could scamper up and down. Forgetting all about Rawlins, he carefully grabbed the cat around her waist, pulled her back, then carried her inside.

Besides, it was time to get ready, and he for one was going to take a shower, determined to wash the day and that man out of his mind, at least for a few short hours.

Parked on the street in front of Todd's building, Rawlins didn't know what in the hell he should do, go up to Todd's apartment or stay down here in his car.

Of course he wanted to do the first. Of course he wanted to go up there and finish this off, this argument disguised as polite—well, okay, so it wasn't so polite—dinner discussion. Shit, it had been just like Todd to snap at him and storm away instead of finishing things off. That guy could be a real drama queen when he wanted. From his work in the media he knew how to sensationalize the facts, how to focus on certain things to bring undue attention to one particular detail and blow it out of proportion. Rawlins just couldn't compete, and they both knew it. But what in the hell had Todd been talking about? A date?

Shifting in his seat, Rawlins tugged at his mustache. Todd didn't know about Andrew, did he? He couldn't, could he? But then why all the strange questions? Why the odd mood? It was almost like Todd had been leading Rawlins, trying to trick him into tipping a card or saying something inopportune. So what else was new? It was, however, exactly why Rawlins didn't just head up to the condo right now, because he was terrified Todd somehow knew and things would blow wide open.

Of course Todd was up there, Rawlins knew that for a fact. After Todd had stormed out of the restaurant, Rawlins had grabbed a carry-out box, dumped his pizza in it, and then charged out after him. By the time he'd gotten to the parking lot, however, Todd was just pulling into the street. Not by any means unfamiliar with getaways, if this in fact was one, Rawlins scrambled into his car, drove down the side street, and caught up with Todd, which had proved no difficult feat. As he tailed Todd around the northern end of Lake of the Isles, Rawlins had soon discerned that Todd was going home. Yet instead of hurrying up and trying to get Todd to pull over, Rawlins had kept his distance, letting one and then two cars slip in front of him. He could have even been very nineties and called from his car to Todd's, but he chose silence as the safest course. He wanted desperately to talk to Todd but he was terrified of what they'd get into, specifically the subject of Andrew Lyman.

Sitting in his parked car, he reached across the seat of the Taurus and flipped open the lid of the takeout box. And as if this truly were a stakeout, he started eating, only now it was designer pizza instead of donuts and coffee. His meal was only less than reasonably warm, and he gobbled down a single slice in two or three bites. He was only halfway through a second slice when he licked his right fingertips clean and reached into the pocket of his leather jacket and pulled it out, Andrew's diary, that small spiral-bound notebook with a slick red cover.

It was not something Rawlins had been looking for, sex with Andrew or any other boy for that matter. But now this diary and God only knew what else were lying around like time bombs waiting to go off and ruin Rawlins's life and career. It wasn't merely that Rawlins was more than twenty years older than Andrew either. No, that was far too simple. Just this afternoon Rawlins had reread the Minnesota Statutes, and the very thing he'd feared had jumped right out at him: criminal sexual conduct in the third degree. Yes, Andrew had been at least sixteen but less than eighteen and Rawlins was not only more than forty-eight months older, he was also in a position of authority. The allegations alone could ruin Rawlins and set back by ten years the progress gays and lesbians had made on the police force.

He'd read only a line or two here and there, and he now opened the diary and thumbed through the first pages. There were pages about Andrew's trip to Minneapolis, how Jordy and he had hitchhiked here, what they found, where they stayed, things about his parents and how he hated his father and never wanted to see him again, then pages and pages about his relationship with Jordy, who seemed to want to control every aspect of Andrew's life. Rawlins raced through it all, and then his eyes finally skidded to a stop when he saw the first mention of his own name written on the fine lines. There it was, as incriminating as possible.

> I had my first date with Steve Rawlins. He's a cop, he's got dark hair and beautiful eyes and he's hairy, and I think I'm in love. I mean, big love. And what's so cool is that I think he likes me too. No, I'm sure of it. He took me out and paid and everything and now he wants to see me again. I can't wait. I can't wait to have sex with him—I'm certain we will, I'm certain he wants me.

That little shit, thought Rawlins. That stupid little shit. That hadn't been a date. Yes, Andrew was enormously handsome. Yes, he had the body of a young god. And, yes, Rawlins had noticed all of that and then some, from his broad chest to his slim hips to the bulge in his jeans. But that hadn't been a date. Hell, no. Rawlins hadn't taken him to lunch because he wanted to get in his pants. No, he'd taken him to lunch because he recognized a kid who needed help, who needed direction. He was a runaway and he was a good kid, and Rawlins didn't want to see him flush his whole life away just because he was having trouble with his family over his sexuality. That was the whole idea of being a mentor to a young gay person, the chance to offer advice and direction and support to a kid who couldn't get it anywhere else.

But . . .

There was more about Jordy. Lots more. They were living in a ratty old apartment along with six other young guys, and Jordy was becoming more demanding, more controlling. Andrew wrote how hard it was to get away from him, even for an hour or two. One night Andrew went out with some other kids and snuck into a gay bar and danced and danced and danced. And Jordy went ballistic. It was shortly after that that Andrew took the job as the caretaker for the apartment buildings.

I love Jordy but I have to get away from him. He's just always in my face. He just never quits, never gives me any space.

Andrew then went on to write about his new apartment and how great it was. It was so cool, so great. His own place. Not that big, but wonderful. He was out of the closet and on his own. He was a real adult now.

I had to do this, I had to break from Jordy. When I told him I was moving out he cried and cried, begged me not to go, begged me to let him come with me. I was really firm. I told him no. I said I just needed some space. He kept pushing, saying how much he loved me, that he couldn't let me go, and asking if there was someone else. I kind of just sort of said there was. That's when the shit hit the fan. He hit me, started beating on me. And I told him to stop, to get away. I punched him real hard, started screaming to leave me alone, to get away. I told him my new boyfriend was a cop and he'd arrest Jordy if he so much as touched me again.

Oh, fuck. Rawlins lowered the diary to his lap, sat there staring out the windshield. He forgot about the pizza, forgot about where he was. And he didn't see the dark night all around him. No, instead he was seeing it all so clearly for the first time. A setup, that was what it was. Andrew had been plotting and setting this thing up all along. How could Rawlins have been so stupid, so naive? Why hadn't he seen it in those dreamy blue eyes, all that want and lust?

I'm in love, big love. Rawlins took me out for lunch again and we talked and talked.

Right, we talked about your future, about going to law school. Or was your interest all bullshit?

And I think I had a hard-on the whole time. I brushed his arm, felt the fur there, the muscles. God, he just drives me crazy. He's just so butch. Rawlins Rawlins Rawlins. He's all I think about, all I dream about. I told him I have a diary, that I write everything in it, and I know he knows that I'm writing all about him. It's going to be so good, me and him. I can't wait to get in bed with him. I know he wants me too. I can see it in his eyes, sense it in his voice, hear it behind his words. Actually, I think it's going to happen tomorrow. I invited him over, told him I needed some help moving some furniture, but when he comes . . .

Oh, shit, cursed Rawlins, throwing the diary on the seat next to him. One big lie. One big plot. How could Rawlins explain? How could he make anyone believe what had really happened? Yes, he'd gone over to Andrew's apartment, and all by himself too, which had been stupid. He'd gone over there just hours before Andrew was killed. And, yes, Andrew had been all over him, not just throwing himself into Rawlins's arms and kissing him, not just rubbing Rawlins's crotch, but dropping his pants and exposing his wildly lustful self.

Oh, God. Rawlins had been such a fool. Such an idiot. Why hadn't he seen it coming? And now? Now what? Andrew hadn't been crazy, not by any means. No, he'd been a kid, lost and lonely, tossed out of his home and frightened, seeing Rawlins as some kind of hero, some kind of savior. And Rawlins now understood that, just as he understood that Andrew's crush on him was just a desperate grab for something stable and secure in a world awash with confusion.

He grabbed another piece of pizza, crammed it into his mouth, and started chomping down bite after bite without even tasting the artichoke. What should he do? He should go right up there, right up to Todd's apartment, and tell him the whole thing. At the least it seemed as if Todd already suspected, so Rawlins should just go up there and blurt it all out: I fucked up, I got myself into a bad situation, and I need the advice of the person I love more than anything or anyone else. Help me, tell me what to do.

Oh, God, how he loved Todd. He just didn't know how to describe it, the peace that he felt when they were together. Or rather the peace he usually felt but hadn't, not since the night Andrew was murdered. Ever since then Rawlins had felt as if he were standing on the edge of a cliff ready to be pushed off.

He gobbled the last bit of artichoke off the piece, then tossed the crust back in the container. Yes, that was exactly what he had to do, go right up there and, as his mother would say, have a good old-fashioned heart to heart. Todd would help him sort it out, Todd would tell him how to handle this. And then maybe they could start over, maybe they could even go out for dinner again and get things right back on track. Or maybe . . . maybe they'd just have some wine and crawl into bed.

Energized, Rawlins checked himself in the mirror, then climbed out and hurried toward the glass lobby. He glanced up, wondered which lit window was Todd's. And he wondered too how far away they were from the next big step in their relationship. For Todd, who kept close track of his finances, that meant getting a joint checking account, but for Rawlins that meant moving in together. After all, wasn't sharing the same legal address about as close as a gay couple could come to getting married?

He was just entering the glass doors when he saw a familiar vehicle come barreling down the driveway from the garage. Todd? Rawlins was just about to dash outside when he caught a glimpse of him and noted right away that he'd gotten himself all slicked up. No, Todd couldn't have a date. He couldn't, he wouldn't do that to him, really go out with some other guy. Or . . . or had that been why he'd been acting so weird tonight?

It was as if he'd been punched in the gut and all the air knocked out of him. Rawlins just stood there, his feet cemented to the floor, watching as Todd sped past the lobby. The house, the joint checking account—all of their hopes and plans whooshed through Rawlins's head.

Fuck. The bastard really did have a date.

And then in a bitter rush of jealousy he was pushing his way out the door, charging to the street, and leaping into his car. He'd followed Todd here, and he damn well wasn't going to stop now.

Chapter 20

Displaying his Midwestern punctuality, Todd parked on the street, then got out and approached the iron gate at precisely nine. Even in the dark he recognized the place, a yellow brick mansion sitting prominently on Lowry Hill and right on the edge of downtown. The house, just up the hill and a few blocks west of the Walker Art Center and the Guthrie Theater, was one of the few gated residences within the city limits. Hadn't Todd even heard there was a pool in the basement?

And Tim Chase was in there? And they were about to meet?

The sheer strangeness of it wiped everything from Todd's mind, including, in particular, Rawlins. Relieved to escape his troubles, at least for a few hours, Todd went up to the iron gate that was painted a shiny black, tested it, and found it locked. Then he saw the small brass intercom box and pressed a button.

A moment later a deep voice from the box cracked and snapped as it said, "May I help you?"

"Yes, my name's Todd Mills. I have an appointment to see Mr. Chase."

"Certainly."

The gate vibrated with a deep electric buzz, and Todd pushed it open.

He'd spent a lot of time thinking about how he would dress. While a suit had been appropriate for his interview with someone like Congressman Johnny Clariton, it was definitely out for tonight as too uptight, too conservative. Todd likewise nixed a sport coat and tie as too nerdy, too unhip. He thought about jeans but didn't want to appear too informal or unprofessional. In the end, he opted for his most casual but hippest-looking shirt—and also his most expensive—that some New York designer had conceived of in green and brown and black, a black leather belt, and fine black wool pants that made Todd look as slim as a model. He topped it all off with his black leather jacket, the most expensive article of clothing he'd ever bought, which hung perfectly from his broad shoulders.

As he followed a brick walk straight up to the house, he saw the massive door in the center and two large rooms symmetrically positioned on either side of the house. Everything was lit up, the tasteful lights along the walk, all the rooms downstairs, and every single window on the second floor. How many people were staying here, just Tim Chase, or an entire entourage? Was he going to be one of those stars who moved around the world in larger-than-life style, or would he be one of those whom you occasionally heard about, someone who was as real as he was down-to-earth? The power that the American public gave over to the stars of Hollywood had always amazed Todd. They were our de facto aristocracy, as American as anything could possibly be because their positions were made, not created, and their titles lasted only as long as they curried favor.

So was Todd going to do it? Was he really going to ask Tim Chase if he was gay? Perhaps, but definitely not in so many words.

He climbed the front steps and approached a huge front door filled with stained glass in a rich pattern of red, green, and yellow leaves and flowers. Todd didn't know much about these things, but he wouldn't have been surprised if it was the work of Tiffany or some other East Coast artisan. After all, the wealthy of the Midwest had always been eager to deny the corn and the forests and the coal that had made them rich, relying on more worldly acquisitions to prove their class and sophistication.

When Todd was only some four feet away the door began to pull open.

"Come in, please," said a large man with a shaved head.

"Thank you."

Todd quickly looked him up and down, saw that he was wearing black leather boots, black jeans, and a simple white shirt that was perfectly pressed. This guy was no butler, no personal valet. No, he was Tim Chase's bodyguard, for the life of the rich and famous didn't come without its ball and chain, namely life in a gilded cage and with hired muscle always at hand. No matter the wealth and the toys it bought, Todd didn't know how they could stand it, living under such constant scrutiny.

"This way, Mr. Mills," said the man in a deep, courteous voice.

Todd followed the guy through an enormous center hall that alone was the size of many smaller houses and lined with deep, rich mahogany paneling. They turned immediately left into a living room that was borderline gaudy and by no means whatsoever cozy; Todd's friend Jeff, a banker and a drag queen, would have called it early whorehouse. The ceiling soared a good fourteen feet and a huge, ornate marble fireplace and mantel—definitely not from Minnesota, Wisconsin, or Iowa, but surely cut out of some French castle—dominated the center wall. Three expansive couches covered in dark, heavy floral fabric were placed in a U around the fireplace and a glass coffee table the size of a small billiard table sat in the middle. Huge old oil paintings, over a half-dozen and each of them perfectly lit, hung in strategic locations. Looking at them, Todd guessed they'd been chosen perhaps not because of their artistic merit but, like the old books interior designers bought by the yard, because the meadows and the mountains and the châteaux they portrayed looked so very old, so *très riche.*

"It'll be just a moment," said the bodyguard, who stood against one wall.

"Thank you."

Suddenly Todd realized what was missing: people. If nothing else he'd been expecting to walk into a group of people. Melissa, the Tim Chase publicist. Some young guy, the Tim Chase assistant. Someone else, the Tim Chase manager. For hours Todd had been imagining some kind of committee that would, very L.A. style, hand him a glass of wine, smile and laugh, tell him all sorts of wonderful things, pretend that they loved Todd, all the while silently judging him, wondering if he would do, if in fact he suited their purposes. Yes, he expected to be greeted not by a bunch of fake people, but by a group of extraordinarily casual-appearing people who were in all actuality vicious guards, the Hollywood variety, with one job and one job only: the protection of the Tim Chase franchise. Yes, he expected the: I love you, you're great, this is wonderful, fabulous, now read my smile: You dumb fuck, you're nothing.

Instead there was no one except Mr. Muscle.

At a loss, Todd stood in the middle of the enormous room, looking at the furniture that was too new to be old money and the paintings that were too safe to be masterpieces, when he heard steps from somewhere else in the house. Todd turned and looked at the hired thug, who was undoubtedly good at tossing out people but who needed a few quarters of finishing school. From the quick, light steps Todd presumed it had to be her, Melissa. Looking past the massive guy, Todd stared into the entry hall that was the size of a ballroom.

And suddenly there he was.

It wasn't her. It wasn't Melissa or any other young woman. It was him. At first Todd thought his eyes were failing. He just looked so . . . so small. He came racing around a corner, sliding on the oak floor in white athletic socks as if this weren't some huge mansion and he weren't one of the most well known stars in the whole universe. Wearing faded blue jeans, a white T-shirt, and an untucked and unbuttoned denim shirt, Tim Chase just looked like he was in any old home and he was just any old regular guy. No, wait. Hell, thought Todd. Look at that smile. Those teeth. That electrifying grin that could and had charmed gazillions, both male and female.

"Thanks for letting him in, Vic," he said to Mr. Muscle. And then approaching Todd, he held out his hand. "Hi, I'm Tim Chase."

Much later, Todd would kick himself for not saying something like, No shit. Or, Gee, I thought you were John Travolta. Or, And I'm Bill Clinton.

Instead he was barely able to mumble, "Nice to meet you. I'm Todd Mills."

When their hands met in a formal handshake, Todd was surprised by more than a couple of things. First, he was surprised at how short and fast his own breathing had become. Second, he was impressed by the firmness of Tim Chase's grasp, how he squeezed Todd's hand so hard, so very guylike. Third and most important, the eyes. Oh, my God, thought Todd. What gorgeous brown eyes. And they were looking right at him. No, he realized, they were peering deep into him, fishing for some kind of truth, and Todd was staring right back. It lasted for just a second or two, but it was a moment much too long. Simultaneously and inexplicably, Todd's stomach tightened and his heart seemed to skip a beat. And it scared the hell out of Todd, that rush, that jolt. He knew what that was—his "gaydar" flashing "alert, alert." It was, however, more profound than a simple feeling or a mere sense. It was in fact a physical reaction. Holy shit.

The star asked, "Are you hungry?"

Todd just stared at him.

"God, why do I have this effect on people?" He lifted his right hand in front of Todd's face and snapped his fingers. "Sushi? Do you like sushi?"

Effect? No, thought Todd. He doesn't understand just what he's exuding.

Todd cleared his throat, forced himself to say, "Sushi's great."

"Vic," he said, turning to the large man, who still stood on the edge of the living room. "Would you mind playing meals on wheels again?"

"Of course."

"Get the same combination plate you did last night, okay? Oh, and their eel's great, so get some extra."

"Extra pickled ginger too?"

"That's my man."

As Vic left the room, Chase turned back to Todd, and said, "And here you've still got your coat on. Vic's almost perfect, but he's never been to butler camp."

Slipping off his leather jacket, Todd couldn't help but grin.

"Oh, this is nice. Very soft," said Chase as he took Todd's coat and carefully laid it on the back of one of the sofas. "Who would have thought you could get good sushi in the Midwest, huh? I mean, when I grew up in Milwaukee the exotic foods were chili and Reuben sandwiches."

"Just like it was in Chicago."

"You from there? Great place. Lots of fun."

Todd shrugged and didn't know why he said it, why he would divulge anything so quickly. "Yeah, but too many memories, and not enough of 'em good."

"Hey, that's exactly how I feel about Milwaukee." He took a deep breath and then sighed. "Some hard shit, I'll tell you that much."

He was talking family dirt. Divorce. Poverty. His mother's treatment and his taking all the jobs. Todd had read all about the hard times of Tim Chase, the stuff that made him tough and resilient, the stuff that made for good publicity copy. And there it now was, lying both on the surface of his soul and the surface of their conversation. Todd didn't know why, but it suddenly struck him that he liked this guy. He just seemed very real.

"So Melissa made me promise I'd get the formal stuff right on the table," continued Chase with one of those smiles that could disarm a nuclear warhead. "Namely, all this tonight is completely off the record. Nothing recorded, nothing quoted. No stories repeated. This is just a chance, you know, to talk. A chance for us to get to know each other."

"Sure," replied Todd, at the same time wondering why in the world Tim Chase would want to get to know him.

"And then . . . then we'll see."

"She won't be here tonight?"

"Melissa? No."

"What about an assistant or . . ."

"I can take care of myself, if that's what you mean, and they sure as hell know it. I mean, after all, I do pay them."

"Sorry, I just didn't know what to expect. She didn't really tell me."

"That's my Melissa, Miss Control herself." Tim rubbed his hands together, and said, "How about something to drink? A beer? Some wine?"

"Wine would be great."

"Come on."

Tim turned, spinning quickly on his stocking feet, and starting off. As Todd followed him from the living room and back through the entry, Todd thought, yes, this guy is gorgeous. Actually, more cute than gorgeous, with that perfect brown hair that flopped about, that smile that glowed. He was a real star; Todd felt that, already sensed that he was in the presence of one. He was normal size, not larger than life. Actually about the same height as Todd. And he was a bit stockier than Todd had imagined. But he looked to be in perfect shape, the shoulders broad and muscular, the legs in those tight jeans strong and athletic.

"How about this joint, huh?" said Tim as he led the way into the dining room. "We're renting it from some cosmetics queen and she's got it all dolled up."

"It's huge."

"No shit. I had to use my cell phone to find Gwen a couple of hours ago," he said with an easy laugh. "She was in the den."

"I heard there was a swimming pool in the basement. Is that true?"

"Yep. All tiled and everything. And there's a billiard room up here. You like pool?"

"Sure."

"Good, we'll shoot some."

The dining room was a tad more intimate, a smaller room with a long wooden table for a crowd, a carved plaster ceiling, another stolen marble fireplace, and a Venetian chandelier that had blue and pink baubles protruding every which way. From there they passed into a breakfast room with a tiled floor and lots of leaded glass windows; Todd easily imagined the robber baron who'd built this place taking his morning coffee out here. And then they turned left into an enormous modern kitchen that stretched all the way along the side of the house.

Immediately a small voice shouted, "Daddy!"

"Jack!"

Clutching the remnants of a chocolate chip cookie, a young boy, perhaps no older than three, came charging across the white floor. Tim scooped him up and kissed him on the neck.

"How's my best boy?"

"Good!"

"Well, there you are," said a woman who stood at the sink, her goldish-brown hair put up in a lazy bun. "He wants to say good night."

This was his boy, Todd understood. And that was his wife. That beautiful young woman in the jeans and oversized sweatshirt was *the* Gwen Owens. When he'd seen her accepting her Oscar her hair had been professionally done, her makeup perfectly applied, and she'd worn a designer gown that had made her look like a goddess, but there was no mistaking her pale complexion, her small mouth, and the gentle eyes. Standing at the sink like any ordinary slob, that was she, one of the hottest female stars in moviedom. And here they both were, Tim and Gwen, the legendary couple.

Looking past her, Todd saw a trim, handsome woman with the short brown hair sitting on the countertop. So who was she?

"Well, it's that time, is it, little man?" said Chase, hugging his son. "Give me a big kiss and a big hug. I'll see you in the morning. I love you."

"Love you too," replied the boy.

"Gwen, this is Todd Mills. Todd, this is my wife, Gwen Owens. She came out for a while so I wouldn't get lonely—and to keep me out of trouble."

"And this," said Gwen, gesturing to the attractive young woman, "is the lovely Maggie, my—"

Tim cut in, saying, "Todd's a reporter for a local TV station."

"Oh, is that right?" she said with a broad smile and without missing a beat. "Well, as I was saying, this is Maggie, our lovely nanny."

Todd said, "Nice to meet you."

"Likewise," replied Maggie, grinning from where she sat.

Our lovely nanny? Had something just happened here? A warning telegraphed?

"Come on, pumpkin," beckoned Gwen, walking over and lifting her young son from Tim's arms. "Time to hit the hay." She leaned forward and pecked Tim on the cheek. "I love you, sweetheart."

"Ditto," he said, returning the kiss.

"Nice to meet you, Todd." With a wink, she added, "Now, don't keep him up too late. He's got to be on the set at six tomorrow morning. And God knows it's hard for anyone, male or female, to look beautiful at that hour."

With her son in her arms, Gwen headed toward the back of the kitchen and presumably another staircase. Just as Gwen passed Maggie, her young son began twisting and squirming.

"I want my other mommy too!"

"Oh, don't worry, she's coming," assured Gwen.

Todd stood perfectly still, sucking it all in, trying to comprehend what was really going on in this household. He glanced at Gwen, who didn't seem the least bit fazed by the child's words, and then Todd watched as Maggie hopped off the counter and followed after them. When he looked over at Tim, however, he saw the other man looking straight at him.

"Kids," said Chase. "Maggie's been with us since the day he was born. She travels everywhere with us too."

"Really?"

"Yeah, and she's been a real lifesaver."

So Maggie probably was like a second mom to the boy. Or was she really? Could little Jack have two mommies? After all, children were not only remarkably perceptive, they were also naturally honest, brutally so.

Tim said, "What do you want, white or red?"

"Red if you've got it."

"By the case." Chase reached into a cabinet and pulled out two large wineglasses. "Actually, I'll open a bottle of Jack's wine."

"Your son has his own label?"

"No. Jack as in Jack Nicholson. We named our boy after him—he's his godfather too. And Jack Nicholson has a vineyard he thinks is the greatest on earth, which isn't surprising since he thinks he's the greatest piece of shit on earth. And maybe he is. Anyway, he sends us a couple of cases of his wine every year for Christmas, and it's actually pretty good."

"Oh."

Like what was Todd supposed to say, how was he supposed to keep up with that kind of casual talk? Tell him that two years ago he got a Butterball turkey from the station manager?

Todd watched his every move, judged his every word, from the way he pulled a bottle from the cabinet and opened it with ease, to the toast he made to their good health. It was weird, there was no doubt about it. It was as if he'd walked through a door and was having a totally normal conversation with Michael Jackson and that he found him just a regular old guy. But that's in fact how Tim Chase appeared. Normal. It was that sense of ease that so many journalists had written about, that nice guy quality that sort of couldn't help but come through the dazzling smile. Or was that all a facade? This guy was an actor. He was a professional at creating illusion. And that was what acting was all about, the craft and art of making people believe that what they were seeing was the absolute truth.

"Come on, let's go shoot some pool," said Chase, touching Todd on the elbow. "Say, I bet you're wondering why we selected you of all the local journalists for a possible interview."

"Well, that thought had crossed my mind."

"I'll be perfectly frank, it's because you're gay."

Chapter 21

Standing in the back hall, his muscular body pressed against a line of coats hanging from hooks, the bald man listened to their conversation. No, thought Vic, he didn't like this, not one bit. Gwen wasn't too bad, but Tim always said too much. Always. Which made Vic's own job that much more difficult.

Now that Gwen and Maggie and the boy had gone the other way down the hall and up the back staircase, he could move closer. He had, from years of Tai Chi, fine control of every muscle, and he silently inched around some boots, past an umbrella, around a nylon parka, and right up to the edge of the kitchen door. No, he thought, there was no way they knew he was back here. No way at all.

He heard the pop of a wine bottle, the clinking of glasses. And he heard Tim turning on the charm, per usual. A real master at that, no doubt about it. But it made Vic nervous as hell. He didn't think there was any way this Todd Mills could know anything. Maybe he suspected, perhaps he just wondered. But this wasn't good, not by any means, having someone from the media lurking here inside the house.

Listening to every word of their chatter, he then discerned them heading off to play pool. Well, he thought, there was nothing to do now. Whatever happened was out of his control.

And hoping no damage would be done before he returned with the sushi, he turned down the narrow hall and started for the garage.

Chapter 22

Carrying the bottle of wine as well as his glass, Tim led Todd through the living room and into the billiard room, which was of course a chamber of grand proportions with the same soaring ceiling. Two huge leaded glass windows filled one of the walls, while on the others hung random antelope and deer heads, a six-foot-long rattlesnake skin, and a pair of longhorns, all trophies of when men were men. Squarely planted in the middle, with a brass light fixture hanging low over it, was a Victorian billiard table, a huge thing crafted of carved mahogany. Its surface was covered with a field of rich green felt, and from the six pockets hung woven leather pouches. This was a gentleman's room, a manly man's place to discuss money and hunting and port. And tonight, the mysteries of sexuality.

Todd sipped his wine as he leaned against the edge of the billiard table, then couldn't stop himself from saying, "Gee, and here I was hoping your people had contacted me because of my talents and abilities as a journalist, not because of my sexual orientation."

"Please, don't be offended."

"For being gay?"

"No," replied Chase looking at him with an oddly seductive grin, "for my wanting to use you."

What the hell did he mean by that? It gave Todd a start, not only the way Tim Chase said it, but also the way his eyes kept scanning Todd. Was double entendre the second language of this household?

Determined not to lose his own ground, Todd said, "I'm afraid you're going to have to be a little more specific."

"What I mean is that I wanted to meet with and talk to a successful gay person from the Midwest. Everybody and their brother at
a studio fiddles with a script, but it's me that has his neck on the line.
They're a bunch of West Coast people—and granted, a whole lot of
them are homosexual—but it's me who's going to have to convince an
audience not only that I'm gay, but that I'm from here."

"Oh, so I'm research."

"In so many words, sure."

"But why? You're from the Midwest." Did he, Todd wondered,
dare? "But I can see your concern. After all, there've been all those
nasty little rumors, haven't there? I mean, isn't everyone curious if you
are in fact gay?"

"Ohhh, aren't you the direct one? And, yes, that's been the sixty-
four thousand dollar question: Where does Tim Chase put his cock?"
he said with a laugh. "Good God, I'll never live it down, just like
Richard Gere will never live down that apocryphal pesky rodent story."

"Yeah, he probably won't."

"Do you know why they put Princess Di on the cover of so many
issues of *People* magazine? Because those issues always sold millions.
And do you know why all the tabloids put Tim Chase and his love life
on the cover? Because those issues always sell out. Which leads me to
the second reason I wanted to meet with you. For this movie I'd like
ultimately to be interviewed by someone who's gay. I want to meet the
doubters head on so that they can see there's no conspiracy of silence."

So how the hell was Todd supposed to understand all this . . . this
babble, this elongated non-answer? In a roundabout way was he saying no, he wasn't gay, or was he just successfully evading the question?

Tim led Todd to a wooden wall rack and they chose their
weapons, the finest of long straight cues. At his host's insistence, Todd
racked up the balls into a tight triangle, and then broke them, sinking
a striped ball. Tim followed, making a difficult shot into a side pocket,
then missing a second one. They played on, alternating turns and sipping Jack Nicholson wine.

And it was Todd, who by personality as well as by profession returned to risqué waters, asking, "So what do you want to know about a gay man in the Midwest?"

Tim completed a shot, sinking a solid in a corner pocket, and replied in a near-businesslike way, "I want to know about your work, how long you've been at the present station and what kind of stories you usually cover. I want to know what it's like being openly gay at work . . . and how long you've been out. And I want to know if you're out to your parents, and of course all about your love life."

"Well . . ."

Todd went through it all, answering each of his questions in detail. He started with his college years, telling Chase all about his dear love and dear friend Janice, who also turned out to be queer. He talked about being in the closet, about marrying Karen, then being terrified that viewers would find out and his career would be flushed down the toilet. And he talked about doing tricks on the side, wherever, however he could get them. And then Michael and Rawlins.

They finished one game, started on another. And refilled their glasses. Tim took it in, every facet of Todd's life.

"You were married?" asked Chase as Todd neared the end.

"Yeah, for a number of years." He hesitated, then added, "And I've got a kid. A son."

"No shit. How old?"

"Well . . . it happened when I was in college, so actually he's in his early twenties now."

"Wow."

"Unfortunately I don't know him very well. It's a long story, and something I need to take care of, but . . ."

No, thought Todd, I'm not going to toss in the fact that my son has a daughter, which obviously means I'm also a grandfather. Instead he went on to tell the story of his coming out, which was when Todd realized he had Tim Chase completely hooked. As Todd told the star how he was outed when Michael was murdered, Tim put down his pool cue, picked up his glass of wine, and stared at Todd, his face etched with sympathy and understanding.

"Oh, my God," Tim muttered several times throughout the telling. "How horrible. It must have been . . ."

"Hard, but ultimately good."

Why was it, Todd wondered, that coming-out stories held such universal appeal to gay men? Was it simply the common experience? The same plunging of the soul for the inner truth, a truth of character that straight people were rarely forced to discover? And why did it seem that Tim Chase was now listening to Todd's story, judging it for how it might reflect on his own life? Was he vicariously understanding what it would be like for him to come out, to put everything he had worked for at risk simply so that he could assert his own identity and inner sense of honesty? Or was he simply a truly kind man?

Tim Chase was already one of the very biggest stars, the kind like Henry Fonda and Cary Grant, a star who was destined to live on as an icon for generations. Todd, in comparison, was a mere speck, if that, yet as he talked Todd couldn't help but feel that they had something in common. No, Todd wasn't particularly intuitive, not by any means, yet he couldn't help but think they were very similar in one regard, that they both held a deep-seated fear of what people thought of them. Without any evidence and despite knowing the man but for a very short while, Todd supposed that Tim Chase had gone into acting not only as a way of escaping himself, but as a way of projecting a larger-than-life image of the person he longed to be: a true hero, a true heterosexual hero. Maybe he was straight, maybe he wasn't, Todd had no answer to that simple question, but he did know that Hollywood was a citadel of homophobia, a place where people feared one thing almost above all others: that a particular truth would kill their careers.

The sushi arrived. Vic, the bodyguard, didn't make much of a waiter, but he brought in two Styrofoam containers and then silently disappeared. Todd and Tim started in on the food, and then Tim dashed off for another bottle of Nicholson's best. As Tim poured Todd his third and soon fourth glass of wine, Todd wondered if Chase felt it too, this sense that the two of them could be genuine friends. Or did Chase just naturally exude that aura, was that part of his star charm, the ability to make everyone feel comfortable around him? Was the magic of his appeal simply based on his ability to make everyone like him?

"So what about your love life?" asked Tim, stuffing a tuna roll into his mouth. "You mentioned this guy, this cop. Is he your Mr. Wonderful?"

Todd picked up a California roll, draped it with a piece of pickled ginger, then dipped it in wasabi and soy sauce. As he took a bite, he glanced at the other man, who was bent over and focusing on a shot. Could Chase be checking Todd out to see if he was available, or was he really just asking about Todd's life? And how should Todd answer? What the hell was going on here?

"Rawlins and I are pretty involved." His mood increasingly dictated by the wine, Todd decided to leave the door open, and he added, "But we've recently run into a major bump."

"I see."

Todd found himself looking at Tim Chase's broad hands, his muscular wrists. And the clean-shaven cheeks. He studied the other man's eyes and eyebrows. His ears, the back of his neck.

And then he turned away, reached for his glass of wine.

"Your shot," said Chase.

As he took a sip, then put down the glass and reached for his pool cue, Todd realized he could ask the one question he loved to ask straight people—if in fact Chase was straight. In an attempt to keep the issue on the table, he could pose the fairly non-threatening: Have you ever had a same-sex encounter? Probably sixty or seventy percent of the men Todd had asked had said yes, but how would Chase respond?

Instead, Todd backed down. "So do you think you'll have a hard time playing a gay man?"

"No. I mean, why should I? I'm an actor. I've played lawyers, I've played murderers. And could I defend someone in court? Hell, no. Could I kill someone? Absolutely not. This is just a continuation of my work, that's all."

"But you don't think you'll have any trouble pulling it off?"

Somewhere off in this huge house the phone rang, and it made Todd realize how utterly quiet it had been up to this point. There'd been no music, no distant voices. Only the slow dance of their conversation and the occasional chattering of pool balls.

Staring off into the rest of the house, Tim said, "Shit, I wonder who that is. Hardly anyone has this number." When someone picked it up midway through the third ring, he shrugged and said, "Oh, well."

Todd leaned over, focused on a red striped ball that was hugging the side. If he did it carefully enough he could just tap it with the white ball and get it to roll slowly to the corner pocket. Squinting, he took careful aim, then took a shot, and moments later the ball slipped into the pocket.

"Very nice," said Chase.

Todd came around, saw that the green striped ball was his only chance. But how the hell was he going to get it in that far corner? With force or a slight tap? Squinting, he bent over. And then felt hands on his hips. His entire body tensed, his heart flew into a rush of a panic.

Slowly enveloping him from behind, Tim Chase said, "So what do you think, can I pull it off?"

"I . . . I . . ."

"Don't forget, TV boy, this is off the record."

Todd took a deep breath, felt the hands come around his hips and move seductively across his waist, then he quietly gasped, "Maybe."

Todd felt the other man's crotch press against his ass, and Todd's body rushed with a double shot of fear and desire as powerful as a tall glass of tequila. The pool cue rolled out of his hands, dropped onto the green felt. And he stood motionless as Tim Chase started to dry hump him from behind. Jesus Christ, was this really happening?

"You've got a nice body." He kissed Todd on the back, once, twice, then slowly moved his hand upward to Todd's chest, and said, "I think this is how you make love to another man, right?"

"Yeah, I think . . . I think, ah, you've got the hang of it."

Oh, fuck. Was he playing with Todd or really coming on to him?

Was one of America's biggest idols, the same star Todd had seen on the huge silver screen, now riding him from behind with true lust or—

"Just let me do the work," cooed Chase into Todd's right ear.

Like silky magic, Chase's broad hand slid down Todd's stomach, over his belt buckle, then flew briefly across his lusty crotch. Oh, my God, what was going on here? This guy's wife was right upstairs. Rawlins was probably waiting for him at home. But . . . but this guy was so sexy. So amazingly gorgeous. And if Rawlins had been screwing around, why the hell shouldn't he? They weren't married. There was no dictum that said, no, don't do this. Right. This was the benefit of being gay, of never being bound, legally or otherwise, to another, of . . .

From behind Chase grabbed onto Todd's left nipple and twisted. The delight shot through him, and he thought, if this is a game, I'm not going to be his toy. And he thrust back with his ass, nudging Chase slightly away, then spun around. Their eyes caught and held and it scared the crap out of Todd. The next second they were back together, clutching each other. Todd felt Chase's lips on his neck, felt his tongue drawing a moist line upward to his chin. And Todd was rubbing his hand across that hard stomach, not merely massaging it, but determined to probe beneath the belt, to read the only true thermometer of what was now—

A voice from the edge of the room said, "The reviewers have always said my timing is my best quality. I almost think they're right, don't you?"

As if Todd had been caught stealing a bucket of priceless jewels, he flew back against the pool table. Glancing over, he saw her, Gwen Owens. She was standing in the doorway, leaning against the jamb, a wily smile on her face, the same smile in fact that he'd seen her sport at the Academy Awards. He turned, looked at Tim Chase, who was grinning back at her. What was this, some kind of dream?

Chase wiped his mouth with the back of his right hand, and said, "Just doing a little rehearsing, sweetheart."

"Of course you are. After all, we all know what a stickler you are for details." She shrugged, turned, and sauntered off, calling over her shoulder, "Oh, and Brian's on the phone. Says there's something wrong with the script, something that you guys have to work out tonight so the shooting schedule doesn't get all fucked tomorrow. Actually, I wouldn't be surprised if he wants to come right over."

Turning to Todd, his mouth pursed in a naughty grin, Tim said, "Oh, brother, that's the director. Sorry, but I gotta take this call. I'm afraid it's going to be a while, it always is with Brian. Do you mind letting yourself out?"

"Ah . . . ah, no . . ."

The naughty grin blossoming into one of his megawatt smiles, Tim Chase asked, "So what do you think, can I pull it off, can I act the role of a gay man? Did I convince you? I did, didn't I?"

Todd stood there—was that all this was, just a game?—and before he could reply Tim Chase turned and trotted out of the billiard room. Had any of this really happened? Todd looked over at the pool table, saw his cue lying there. He glanced at the half-eaten sushi. Yes, he'd just met with Tim Chase. They'd had wine. And there, those were their wineglasses. And—

Ducking his head back in, Tim proffered a small, naughty grin. "Say, I got a couple of more research questions for you. Why don't you come back tomorrow night, say about seven thirty? How's that sound?"

Wondering what in the hell he meant by that, at first Todd said nothing, just stared at him, and then hating himself, eagerly replied, "Sure."

Chapter 23

Sitting in his grandfather's worn red leather chair in the living room of his own apartment, Rawlins took a long drink of beer and tumbled into a black hole of worry. What would he do without Todd? Was he destined to always be alone? Was the stereotype of the lonely old queen prophetic? Oh, God. He didn't know when or if HIV would eventually overtake his life, and that of course worried the hell out of him, but he'd always feared the double curse of growing old and being lonely.

Just a short while ago he'd followed Todd all the way to that huge house on Mount Curve. He'd watched Todd, all dressed up in his hippest, get out of his car and go up to the gate, and then proceed to the massive front door. At first Rawlins told himself that Todd was merely going to a party, but then he realized there were scant cars on the street and that, apparently, no one else was coming. So who lived there? Was it some wealthy homosexual, some Spam heir or plastic surgeon from the Mayo or one of the queens who'd sold a gajillion of those ceramic Christmas houses? Was some fag with buckets of money trying to steal handsome Todd away from him, a lowly cop whose health was questionable?

Rawlins, whose temper could be rageful, had been about to go up there and either shove his way through the gate or climb over the fence. The anxiety had been building like steam in a boiling kettle, and he pictured himself bursting into the huge house. Then, however, the gate on the drive had opened and a white car had come speeding out. It was so dark that Rawlins thought Todd was in the passenger seat, and so, madder than hell, he'd sped after the vehicle. At the very first stop sign on the next block, Rawlins had pulled up alongside the car and stared right in, only to look at a man with a shaved head, who was the only one in the vehicle. As that car then sped away, Rawlins pulled over, shook his head in disgust, then pressed on the gas and somehow managed to get himself to his home, this apartment on the second floor of a duplex.

No, I won't cave, thought Rawlins, now sitting there. I won't go to Todd's, not tonight. They hadn't slept apart in months, but Rawlins wasn't going to give. He didn't want to lie next to Todd and wonder where he'd been, what he'd done, whom he'd perhaps kissed, because of course he'd go absolutely and completely ballistic. He also couldn't go there because . . . oh, shit . . . because he didn't want to tell him about Andrew. Yes, the next time Rawlins saw Todd he'd have no choice. He was going to have to tell Todd exactly what had happened on that afternoon only hours before that young kid was killed.

Oh, shit. How could he have been so stupid?

Rawlins ran his left hand through his short dark hair and pulled at the roots. Clutching the cool beer bottle in his right, he raised it to his mouth and took another swig. And then he got up and went to his old brown leather coat, which hung on the back of one of the old chairs at the dinner table. He reached into the inside pocket and pulled out the small spiral notebook. Staring at the small booklet that contained so many confessions, so many fears, so many hopes, Rawlins recalled their last conversation that had taken place early that afternoon.

"You don't understand," Andrew had said as tears filled those beautiful blue eyes. "My entire life is so unbelievably fucked up. You're the only good thing. Don't you understand how much I need you?"

"But, Andrew . . ." Rawlins had tried to protest.

"You can't imagine what happened today. You can't imagine who came by this morning. I mean, I just want to kill myself. I just want to throw a belt over that pipe up there and just string my—"

"Stop it! Don't talk like that! You're fine. Everything's going to be okay."

"But—"

And then Andrew was falling into Rawlins's arms. No longer the butch farm boy, he was sobbing like a lost child.

Yes, that was how it had happened, how it had begun. Rawlins should have just turned and walked out of there. No, he should have flown as fast as a bat out of hell. But how could he have left him? He was so upset, so lost. Rawlins remembered looking up, seeing that old pipe, and imagining Andrew hanging himself. Everyone had let that kid down, and Rawlins was determined not to, particularly when he was at his lowest low. But then Andrew had started it, groping Rawlins, rubbing his chest, kissing him, and ripping open his own pants and broadcasting his own eagerness.

Recalling that net of seduction that Andrew had thrown over him, Rawlins now clutched the diary and returned to the old red leather chair. But wait, thought Rawlins. He'd been so focused on those few minutes that had followed, so terrified what the police department and Todd and the world would think—if in fact they ever found out— that he'd all but forgotten what Andrew had said: "You can't imagine what happened. You can't imagine who came by this morning."

What the hell had Andrew been talking about? Who could that have been? And could it, Rawlins now wondered, somehow be related to the murder that had taken place a mere few hours later? Absolutely. And could that secret be hidden here in these pages of a lost boy's confession? Quite possibly.

His hands all but shaking, Rawlins flipped through the diary, stopping at that fateful day.

> The only true love of my life will be here in a few hours. He means so much to me, so much more than Jordy ever did. And today I'm going to tell Rawlins how much I love him, how much I need him. Especially after today.

Reading those words, Rawlins shook his head. Obviously he'd done something to encourage Andrew, but what? What words, what looks? What false messages of interest had he broadcast?

I need him now more than anything because now I under-
stand everything and just how perverted this world really is. I
don't know if I can take it. The truths of this world are too weird,
too twisted.

Rawlins remembered the first crush he'd ever had on another
man, his high school gym teacher. All but nine years older than
Rawlins, who'd been seventeen at the time, he thought Mr. Stevens
was the handsomest, sexiest thing around, his voice so deep, his arms
so powerful. He'd fantasized the two of them going out, having a couple of beers, and then . . . But of course Mr. Stevens had been
straight, nothing had even remotely happened, and he had, in fact,
gotten married the next year.

This morning I was out in front of the apartment building,
just raking like I was supposed to. That's when I noticed that
guy—he was sitting in a car and staring at me. He scared me
right away because he was kind of creepy-looking. He was bald
and wearing sunglasses and he didn't look very friendly. I just
kept raking, but he didn't take his eyes off me. Finally I heard
this car door shut, and I looked up and saw him coming over. I
kind of wanted to run, and I was about to when he called out
my name.
"Andy, you're Andy, aren't you?"
I didn't say anything. I mean, I was sure I never saw him be-
fore. I mean, I've done it three times exactly. Three times I took
money—once this married guy paid me fifty bucks to let him
suck me. Another time this guy, this businessman, was here for
some kind of dentist convention, and he paid me seventy-five to
go back to his hotel room. Then another time, this old guy, he
was gay for sure, he paid me twenty-five bucks just to let him
watch me jerk off. But what was I supposed to do? I was hun-
gry. I needed the money. But this guy, all I could think was,
Who's that old troll?

And then he said, "You got to be Andy—you look just like your dad."

I kind of freaked. I mean, I probably shoulda just taken off. Instead I just kind of tried to look, you know, tough.

And even though I thought my heart was going to pop out of my chest, I said, "Who the fuck are you?"

I mean, I thought he was a cop. Or a detective, someone they hired to come find me.

He said, "A very old friend of your dad, that's who, you little shit."

I stared at him, and at first I didn't know what to say, then finally, "How did you find me?"

It turns out that Jordy Weaver is a bigger idiot than I ever thought. Last night he was all upset—all upset about me, probably—and that idiot called home. He probably was bawling to his parents that he wanted to come home or something. What a wuss. And then Mr. Weaver called my house and talked to my dad and apparently told him where Jordy was living. Dad then asked this guy to come up here and check on me. He went to Jordy's, and then that fucking turd sent him right over here, thank you very much, Mr. Jordy Fairy Weaver.

Yes, thought Rawlins. He should have already done it, but first thing tomorrow morning he'd find Jordy and get a formal statement from him.

So this guy asks if I'm alright, and I say yes. He said my dad is all worried about me. Well, that was a crock of shit, I knew that right away. My mom maybe, but not Dad, not after he beat the crap out of me. You know, so I'm looking at this guy, thinking what is he really here for?

And so I say, "Dad said he never wanted to see me again, and I don't ever want to see him either."

"You know what, Andy, maybe you'll understand some day."

"Understand what?"

"Things, that's all."

"Well, if she wants to know, you can tell my mom I'm fine. Now I gotta get back to work."

And then this guy, he goes and pulls a hundred dollar bill from his wallet. Like no way. No way am I going to go to bed with him. Fuck! What a disgusting pig.

"I don't want your money," I tell him.

"Please, your dad is a special friend of mine. We've known each other since we were kids. He just asked me to drive by where you were living, he didn't want me to stop, but then I saw you out here, and—"

"I've never seen you before. If you're my dad's friend, then why haven't I ever seen you? You've never been at our farm, have you? And I've never seen you in town. So who the fuck are you?"

This bald guy, he looks down at the ground, and then he says, "He's going to shoot me for doing this, but there's something you have to know."

The way he said it really scared me, and I asked, "What's . . . what's that?"

"Do you promise you won't tell him I told you?"

"Sure," I answered even though I knew I was lying.

"You swear?"

"Yeah, I swear. Now tell me! What is it?"

And then he tells me. He just blurts it out. It just takes one little sentence, that's all, and then everything's ruined.

"You're a fucking liar!" I yell at him.

"I'm sure it's kind of a shock, I—"

"You're wrong!"

"No, Andy, I'm not. I wouldn't lie about something like that."

"No!"

I threw my rake at him and then ran inside. He tried to come after me, but I pulled the front door shut and locked it. He was banging on the door, yelling at me to let him in, but I didn't.

I never wanted to see that jerk again. I mean, I couldn't believe it. There had to be a mistake. It had to be a lie. I started crying and I ran right to my apartment. I like threw myself on my bed. What was I supposed to do? Believe him? But . . .

I mean, I had to know. I had to know for sure. So what did I do? I called Dad. I called him on his cell phone. He was out on the tractor, tilling the south field, and he picked up right away.

"Is it true, Dad?" I yelled into the receiver.

"Andy? Andy, is that you?"

"This guy, he just came here, and he said . . . said something bad about you," I began, breaking my promise. "Is it true? Do you know him and is he telling the truth?"

At first there was nothing, like I hit him in the stomach or something. And then he started screaming and yelling at the top of his lungs.

"Are you crazy? Of course it's not true! And . . . and if you ever say anything like that again, God damn it, I'll kill you with my very own hands!"

"Oh, my God . . . it is true, isn't it?"

"You little—"

And then I hung up. I just sort of dropped the phone. For the first time in my life everything made sense. I saw how all of us fit together, Mom and Dad, me, my sisters. Now I knew why he hit me so hard in the barn, why he went so crazy. Everything made sense, yet nothing did.

I still can't believe it. In fact, I can't even write it down. I mean, if anyone ever found this diary and read it, then they'd know what my dad's been doing. And then . . . then Dad really would come after me and kill me. For sure.

God, I'm so afraid . . .

Afraid? Afraid of what?

On the one hand, thought Rawlins, nothing made sense. On the other, everything did. Now he knew why Andrew had been so desperate, why he had been so needy and clingy. Now he understood why Andrew had so wanted to fall into Rawlins's arms. His father had threatened his life, and Andrew had wanted love. He'd wanted comfort, he'd wanted solace. Desperately confused, Andrew had needed all of that. The only mistake he'd made, however, was that he'd tangled it all up with sex, which was so often the case with kids, gay or straight, male or female, for they too often lacked any other way to say: I need comfort. But then why should they? Hell, most adults didn't know how to say those three simple words either.

It was as horrible as it was pathetic. If only he'd known, Rawlins told himself. If only Andrew had come right out and said something. If only he'd told Rawlins what his father was involved in then maybe he could have helped.

So, mused Rawlins, holding the diary in his lap and now staring at the blank white wall across the room. Late morning of the day Andrew was murdered, a bald man had come to see him and dropped a major-league bomb. And then Andrew had called his father, and the father had in no uncertain ways threatened his very own son. So had either one of these men come to Andrew's apartment later in the day, blindfolded him, and cut his throat? Had the bald man returned, furious that he'd broken his promise and talked to his father? Or had Andrew's own father come up, knowing that there was but one way to keep silent the truth, whatever it was?

Oh, God, thought Rawlins. Could the world really be that horrible that a father would harm his son?

Chapter 24

As he sat outside the coffee shop, the night air chilly and damp, Jordy Weaver couldn't help but feel as if somebody's eyes were tracking his every move. He wanted to be out here, away from all of them, those gay people inside the cafe who were talking and gabbing and laughing as if they didn't have a care in the world, but who was that in the car across the street? Who was that guy and why did it seem he was just waiting? But waiting for what? Some hustler and a midnight blow job? A chance encounter with another desperate soul? Or could he, Jordy wondered as he sipped his coffee, be waiting especially for me?

The Octopus Cafe, just on the edge of downtown Minneapolis, had once been a car wash known by almost the same name. In fact, the very namesake creature still sat on a pole high above Jordy, only now its multiple arms didn't hold sponges and buckets but coffee cups, lots of them. It was a popular place among queer people, not too far from the gay bars, of which the Twin Cities had a particularly odd dearth, and only a few blocks from Loring Park, known for its after-hours cruising. Tonight, as the bars began to empty, the cafe was getting more and more packed with men waiting for this evening's sidewalk sale. After all, who wanted to be out this late and end up in bed with naught?

Look at them all, thought Jordy, peering in through the large glass garage door from which freshly scrubbed cars had once exited. Look at all those men sitting in there gabbing away about this and that, none of it important. Do I want to be like them, those scuzzy homos? Do I want to end up like that, smoking and drinking and doing drugs and fucking everything in sight . . . and getting killed? Right, now Jordy knew it for sure. If you were gay you either got AIDS or you got your throat slit. Oh, shit, why couldn't he just be normal? Maybe he could change, get rid of this thing inside him. He'd heard about such religious organizations that took you in and made you straight. Maybe he should give it a try.

In the distance he saw the sky pulse spasmodically with lightning, then soon thereafter heard the deep grumbling of thunder. Oh, God, he couldn't believe this. All he'd ever wanted was Andrew, but now he was gone forever. First Andrew had moved away from him, taking that job and getting his very own apartment, then he started seeing that cop, and now . . . now . . .

No, Andrew was never coming back. Never. He was dead, dead, dead. Jordy wondered if there was going to be a funeral back in their hometown or if his parents were going to keep the shame of their lives all secret and everything. If there was a funeral, Jordy wondered if he'd be invited, but then realized that, no, of course he wouldn't be. Andrew's parents probably wanted to see him in the grave too. They probably even blamed him, Jordy Weaver, for what happened to their son, and maybe, just maybe, they were right. At least it hadn't been him who had started it all. Nope, it had been Andrew. He'd been the one to first bring up sex. The first one to pounce.

Tears filled his eyes yet again, and he bent over his coffee, which was getting colder by the second. He bowed his head and his long silky light brown hair fell forward, covering his face. Who would've ever imagined that something like this would happen to one of them? He remembered the first time they'd done it, Andrew and he. It had been something like two years ago when Andrew had come for a sleep-over. They'd just started goofing around—"I'm kind of horny, how about you?" Andrew had asked. One thing sort of led to another, and then they realized what they really had in common. They'd done it another six or seven times—in the attic above Jordy's parents' garage, in the hayloft in Andrew's barn, once in a car—before they got caught and the shit really hit the fan. After that it had been Jordy's idea for the two of them to run away, to come all the way up here. Jordy had thought he was so cool, so smart, coming up with that plan, but it proved to be the stupidest thing. Shit, fuck, piss. This was all his fault. Andrew would never have gotten himself killed if they hadn't come up here to The Cities.

"You okay?" said a deep voice.

Jordy looked up and saw some guy with a rough, bearded face staring down at him. Oh, God, was that him, the guy who'd been watching him from across the street? No, he didn't think so, but whoever he was, this guy was a major creep too. He wore a black leather vest and tight black leather pants, the crotch of which looked like it had been stuffed with a week's worth of socks. Fuck, what a pig. Why were these older guys always hitting on him? Was it because his face was so boyish, because his tall body was so reedlike?

"You're going to catch cold sitting out here, kid. Come on inside and I'll buy you another cup of coffee."

Well . . . well, maybe, thought Jordy. Maybe the guy was just being nice. Maybe he really wanted to help. He wasn't that bad, actually. His voice was gentle enough, the eyes likewise sweet. And it was going to rain. But then Jordy remembered exactly what happened to Andrew, and he shook his head and looked away. No fucking way.

"No thanks."

"You sure? It's fixing to rain. You're gonna get soaked out here, you know."

"I said no, so just leave me alone, alright?"

With that the guy turned toward the door, saying, "Hey, listen, you little shit, I was only trying to be nice."

Under his breath, Jordy muttered, "Yeah, right."

Jordy raised his cup, downed the last bit of now completely cold coffee, then turned and looked down the dark empty street. That car was still parked there, but what about the guy? Was he still behind the wheel? At first Jordy couldn't tell, but then a dark shadow moved inside the vehicle. Yes, he was sitting there. And he was looking right this way.

Jordy just had to get the fuck out of here. Not just this place, not simply this stupid coffee shop, but The Cities. He wished he could do it all over again, these past few months. He wished he'd never left home, and the next moment he was on his feet, pinning his old wool coat shut with one hand. He didn't have a car. He didn't have a bike. And he didn't even have enough money to spend on a bus, which at this hour would be a long wait, anyway. It was going to take, he knew, at least forty minutes for him to walk, which meant it would be after one in the morning by the time he got back to that shithole of an apartment he shared with all those kids. He wondered how many would be sacked out there tonight, four or five, or ten or twelve. At least no one had better be in his bed, that was for fucking sure.

Heading south on LaSalle Avenue, he saw the sky again throb with lightning, and he wondered if he would in fact make it home before the storm hit. Picking up his pace, his straight, long hair bounced with each of his strides. He was a beanpole of a kid, slightly over six feet tall with a frame that desperately needed another thirty or so pounds. Or at least that was what Andrew always said. Andrew, who promised to take Jordy to the gym and help him work out, pump some iron. Right, Andrew, who had promised so many things, namely that they'd always be together.

"We'll get those arms all beefed up, you'll see," Andrew had once said, lying naked in bed next to him and squeezing Jordy's twiggy arms. "We'll go work out every day, and you'll see, you'll get some muscle."

Yeah, sure. And someday we'll actually cross the Minnesota border, which neither of them had ever done. Forget the Dakotas, forget Iowa. Chicago, that was Andrew's big dream.

"I hear they have some rocking dance places down there."

"Yeah, sure they do. I've heard all about 'em. They're supposed to be incredible, but how the hell would we get in? Anyone who takes one look at me knows I'm underage."

"I don't know, we'll get some fake IDs or something."

A stream of cars whooshed past Jordy, and tears came again to his eyes. He was such a sissy, he knew, but he couldn't help himself, couldn't stop crying. Beautiful Andrew. His beautiful Andrew. Dead, his throat slit. He bit his lip, tried to force the image out of his mind. Why? Why the fuck why?

Suddenly he sensed a car slowing. He glanced back, saw a brown Ford Explorer come to a crawl by his side, and then everything inside him went tense. Was this the guy he'd seen parked down the street from the cafe? The next moment the passenger window slowly descended with a deep electric hum. Jordy looked in, saw a heavy man with gray hair behind the wheel. He was wearing a white shirt and a fancy suit. And he was rubbing his crotch nice and slow.

"It's awfully late," he said, his voice all deep and lusty. "You need a lift, kid? I'll take you wherever you want to go. You want to get in?"

"No," snapped Jordy as he kept walking.

"How about fifty bucks? You need that? I bet you do, don't you? How about fifty, will that do?"

With glaring eyes, Jordy looked into the truck, saw the guy reach into his suit coat and pull out his wallet. In the light from a nearby lamppost he also saw the glint of gold on his left ring finger.

"Fuck you, you old fart!" shouted Jordy, who then honkered up a good wad and spit it through the window onto the guy's fat thigh. "Why don't you go home to the suburbs and fuck your stupid wife, huh? Why the fuck are you out here looking for cock?"

The guy stomped on the gas, and the vehicle flew away, but not before Jordy was able to kick the side door. And as the stranger hightailed it, Jordy wondered just who he was, really some married suburban creep or an undercover cop hoping for a bust. The cops were doing that, they were, going after kids. He'd heard all about it. Just last week the whole DQ had been buzzing because some kid had gotten scooped up by the cops for hustling. Well, Jordy had never done it, sold himself, and he never would. All he wanted was . . .

Shit, but Andrew was gone.

From somewhere back along the street he heard a car door slam, and Jordy turned, scanned the parked cars, the empty sidewalk. It was a little late and this neighborhood wasn't the best, that was for sure. He heard footsteps but couldn't see anyone. Looking at the tall redbrick apartment buildings that were packed in right up to the side-walk, he saw maybe three or four lights on.

Clenching his arms around his chest, he hurried on, crossing onto a bridge that led over the freeway. The wind was stronger here, the chill more biting, and he looked over the edge, saw the anonymous cars hurling along at insane speeds. It crossed his mind that the guy in the Ford Explorer might circle around and come after him—this time no longer offering money—and so he glanced over his shoulder. He saw headlights barreling down on him, but they were from a small car, he could see that right away. There was something else, though. Or rather someone else—just a half-block back a figure was hurrying along the sidewalk as well. Some guy, that was all he could really tell. Where the hell, wondered Jordy, had he come from?

Walking still faster, Jordy pushed on. Out of nowhere a sprinkle of rain came, spraying chilly water across his face. Shit, he realized, the storm was going to come sooner than he thought. Just a couple of seconds later the sprinkle turned into a steady rain, and Jordy pinched his collar shut, bowed his head even more, and broke into a quick trot. Scurrying across the bridge, he glanced back, saw the dark figure behind him break into a run as well. Holy shit, he thought. He's following me. It's probably the same guy who'd been watching back at the cafe, and it very well might be the same guy who got Andrew. And now he's going to do it, he's going to get me too.

There was a crack of lightning and an almost instant explosion of thunder, and Jordy started running as fast as he could. As if a single huge switch had been flicked on, the rain came down in sheets, now falling so hard that Jordy could barely see the other end of the bridge. But then what? Where would he go from there, how would he get away? Maybe there was a bar up there. Or a grocery store. Just some-place that was open that he could duck into.

He glanced over the bridge, saw the freeway traffic below now crawling along through the storm. Wiping the water from his brow, he checked over his shoulder yet again. Oh, shit, the guy was gaining on him! What if he didn't just have a knife? What if he had a gun? Oh,

God, thought Jordy, now running as hard as he could. Why had he ever left home? Why had he ever run away? He just wanted to be back there, back with his parents and his brother and their dog. He'd never do it again, never have sex with another guy, never get in trouble, if only he could get back home. Please, God! Please, just don't let this guy get me too!

Reaching the far end of the bridge, he looked up the street, but through the pouring rain all he could see were apartment buildings and some big old houses, all of them dark and lifeless. There were no businesses, not as far as he could see, no public place he could duck into. No, those were all on Nicollet and this was LaSalle. Looking back, he saw the guy charging through the rain right at him. Oh, shit, Jordy was never going to be able to outrun this guy, never. He climbed up on the railing of the bridge, saw the steep bank and the edge of the freeway below. There were cars down there and people. He could slide all the way down. Someone would stop. Someone would help.

Only ten or fifteen feet away now, the stranger started shouting, yelling, "Hey!"

Through the pouring rain Jordy glanced back, thought he recognized him, and cried, "You're not going to get me too!"

But then the man was upon him, and the next moment Jordy was tumbling head over foot down the steep hill and into the busy stream of traffic below.

Chapter 25

Way in the distance and far to the east, Martha Lyman saw the late night sky spark and snap with a bravado show of lightning. Not just one or two pops, but a bunch of them, one right after the other. Yes, she thought, leaning on the fence behind her house and gazing across their farm at the huge storm, someplace was getting hammered. Someplace like The Cities. And Andy, her Andy, was up there beneath that storm, his body covered by a white sheet and stored in some refrigerator.

She couldn't sleep, not with the image of her dead son burned into her mind. In fact, she wondered if she'd ever be able to sleep again. How could she? How could she when all she could see whenever she closed her eyes was the ashen face of her boy? Oh, Andy. He was never that pale, not her baby. He used to be so tan from being outside, from working the fields. His skin was so rich and healthy-looking, his hair so golden blond. What a handsome boy. Her pride. Often she just looked at him, marveled at his strength and his beauty and his youth, and she'd think: Good God, did such a handsome boy come out of me? Did I really make him?

She was glad she went up there today, glad she drove all the way up to The Cities. She had to see him one more time, especially before they hacked him apart. Just hours after she'd left they were supposed to have started the autopsy, cracking his chest wide open, pulling his insides out and slipping all that mess into plastic bags. The very thought of it was more than she could bear, butchering her boy up like he was a side of beef. She asked them not to, pleaded with the detec-

tive to leave her boy alone, that he was dead and nothing was bringing him back, but he told her that he had no choice. It was the law. An
autopsy was required when someone died of unnatural causes. Good
Lord, what a final indignity, being split open by some total stranger.

Aside from the lights that continued to pound in the distant sky,
Martha saw headlights way down the road and coming this way. Was
it him? Was her husband finally coming back? It had to be going on
two or three. Two or three in the morning, and she was still the only
one home.

After she'd been at the morgue, she'd been interviewed by the police. But after that Martha really wasn't sure what she'd done.
Somehow she got into the skyway system downtown and just started
rambling around the indoor system of walkways and pedestrian
bridges. Eventually she'd found her car. And then she'd just started
driving. It had taken her hours to get home, and when she did there
was no one here, neither her daughters nor her husband. Only a simple note.

> Martha—
> I've taken the girls to their grandmother's for the night. I'll
> be back later, I don't know when.
> John

So was this him, was that his truck now speeding this way? Her
eyes, dazed and achingly tired, focused on the vehicle, watched it as
it flew across the flat terrain that stretched nearly as far as the eye
could see. But it didn't slow as it neared their farm. Rather, as if she
and her life hadn't ever existed, it just went flying right on by, disap-
pearing into the depth of the night.

When she'd come home to no one Martha had in one simple moment realized that the life she had known would never exist again, that
it was gone forever. She'd picked up the note and understood that her
husband could have been and probably had been gone all day. He
hadn't put a time when he'd left, nor had he said when he'd be back.

And looking around the farm, she saw that nothing had been done. The tractor was just where it had been this morning, over by the metal pole barn. There had been no more tilling, no more bailing. She'd looked around, calmly taken it all in, and it just came to her, easily and simply: I want a divorce.

Yes, she thought hanging on to the white fence, that was going to be the fallout from all this, the complete and utter dissolution of their little family. It wasn't Andy's fault, not at all, but the trauma of coming to terms with his being gay and running away had forced upon them a test of greater magnitude than she could ever have imagined. Sure, it was a test they might not ever have faced, and certainly one they need not have taken. And if they hadn't, they probably would have just marched on, working the farm, raising their kids, and growing old together. Or maybe, just maybe, it wasn't a test at all. Maybe all of these travails had simply shone a light on the truths she had previously chosen not to see. Whatever. Without all of this, though, she doubted anything would have changed. But instead everything had, most definitely so, especially now with young Andy's death. It was just kind of one of those before and after things. Tonight she saw everything quite clearly, just who her husband was to her, what role he really played in her life, how much she could or couldn't depend upon him. And she understood that all of this was a storm too great for them to handle, that this was something from which their marriage could not and would never recover.

So where had he gone, and where was he now?

It was not a question of dark jealousy, not even one of bitter curiosity, but merely a point in need of simple clarification. That was the lie. His lie. And she'd chosen to ignore it, turned away, pretending not to see something that was lying right before her. Why had she thought to never question him? Because she was afraid of the answer? John, her husband of almost twenty years, hadn't gone with her today to identify the body of their murdered son, and he wasn't home tonight when she was drowning and needed him more than ever. And suddenly it all made sense. All those stupid stories. Martha, I'm going to go look at a small feedlot this morning, I think it might be a great investment, but, don't worry, I should be back by dinner. Sweetheart, there's a tractor I'm thinking about buying, don't hold lunch. Honey, I'm going to play some poker with the guys, don't you wait up on me, okay? At least once or twice a month something like that came up, and not once had she ever doubted him. You fool, she told herself. You absolute fool.

So who was she?

Chapter 26

The following morning Todd still wasn't sure who he should be more flipped out about, his lover, Steve Rawlins, or film sensation Tim Chase. Sitting at his desk in his small office at WLAK, he sipped a cup of coffee and stared at the list of e-mail on his computer screen. Presuming that he'd be assigned a follow-up piece on the Lyman murder for tonight's six o'clock, he had a pile of work. All of that, however, seemed oddly remote and definitely not of interest.

Todd hadn't been simply glad that Rawlins had chosen not to stay at the condo last night, he'd been relieved. Coming home, Todd had checked his answering machine, finding just a single message from Rawlins saying not to expect him tonight. While that could have meant that he'd be working late on the Lyman murder, Todd didn't take it as such. Yes, for more than one reason they needed a breather, and apparently both of them knew that.

So was Tim Chase gay or wasn't he? And had he or hadn't he been hitting on Todd?

The way straight men reacted around gay men varied in a most predictable way. Though by no means a majority, there were straights who were entirely comfortable and cool with it, guys who weren't the least bit threatened by the presence of homosexuals. Not only were they the most secure in their sexuality, they were also the straightest. Simply, it was a non-issue, primarily because they instinctively knew that territory was one where they'd never travel. On the other hand, there were men, a great many actually, who just couldn't handle it, who felt deeply threatened. At a mixed party, they tended to steer clear of gays, cling to their wives, or just get obnoxiously fidgety, as if they might be attacked and raped by a queer at any moment. This second group, Todd believed, tended to be composed of guys who'd done it once with another guy, usually as kids, and they were still deeply ashamed and terrified about what it meant, when all it really did mean was that they'd been trying to understand how their bodies worked. There was, after all, nothing much weirder than a penis, this thing that grew into a hunk of rock-hard salami in the heat of the moment, then shrank into a piece of limp macaroni when, say, swimming in Lake Superior. It was this second bunch, those who were the most threatened, that Todd had always found the most obnoxious, guys that used homophobia as a means of defending their heterosexuality. Didn't they realize that there was nothing less appealing to a gay man than another who sported his sexuality as comfortably as a nerd wearing Jockeys that were four sizes too small?

And then . . . then there were straight men who enjoyed the company of gay men. Perhaps they were among the lucky few who saw sexuality as not a binary thing, not an either/or, straight or gay kind of fixed deal, but something much more fluid. Maybe they enjoyed the broader interests of gays, interests that ran the gamut from the traditional male territories of baseball, football, and grilling all the way to cooking, gardening, and opera. Or maybe they just enjoyed the flirt, being admired, even sought after.

So in which group did Tim Chase belong? Any of the above? Or none?

No, thought Todd, if Chase was straight, he definitely belonged to the latter group. That guy was a flirt, a tease. Or was that not it at all? Perhaps he was merely a master at making not simply everyone and anyone like him, but love and desire him. Perhaps the sexual chemistry he put out was the true secret of his charm and broad appeal.

But those hands—so strong. Those hips—so lean. And the face— so gorgeous. His heart even now charging with lusty excitement, Todd recalled looking into Tim Chase's eyes and how the gaze had stayed steady and deep for that all-telling split second too long. Todd's gay-dar warning had gone off major league, wailing as loud as a Berlin air raid siren. Oh, brother, if that guy wasn't gay then . . . then . . .

But what about Gwen Owens? Did she know? Was it just some-thing she tolerated, a dally she put up with as dutifully as a president's first lady? If her husband was indeed gay, though, Gwen had to know. It could be no other way. She certainly wasn't that dumb, nor were her own handlers, who were certainly crafting her career every bit as care-fully and masterfully as her husband's. But why would one of the most beautiful, most successful actresses in the world put up with it? Why would she play his beard, unless of course he was playing hers as well? Could theirs be a match made only in Hollywood?

Like an obsessed courtier—had Chase really been rehearsing or had he been in the early steps of seducing Todd?—Todd had to know everything. Not just the box office deals, the star parties, and the lav-ish banquets and homes and cars and yachts and horses. No, Todd had to know all the dirt, which pretty much boiled it down to one thing, the only scandal to publicly break through the perfect veneer of Tim Chase, Inc.

Forgetting all about Rawlins and the murder of the young man, Todd turned to his briefcase and pulled out the thick manila folder containing the stack of articles he'd collected on Tim Chase. Flipping through them, he paused at one of the bios which not only made ex-tensive mention of his mother, but used her full name. God, thought Todd, wouldn't he love to talk to her? Wouldn't he love to hear what she had to say about her son, Mr. Wonderful? But how in the world would he get her phone number? It just might be buried somewhere in the layers of information of Lexis-Nexis, but that was doubtful. He could try one of the other search engines. Or he might ask Rawlins if he'd check the National Crime Information Computer, though Rawlins, Mr. Ethical, sure as hell wouldn't do anything like use the NCIC to dig up any dirt for someone in the media.

Skipping the mother as a bad idea, Todd continued through the stack. There were a few articles from the *Los Angeles Times,* an interesting profile of the moneyed star in *The Wall Street Journal,* a couple of more articles from some smaller regional papers. And then the bombshell article from the supermarket tabloid *The National Times,* with the searing headline, "Mean Queen Chase Denies 7 Year Gay Romance & Buries Boyfriend in Poverty." Not even trying to stop himself, Todd tore through the piece, reading all over again about the supposed romance between Tim Chase and the handsome blond Rob Scott. In searing judgmental prose, the journalist described their great love, which had begun before his marriage to actress Gwen Owens and then continued right on until, for some unknown reason, everything exploded in a ball of fury. Apparently Chase, otherwise known for his even temper and kind disposition, totally lost it. One neighbor claimed he heard Chase screaming at Scott, another claimed the police were called, and a nurse from a nearby hospital said she treated Rob Scott for bruises to his mouth and left eye on that very day. The writer went on to detail how the following day Chase's bodyguards, under the direct instructions of Tim Chase himself, had then kicked Rob Scott out of the condo the star had bought as their little love nest, allowing Scott to take no more than a single suitcase of clothing.

What a bitch, thought Todd. If this was really true, then the tabloid was certainly right, Tim Chase was in fact a mean fucking queen. But what had happened? If this was all true, what had ignited the situation, what had caused the alleged love affair to blow up? And if Rob Scott had really been Tim Chase's lover, what had Scott been trying to do by selling the story to *The National Times* for one hundred grand—simply make a pile of money or get revenge? Or both?

Todd wanted to see pictures, none of which was here of course because he'd pulled virtually all of these articles in this folder from Lexis-Nexis, which reprinted articles only in simple text. There were no telltale graphics, no sizzling snapshots, yet Todd wanted to see visual proof. Famous for its paparazzi-style photographs, *The National Times*—or *The National Dirt,* as it was so often called—was sure to have printed some doozies. And flipping to one of the last articles, which another paper had done as a follow-up to the lawsuit Chase had brought against *The National Times,* Todd saw that mention was even made of scandalous photos of the actor in the arms of another man. Chase's lawyers had been furious over this, claiming that the pictures were nothing but fakes, images that had been doctored on a computer.

"Go on the Net," the star's lawyer had fumed. "See what's out there. Look at some of that porn and you'll see what they can do, moving body parts this way and that. This is no different. This is just some sicko's wishful thinking. We're going to win this case, and we're going to win big. You'll see, my client will be vindicated."

However, the journalist who had written the original story, Marla Glore, stuck by it all, ranting at one point about the vast conspiracy of silence from, in particular, the Los Angeles media.

"They won't comment even though what I've written is the truth—and they know it too," Glore had heatedly said. "What it boils down to is that they're not only afraid of the major studios, they're also terrified of being blacklisted by the Hollywood public relations firms."

But in the end, after a short trial, Chase was, in fact, "vindicated" to the tune of over eight million dollars, which of course the star needed about as much as a hole in the head.

Todd turned to the last article, again a follow-up to the lawsuit, that *People* magazine ran as their cover story. The gist was that, yes, it's been proven now. Tim's our guy, he's straight and in love, a wonderful actor, a smashing husband, an adoring father. America is safe. He's vanquished over evil. He's our prince.

It kind of made Todd's stomach turn. It just felt too forced, too contrived, like the Christmas all of us dreamed of but never had. Yes, as a culture we wanted and needed someone like Tim Chase, whose image, albeit secretly manufactured, embodied so much of what we wanted for ourselves as well as for our country.

Knowing his next step, Todd picked up the phone and dialed information for New York City. He didn't know why, but he assumed, and correctly so, that *The National Times* was located right in the heart of it all, Manhattan. Moments later he had their number, which he dialed.

"Good morning, *The National Times,*" said a hurried operator who sounded as if she'd drunk a few too many pots of coffee.

"Marla Glore, please," requested Todd.

"Marla Glore . . . Marla Glore . . . hmmm," she said as she obviously typed the name into a computer. "Listen, I'm sorry, I'm checking but there's no one here by that name. Nope, sorry, no one."

"She's one of your journalists."

"Well, I'm sorry, doll, but I'm checking and I don't show anyone listed by the name of G-L-O-R-E."

So obviously she was long gone or was a freelancer. Either was a distinct possibility.

"Then could I speak to someone in your editorial department?"

"Like who? We got lots of people in editorial."

At first he drew a blank, and then Todd blurted, "How about the senior editor?"

"That'll be your Suzanne Levine. One moment and I'll—"

She spoke and worked so quickly that she unknowingly cut herself off. Nevertheless, seconds later there was a long ring, followed by a second, which made Todd think that he'd fallen into the netherworld of voice mail. Much to his relief, someone picked up after the third ring.

"Suzanne Levine."

"Hi," began Todd, realizing he didn't have any kind of ruse prepared, as was so often needed when trying to hunt someone down. "I'm looking for one of your journalists, a writer by the name of Marla Glore."

"Oh, Marla," she said, more than a trace of sadness creeping into her voice. "I'm sorry, she doesn't work here anymore."

So had she burned out on tabloid reporting and quit or had she been fired? Todd was willing to bet on the second, that management had been willing to stand behind one of their writers only to a certain point, which definitely hadn't been up to $8.5 million.

"Do you have any idea how I could find her?" asked Todd.

"No, I'm sorry, I'm not allowed to give out any information."

"I see . . ." All the different stories he could say whizzed through his mind, such as telling her he wanted her to do a story for his magazine to claiming he was an old college pal, but he opted for the simple truth. "I just want to ask her a couple of questions. I work for WLAK-TV in Minneapolis, and—"

"Minneapolis? Are you calling from out there? Wow, I'm from St. Paul, from Highland Park, actually."

Bingo, thought Todd with a confident grin. The Minnesota Mafia. There was hardly anything or anyone more reliable. Maybe it was the cold, perhaps it was the common experience of the extreme winter that was the great equalizer.

"How are things out there?" she asked. "How's the weather? Is it cold yet? No, wait, it's too early."

"Oh, please," said Todd, choosing his words carefully in order to spike her nostalgia, "the State Fair ended only a few weeks ago."

"Oh, for fun, the State Fair!" she said in a perfect Minnesota accent, all of which was happening at the back of her nose. "Oh, I want a corn dog! I want some mini-donuts!"

"All I want is a phone number."

"Jeez."

"Any chance? I just want to talk to her about a story she did." Todd added, "I'm doing a story on Tim Chase, the actor."

"He's out there?"

"Yeah, he's filming a movie here."

"Wow."

When she failed to say anything, Todd jumped in, "I really do work for WLAK. I'm their investigative reporter, and I can give you my phone number here if you want to call me back just to verify."

"No, no, I believe you." There was a moment of pensive silence, and then Suzanne Levine said, "Listen, I wish I could tell you that Marla's a freelancer now and that she lives in Park Slope, but I can't. I mean, I can't give you her number or tell you where to find her because I don't know. The last I heard was that she moved to New Mexico. Santa Fe, maybe. Or was it Taos?"

So, thought Todd, she really did get canned. *The National Times* had probably dumped her only minutes after the judge's announcement. And by the end of the trial, during which she and her reputation had surely been pummeled and trampled, she was probably so burned out that she had perhaps gone off in search of a new career, like waitressing.

As his Polish father used to say, "You must follow your tongue," meaning if you ask enough questions you'll get where you need to go.

He said, "That's too bad. I've read the article she did on him—"

"The lawsuit one. Yeah, that whole thing was unfortunate, to say the least."

"—and I was just hoping to ask her a few questions."

"Well, if Marla were here, I'm sure she'd love to talk to you. She was pretty bitter about all that when she left here, I'll tell you that much."

"Actually," said Todd, "I got a copy of her story off Lexis-Nexis, so there aren't any pictures with it."

"Of course not."

"And I don't think I can get any back copies of your paper at the library."

She laughed. "I really don't think so, either. I think the only places that stock us, particularly in the Midwest, are supermarkets and drugstores. And correct me if I'm wrong, but they don't have archives."

"But how about you all, do you have back issues? Would it be possible to get a copy of the original Tim Chase story, photos and all?"

"Now, that I can do," cheerfully said Suzanne Levine. "When do you want it, for morning or afternoon delivery? I'll Fed-Ex it out right away."

Chapter 27

The Hennepin County Medical Center was a monolithic, eight-story hospital built in the late seventies, a sprawling building that sat on the edge of downtown Minneapolis like a gigantic beetle. Fortunately for Jordy Weaver, thought Rawlins, as he hurried into the beige concrete complex, it had the best trauma center in the Twin Cities area.

Once inside it took Rawlins no less than ten minutes to wind his way through the corridors to the intensive care ward, where he was directed down the hall to the second room on the right. Just as he approached the room, a short African-American man in a white robe stepped out, quietly pulling the door shut behind him.

"Excuse me," said Rawlins, reaching into his leather coat for his badge. "I'm Sergeant Steve Rawlins with the Homicide Division of the Minneapolis Police Department, and I'm looking for Jordy Weaver."

The man had a round face and short hair, small eyes, and a serious look on his face, and he held out his hand and said, "I'm Dr. Nevin, his doctor. Jordan's right here."

Taking several steps, he led Rawlins to a large plate glass window. Lying on the other side was Jordy, his head swathed in gauze, his left arm packed in a cast, and his left leg swaddled in a mass of gauze and splints. His face, of which little was showing, was pocked with bruises, and a clear tube ran out of one nostril. All around him were a host of electronic monitors, their lights pulsing with regularity, which actually were the only indication that the otherwise lifeless body wasn't dead.

"Oh, my God," muttered Rawlins, staring in and barely able to recognize Jordy. "Is he going to be alright?"

"He's a very lucky man. Lucky that they got him here so quickly and lucky that he's so young. When he came in last night I thought we were going to have to amputate his leg, but I think we'll be able to save it. I operated on him about three hours ago and it looks like, with a great deal of therapy, he'll be able to walk. It will be a long recovery, however."

"Is that all? Is that—"

"Well, he also has a concussion and a broken left arm, but neither of them is life threatening. From what I understand, however, if the car that hit him had been going any faster he would have been killed on the spot. I think everyone had slowed because of the heavy rain, again a lucky break, per se."

"I'm sure this isn't a good time, but I need to talk to him. It involves a murder case, so obviously it's very important."

"Well, as you can see, that's impossible. He's only been out of surgery for a few hours."

"Can I come back later this morning? Or how about after lunch?"

"Oh, no, not nearly that soon. He's on a great deal of medication, you see. Sort of a drug-induced coma, and hopefully he won't wake up until later tonight, perhaps tomorrow." Dr. Nevin lowered his hands into the pockets of his robe and gazed through the glass at the young man. "Trust me, he's a very lucky fellow, but he's going to be in a lot of pain. The longer he's out the better off he'll be."

But Rawlins needed to talk to him. And he needed to talk to him now if for no other reason than to find out if this horrible accident was somehow connected to the murder of Andrew Lyman. Yes, Jordy had somehow managed to survive his fall from the bridge onto the freeway, but was that not at all the intent? Could his life in fact still be in danger?

The first time Rawlins and Andrew had lunch, Rawlins had picked him up at the apartment, a kind of queer teen flophouse, where he'd been living with Jordy and all those other kids. Then first thing this morning, hoping to interview Jordy regarding the death of his close friend and to see just what he might or might not know about Andrew's father, Rawlins had gone directly there. Instead of finding Jordy, however, Rawlins had found a handful of kids huddled around a ratty old kitchen table, terrified of what had happened to one of their own. All that they knew was what the police, who had found an envelope with Jordy's address in his coat pocket, had told them around six this morning that Jordy had fallen off the LaSalle Avenue Bridge right into traffic on Interstate 94 and that he was in the hospital in intensive care. A couple of kids were praying that it wasn't a suicide attempt, particularly since another of their DQ pals had killed himself a mere two months ago.

"But Jordy wouldn't have tried to kill himself, I just know it," one young man with short, short hair and a pierced nose had said. "We've been doing all these sessions, all this talking about queer teen suicide and . . . and . . . he wouldn't have let us down like that, I just know it."

"Yeah, but he was so upset about Andrew," another had protested as he leaned against the refrigerator. "First Andrew moved out, and then he was killed. Jordy was really flipped out, I mean really freaked."

Still another, a young guy with red hair and patches of freckles on both cheeks, said, "But if it wasn't suicide, then what the fuck happened? I mean, hello, you just don't fucking fall off a freeway bridge. Couldn't the same guy who killed Andrew have gone after Jordy?"

"Oh, shit."

"Oh, fuck."

"We gotta stick together."

Rawlins in turn had raced down here to HCMC, all the while wondering if Jordy had purposely jumped from the LaSalle bridge or if he'd been thrown or somehow pushed. For Jordy's safety, he had to presume the worst.

"As I told you," said Rawlins now as he pulled out his business card and handed it to Dr. Nevin, "this might be related to an ongoing murder investigation, so I'm going to give you my number. It's very important that you or anyone on your staff call me as soon as Jordy wakes up and is able to talk."

"Of course. I'll leave those instructions at the nurse's desk."

"In the meantime, for the safety of your patient, I'm going to have a police officer posted outside this door. I want no one to go in except you and your staff."

"I see," he said, his eyebrows rising in controlled surprise. "What about family? I believe we got his home address off his driver's license and that our office has contacted his parents. If I'm not mistaken, they're on the way here."

"That's fine. The police officer will need to check some identification. But again, I need to talk to him as soon as he wakes."

"Certainly."

Rawlins glanced in at Jordy, wondered what truths were waiting to be told, then said, "I'll be staying until we can get an officer posted."

An hour later Rawlins was at his desk on the second floor of City Hall. There was any variety of things to be done on the Lyman case, from checking to see when the final autopsy report would be in, to finding how long the DNA typing would take on the semen samples. Actually, the first thing Rawlins had to do was find his partner, Neal Foster, and tell him about Jordy Weaver. Quite possibly, he also needed to tell Foster that Andrew had been threatened by his father. But how the hell was Rawlins going to do that without bringing up the diary? Perhaps he could get around it somehow. Perhaps he could say that he'd heard something about Andrew's father from one of the kids down at the DQ.

Oh, shit, thought Rawlins. He had to come up with something like that, something to keep secret the revealing passages Andrew had written about Rawlins. He was, Rawlins knew, between the proverbial rock and a hard place, and he had virtually no idea how he was going to get out. Unfortunately, his problems with Todd seemed minor in comparison. Still, he was obviously going to have to speak to Foster sometime today. They were partners, after all. And they were going to have to draw up a plan of attack on this investigation, as well as write up some kind of progress report to submit to their boss, Lieutenant Holbrook. Among the many things that needed to be discussed was the black mask that had been covering Andrew's eyes and whether they should continue to withhold that detail from the public. With all that in mind and not knowing whether Foster was just downstairs or still in bed at home, Rawlins picked up his phone and dialed Foster's pager.

Yes, he thought, as he waited for the call back, this was a fine mess. If it ever got out, how the hell was he going to explain his involvement with Andrew Lyman? Better yet, who would believe him if he said nothing happened? Andrew's stupid diary, his silly confessions, were nearly enough not simply to get Rawlins fired from the force but thrown in jail. A gay cop involved with a runaway minor? It screamed rape. It screamed headlines. And guilty or not, it screamed witch hunt and the end of Rawlins's career.

The phone rang more quickly than Rawlins anticipated, and he snatched the black phone from its cradle.

"Sergeant Steve Rawlins."

"Hi, . . . it's, ah, me again."

No, it definitely wasn't Foster. And, no, it surely wasn't Todd. It was some guy, his voice a tad meek, a bit unsteady, and at first Rawlins's mind went blank. The next instant he was very alert. It was him, the tipster. And the moment after that, Rawlins was telling himself to keep calm, be cool. He'd lose him if he scared him again, and he couldn't afford that.

"Is this my friend?" began Rawlins, as he quickly slid open his top desk drawer and pulled out a small black tape recorder and a long wire with a suction cup dangling from one end.

"Yeah, it's me, the guy who saw that other guy down at Lake Harriet. I . . . I saw in the paper that you found something, that you took my tip and that you guys went down there and everything."

"That's right. And we all owe you a big thanks. Obviously we would never have found anything without your help."

Working as quietly as possible, Rawlins plugged one end of the wire into the tape recorder and then slapped the other end with its small suction cup onto the phone's receiver. Even though this specific conversation wouldn't be admissible in a court of law because the witness didn't know he was being taped, Rawlins pushed the record button. At this point he needed anything and everything for his own hunt, and he sat back, telling himself to just sound cool, relaxed. Obviously this guy's calling back because he's pleased with what happened, how things went, and you've got to make him believe not only that he's a hero, but that you need him. Which was more true than ever.

"So was that it? Was that the hunting knife that was used to kill that kid? I mean, I hope you're able to nail whoever did it."

"Well, we did find it right where you said it would be, but we've got a ways to go." As he spoke, Rawlins pulled out a yellow notepad, jotted down the time, then proceeded to take notes. "We found evidence of blood on the blade, and we also were able to get some blood samples from the nooks and crannies of the handle."

"Wow."

"Yeah, it's great. Our initial report shows that the blood type matches Andrew Lyman's, but it's going to take awhile to get a DNA report. We're going to expedite it, but it's still going to take a week or so. Fortunately the weapon wasn't in the water that long and we were able to get a couple of good fingerprints too, which is the really great news. Apparently there was some sort of oily substance on the handle that didn't wash off."

"Oh, good. I'm glad." Over some kind of background noise, the guy added, "You know what, there's something else."

"Really?"

Rawlins closed his eyes and focused not only on the voice but also on the background noise. Was that a car? A bus or a truck? Exactly. The guy was outside, probably calling from some pay phone. Chances were he was even here downtown, perhaps only a matter of a few blocks away. God, what Rawlins wouldn't give to get a trace on this and have the guy picked up. After all, who was to say this wasn't their guy, that this story wasn't all a fabrication?

Rawlins asked, "So what have you got?"

"Well, you know, I was down there in those bushes and . . . and I saw that guy. The bald guy I told you about."

"Right. A muscular guy with a bald head," said Rawlins, writing that down.

"Yeah, he was down at the lake and I watched him throw the knife into the water." He broke off as the blast of a car horn drowned him out. "In case you were wondering, I'm calling from a pay phone. Like I said, I don't want this call to be traced. I'm sorry, I just can't be more involved than I already am."

In other words, you're a big closet case. Perhaps you're married, perhaps not. And rather than risk telling your friends and family that you're gay, you're more than willing to risk your health and safety by sneaking into the woods and having anonymous sex.

"That's okay," said Rawlins at the same time trying to figure out how he could in fact do just that, get him involved. "Go on."

"Well, there was that car. Like I think I said, it was a Saab. I mean, I'm sure of that."

"Tell me again what it looked like."

"It was white with a black roof, so it was a convertible. I'm sure about that. And I remember looking at the back license plate."

Rawlins wrote down a couple of notes, then bent forward, lowering his forehead into his left hand. Oh, dear God in heaven, please let this be it. Tell me this guy, whoever he is, has a photographic memory.

"Did you get a number?" asked Rawlins.

"No, but it wasn't from here."

"What do you mean?"

"It wasn't a Minnesota plate. It was from California."

"You're sure?"

"I'm positive." The caller paused, then asked, "Will any of that help?"

"Absolutely. A white convertible Saab with California plates—yes, that will definitely give us something to look out for. I'm sure we'll put out an alert. Who knows if we'll be able to find anything, or even if the car is still in the state, but . . . but we'll try our damnedest."

Okay, how was he going to handle this? How was he going to hook this guy and lure him in? Notwithstanding that, first and foremost they had to rule him out as the perpetrator; the prosecuting attorney would want this guy's sworn testimony of what he'd seen. He was at this point their only lead, and they needed to make the most of him. If they were able to get an ID from the fingerprint, then they'd need this tipster to identify the man he'd seen throwing the weapon into Lake Harriet. If the fingerprint didn't lead anywhere, then Rawlins would have to arrange a photo lineup and see if the tipster could identify anyone.

But how? How was he going to get him to come in, per se, from the cold world of the closet?

Rawlins said, "You know, I'd really like to get together with you sometime and thank you in person. I'd like to meet you and talk about this. Can I take you out for a cup of coffee or a beer?"

"Oh, I don't know. I really don't think that's a good idea."

"How about it, huh? Just a cup of coffee? A beer? Something quick and simple? You name the place."

"This isn't like a trick, is it? You're not going to like arrest me and make me come down to the police station and interrogate me, are you? I mean, I didn't do anything illegal."

"Of course not," replied Rawlins, wondering if this guy had more to worry about than his sexuality. "You've just been very helpful and I want to meet you, that's all."

"But I've already told you everything I saw."

"I know. Listen, all I want to do is get together. Maybe later, if you want to make a formal statement or anything, then that would be your decision. Totally your decision."

"Well . . ."

"Trust me, no pressure. You just name the time and place, I'll be there."

"Well, okay. How about seven tonight at Jam's. Do you know where that is, out on Excelsior Boulevard?"

"Sure," replied Rawlins with a smile, for he'd been to the bar more than several times. "I'll see you at Jam's at nine tonight. Don't forget, the drinks are on me."

"Alright." The tipster hesitated, then added, "Listen, I should tell you that I'm a photographer and that I've been working on . . . on, well, a story. The reason I saw that guy down at the lake is because I followed him there. So I'm positive about the car. And . . . and I think you know where to look for it too."

"I'm sorry, I'm not sure I understand."

"I saw you down at the lake yesterday—I asked some cop and he pointed you out. And . . . and then I saw you last night as well."

"Wh—"

"I'll explain tonight."

The tipster hung up, and Rawlins just sat there holding the receiver until the dial tone started blaring in his ear. This guy was a photographer who'd followed the bald man down to Lake Harriet and watched him throw a knife into the water. Then the guy had been down at the lake again when they'd recovered the knife. And he'd seen Rawlins last night as well? But how was that possible? And where?

Holy shit. Rawlins stared down at his notes. It hadn't clicked, not until just now, but hadn't he himself seen that very same car, a white Saab, just yesterday evening?

Chapter 28

The murder of Andrew Lyman was a hot story that was getting cooler by the moment, or so thought WLAK management. And it was no-body's fault but Todd's, for instead of attending this morning's editorial meeting and fighting for his story, he'd been on the phone tracking down an old issue of *The National Times*. Consequently, he didn't get one of the top slots, but was instead told to prepare a twenty-second VOSOT that would probably run just prior to the weather.

You idiot, he told himself.

Sitting in one of the dark edit bays, a small glassed-in chamber packed with monitors and tape players and a bizarre assortment of control equipment, Todd tried to think of a way to come at this. But that was the problem, he was having trouble thinking, or more specifically, focusing on the who and the why and the what of Andrew Lyman's death. To do a good story you had to obsess about it. You had to grab hold and not let go. And today he was having trouble doing just that. Distracted by his problems with Rawlins as well as his encounter with Tim Chase, Todd had lost the thread of the story. And right now he felt as if it were gone for good.

Okay, he told himself. Just go back to the beginning. Sort through it all. Look at everything. It'll come back. You'll get it.

He glanced at his watch, saw that it was pushing noon. Tensing, he realized how little time there was until the six o'clock show. Shit. Not only didn't he have a thing ready, he didn't have a clear idea for a story or even an angle. He'd never been in this position before, but he knew enough to be sure that he was headed for certain disaster.

Trying not to panic, he took a deep breath and recounted to himself the sequence of events over the past few days. Andrew Lyman had been killed the day before yesterday, his throat slit early that evening, though as far as Todd knew, the exact time of death had yet to be fixed. He'd covered the event, arriving at the scene shortly after nine-thirty P.M. and finding a host of media already there. Trying to differentiate his coverage, Todd had done the lead story for the ten o'clock live from the Domain of Queers. Then yesterday the big breakthrough had been the discovery, thanks to an anonymous tip, of the possible murder weapon, a hunting knife found at the bottom of Lake Harriet. Getting taped footage of that, Todd had done a VOSOT for the five o'clock and then a taped package for the six. And now today? Certainly the autopsy report would be done at some point this morning, but the authorities might not make the results public right away. Likewise, the police might also not release any information regarding search warrants and if any had been filed, which would indicate, of course, which direction this thing might be going and, most important of all, if they had any suspects in mind.

But what if they did release the autopsy report and there was nothing much of interest beyond the time of death? What then? The next big break after that probably wouldn't be until the initial lab reports on the knife were back, and God only knew when that would be. Modern science might pull a rabbit out of the hat, but the weapon had been underwater for at least eighteen hours, so Todd didn't think it too promising. As they stood at the lake yesterday afternoon, Rawlins had said he doubted they'd be able to use Luminol to detect evidence of blood proteins, but that they might use Kamazi Blue, another chemical. He'd said something about that and funky orange glasses and a light spectrum that would show if there'd been blood on it. He'd also mentioned the possibility that they might be able to simply do a visual. So had they? And had they found anything? Perhaps, but these things always took an annoyingly long time. If they were able to find a trace of blood they might be able to get a blood type, but DNA testing usually took at least three weeks and often longer, particularly if a rush wasn't put on it. After all, the new serology lab had been overwhelmed since it opened—on average there was a murder every two days in the seven county metro area. On top of that, DNA typing was now being used in a far broader range of criminal investigations, from rapes to aggravated assaults, all of which demanded time.

Todd's surest way to get the latest information was, of course, simply to call Rawlins. He was hesitant to do just that, however, because what they really needed to discuss wasn't lab results or search warrants, but their relationship. They needed to discuss where they were headed, what they wanted, what each of them needed, and they needed to be perfectly honest about trysts that included Andrew Lyman. And, Todd thought, quite possibly Tim Chase. After all, Todd had no idea really what had happened last night between him and the actor, and he certainly had no idea what would happen tonight, but if Todd was expecting honesty he was certainly going to have to deliver it as well. Which he was kind of dreading. Perhaps a way of circumventing Rawlins was to call Neal Foster and ask him what was the very latest on the Lyman case. If Todd was going to do that, though, he had to do it soon.

And if there wasn't any breaking news?

Todd's own rule of thumb, one that he always came back to when he was lost, was: What is it the audience wants to know? When it came to murder, of course, people were always fascinated by the details of true crime, first and foremost who did it and why. And while in this case no one yet knew either of those, maybe Todd should do a piece on exactly what the police were doing to answer those questions. Perhaps first he should focus on the knife and what the authorities were doing to determine if it was in fact the weapon that had been used to kill Andrew Lyman. Sure, there was still time this afternoon to whip up a piece on the various forces of technology, including Luminol, Kamazi Blue, DNA testing, and what they'd be looking for down at the serology lab. In fact, maybe Todd should do his report from the lab itself. Having just invested millions in the facility, Minnesota was one of the few states that could do its own DNA work. Maybe Todd should nab Bradley and the two of them could head down there, perhaps even interview a few of the technicians and get them to explain exactly what they were doing regarding the Lyman case. All in all not a bad idea.

However, as long as he was there in the edit booth, as long as he had all the tapes right in front of him, he decided to review not simply his report from the first night or yesterday's package, but also all of the footage they had thus far. It was another one of his tricks, a way of getting him back in the groove of a story and also a way to help him remember exactly what they already had on tape, some of which he might choose to use for tonight's report.

Popping the first Beta tape into a machine, Todd hit play and watched as a cloud of snow filled a monitor. Moments later the footage from that first night appeared on the screen, images from Bradley's handheld camera directly from the scene. There were some shots of cops, including a group of officers standing there talking, others hurrying into the building, still others holding back the crowd that was craning to see what had happened. Then, just as Todd had asked for, there was the footage of the real estate, various shots consisting mostly of the yellow brick apartment building where Andrew Lyman was killed, but also including a few quick shots of the neighborhood. And finally there were a good number of shots of the crowd, people gawking, some shaking their heads, others, wearing sweatshirts and jackets and bathrobes, gathered around in small groups. In one of these Todd quickly caught a glimpse of Jordy, and he realized that that must have been just before the young man tried to push past the police line. Bradley, of course, had overshot and had laid down not quite four minutes of tape, all of which was sent via the ENG truck and a relay of microwave towers back to WLAK, where it was in turn edited for Todd's voice-over.

Watching his report from in front of the Domain of Queers, Todd realized that he was lax in following up on that. He needed to do a little digging around there. There might or might not be enough material to do a story on the DQ and Andrew Lyman, but in any case he needed to get his butt back over there and talk to some of the kids, most notably Jordy Weaver. Then again, even if he could track down Jordy, did Todd even want to hear what the young man had to say about Andrew and Rawlins? Could there possibly be anything left to say? And how relevant could that be to Andrew's murder, anyway? Hardly, thought Todd. Rawlins might have slept with him, which would have been stupid enough, but Rawlins was no murderer, of that Todd was positive. With all that in mind, however, how much did Rawlins really know about what happened to Andrew?

No wonder, thought Todd, ejecting that tape and moving on to the next, Todd was having trouble focusing on this. There was just too much crap to deal with, or to be more exact, too much crap he didn't want to deal with. Perhaps . . . perhaps the best thing at this point would be to really have it out with Rawlins, to level with him and tell him exactly what Jordy had said.

As the last of the footage came up, the monitor filled with the image of Lake Harriet and the divers and lone boat of the Hennepin County Sheriff. Todd and Bradley had arrived almost too late to get anything, but Bradley had managed to get some shots of the divers as they climbed back in the boat and then headed for the small pier by the band shell. Needing more for his report, Todd had asked the photographer to get as much other footage as possible, and Todd now watched this complete, unedited tape. Yes, there was the police and their cars, including that of the Hennepin County Sheriff. And, yes, there was Rawlins standing there on the beach and looking pensive. Quite so, actually.

Hitting the pause button, Todd stared at the frozen image of Rawlins. What was going through his mind right then? Why did he look so very concerned, so very distraught? Todd knew Rawlins took his work with the utmost seriousness, but was he this involved in all his cases? Shaking his head, Todd felt himself wondering exactly what had happened between Andrew and Rawlins, and exactly how long it, whatever "it" was, had been going on. There couldn't have been any kind of emotional attachment, at least not a deep one, could there have been? What about all those times that Rawlins had told Todd those three—"I love you"—magical words? If there'd been any kind of silver lining to Rawlins's health crisis it had been both his and Todd's distinct appreciation not only for the meaning of life, but the meaning and appreciation of their relationship. Or so Todd had thought.

Knowing he had to move on and pull something together, Todd let the tape roll on and watched the remainder of Bradley's footage, which primarily consisted of gawkers. He watched as Bradley's camera focused on two young blond moms as they stopped with their strollers, shook their heads and rolled on. Next there was a bicyclist who paused and stared. And then Todd watched as two older women stood there pointing and gabbing, obviously trying to decide what was what and if the world had truly gone to hell in a handbasket. Standing next to them were two younger men, one with a German shepherd, who seemed to be listening to the women's conversation, and a youngish man in sunglasses and a jeans jacket who obviously realized he was being photographed and quickly turned away. The two women, true Minnesotans, just stood there, blabbing and speculating. If only Bradley had gotten the audio—now that would have been perfect. But this would do quite well.

Todd reversed the tape, then froze it. Yes, the guy standing there with his dog, the other turning away in perhaps disgust, and the two women standing in their fashionable jogging suits, hands raised, mouths open, exemplified it all, both the public's disgust and the public's fascination with the crimes eating at this world.

This, thought Todd, would be his opening image for his piece on tonight's news. He would begin here with the curiosity and then conclude with the facts at the serology lab on University Avenue in St. Paul.

Through the glass walls of the edit bay, he suddenly saw one of their interns, Scott, rushing down the dark, narrow hall. A handsome kid with brown hair and lots of energy, he waved to Todd and tapped once on the glass door.

"What's up?" asked Todd, cracking the door.

"You got a page from the front desk—they said it was a phone call. I knew you were down here, so . . ."

"Thanks."

A page meant one of two things, either it was someone too important to be dumped into voice mail, or someone too insistent. Wondering just who it was—Rawlins?—Todd rolled his chair over to the phone and called the front desk.

"One moment, Mr. Mills," said Renee, the receptionist, "and I'll connect you."

There was a pause and a click, and a moment later Todd said, "Hello, this is Todd Mills."

"Oh, hi," said a deep, gruff voice. "I, ah . . . ah . . . I need to talk to you."

Everybody had a story. And everybody wanted their story on TV. So while Todd assumed it was one of those—someone trying to get his fifteen minutes of fame—and was tempted to slough it off, he knew better.

"Who's calling, please?"

"Sure. It's me, John Lyman."

Almost nothing could have changed things more, and in a snap the guy had Todd's full attention. Oh, shit, wondered Todd, was it really him?

"Andrew's father?"

There was a long pause and a deep sigh before the caller said, "Yeah."

Todd ran his left hand through his hair and tried not to betray his surprise, at least not audibly. Either this guy, whom he'd never met, was calling with information regarding his son, or he was calling to yell at Todd, which, unfortunately, was the far more likely of the two. It flashed through Todd's mind: he's pissed as hell at what I've said on the air about Andrew's murder.

Bracing himself for the expected lashing, which, unfortunately, was all too common—if you got one detail wrong, people went ballistic—Todd said, "What can I do for you?"

"Listen, I need to talk with you. There's something . . . well, I guess, there's something I . . . I need to tell you, something I need to tell . . . tell someone." He paused, then muttered simply, "Oh, Lord."

Sensing something much different than anger—defeat?—Todd leaned forward and concentrated on his caller's every word. "Go ahead, I'm listening."

"Well, actually, it's not something I can talk about right now. Not on the phone, anyways."

"Do you want to meet? I'd be happy to get together."

"Yeah, that'd be okay."

"Just tell me when and where."

"Okay, ah . . . well, I'm coming to The Cities this afternoon. I have to go to the fairgrounds over in Saint Paul. I left a saddle up there during the fair. Can you meet me in the horse barn, say around five?"

"Sure, five in the horse barn," replied Todd, wondering what in the hell he was getting himself into.

"Go in the door right across from the cattle barn, it'll be open."

"I'll be there."

Chapter 29

Tim Chase sat at the dinette table in his trailer, his elbows on the table, his head bowed against his hands, which were clenched in tight fists. Was this the disaster that he had been fearing all these years? Was his world, which had been so carefully crafted, about to collapse in a heap of rubbish?

There was a light knock on the aluminum door, and a small voice said, "Five minutes."

Chase half turned, and shouted, "Fuck off!"

The minion, one of the many that lurked in the coattails of his fame, scurried away.

He didn't care what the director insisted on. He didn't care what scene it was or how much he was needed. He didn't give a shit how much each minute of shooting was costing, he couldn't do it. They could just fucking well wait. Oh, shit. He just couldn't go out there and pretend everything was fine when actually everything was completely screwed up. There was no way in hell he was in the mood to act, no way in hell he could get into the mind of another.

There was another knock, this one heavier, and a deep voice that said, "It's me, Vic."

"Yeah."

Not moving, not lifting his head in the least, Chase listened as his bodyguard opened the door and stepped into the trailer, which moved slightly under his weight. Chase wanted to kill this guy, he wanted to chop off his head right here and now. And he probably should.

Chase waited a long moment before, in a low, even voice, saying, "I didn't see the local news last night, Vic. I mean, I really didn't have much reason to watch it. How about you? Did you catch it?"

"No, sir."

"And I really didn't have much reason to read the local newspaper this morning. Even though I was up awfully early I did read the first section of *The New York Times*. Oh, and during makeup I glanced at *Variety*, just sort of skimmed through it. But you know, I'm only here for a little while and I'm kind of busy, so why would I read the local paper, right? Am I right?"

"Correct, but—"

"Shut the fuck up, you moron!" said Chase, slamming his right fist on the dinette table, which sent a powerful rattle rippling through the entire trailer. "Can you imagine my surprise when just a half hour ago I'm eating my turkey sandwich in the canteen and I glance over at the local paper and there's a big article about a knife found in some fucking lake? There's even a picture of the sheriff's divers fishing it out. Someone called it in, apparently. A tip. And now they're looking at it as a potential murder weapon for that kid. Shocking, wouldn't you say?"

"I read the piece."

"Oh, you did, did you?"

"Yes, sir."

"And let me guess, that was the knife, right? I mean, as soon as I read about it I just had this hunch. That was it, wasn't it?"

"Yes, sir."

With fey curiosity, Tim looked at him with a shrug. "So what'd you think, Vic? No prob? No big deal?"

"I can explain."

"Bullshit you can explain! There's nothing to explain—you fucked up everything!" He jumped to his feet, looked at the stupid oaf, then turned and leaned against the cheap kitchen counter. "God, you're a moron! A big, fucking dumb moron! I told you to take it out of my car and get rid of it. I told—"

"I went down there and—"

"Shut up before I fire you! And don't you dare interrupt me again!"

Trying not to panic, Chase told himself to just calm down, to keep a grip on things. But how could he when his arch-nemesis, the media, was dancing at the gates? God, all they had to do was get a hold of this one and the world would be screaming for his head. He'd spent so much time worrying, fearing the day when the truth got out. He was the prince of sex and money and power, and any and every Joe Schmoe reporter in the world would love to crucify him on this one.

"I told you to throw it away where no one would ever find it, and the next thing I know it's on the front page of the Minneapolis paper. What are you trying to do, ruin me completely? What the fuck did you do, just go down to that lake, park your car, and throw it in the water?"

Vic jammed his hands into his pockets and turned away. "I took every precaution."

"Precaution? *Precaution?* Jesus Christ, why didn't you just point the cops in my direction? Do you know what this means? Do you have any idea what kind of trouble this could be?"

"I was sure no one saw me."

"But someone did, right? Someone saw you throw that knife into the lake—which means they can probably identify you too." Chase leaned back and pulled at his hair, and as calmly as a madman, said, "What about my Land Rover? Did you get it cleaned like I asked?"

"Yes, I did that yesterday while you were here on the set."

"And tell me what they said down at the car wash. Any of the guys say anything about that little red puddle in the back? Anyone say, Gee, Mr. Vic, is this blood back here? Anyone say that, did they, huh?"

"No, sir. I washed it before I went down there."

"Oh, did you?"

"I can assure you that no one's going to find out, that no one's going to be able to trace it back to you."

"Right."

But if they do, thought Tim, glaring at this idiot, I'm going to deny everything. I'm going to say I never met that kid and that I know nothing about the knife. After all, who would they believe, Tim Chase or some glorified bouncer with a criminal record? Exactly. All they had to do was learn about Vic's past and all suspicion would get dumped upon him.

"You know, I should just fire you now. For starters, I'm not going to take the fall for this, I'm just not. Second of all, the guys back in Hollywood won't let me go down—I'm just worth too much to them."

"As I said, I'm sorry."

"A heartfelt apology—isn't that sweet? I am so, like, touched, ya know?" Chase shook his head in disgust. "Why are there so many morons in the world? And why do they all work for me?"

"I'm sure I don't know."

"Well, you pull one more stunt like this and you'll be working as a bouncer at the scuzziest gay bar in the world, I guarantee you that. I'm paying you a fucking fortune to get me exactly what I like and what I want and to make sure there's no way in hell anyone finds out. One more screwup and you're out. Clear?"

"Yes, sir."

But now, of course, there was no time to waste. They had to move, Chase knew from experience, and move quickly before the cops or worse, the media, descended upon them.

"Okay, I want to get the cars out of the picture. First I want you to take my Land Rover back to the dealership and lease me another one. Tell them something like some newspaper guy has identified the car as mine and he's been tailing me all the time, so I need another color or another model or something." He put his hand to his mouth. "No, wait, this is better. First take my car—the keys are around here someplace—and drive it back to the house and just park it in the garage and leave it there. Don't let anyone else have the keys. Then go back to the dealership and just buy the fucking thing. Get a check from my accountant and just do it."

"Sure."

"Then buy another Land Rover that's exactly the same—same model, same year. And make sure it's the same white, that's very important. And don't buy it there, do you understand?"

"Yes."

"Go to another dealership. There's got to be two in this rinky-dink town. So go and get another identical Land Rover, and that's the one I'll use. If there are any questions then at least it will be clean."

"What about my car?"

"Yes, of course . . ." He thought for a second, and said, "Put it in the garage along with mine. Wait, better yet, go out and rent a garage at one of those self-storage places and put your car in there until we're through here, until you're ready to drive straight out of town. Then this afternoon go to another car dealership—what are you driving, a white Saab?"

"Right. A white Saab convertible."

"Fine, then go to a Saab dealership and lease one for yourself. You can bill me. But get a totally different color. Make it green or whatever you want, I don't care. Just different. And make it a four-door or something like that."

"Sure."

Breaking their conversation came yet another knock on the flimsy door, and a voice that was at once both annoyed and saccharine, saying, "Tim, it's me, Brian. Is there a problem? Are you alright? Can I come in and talk?"

Chase rubbed his eyes and groaned. It was the film's director coming to take his temperature, or more specifically to see what the hell was holding him up. If he only knew.

"Go on, get out of here," muttered Tim to Vic. "And tell Brian I'll be right there. Tell him I'm in the john."

And Chase did just that, escaped to the bathroom, taking a quick two steps into the coffin-sized room and sealing the door behind him. More often than not a chamber like this was his only escape, his last place of refuge. Such was the price of stardom, he thought, as he leaned against the sink and slumped against the cold vinyl wall. At least here he could lock everyone out and no one would come banging on the door every five fucking minutes wondering if he was okay.

With any luck this might work. With any luck . . .

He thought about the beautiful farm boy, his hair so blond, his face so pure and young, and that body, so broad and powerful. He remembered when Vic had first brought him by, how he'd paraded him past for Tim's approval. And he knew it right away, knew that, yes, that one would do quite well, thank you very much. He was just so naturally pretty, so naturally masculine. You didn't find kids like that back in California, not at all. They were into too many things, fads and trends from body piercings to tattoos. But not that kid. He was untouched. A Lolita of boyness. Yet what a mistake. What a huge fucking mistake.

Suddenly he both heard and felt quick steps trooping through the trailer. The next moment there was a rap on the bathroom door.

"Tim, it's me, Brian. Are you okay? You're not sick or anything, are you? You want me to get the doctor?"

Standing there, Chase clutched his fists and tried not to scream.

"For God's sake, I'm going potty, do you mind?"

"Well . . . well, how long are you going to be? We're all waiting."

"Let me think here. I've never been a very good judge of these things. How about five minutes? That good for you?"

"Sure. Five minutes, that's great," replied Brian. "Thank you. Thank you very much."

"You're most certainly welcome."

Sealed in the tiny room, Tim heard the director retreat, his hasty footsteps beating their way through the trailer. And then, with a sigh of relief, Tim sensed the outer door open and close.

Okay, he thought, as he rubbed his brow. The cars were taken care of, or would be soon, provided that Vic didn't screw up again. Now all he had to worry about was, of course, the media.

Chapter 30

"So I was parked right about here," explained Rawlins to his partner, Neal Foster, "when I saw this car come out of there."

From the front seat of his Taurus, Rawlins pointed to the large black iron gates of the driveway. It was early afternoon, the sun was breaking through the clouds, and the shiny black metal glistened, broadcasting an image of wealth and privacy. Past the gates and the fence, past the rich green lawn and thick bushes quietly sat the huge house. Though it was the size of a small hotel and though the grounds were impeccably manicured, the structure and its grounds were deserted.

"About what time was this?" asked Foster, seated next to him.

"Nine last night, maybe a little after."

"And what were you doing here?"

"To be perfectly frank, it's a long story, so let's not get into—"

"Ah, sounds like relationship problems to me. Right? Am I right?" Knowing he was dead on target, Foster grinned, entirely proud of his sleuthing abilities. "In my humble opinion, that's how stories always get long. Or complicated, anyway."

"Whatever," replied Rawlins with a reticent shrug.

No, he didn't want to get into it, and he wouldn't, at least not until he had to. The important thing was that last night he'd been parked right here, right out front of this big house, and he'd seen a white convertible Saab come barreling through those gates and down this street. And the vehicle did have California plates, Rawlins was sure of that,

just as he was sure that the driver was bald. But could it all be so easily solved?

"I want to know who the tipster is and just how and why he knows
so much," said Rawlins. "He was obviously here last night because he
saw me, but why? Why would he be hanging around this place?"

"He said he was a photographer?"

"Yeah." Wondering who in the name of hell Todd had visited inside the mansion last night, Rawlins added, "And I want to know
whose house this is, anyway. It has to belong to someone important."

"So no big deal. We're cops, we can find that out pretty damn easy."

Not hesitating, Foster reached for the radio, which was mounted
on the slender transmission hump between the front seats. He
grabbed the microphone and, because this wasn't an emergency,
called not dispatch but Channel 7, their information channel.

He said, "Car 1110"

Through the small speaker beneath the dash, a woman's voice
warbled: "Go ahead, Car 1110."

"I need a reverse directory check."

As Foster read off the address, Rawlins wondered how long this
was going to take, either seconds or minutes. There was never any
telling. If checking the phone records didn't work for some reason,
then they could always use the cell phone to call another department
to see to whom the water bill was sent. But apparently that wasn't
going to be necessary.

The woman's voice on the radio said, "Car 1110?"

"1110," answered Foster.

"That residence is listed as belonging to Suzanne Buttons."

"Buttons?"

"Yes. That's boy-up-top-top—"

"Copy." With a shrug, Foster hung up, then turned to Rawlins.
"Doesn't ring any bells for me. How about you?"

Of course it did. She was no department store heir. No lumber or
grain scion, of which there was still a wide smattering in the Twin
Cities. No nouveau computer millionaire either. Rawlins had read all

about her in the newspaper, and Suzanne Buttons, who'd made every penny of her own money, was famous and filthy rich for an entirely different reason.

"Makeup," said Rawlins. "She's the queen saleswoman of a direct sales cosmetics line. I think she's something like their biggest grossing sales rep in the country, maybe the world."

"You mean one of those pink Cadillac millionaires?"

"Different company but same idea."

Which didn't tell them a whole lot about what was going on here. Or, thought Rawlins, why Todd would have been here last night, unless of course Todd had simply been working on a story. Which was a possibility. It would be just like Todd to have said he had a date, implying so very much, when in actuality that date could have simply been an interview. But if it had been an interview, what was Todd looking into? What scam or crime had piqued his reporterly instincts? And just who had he seen?

Grabbing his cell phone from the seat, Rawlins said, "I'm going to call CID and see if there've been any police calls on this address."

He punched in the number, and the receptionist answered, saying, "Criminal Investigation Division."

"Hi, Donna, this is Steve Rawlins. Can you get me someone in Homicide? Anyone there?"

"Sure. I think Lewis is in."

There was a click on the line, and a moment later, a woman picked up saying, "Homicide, this is Sergeant Lewis."

"Hey, Kathy, this is Rawlins. We're parked outside a residence in south Minneapolis, and I was wondering if you could check to see if there've been any police calls at this address. I'd be interested in the last year—oh, and whose name might be on it."

"Sure, but I'm right in the middle of something. Let me call you back in five."

"Great," said Rawlins, who then gave her the address as well as his cell phone number.

No sooner had Rawlins hung up, than Foster ran his left hand over his craggy face, and said, "You gotta back up a little bit, Rawlins. If we're going to figure this out, you gotta tell me what you were doing here last night. Just some general information, that's all I'm asking for."

The problem, of course, was that there wasn't much more to tell. Squirming in his seat, Rawlins stared at the yellow brick mansion that was bathed in the bright, cool light. Did he really want to drag Todd into this, or was the cat already out?

"Okay," began Rawlins hesitantly, "you're right. Todd and I are having problems, but I really don't want to get into it. Not just yet, anyway—I mean, I'd like to keep this simple. But I was out here last night, and—"

"And he was in there? Todd was inside the house?"

Oh, shit, thought Rawlins, Foster was a bulldog of an investigator, and a great one too. One chomp into something and he never let go.

"Yeah, right, Todd was in there."

"And?"

"Well, so I'm sitting right about in this exact spot when a white Saab came pulling out. I was rather curious who was in the car. Actually, I thought Todd was with some guy, so I followed it for a block and then pulled up alongside it. Okay, maybe it was a little stupid of me, but I did it."

"And?"

"And . . . and there was only one person in it. Some guy—big, bald. And that was it. I looked at him, he glanced briefly at me, and then I drove on."

"Can you ID this guy?"

"Sure, I think so."

"Good." Returning to the Achilles' heel of this, Foster asked, "But Todd is involved in this somehow?"

"Not involved, not that I can see, anyway, but he was here last night, obviously meeting with someone."

"Have you talked to him about it? Have you asked him why he was here? I mean, that would be the logical place to start."

"Yeah, of course, but . . ." Rawlins shook his head. "Oh, shit, Todd and I've got a few things we need to talk about, and I really don't—"

"Hey," interrupted Foster, raising his right hand and pointing across the street. "Looks like something's going on at the Magic Kingdom."

Rawlins looked over, saw the wrought iron gates begin to swing automatically open in a grand, manorlike way. Spying no car, he turned and looked up the street, then glanced in his rearview mirror. Nothing. Turning his attention back to the house, at first all appeared quiet, even desolate. The next moment a car came speeding up from behind the north wing of the house.

"Wait a minute . . . wait a minute . . ." muttered Rawlins, his eyes trained on a white vehicle. "This could be our lucky day."

"Is that it?"

It was white. It had a black roof. And, yes, it was a Saab.

"Yep," replied Rawlins, watching as it rushed up to the stately gates, then passed through and turned right. "And it's coming this way."

"Look at me, Rawlins," commanded his partner. "You were here last night, and this guy can probably recognize you too. After all, you drove right up alongside his car. So just play along and look right at me so that he can't see your face. We're just sitting here, talking, gabbing, minding our own business, right? Right?"

Trying to obscure his face, Rawlins ran his left hand through his hair and turned toward Foster, at the same time demanding, "Can you see who's driving? Is it him, a bald guy?"

"Can't see, not yet. It's a white Saab, black convertible roof, no doubt about that. Just one guy in the car. He's coming this way. Don't look over, Rawlins. I think he's checking us out. He's got sunglasses on, so I can't really tell, but I think he's looking this way. And . . . and . . . yes, big guy, completely bald. Maybe his head is shaved, but it's gotta be him, the same guy you saw last night."

Forcing himself not to turn around as he heard the car go shooting past, Rawlins demanded, "What about the plates? Are they California?"

"Ah . . . you bet."

"Can you get a number?"

"Okay, okay, okay . . . let me see. Got it!" said Foster, who quickly started jotting it down.

"Excellent."

His eyes still on the speeding vehicle, Foster added, "Yeah, but I think we've been made."

"Oh, my God, that tip caller was just a little gold mine of information." Rawlins reached for the ignition. "Shall we?"

"Yeah, like right now."

Rawlins brought his car to a roar of a start, then stomped on the gas and steered the Taurus in a screeching U-turn. As he did so, Foster reached again for the radio, this time calling dispatch.

"Car 1110."

"Go ahead, Car 1110."

"Emergency check on a California plate," he said, and then read off the plate number.

As before, Rawlins knew this could be instant information—data the computer could retrieve in seconds—or something that could take ten minutes or more to access. In the meantime, they couldn't lose him, and Rawlins didn't waste a moment speeding after the Saab, which had already disappeared around one of the undulating bends of Mount Curve. He passed a towering, castlelike house on his left, a redbrick mansion with a slate roof on his right, then came around a slope and saw nothing, only a quiet street lined with huge homes and the last of the century's majestic elms.

"Shit," muttered Rawlins.

With the microphone in hand, Foster calmly pointed ahead, saying, "I bet he turned left just up there."

It was, actually, the only possibility, and Rawlins raced toward the next street, braking at the last moment, then swooping around the corner much too fast. And there was the white Saab, accelerating with each moment and shooting down the perfectly straight block, which was lined with tall clapboard houses with Midwesternly front porches.

Noting how fast the Saab was shooting along, Rawlins, pressing the gas pedal to the floor, said, "Obviously you were right—he made us as soon as he came out the gates."

"So he's worried enough to be on the lookout, which means things are getting curiouser and curiouser."

"Yeah." As the Saab approached the intersection ahead, Rawlins asked, "So what do we do, pull him over?"

"He's speeding, that's for sure. We could ticket him for that and reckless endangerment. You got a kojack with you?"

"It's right here," replied Rawlins, reaching under his seat and pulling out a small red bubble of a light.

Into the microphone, Foster said, "Car 1110."

"Go ahead, Car 1110."

"Any information on that plate check?"

The voice over the radio speaker replied, "Still checking."

Their computer was linked to the NCIC, which in turn would check the California Department of Transportation's records in Sacramento. So they should be able to get a name on this guy, but then they'd have to call down to Criminal History, which was part of the court services division, to see if he had any record.

Tossing the end of the kojack light at Foster, Rawlins said, "Get this thing plugged in, would you?"

As he grabbed the end and crammed it into the cigarette lighter, Foster said, "This guy's scared shitless, there's no doubt about it. Think we should call for a marked squad?"

"Yeah."

Up ahead a long yellow school bus rumbled through the intersection. The Saab's brake lights flashed red, and then the bald man turned left, following after the bus, his tires squealing as he barely made the turn. In an instant he disappeared around a white house with a tall stand of lilacs.

As they neared the cross street, Foster placed one hand on the dash. "How's this thing corner?"

"We'll find out," replied Rawlins.

Rawlins rolled down his window and was about to reach out and slap the kojack light and its magnetic base on the roof, but there wasn't enough time. Instead, he clutched the steering wheel with both hands and swerved as far right as he could. Like a race driver approaching a difficult turn, Rawlins didn't brake but only let up on the gas. Then swooping to the left in as wide a turn as possible, his tires screamed and the car dipped deeply to the opposite side. It suddenly became clear that he was going too fast, that he might not be able to control the car, and Rawlins was tempted to tap the brakes but didn't for fear of rolling. All he could do was clutch the wheel, hold it steady, and as he did so, he checked the streets feeding into the intersection, relieved at least that no one was approaching. But he couldn't do it, couldn't quite control the car, and the lighter rear end of the vehicle started fishtailing out to the side. He punched the brakes once, then let up.

"Damn it!" cursed Rawlins.

With a large scream of burning rubber, they skidded sideways into the intersection. Rawlins leaned hard against the steering wheel, his powerful arms battling the force. He glanced over, realized that they were sliding toward a red fire hydrant standing firmly on the corner. He had no choice but to trounce on the brake. They swirled around a hundred and eighty degrees, then in one noisy second came to a jerk of a halt.

His eyes wide, Foster looked straight at Rawlins, and said, "Well, don't stop now!"

Rawlins took a deep breath, pressed down on the gas, then spun the steering wheel in the opposite direction. In a moment they were whipping around, once again in pursuit of the white Saab, which had just soared past the yellow school bus like a hawk swooping past a hare.

The radio cracked, and the dispatcher called, "Car 1110?"

Lifting the microphone to his mouth, Foster said, "1110."

"That California plate comes back clear. A white 1998 two-door convertible Saab, registered to Victor Michael Radzinsky, DOB August 23, 1959, of Santa Monica, California."

"Copy." Foster glanced at Rawlins, saying, "That's got to be him. Do we need a driver's license check?"

Rawlins nodded, wanting it all—height, weight, eye color—and said, "Yeah, let's get as good a physical description as possible."

"Car 1110," said Foster into the microphone.

"Go ahead, 1110."

"DL check Victor Michael Radzinsky."

"Copy."

As they quickly gained on the bus, Rawlins leaned slightly to the left and peered around the side of the bus. There was no doubt about it, the Saab was racing faster than ever down the street.

"He's getting away—call it in!"

Foster said, "Car 1110."

"Go ahead, 1110."

"We're in pursuit of a possible homicide suspect and need marked assistance."

As Foster gave them the approximate location, Rawlins reached into his lap and grabbed the kojack light. Lifting it out the window, he realized the cord was tangled, and so he glanced out, tried to ascertain how he could get it up and on the roof.

Foster shouted, "Jesus!"

Rawlins's heart shot up the back of his throat. The reason he'd been gaining so quickly on the school bus was because it was stopped now only a matter of feet before him. He swerved to the left to bypass it, but then the bus driver extended the red stop sign on the side of the bus. The next instant a young girl with glasses and a ponytail stepped out from in front of the bus. Using both feet, Rawlins plunged down on the brake, and the car immediately bucked and started screeching. But there wasn't enough space, Rawlins could see that right away, knew it as soon as the girl turned toward him, eyes and mouth wide open, her small body frozen in fear. He twisted the wheel to the left, the car veered across the lane, then shot over the curb with a horrendous thud and flew a foot or two in the air.

And then came to an awkward halt on the sidewalk.

Rawlins took a deep breath, leaned forward, bowing his head onto the steering wheel. A moment later he reached down and turned off the ignition.

"Hail Mary," mumbled Foster. "Just let me live until the day I retire."

"Oh, my God," said Rawlins, shaking his head. "I usually do a little better than that."

"Sure you do."

He looked down the street, saw the Saab now a block or more away and growing more distant by the moment. No, there was no stopping him now, even if a marked squad was in the immediate area. But now at least they had a name to go with the face, and a plate number to go with the car.

Out of nowhere a woman came screaming onto the sidewalk, her eyes spitting hate at Rawlins as she ran past the car. She charged into the street, lunging for the little girl, who still stood quite paralyzed on the pavement and who, upon seeing her mother, broke into a siren of tears. Rawlins let out a deep sigh. No, this hadn't ended in total disaster. And thank God for that.

Suddenly the inside of the Taurus was filled with a ringing. Rawlins felt his jacket, found nothing, then searched the seat next to him. He found the telephone on the floor beneath his left foot.

"Watch," he said as he stretched to pick it up, "it'll be my mother." Flipping open his cell phone, he said, "Yeah, this is Rawlins."

"Hey, it's me," said Kathy Lewis, the investigator. "Actually there was a police call to that address—just last week, as a matter of fact."

All he could muster was a banal, "Really?"

"Yeah, but here's the interesting part—you know who lives there?"

"Suzanne Buttons is listed as the owner."

"Well, maybe, but right now it's leased out to some huge Hollywood star who's in town making a movie."

Knowing but wanting confirmation, Rawlins said, "Some huge Hollywood star like who?"

"Grab this: Tim Chase."

"No shit. So what about the complaint? Was it made by him?"

"No, the call was made by Maggie Eastman, who called about a photographer who was—"

"About who?"

"A photographer. Apparently some guy with a camera was lurking around the property."

"No kidding."

"Yeah, but by the time two police officers arrived the guy was long gone." Sergeant Lewis added, "Sounds like it was one of those paparazzi guys, you know, trying to get a picture of Tim Chase or something."

"You know what," replied Rawlins, as things were becoming clearer, "I think you're exactly right."

Chapter 31

The Minnesota State Fair—the "Great Minnesota Get-Together"—was supposedly the largest twelve-day fair in the country, with an attendance of nearly two million people. It was also one of the most tacky events on the face of the earth, featuring combines and tractors, chickens, rabbits, gargantuan swine, pop stars from Bonnie Raitt to Wynonna Judd, fireworks, roller coasters, and a riot of food from deep-fried cheese curds to corn dogs and fried ice cream on a stick, not to mention a semi-truck of all-you-can-drink milk. Todd had gone nearly every year since he'd moved to Minnesota and oddly, like so many gay men, always ended up at the Dairy Pavilion with its butter sculptures of Princess Kay of the Milky Way and her smiling attendants. Which, he thought, said a lot about gay stereotypes.

Turning off of Snelling Avenue, Todd drove through the green-and-blue entry gates that only three or four weeks ago were swarming with pedestrians pushing to get in. He headed directly up one of the main boulevards, finding not a mass of people but a huge, deserted street lined on either side with food shacks now boarded up for the year. Where recently upward of two hundred thousand people had strolled each day, there was now virtually no one, a ghost town of fun. It was weird, Todd had never seen the place abandoned, per se, let alone driven right through the four hundred acre site.

He passed the grandstand where horses raced and where rock and country-western stars performed, then veered off to the left. On one side stood a Quonset hut topped by a steeple, which promised the best church breakfast ever, followed by a dark green shack in the shape of a bell pepper, which advertised its fare, deep-fried of course. Then came the Root Beer Hut and a foot-long chili dog place. Todd took a right at Tiny Tim Donuts and headed straight down toward a sea of pavement, now completely empty but which had so recently boasted the Mighty Midway, an extravaganza of amusement rides and arcade games.

Human beings, of course, weren't the only fair guests. Todd had recently read that something like ten thousand animals also attended, exhibiting and competing for the biggest, the tallest, the fattest, and the fastest of breed, and Todd now entered their territory. Large buildings appeared, marked simply SHEEP, POULTRY, SWINE BARN, CATTLE BARN, and finally HORSES.

Glancing down the street, Todd saw that it was totally empty except for one pile of horse manure and an empty black pickup truck. Obviously, he thought as he parked, John Lyman was waiting inside. Not at all pleased with how deserted the area was, Todd grabbed his cellular phone and climbed out.

The horse barn was, according to the sign, a WPA building built in 1937 of thick concrete and decorated here and there with small friezes of horses. An odd greenish-beige color with high windows, the building's large main doors were pulled down and it appeared totally closed for the year. Approaching the structure, however, Todd saw a small door set in an alcove. He pulled open the screen door, tested the wooden door, and found it unlocked. Stepping inside with his phone in hand, he turned a corner and found himself in a huge empty space. Gone were the quarter horses and draft horses, the 4-H exhibits, the breeders, the farm kids, and the straw strewn everywhere.

"John?" called Todd, peering through the dim, dirty light. "John Lyman?"

Taking several steps across the cold concrete, Todd realized he shouldn't have agreed to meet here. Not in a place so void of activity. No, he should have been more heads-up, should have insisted they meet in a place full of people. Glancing around the dank building,

Todd wondered why John Lyman wanted to meet and just how angry he might be.

"Hello?"

A gust of wind shot into the building, the door slammed shut, and Todd jumped. From overhead came a deep flurry—a sparrow, perhaps locked in here since the end of the fair and somehow not yet starved to death. And then finally he heard the soft but distinct shuffle of leather across concrete.

Todd turned to a line of wooden stalls along one side of the barn, and called, "John?"

After a long moment came more shuffling, and then, "Yeah, down here."

Perhaps Todd was a fool, perhaps he should have just turned and headed out of there, but he didn't really think he had much choice. Andrew Lyman was dead, and the boy's father wanted to talk to him. Either he had news for Todd about his son's death—an overlooked fact, perchance—or he was going to lash out at Todd for his coverage. Or maybe, just maybe John Lyman had sought out Todd for an entirely different reason. Could it be possible that he knew something about his son's involvement with Rawlins?

The stalls were made of thick, heavy wood with huge sliding doors and heavy metal bars at the top, perfect for containing the most malcontent of stallions. Approaching the sixth or seventh stall, Todd heard movement from within and cautiously approached the opening. Looking in he saw the back of a large man standing there as he wiped down something. As Todd's eyes adjusted to the faint light, he saw what John Lyman was attending to.

"This isn't the greatest saddle, not by any means," Lyman said, his voice low and pained, "but I won it during my very first cutting competition something like twenty, maybe twenty-three years ago. It's brought me and my cutting horses good luck all this time . . . up until now. I didn't just lose during the competition this year, I was the laughing stock of the whole fucking State Fair rodeo. I mean, I've just up and lost the knack."

"I'm sorry."

"These are hard times for me. Real hard. Farming sure as hell ain't getting any easier. My family has gone and fallen apart. And now my only boy's dead, murdered because . . . because . . ."

He wore cowboy boots and jeans and a khaki jacket that was obviously too small, something that had perhaps once fit around him but would never again. He was a big man, not just tall, but overweight. And between the top of his blue check shirt and his green cap the skin of his neck was red and aged from years in the field.

What could Todd say? How, wondered Todd, clutching his phone in his sweaty hand, could he comfort this stranger?

Breaking the silence, John said, "The night I found out my boy was gay was the night I nearly beat him to death. And I would've, too, if my wife hadn't stopped me. I was so angry at him. I was so upset. I mean, I failed that boy. I wanted him to be happy and healthy. I wanted him to have a good, decent life. I wanted—"

"I met him, you know. And he was a good boy. He was happy and healthy too. And decent." In all his infinite wisdom, Todd couldn't keep his mouth shut. "He was all of that, plus gay."

"Maybe. Maybe he was. But, oh, Lord Jesus, I tried. I just didn't want that for him, that life. It's not good, not right. I saw it coming of course. I knew he was a homo. Knew it years ago, but—"

"It's not your fault. It's no one's fault. It's just a matter of fact that your son was gay. There's nothing to be ashamed of."

"Shit . . . You know why I beat my boy that night? You know why?" asked John Lyman, turning around for the first time.

Todd saw a face that was worn and fallen. And eyes that were red and glistening. How much, wondered Todd, had he had to drink? Or wait, was he not drunk? Were his eyes red with tears?

"No," replied Todd. "Why?"

"I beat my boy because I was trying to beat out of him what I hated most about myself, that's why."

It took Todd a half-second to comprehend what he was saying, for he'd never heard someone place their sexuality in so awful a context. But he was saying that, wasn't he?

"Can you be a little more specific?"

"Well, I'm married, but . . ." He closed his eyes, shook his head. "Let's just say I haven't been faithful to my wife."

Todd understood perfectly now. Understood that John Lyman would sooner kill himself than say he was gay. There was obviously no way in hell he was going to say he was homosexual, queer, a fairy, a pansy, a fudge packer, a corn holer, or whatever the kids these days said so easily but that not so very long ago all but equaled death, and in fact sometimes still did. John Lyman had lived an isolated life in rural Minnesota, obviously terrified of his personal truth, and that he had said as much as he had to Todd was amazing. Then again, it had taken the death of his son to pry open his closet this much.

Still, Todd knew of the profound difference between the unspoken and the spoken truth, and so he asked it in as non-threatening a manner as he could, saying, "You mean you've been having a same-sex affair?"

Nodding as he stared at the floor of the stall, John Lyman said, "I been seeing the same guy ever since high school."

"Really?"

"Not all that much, not really. Maybe three or four times a year. Sometimes more."

So, like father, like son. Incredible.

But why was he telling Todd this? Because Todd was openly gay? Because he had perhaps witnessed Todd's own outing live on TV? Perhaps. Perhaps even though Todd was a complete stranger he saw him as an isle of safety, even compassion. After all, didn't we all just want to be understood?

"This is obviously a very difficult time for you," said Todd. "Is there anything I can do? Anyway I can help?"

John Lyman nodded, closed his eyes, and said nothing.

"How?" asked Todd.

"Shit, I wondered if it was really going to come to this, if I could actually go through with it."

He sighed deeply, reached into the right pocket of his khaki jacket, and pulled out something small and metal. At first in the faint light Todd could only make out a mellow glint of metal. Then he saw something round and long. A barrel.

"Hey, wait a minute," said Todd, taking a half-step back.

This, of course, was what he feared. Something exactly like this. He glanced around, saw nothing, realized that the only thing he had to defend himself with was the stupid phone.

"We can talk this out," insisted Todd.

"You don't understand, there's nothing to talk about."

"You don't have to do it, John. I know these are bad times, but you don't have to hurt anyone. There are other ways."

Raising the gun, he said, "No, I'm afraid there aren't. I been thinking and thinking, and I got no choice."

"John, wait. Please."

Todd was worse than a sitting duck. He could make a break for it. He could tear for the door, and perhaps he'd make it. Then again, thought Todd, his heart taking off at a gallop, he probably wouldn't. John Lyman was sure to be a good shot.

"Why?" demanded Todd.

"Because I can't face it, the truth."

"But—"

"And if it ever comes up I want you to go see my wife."

"Do what?"

"Go see my wife, Martha."

Suddenly this wasn't making any sense. Was this perhaps not headed in the very direction that Todd feared?

"What do you mean?"

Raising the gun higher, Lyman said, "I want you to tell her how much I loved her. Tell her in my heart I was true to her."

As Todd watched Lyman's elbow bend he suddenly understood. Oh, God. He'd called Todd here for a kind of last confession.

"John, don't."

"There's no other way. I got no other choice."

"Your son's dead, don't make things worse."

Lyman lifted the handgun to his right temple and slowly let his eyes drift shut. "It's all my fault too. Somehow I made that boy a homo. And . . . and I definitely drove him away from his home. He's . . . he's dead because of me."

Tears started rolling from his eyes, big, fat drops that traveled down his large cheeks. No, he didn't want this. He really didn't. And Todd knew what he had to do, just keep him talking.

"No," said Todd, "he's dead because some insane person killed him."

"If I hadn't drove him away he'd still be alive. He shoulda been home with us. He woulda been safe there. None of this woulda happened."

The other man's trigger finger started to flinch, and Todd knew he'd lost, that there was no way of stopping this, that Andrew Lyman's death was going to be like a chain accident, one death piled upon another. And all for nothing.

The phone.

There was nothing else Todd could do. No other course, none that he could see. And so, as John Lyman stood there with the pistol to his right temple, Todd slowly brought back his arm. This was perhaps the stupidest thing, but he was determined to do something, anything, to change the course of the next few seconds. Wasting not a moment, Todd tossed the small black phone at the other man.

"It's for you, John!"

John's eyes popped open in surprise and instinctively he reached out to catch the little plastic phone hurtling his way. And catch it he did, the small phone clattering against the barrel of the gun.

Desperate, Todd blurted, "If you shoot yourself, you know what I'm going to do? I'm going to do a story on television about you and your son. I'm going to say that Andrew was an incest victim. I'm going to say that you had sex with him."

"That's not true!"

"Of course it's not, but that's what I'm going to say. And that's what the world will think because you'll be dead and you'll have no way of defending yourself."

"No!"

"I'll do it. If you kill yourself, that's what I'm going to do." Oh, Christ, what was Todd about to unleash? "But if you don't hurt yourself, if you push through all of this, then all I'll do is tell the truth, that you loved your—"

"You bastard!"

Lyman threw Todd's cellular phone to the floor, smashing it in a half-dozen pieces, and then charged forward, a bull of a man overflowing with rage and self-hatred. Todd, seeing the gun aimed at him, leapt to the side, and an instant later a bullet blasted deep into the thick wood of the stall. But rather than running for the door, Todd twisted around and used his foot to trip Lyman just as he came rushing out. Lyman fell forward, landing on the hard concrete floor with a deep groan, and the gun flew from his hand and went sailing through the air. Racing after it, Todd bent down, grabbed the butt of the gun, and scooped it up.

"You asshole!" roared Lyman as he scrambled across the floor. "I'm gonna kill you!"

Just then a hand locked onto Todd's left ankle and pulled with the force of a draft horse. Before Todd knew it, he went flying forward and the gun went hurtling out of his hand. He landed smack on his stomach and all the air exploded out of him. He knew he had to move, to get out of there, but he couldn't breathe, couldn't even manage to push himself onto his hands and knees. And the next moment Lyman was pulling him back. Todd managed to twist over, to cover his face, as Lyman lunged at him, striking Todd on the chin once, twice. Todd tried to curl into a ball to protect himself, but it was too late. Before he even had time to think, his head exploded with a blast of pain and everything plunged into quiet darkness.

Chapter 32

Rawlins was the first one to crack.

All afternoon as he'd been going about his work he'd been wondering if Todd would call and perhaps chat awhile, maybe even apologize or simply, without admitting guilt, voice his regret for their argument last night. Actually, Rawlins half expected Todd would phone and insist they get together if not sometime this afternoon, then certainly for dinner. But now, checking his watch as he sat in his cubicle at CID, it was after six o'clock and of course Todd hadn't called, which really didn't come as any great surprise to Rawlins. Todd was that stubborn. That resolute. Or more to the point, that determined to be in control.

Well, screw the bastard.

Rawlins had caved not quite an hour ago. He didn't know what he was going to say, he didn't actually know what he wanted to happen, but he couldn't stand this separation, this odd quiet between them. Over the course of their young relationship they hadn't argued that much, but they'd certainly never run into a stupid brick wall like this one. And it was this silence that scared Rawlins, because for the first time there didn't seem any desire on Todd's part to work through their differences. What was going on? Could Todd really have gone on a date last night? Might he be sneaking out of their relationship? Yes, it was certainly possible.

From his desk on the second floor of City Hall, Rawlins had first tried Todd about forty-five minutes ago, calling him at WLAK. When he'd been dumped into voice mail, Rawlins hadn't left a message but simply hung up. He'd then tried Todd's condo, where he'd reached an answering machine and likewise left no message. Finally he'd called Todd's cell phone, which just rang and rang until some recorded message came on stating in much too bright a voice that, thank you very much, the phone was either turned off or out of range. The frustration brewing, Rawlins went for a cup of coffee, then returned to his desk some twenty minutes later and tried all the numbers again, yet again had no luck. It wasn't that unusual, Rawlins supposed. He could almost always get Todd on the phone, particularly if he called him on his cellular, but there were those times when Todd was doing an interview, when he was in an editorial meeting, or when he was in the studio doing some taping.

Frustrated, Rawlins compulsively tried the numbers a third time. When he still had no success, Rawlins began to wonder if Todd was doing this on purpose. Could he be avoiding Rawlins? Perhaps, even probably. He had caller ID on his cell phone—who knew, maybe even on his phone at work as well—and it would be just like the son of a bitch to take note that it was Rawlins calling and not pick up.

Damn him.

That bit of paranoia—the distinct possibility that Todd was avoiding him—started twirling in Rawlins's mind until it reached tornadic confusion. He got up and started pacing up and down CID, from Homicide all the way down to Juvenile. And he kept at it for a good ten minutes until he came up with an idea. Calling the front desk at WLAK, he asked for Nan, the six o'clock producer whom he'd met on several occasions.

"I'm sorry," replied the receptionist, "but she's busy with the evening news right now."

Rawlins glanced at his watch, saw that it was not quite six-thirty. Oh, shit, was it that simple? Was that why Todd had been unreachable, he'd been busy with the evening news?

"Well, tell her Steve Rawlins called. And tell her it's an emergency. Here's my number," he said, determined to figure this out. "Okay, you got it? Just make sure she calls me right away."

He sat there, rubbing his face and wondering what the hell he was going to do next, when just a few minutes later his desk phone rang, and he grabbed it, saying, "Homicide, this is Sergeant Rawlins."

"Where the hell is he?"

"Nan?"

"Yeah, it's me. Where the hell's Todd?" she ranted. "He was supposed to be on at six and he just blew us off. I mean, blew us off completely. Unbelievable. Let me tell you he's got a lot of people really pissed at him. You just can't do that. Do you know how hard it was to fill his slot just minutes before we were supposed to go on? Do you? I mean, what the hell was he thinking? What the hell happened?"

"Actually, Nan, I don't know. I don't have any idea," replied Rawlins, his tone a bit sheepish. "That's why I called—I was hoping you could tell me. I haven't been able to find him either."

"But . . . but . . ." As if seizing on a novel idea, she said, "God, I hope he's okay, I hope nothing happened."

"Me too," replied Rawlins, his anger quickly dissipating, only to be replaced by a deep current of worry.

They agreed to keep in touch and then hung up. Rawlins immediately picked the phone back up and dialed all of Todd's numbers yet one more time, this time leaving a message at home and work.

"Todd, it's me, Rawlins. Where are you? I'm kind of worried. I've got my cell phone with me—call me as soon as you can."

There was, thought Rawlins, shrugging as he hung up, nothing more he could do, at least not before his seven o'clock meeting.

Chapter 33

It was the concrete that woke Todd.

Cool and smooth against his left cheek, it was as refreshing as a cold, damp washcloth on a hot summer day. And just as invigorating. His eyes fluttered, then popped open. Lying on his side, he didn't move, just gazed around at the huge empty space and saw a small bird, a sparrow, flutter toward a window and bang its body over and over against the glass.

Where the hell was he?

The stale odor of horse manure and straw sparked the memory that his eyes could not. He was at the State Fair in the horse barn. And his head hurt like hell. Right, he'd come here to meet John Lyman, and then . . . then . . .

Using both hands, he pushed himself up and then sat there, looking around, sure that John Lyman's body would be lying just a few feet away, bloody and lifeless. Instead there was no one and nothing. Todd turned toward the horse stall against the far wall, wondered if he'd done it in there, gone back to the small space and blown his brains out. Groaning and rubbing his head, Todd got up and started moving slowly, not at all eager to discover someone's remains.

"John?" he called rather feebly.

As he approached the stall he expected to see the large man laid out within the four heavy wooden walls of the stall. Instead, except for Todd's cell phone, which lay smashed in pieces, it was perfectly empty.

There was no sign of John Lyman, nor for that matter the saddle he had so lovingly tended.

Leaning against the stall, Todd touched the side of his head and felt the epicenter of the pain, which, like a hangover, was thick and nauseating and rippled from his head to his stomach. At least Lyman wasn't dead. At least Todd had prevented that—although perhaps only temporarily. And that, Todd thought, was a good point, for if Lyman hadn't killed himself in here, then perhaps he'd gone off and done the deed elsewhere. Perhaps he'd stormed out and done it in the front seat of his truck. Pretty.

As his senses regrouped he realized he had to get to the station. He had a broadcast to do. Checking his watch, he stared at the small face and thin hands. Oh, shit. It was a quarter past six. He hadn't lain on the concrete for five or ten minutes, but almost an hour.

Panicking, he bent down and started grabbing at the pieces of his cell phone, the main body right in front of him, the battery over on one side of the stall, and then a couple of small pieces scattered like marbles. His hands shaking, Todd tried cramming the battery in, but it wouldn't stay. He jammed something into something, but the plastic body was entirely cracked. It was beyond hopeless.

Clearly, he'd missed his spot. There was going to be hell to pay for this, but what could he do? It was, he thought as his head throbbed, already too late to simply warn them.

Turning, he started for the door, moving none too fast. As he stepped out into the evening light, he saw his Cherokee sitting right where he had left it. John Lyman's pickup, however, was gone, which meant, of course, that he'd been alive when he'd left. Thank God for small miracles.

Todd rubbed his brow, went around and unlocked his truck. He tossed the broken pieces of his cell phone on the passenger seat and climbed in. What he needed now was a long, hot shower. And then? Something about seven-thirty. Right, he was supposed to do something. Be somewhere. Meet someone.

Of course. He had a date with Tim Chase.

Chapter 34

Slipping his cell phone into the pocket of his jacket, Rawlins headed across the rough, potholed parking lot. His first major worry of the night was Todd and if he was alright. His second was this guy, the witness, and if he was actually going to show.

Jam's was a freestanding building, a green box of a place with black glass windows on one side and a pair of red neon cowboy boots on the roof. Known for its country music DJ, its tiny dance floor, and its half-dozen pool tables, it was a popular pickup bar, and Rawlins wasn't at all surprised that the witness had suggested it.

So who the hell was this guy? Was he not a closet queen but a photographer who regularly sold his pictures to the tabloids? Was the answer that simple?

As he approached the door, Rawlins casually glanced around the crumbling parking lot. He should have, he realized, done this a bit differently. He should have sat in his car for a few minutes and jotted down as many license plates as he could have. Instead he took quick note of the fifteen or so cars scattered about—a couple of Ford Explorers, three pickup trucks, a Honda Accord, and a few other sedans.

Pulling open the door, Rawlins entered a small lobby with a couple of pay phones hanging on the wall to his left. It was two minutes to seven. He proceeded to a broad, open doorway and gazed into the main room, which was dark and faintly smoky. Glancing to his right, Rawlins saw two of the pool tables in use. He then peered to the left, saw some tables and chairs, the bar, and off in the dark distance the quiet dance floor. Here and there were couples, men and women drinking and gabbing, and a few men who'd obviously met after work for a beer. All in all it was fairly quiet; the real action wouldn't begin for several more hours. Rawlins stood for a long moment, surveying the scene and noting that there wasn't any lone person here by himself. And that unto itself, Rawlins knew from experience, didn't bode well. A tipster like this was either here exactly on time or not at all.

Scanning the dark room, Rawlins made his way to the bar, where he sat on a tall stool.

"What can I get you?" asked the bartender, a trim, handsome woman with long brown hair and a quick Minnesota smile.

"A Leinie."

"You bet."

As she pulled him a draught Leinenkugel's, Rawlins turned on the stool, again looking casually over the room and toward the doorway. No one was looking his way, nor even paying him the slightest bit of attention.

"You want to run a tab?" asked the bartender, sliding the tall glass of beer to him.

"Yeah." Rawlins took it, then asked, "I'm supposed to meet someone here, you haven't by chance—"

"Male or female?"

"A guy."

"What's he look like?"

"Actually, I don't know. We've never met before."

"Well, there hasn't been anyone waiting around, least not as far as I can tell. You late or something? What time were you supposed to meet?"

"Seven."

She glanced at her wristwatch, then looked up at him and winked. "Drink up, hon. The night's young."

"Whatever."

Sitting sideways with his right arm on the bar, Rawlins kept his attention on the door and sipped his beer. With this few people in the place the bartender surely wouldn't have missed a single man sitting around, which meant the guy had yet to come. So how long would Rawlins give him? A half-hour? If he was going to show, which Rawlins already doubted, he'd certainly make it by seven-thirty.

Glancing down the bar he saw the bartender casually leaning against the back counter. Holding a cigarette to her mouth, she took a long drag, sucking on her vice as if it offered much more than a mere puff of smoke. Not only was the night, as she said, young, it was also slow, and she looked at Rawlins with a generous grin that could be read in the most generous of ways. Rawlins briefly returned the smallest of smiles and immediately averted his eyes. He took a sip of beer and then turned back to the entry.

Come on, buddy. Don't crap out on me.

Rawlins glanced at his watch. At the most two minutes had passed. So where was this guy? And where the hell, of course, was Todd?

Suddenly there was a ringing right against his side, which caused him to jump. His phone. As a few heads turned his way, he put down his beer and snatched the small device out of the pocket of his jacket. Please let it be Todd, he thought. Please let him be okay.

Covering his left ear with one hand, he held the receiver to his right, and said, "This is Sergeant Rawlins."

"Hi."

Rawlins immediately knew it wasn't Todd. His voice was remarkably clear and clean with plenty of resonance, while this one was softer, even timid. It was him, the witness. Damn. From experience Rawlins guessed this guy wasn't calling to say, sorry, I'm going to be a couple of minutes late, just sit tight. He was calling because he wasn't going to show. Shit, thought Rawlins, realizing he was going to have to start tap-dancing real quick before he lost the guy altogether.

"Is this my friend?" asked Rawlins.

"Yeah, it's me."

"I'm here, I'm at Jam's, just waiting for you. Everything okay?"

"Listen, I'm . . . I'm sorry, but I'm not going to make it."

"Really?" said Rawlins, feigning surprise and at the same time shaking his head in frustration. "You know, I can wait if you need a little more time. That's absolutely no problem."

"No . . . no, it's not that. I just can't get any more involved than I already am."

"I only wanted to meet for a drink, that's all, nothing more."

"Yeah, but . . ."

"Trust me," said Rawlins as he glanced over at the bartender, who looked at him and smiled back, "there's nothing to worry about."

"I don't know. I . . ."

With the receiver pressed hard against his ear, Rawlins heard voices—a couple of men laughing—and what sounded like a door slamming shut. So this witness, wherever he was, was again calling from some anonymous phone. Rawlins had to give him that, he was consistent.

Fearing that he'd lose him completely if he kept pushing, Rawlins forced himself to take the conciliatory path, saying, "I just wanted to meet for a quick drink, but if you're uncomfortable with that then let's not. You've been amazingly helpful, and it's absolutely your choice if you want to limit your involvement to the tips you've already given us. I mean, it's more than we could have hoped for. Not everyone's willing to do as much as you've done, that's for sure."

"Thank you," he said, the relief clearly audible. "Thank you very much. I've been working on something, you see, and it's very complicated."

"I don't doubt that."

"I mean, I just don't want to screw things up."

"I see."

Rawlins had to curb his tongue, had to keep himself from asking if the guy was really a professional photographer or if perhaps he was a closet queen who had an obsession with Tim Chase. Yes, thought

Rawlins, if the guy was something like the latter—a stalker perhaps—
that would of course explain why he'd secretly spied so much going on
at the Chase residence. And it would also explain why he was so reticent to meet with Rawlins.

He glanced across the room and saw a couple of guys laughing
and talking as they sat down, then asked, "Is there anything else that
you can remember? Anything else that comes to mind that might be
helpful to us?"

"Um, no, not really. Not that I can think of, anyway. But I'll call
right away if I do think of anything else."

"Good, we'd appreciate that." Fearful that losing him now would
mean losing him forever, Rawlins, trying not to seem desperate, asked,
"Is there any way I can contact you if I have any questions?"

"Well, not really."

"Not even a number I could call, say, just to leave a message?"

"No. Like I said, I just can't get involved."

"Sure, I understand."

Okay, Rawlins told himself. Think. And think fast. Remember
what Foster told you a few months back, that story of an informant in
a drug ring and how Foster had arranged to contact him anonymously?

"Listen, I have an idea." Through the receiver Rawlins could hear
the wail of an ambulance, and he raised his voice, and said, "I want to
think of some way that I can send a signal to you, some kind of signal
that would tell you I need to talk to you. I'm probably going to have
some questions after all."

"Like what? What were you thinking of?"

"How about a cop car? If I want you to call me I'll park an empty
squad car down by Lake Harriet. I'll park it right where you saw that
Saab. Can you check there, say, every day around twelve-thirty for the
next couple of weeks?"

"Sure. Sure, I can do that. I can go down there and check. And if
I see it there, then I'll give you a call as soon as I can."

"Exactly."

"Cool." As the siren ambulance grew closer and louder, the witness said, "Just a minute—I can hardly hear you."

The wail rose and contracted over and over, screaming as the ambulance tore to some emergency. Or was it a fire engine? Whatever type of emergency vehicle it was, it was awfully close, and as Rawlins pressed his small cellular phone to his ear it seemed as if he could hear the siren in both ears. Actually he could, couldn't he? The next instant he held the phone away from his head and realized he could hear the siren just as loudly, which meant it wasn't far away, not by any means.

Dear God.

He looked at the two men who'd just sat down and in one stupid second understood that they'd walked right past the very phone the witness had been using. It was them Rawlins had overheard. Which meant only one thing: the witness had been willing to come only so close.

Over the cry of the siren, Rawlins desperately said, "Hang on one second. I've got one more thing to ask you."

With the phone pressed to his ear, Rawlins was off the bar stool and hurrying across the room. And then he was running. There was no reply from the other end, only the sound of the wail, which was now growing weaker. Rawlins tore toward the entry, dashing around the corner. But there was no one standing there at the pay phones, only one of the receivers, gently swinging to and fro by its long cord. Rawlins glanced at the door, saw it easing shut. Charging forward, he hurled open the door and ran right into the parking lot.

There was no one.

He glanced at each and every car, half-expecting to see one racing off, its tires peeling. All he needed was a license plate number, nothing more. Instead the lot was perfectly quiet. Spinning around, Rawlins looked across Excelsior Boulevard, sure to see someone racing across on foot. Instead the broad concrete road was deserted, virtually so.

Turning from side to side, Rawlins folded up his phone and slipped it back into the pocket of his jacket. The witness had been that close, only a matter of a few yards away, but his paranoia must have made those last few feet seem like a million miles.

"Hey, pal," called a voice.

Rawlins turned, saw the bartender hanging out the half-open door, a smile on her face, her long hair hanging off her right shoulder.

She said, "I hope you're coming back in to pay for that beer. You are, aren't ya? Right?"

Acting the perfect Minnesotan and not belying his frustration, Rawlins replied, "You bet."

Chapter 35

On his way back to his condo, Todd stopped at a gas station and bought two glass bottles of mineral water. One he drank down immediately. The other he pressed against his temple, the chilled, sweaty glass sending a rush of relief through his aching head. He took Interstate 94, crossing the Mississippi, which acted something like a Berlin Wall, dividing one metropolitan area into two capriciously distinct cities that, unlike Berlin, had never possessed any desire to be united. No, old and proud St. Paul wanted nothing to do with its flighty neighbor, and Minneapolis, feeling itself far more dynamic and hip, all but ignored its stodgy sister.

It was approaching seven by the time Todd parked his car and rode the elevator up to his apartment. He let himself in, finally uncapped the second bottle of mineral water, and, sitting on his leather couch, drank it down. A few minutes later he was roused by Girlfriend, who leapt on his lap, purring and rubbing against him as if he were the greatest of gods. Immediately Todd understood that, no, she wasn't all full of sympathy and love. The slut was hungry.

Going into the kitchen, Todd opened a can of cat food and fed Girlfriend, who was swirling about his feet in a Pavlovian frenzy. He then glanced across the kitchen counter and saw the blinking red light of his answering machine. There were two messages. As he could have guessed, the first was from the six o'clock producer, Nan.

"Todd, where the hell are you? It's almost six! You better get your butt in here in the next two seconds or . . . or . . ."

He knew there was going to be hell to pay, he just didn't want to hear about it now, and he fast-forwarded it to the second message. Which was from Rawlins, as he also could have guessed. Of course Todd needed to call him back, he thought as he glanced at the clock on his stove and saw that it was a couple of minutes after seven. Picking up the phone, he started to dial, but then stopped. He put his hand to his forehead, but the number that was always there had, apparently, been beaten out of him. He quickly pulled open a drawer and pulled out his phone list, which was scribbled on a yellow legal pad, and saw the number he thought he'd never forget. When he dialed it, though, it rang busy. He waited no more than five seconds and tried again. Damn, he thought. He was never going to make it to Chase's by seven-thirty. Frustrated, Todd glanced again at the list, saw Rawlins's number down at CID, and called there.

Reaching Rawlins's voice mail, Todd stumbled over his thoughts as he said, "Hey, Rawlins, it's me, Todd. I'm okay . . . I think. It's a long story—I'll tell you later—but obviously we have a lot of things to talk about. Listen, I've got to meet someone in a few minutes. I'll call you back later."

Shaking his head as he hung up, Todd realized he was in no shape to talk on the phone, let alone go to Tim Chase's. Hoping a shower would help, he went straight to his bedroom, where he stripped, then headed for the bathroom. Taking two aspirin, he chased the pills down with water from the tap, and next turned on the shower full blast and climbed in. Thank God, he thought as the water pounded and massaged his head and body, for the seemingly unlimited amount of hot water this building could produce.

A half-hour later he was driving along Mount Curve Avenue, and if he wasn't completely revived, then he was at least coherent. Looking as good as he could on this particular night, he wore black jeans, a blue shirt, and his leather coat, but who was he hoping to impress? And what exactly was he hoping would happen tonight? Recalling the strong embrace and the gentle kisses from the night before, Todd knew damn well.

As he rounded a bend and approached the house, he saw that the street was lined with cars, expensive ones too, from Mercedes to Cadillacs to Range Rovers. Could Tim Chase and Gwen Owens be having a party? Might this not be the intimate evening that Todd had envisioned? Taking the first space, Todd pulled over and parked. Up ahead on the right he saw well-heeled people streaming into a massive Tudor house; one of Tim Chase's neighbors was evidently having quite the bash.

But, no, Todd told himself as he climbed out of his truck, a roll in the hay with Tim Chase wasn't impossible, it was outrageously impossible. Tim Chase wasn't simply one of the most famous actors in the world, he was also gorgeous. And rich. If in fact he was gay—after all, he could have been playing with Todd last night, rehearsing as he said—he could have the most beautiful of queer men. So why in the world would he want Todd, who was not only in his forties and eight or nine years older than him, but also not a stunning, drop-dead Calvin Klein beauty? There was no way. Perhaps Todd was soon going to learn the secrets of Tim Chase's personal life, but, he realized, there was no way in hell they were going to have sex. It just wasn't going to happen.

Besides, there was Rawlins.

Or was there? It seemed quite obvious that Rawlins was not only unable to maintain a monogamous relationship, but that he had also broken their compromise agreement of pledging to tell the truth. So now what? There was nothing else—least of all, no other laws or ceremonies—binding them, so if Todd couldn't count on Rawlins for the simple truth, then did he really want him at all? As he was buzzed through the gate and started up the front walk, Todd realized once again that what he wanted was not a lover whom he could trust in some suburban sense, but someone who couldn't help but be totally honest. Exactly. In a restless world like this one Todd wanted something stable, a rock, someone he could count on. The sad thing was that now it was going to be so very, very tough to get back to the beginning, to what they had before. Love, lust, passion—that was one side of a relationship. The other was trust, honesty, and respect—the three of which operated in a delicate, mysterious balance and that were, once violated, all but impossible to reset. Perhaps time could both repair and restart what Todd and Rawlins had so recently had, but. . . .

As he approached the huge front door, Todd checked his watch, saw that he was almost fifteen minutes overdue. Perhaps that was nothing by the standards of the coasts, but in the Midwest, particularly Minnesota, that was significant. Well, thought Todd, he was just glad to be here.

As he climbed the first of three steps, the door swung open, and there she stood in tight, worn blue jeans and a baggy white T-shirt, Mrs. Tim Chase, better known throughout the world, of course, as Gwen Owens. She wore her beauty as she wore her clothes, with casual ease, and she looked right into Todd's eyes and smiled at him as if they were old friends.

"Hi, Todd, come on in."

"Hi," he said, still feeling nothing short of sheepish for last night's escapades with her husband. "Sorry I'm a few minutes late."

"Don't be silly, you're not at all late. Tim's in the living room—he's been on the phone with his attorney for the last forty minutes. I think he spends half his time either filing a lawsuit or defending himself against one."

"Really?" replied Todd as he passed through the vestibule and into the huge entry hall.

"Yeah," continued Gwen, her walk and manner entirely easy, "now I think he's trying to take some photographer to court, some guy who actually blocked Tim as he was pulling out of a parking space. You know, trapped him so he couldn't move, which really pissed him off. Apparently the photographer was going after a picture of Tim and some guy."

Todd's reporter ears perked up. Some guy? Some guy like who?

"Anyway, you can just go in. He'll be off in a minute." Gwen shut the inner door, then turned and started for the huge staircase at the far end of the entry hall. "Nice to see you. Take care."

"You're not joining us?" he asked with feigned innocence.

"Me? No," she replied with a coy smile as if to say, Who are you trying to kid? "Maggie and I are going out for a while."

What the hell, wondered Todd, did that mean?

From the wood-paneled entry hall, which in itself was as big as a ballroom, Todd headed left into the living room. Tim Chase sat on the large couch facing the fireplace, a telephone to his ear. Glancing over, he raised one hand in a big, familiar hello.

"Okay, Art, that's cool. Yeah, you do that. Get it all written up and Fed-Ex it out. I'll take a look at it right away, just as soon as it gets here. Listen, I gotta go. A friend just stopped by for dinner."

Standing there on the edge of the room, still wearing his black leather coat, Todd couldn't help but take note. A friend? He didn't much feel like one. In fact, for some reason he felt almost uncomfortable and, he realized, certainly more nervous than he had yesterday.

Chase paused as his attorney obviously said something, then added, "Yeah, you too. And say hi to Leslie."

He hung up, dropping the receiver into the base, then puffed up his cheeks and exhaled all at once. A half-second later he turned to Todd, flashing that grin that could light up a city.

"My life is so fucking complicated I can't believe it." As he placed the phone to a side table, he said, "I can't use a cordless phone or even a cellular, at least not for anything serious. I've had people try to listen into my conversations. I mean, they did it to Prince Charles, listened while he supposedly told Camille what's-her-face that he wanted to come back as a Tampax for her use."

"Doesn't sound very appealing to me."

"Straight people—what can I say?" Shaking his head and laughing, Chase pushed himself to his feet. "Hey, where are my manners? Let me take your coat."

Like his wife's, Tim Chase's good looks were by no means forced or contrived, but rather natural, even casual, in an all-American, boyish kind of way. He too wore jeans that were somehow perfectly worn and that fit him like a leather glove. Again, tonight he sported no shoes, only white socks. And a simple shirt, off-white with a light plaid pattern of black threads. His hair was rich and brown and glossy and perfectly cut. And that smile, that unbelievable smile that seemed so genuine, that seemed to say he was glad Todd was here. Could it be true?

As Todd started to lift off his coat, a shot of pain zipped through him, and he flinched and grimaced. He closed his eyes for a moment, realized that he shouldn't have come.

"Hey, are you alright?" asked Chase, coming over.

"Well . . . it's been kind of a long day."

Chase's smile vanished and a look of concern washed over him. He reached for Todd's coat, then peered at the side of Todd's head.

"Man, what did you do, fall off a horse?"

"Something like that, anyway."

"You got a pretty good bruise going on up there." Not hesitating, Chase reached up, gingerly touching Todd's head.

As Chase's fingertips skimmed across his skin, Todd grabbed him by the wrist, and said, "Ouch."

"Sorry. Are you going to be okay?"

"Yeah, I think so, but maybe I shouldn't have come. Maybe I . . . I . . ."

"What the hell happened?"

Todd wondered if he should get into it, but found himself saying, "I've been covering this murder story, the one about the gay kid who was murdered."

His face went blank. "Yeah?"

"Well, I got a call from that kid's father, and—"

"You're kidding?"

"No, and he asked me to meet him and . . . and we kind of got into a scuffle."

"Jesus, you should have called the police."

"I tried. His line was busy."

Tim looked at Todd with a grin. "What?"

"Nothing."

Helping Todd off with his coat, he said, "Let me guess, you didn't win."

"That obvious?"

"Yep. Now, come on, follow me. I know just what will make you feel better."

Without hesitation Chase wrapped his fingers around Todd's wrist and led him toward a dry bar on the side of the room. As they walked Todd looked down, saw that the cuff of Tim's shirt was rolled back a couple of times, exposing a meaty forearm covered with a fine grove of dark hair. In his gut Todd felt something smolder and spark.

The bar was a gilded wooden chest with a green marble top, and on it sat a silver ice bucket cradling a bottle of white wine. Next to that was a plate of artfully arranged food.

"Do you like shellfish?" asked Chase.

"You're belying your Midwestern roots—I've never heard that question anywhere but here."

"Right, this is the land of the tuna fish casserole."

"Up here we don't use such fancy words—we call it a hot dish."

"Ah, Minnesota—call it like it is." Chase laughed. "God, I get so sick of the bullshit in California. This place may be a little naive—"

"The land of the bland, you mean."

"Maybe, but at the same time it's pretty straightforward. I miss that. I'm so sick of people sucking up to me. I'm so sick of people pretending to be my friends. It's just so fake, so unreal, that sometimes, well, I forget who I am."

Todd couldn't resist. "So who are you?"

Looking straight at him, Chase said, "What an odd sense I get from you."

"Don't forget, I'm a reporter, and reporters always have ulterior motives."

"Ah, yes. A good point. So, let me remind you, all of this is still off the record. Agreed?"

"Agreed," replied Todd, knowing that unless he wanted to be shown to the door he had no choice.

"So what we have here is a plate of mussels, first grilled outside, then doused with garlic butter and chopped tomatoes." Tim picked up the plate in one hand, two wineglasses in the other. "Now, grab that bucket of wine and follow me."

"Where are we going?"

"To ease your wounds."

They made a small train, the two of them, Todd following Tim Chase out of the extravagant living room and then down the enormous entry hall toward the back of the house. Todd presumed they were going to a back porch of some sort, yet Todd couldn't help but be suspect.

He asked, "Why are you doing this?"

"Doing what?"

"Being nice to me."

"Because I like you."

No, Todd wasn't going to take this, being baited, and he said, "What the hell does that mean?"

"It means that you're sincere and honest. It means that you don't say pate or terrine or flan or even casserole. You say hot dish. And it means that this wonderful kingdom of fame and fortune in which I live is nothing more than a gilded prison."

"What are you implying, that you're lonely?"

"Yeah, as a matter of fact I am. I'm lonely for intelligent company instead of an army of bimbo wannabes." Throwing a curve, Chase added, "And I want to hang out with a gay man."

"Are you taunting me?"

Glancing over his shoulder with a smirk, he said, "No, I'm playing a gay man from the Midwest and I need to do some homework."

"Oh, so I'm still research?"

"As I am to you."

"Touché."

At the rear of the hall they headed not out the rear door, not up the curving staircase to the right, but down the stairs to the left, which descended in a wide curve. Carrying the frosted wine in the silver bucket, Todd silently followed after the leading man, taking the low, even steps around and down to the basement. Reaching for a brass plate mounted on a wall of mahogany paneling, Tim hit a bank of light switches, the old-fashioned push-button kind, which he poked one after another. Brass sconces came to life, lighting up a room that was filled with the latest gym equipment, from stair machines to racks of free weights. Todd looked around until he saw a wall of French doors and beyond them a swimming pool, the one he'd heard about. Yes, not only did it obviously exist, it was beautiful. And it was no concrete tub, not by any means. Tim led the way over, pulled open two of the glass doors, and exposed a robber baron's swimming pool, none too large, but completely lined with small pearly-white tiles, from the bottom of the pool, up and around the deck, up the walls, and across the ceiling. Four large brass fixtures mounted on the walls lit the chamber.

"Amazing," said Todd.

"Isn't it great? It was built when the house was—1901—but this," said Chase, leaning around to a panel and flicking more switches, "was added a few years ago."

In an instant he brought to life the bubbling power of a hot tub, which sat off the far end of the pool and in front of four French doors that led outside.

"Come on. It'll make you feel great."

Todd glanced over at the swirling mass of water, not sure that any of this was really happening. Biting his trepidation and holding his tongue, he continued after Chase, who made his way along the narrow tile deck. When he reached the far end of the pool, Chase put the plate down on a small metal table, then grabbed a couple of mussels and sucked them down. He groaned with pleasure, put down the wineglasses, then turned and took the wine from Todd.

Pouring them each a glass, he handed one to Todd, then held his up. "Cheers, man."

"To your health."

Taking a sip, Todd eyed Tim Chase as he took a long, luxuriant drink. Then Todd watched as the other started unbuttoning his shirt.

"Don't just stand there," said Chase, pulling his shirt out of his pants. "Come on."

"We're really doing this?"

"Of course."

"But I don't have a suit."

Chase looked at Todd as if he were crazy. "Well, neither do I." He stopped still, snapped his fingers, and said, "Which reminds me."

Moving quickly, Chase went to the four French doors that looked outside and shut the miniblinds that covered them.

"You never know," said Chase. "The yard falls away in the rear of the house and these windows look out over a patio and the backyard. And you never know when some photographer is going to be lurking out there. The last thing I want is my naked ass all over the Internet."

"It's kind of like you're being spied on all the time, isn't it?"

"That's the story of my life."

As Todd watched, the star continued to strip, unbuttoning his shirt, then unzipping his jeans. So? So Todd started to disrobe too. He put down his glass of wine, pulled out his shirttails, and thought how no one was going to believe this. No one. A little smirk crossed his mouth. He was getting naked in that tub of boiling water with Tim Chase? Good fucking grief.

Feeling like a naughty schoolboy, Todd stole a glance out of the corner of his eye, and saw an incredible body, the best that Hollywood could buy. Surely sculpted by a personal trainer, Tim Chase's body was as muscular as it was lean, with every muscle on his arms defined and bulging, a beefy and taut smooth chest, and a six-pack of muscles on his abdomen. More than a box-office body, it was a muscle queen's, and Todd, who was in no shabby shape, paled in comparison.

"The truth of it," said Chase as he peeled away his faded jeans, "is that it's like being in Russia or China or North Korea, with everyone spying on my every move, wanting to report this or that."

Todd reached for the top button of his pants, then started to unzip. "It sounds awful."

"You know what—it is."

Chase was naked in a second, and Todd tried not to stare. Nevertheless, his eyes went right to the target, and he saw a bush of brown pubic hair surrounding what appeared to be not a box-office, larger-than-life organ, but a mere normal-sized penis. Right, thought Todd. He's just a guy. Yet Todd couldn't help watching as the clothes-less Chase placed the plate of mussels by the whirlpool, grabbed his glass of wine, then slowly descended into the hot water.

Todd dropped his pants and underwear, sucked in his waist, then naked, casually took his glass of wine. As he approached the mass of bubbling water he realized Tim wasn't even looking at him. No, he was sitting deep in the water with his head leaned back against the edge and his eyes closed. So either Todd did nothing to elicit his fantasies, he was playing it very, very cool, or . . . or Tim Chase was in fact straight.

Either way, Todd instinctively understood he was about to find out.

Chapter 36

After he paid for his beer at Jam's, Rawlins returned to his car, climbed in, and wondered what in the hell he should do next. He jabbed his car key into the ignition and was about to fire up the engine, but then instead pulled his phone from the pocket of his jacket. Yet again he tried Todd's cell phone and yet again he tried the condo, failing to get an answer at either number. Rawlins then called his voice mail down at CID, finding to his surprise that Todd had in fact called. Pressing the small phone to his ear, Rawlins listened both carefully and nervously.

"Hey, Rawlins, it's me, Todd. I'm okay . . . I think. It's a long story—I'll tell you later—but obviously we have a lot of things to talk about. Listen, I've got to meet someone in a few minutes. I'll call you back later."

More than stunned, Rawlins played the message a second and a third time. What the hell was going on? Unsure, Rawlins flicked off the phone, dropped the slim plastic device onto his lap, then just sat there in the parking lot, as angry as he was fearful that one of the greatest things in his life had already started to unravel. Where the hell was Todd? What was he doing? And what did any of this mean?

His phone began to chirp, which shocked Rawlins out of any kind of funk that he'd been about to tumble into. Praying that it was Todd, he snatched up the receiver.

"Yeah?"

"Hey, it's me, Foster."

"Oh, right, hi."

"Did your guy show yet? Is he with you?"

"What? Ah, no." Grabbing and tugging at his hair with his right hand, Rawlins glanced around the parking lot. "The whole deal kind of fell apart. I'll tell you about it later."

"Well, then, let's do it."

"Do what?"

"Let's do like we talked about. Let's see what we can learn about Victor Michael Radzinsky."

Right, thought Rawlins, now recalling. That was their plan, to go right up to that place. That was what they had discussed. Just a few questions, that was all, namely what connection did Radzinsky have to that house and where was he the night Andrew Lyman was murdered?

"Okay," said Rawlins. "I'll come pick you up. Where are you? Down at City Hall?"

"No, I'm at Christo's getting something to eat. You wanna bite? You had dinner yet?"

"No, I haven't." Rawlins tried to clear his head. "Why don't you order me something? I'll be there in ten minutes."

"Got ya."

Rawlins hung up, dropped the phone on the seat next to him, then started up his car and headed off. A quick bite, then a visit to a house supposedly leased by Tim Chase. At least that would be interesting. Who knew, perhaps he'd even get a chance to meet the star himself.

About an hour later, taking Foster's big brown Crown Victoria, they turned up the gently arching Mount Curve Avenue and found it lined with cars.

"Must be a wedding or something going on," commented Foster as he pulled over and parked.

"Yeah," mumbled Rawlins, scanning the street for either a white Saab or, for that matter, Todd's Jeep Grand Cherokee. "So how are we going to do this?"

"Let's just ask for Victor Radzinsky and take it from there."

"That's not much of a plan."

"You got a better one?"

"No."

When they reached the front iron gate, Rawlins turned the handle and found it, of course, locked. Wondering if this was as far as they were going to get, he then pressed the button on the intercom box.

A moment later a man's deep voice called, "May I help you?"

Rawlins nodded to Foster, who stepped up to the small box and said, "We'd like to speak with Victor Radzinsky. Is he there?"

There was a distinct pause before the voice replied, saying, "Who is this?"

"I'm Sergeant Neal Foster and I'm here with Sergeant Steve Rawlins. We're from the Minneapolis Police Department, and we'd like to ask Mr. Radzinsky a few questions. Can we come in?"

"Ah, just a minute. I'll see."

It was a long minute, three or four actually. Either there was a little conference going on or they'd been blown off, and Rawlins was about to lean on the intercom button again when he heard something up at the house and saw the front door pulled open. And there he was, their guy, Victor Michael Radzinsky, stepping outside. Rawlins recognized him in an instant.

"That's him," said Rawlins quietly, peering through the thick iron bars at the shaved-headed man.

"Well, well, well."

He was a fairly large guy, there was no doubt about that, with a thick neck and broad shoulders. As if he'd been pumping a lot of iron, he walked stiffly, and his dark clothes looked expensive.

Keeping his voice low, Foster said, "Looks like a friendly guy, eh?"

Radzinsky took his own time, stopping just a couple of feet short of the gate. He looked at them in the fading light, cocked his head to the side.

"How may I help you?"

"Are you Victor Michael Radzinsky?" asked Rawlins.

"So?"

"Is that you?"

"Yes, but of what interest is that to you?"

Rawlins pulled out his badge and held it up. "I'm Sergeant Steve Rawlins with the Minneapolis Police Department, and this is my partner, Sergeant Neal Foster."

"Nice to meet you, I'm sure. What can I do for you?"

"For starters," began Foster, "there's speeding and reckless driving. There's also endangerment. Plus there's the fact that you were evading two police officers."

"What?" he asked, cracking a small, nervous smile. "I'm afraid I don't understand."

"That was us behind you this afternoon," said Rawlins. "We were in that silver car, you were in the white Saab."

"That was you chasing me?"

"Yeah, no shit, that was us."

He smiled. He smiled a naughty grin, looked down at the ground, and ran one hand over the moonlike dome of his head.

"I'm very sorry. We've been having some problems and I thought you were someone else."

"Like who?" asked Rawlins.

"A photographer—the so-called paparazzi. Unfortunately, we get them all the time, chasing us in cars, hanging from trees, dressing up like mailmen and coming up to the house. You see, I work for someone very important, someone who's quite—"

"We know, Tim Chase."

"Right. Exactly right. I'm in charge of his security, and I thought you were trying to take pictures of me or something."

Clearly not amused, Foster said, "You nearly sideswiped a school bus. Someone could've been badly hurt."

"Yes, well . . ."

"Mr. Radzinsky," said Rawlins, cutting in, "where were you on the night of September twenty-second?"

"When?"

"That's three nights ago. Where were you at approximately ten-thirty that evening?"

"I don't know. Here, I suppose."

"A witness saw a white Saab with California plates down at Lake Harriet. That car is registered to you, and the witness saw someone who matches your description throw a knife into the water. We've since recovered that knife, and our forensics lab is now testing it to see if that was the weapon used to kill a teenager by the name of Andrew Lyman earlier that—"

"Please, gentlemen," pleaded Radzinsky, smiling nervously and holding up both hands. "You've got the wrong guy."

"I'm not so sure we do."

Foster stepped right up to the gate and grabbed onto one of the bars. "Listen, we need some nice, simple answers."

"And we could," added Rawlins, "arrest you right now for that little escapade this afternoon. Reckless endangerment and evading an officer are two charges that come to mind."

"Is that what you'd like? Shall we take you downtown, where we can have a nice, long, serious talk?"

"Please, let's not be too hasty," replied Radzinsky, reaching up and unlocking the gate. "Perhaps you'd like to come in and speak to my employer, Mr. Chase?"

Chapter 37

It wasn't easy for Todd to relax. In fact, sitting naked in a hot tub with such a famous person made Todd, if anything, more tense. After all, where was this headed and why were they even in here at all?

Placing his wineglass on the edge of the tub, he sank into the hot water all the way up to his neck, paused, then slipped down until it was up to his chin. Directly across from him sat Tim Chase, his head tilted back against a cushion, the water churning and whirling up and around him.

"God, isn't this the greatest?" groaned Chase, his eyes closed and a contented grin on his face. "Did you find the jets?"

Todd reached behind his back, felt a shot of water, and slid over. "Yeah."

"This should make you feel better in no time. Is it hot enough for you? I can turn up the temperature."

"Actually, it's perfect."

"Good."

Todd stared right at him. Or rather he stared right at Chase's body, but the churning bubbles were so thick his eyes couldn't see beneath the surface.

He asked, "Have you been using this thing much?"

"No. This is something like only the second time."

"Really?"

"Yeah, but I have a scene like this in the movie we're shooting. My character, Rich, goes to visit an old friend, who's now married, and they have this sort of awkward encounter in a hot tub."

"Oh, so that's what this is all about," said Todd. "The two of us—you a married man, me gay—in a hot tub. Is that why you suggested this?"

"Well, you did get yourself a little beat-up, but like I've said, I do need to do some more research."

"Ah, the ulterior motive."

"Something like that, anyway." Tim opened his eyes and gazed over at Todd. "Hey, I should ask if you've ever slept with a married man."

Todd thought for a moment, then replied. "I really haven't had that many sexual partners, but I have done it once with a married guy. Well, kind of, that is."

"And?"

"And what?"

"Well, how was it?"

"In a word, humiliating."

And that it most certainly was. Todd recalled the cheesy motel room they rented, the awkward attempt at intimacy, the dirty aftertaste.

"Why was that?" asked Chase.

"Well, it wasn't my idea. Sure, I was attracted to him. He was an old friend in Chicago, Mike, and we got together and went to a Cubs game. Somehow it came up. Somehow he said he was afraid that he might be gay. I told him I had the same worries. Actually, this was when I was married too. I didn't really want to try it, but one thing led to another. I don't know, he really pushed for it. He was quite aggressive."

"So what happened?"

"Of course I had to pay for the motel room because Mike didn't have enough cash and he was afraid his wife would see his credit card bill. Anyway, we went to this dump and . . . and nothing much happened. In the end we both got an answer, each of them different."

"What do you mean?"

"Well, lo and behold, he literally couldn't get it up for another guy."

"But you could?"

"Exactly, which left me kind of excited and exposed in front of a guy who realized he was, after all, straight. It was embarrassing for me, to say the least, and we never spoke again. Last I heard he was still married, but I got divorced soon thereafter."

Todd sat up a bit and twisted around. He grabbed hold of one of the jets and tried to turn it, but the thing wouldn't budge.

"What's the matter?" asked Tim.

"I was just trying to aim this thing but it's stuck."

"Yeah, they can be a little tough. Here, let me help you."

Before Todd knew it, Tim Chase had floated over and the two of them were side by side, their wet arms sliding up against each other as they worked at the jet. In a second the device twisted in one direction.

"There, that's great," said Todd as his heart broke from a walk to a trot.

Todd pulled back, sitting right where he had before. Tim didn't return to the other side, but instead sat down so that his shoulder butted up against Todd's. Todd looked over, saw the other man smiling back, and then, unseen beneath the churning water, felt a hand on his thigh. Against Todd's will, a rush of desire stormed through him and his heart proceeded from trot to gallop.

"Tim," said Todd, his voice low and unsteady, "what are you doing?"

"Research, remember?"

"But—"

"Shh. The trouble with reporters is that they don't know how to listen."

Oh, yes, Todd was aroused, very much so. But he wasn't going to be so exposed and left so stupidly vulnerable like that time so many years ago after the Cubs game. No, and he wasn't going to be used, and he slid his hands down over his crotch. Besides, what did he himself really want and what was he tempting by simply being here?

But then . . .

Then he glanced over at gorgeous Tim Chase and his last de-

fenses vanished. Yes, he could fall real hard for this guy, and a hot little voice in his head cooed: why shouldn't you? After all, Rawlins had
had his fun, so why shouldn't he?

The next moment Todd felt Tim lean over and start kissing him on
the neck, the ear. Todd closed his eyes and tumbled into it, into him.
Yes, he could fall real, real hard.

"Tim, I—"

"If I were a gay man seducing someone else in a hot tub, is this
how I'd do it?"

"Well . . ."

"Well?"

"Yes, I'd say you were doing pretty . . ." Todd felt a hand slither
across his stomach and slide up his chest. ". . . Pretty damn well."

But was this just a game? Was he just being used?

"Tim, maybe I'm too much of a Midwesterner to understand, but
you just gotta tell me if this is what people in Hollywood call research
or . . . " said Todd, trying to throw up a last line of defense. "No, you
just gotta tell me—are you or aren't you gay?"

"Fuck labels."

Right, thought Todd. Screw 'em. And he turned into Tim, embraced him, clutched him in a desperate, almost hungry way. The other
man hugged back, and Todd couldn't believe it, couldn't believe he was
in this mass of swirling water, his heart and his body pounding with
want and lust for him, for Tim Chase, and that Chase was actually returning the passion.

Or was he? Couldn't it all be simply . . . acting?

Determined not to be duped, Todd's hand drifted down the other
man's side and to his waist, groping for that so-called thermometer, determined to know how it would read, knowing that a man's mind and
mouth could lie buckets, but the ever-honest penis could not. And sensing Chase's taut, rippled stomach in the water, Todd lowered his hand,
but Chase, realizing the destination of Todd's wayward grope, scooted
back.

Looking suddenly, even oddly, worried, Chase said, "Just take it easy there, champ."

"But . . ."

"Not too fast, okay?"

Now it was Todd's turn to pull back, and Todd, not without a bit of anger in his voice, softly demanded, "Tim, quit screwing with my head. What's going on here?"

"Off the record?"

"Of course."

"You just never know. I mean, I've just gotten kind of gun-shy, you know? And you—here I am sitting naked with a reporter of a people. I mean, my publicist and my lawyers would have a fit."

"You have nothing to worry about from me. I swear to that."

"I'm sorry, but you don't know what it's like. I've just gotten burned a few too many times."

The way he said it, the way his brow wrinkled and those beautiful eyebrows pinched together—well, Todd didn't doubt him. Not for an instant. Of all the things to feel at this particular moment, the last and the least Todd expected was a flood of pity.

"Really, it's okay. You have my word."

"Thank you," said Chase. "Thank you very much. I have very few safe harbors, very, very few."

Tim reached into the water and pulled up first Todd's right hand and then his left, both of which he clutched between his. Then softly yet firmly he placed his lips on Todd's hands and kissed them, his eyes all the while staring deep into the molten well of Todd's desire. Something, he didn't know what, shot through Todd, and he just sat there, not even flinching, for he found himself transfixed as much by the intensity of the moment as by its lack of pretense. Yes, there sat the two men in that pool of hot water, naked in every sense of the word. Finally, after what almost became a painful length of silence, Tim kissed Todd's hands once again, and then his lips moved, started to explain, to divulge the hidden truth of Tim Chase, Inc. At that very instant, however, every bit of him seized up as a herd of footsteps entered the far end of the pool room.

A deep voice from across the pool gasped, "Oh, shit."

Todd knew that butch, sonorous voice, and as if this were some sort of pathetic soap opera, he spun around, saw not one but three men standing there on the far side of the pool. And one of them, of course, was his erstwhile lover. The next moment, practically flailing in the water, both Todd and Chase were pushing away from each other.

"Rawlins, what . . ." gasped Todd in a panic. "What the hell are you doing here?"

Rawlins stood there, his face frozen in shock. He went to say something, then stopped. He stared at Todd, shook his head, and then turned and stormed out. As the water churned around him, Todd started to get up, but then sank down beneath the churning water, for not only was he nude, his arousal had yet to deflate.

Furious, Chase practically leapt out, shouting, "Vic, what the fuck are you doing barging in?"

"Sorry, but ah . . . we have a situation here."

"No, Vic, we don't have a situation—you do!"

Chapter 38

If there'd been lust in Todd's gut, now there was simply a terribly potent stew of guilt and shame and regret that Todd, in an instant, had been forced to consume in its entirety and that had left him feeling nothing short of sick, sick, sick.

He could barely pull himself out of the whirlpool, let alone stand and pull on his clothes. But he had no choice. The strength of his remorse pushed him onward, and, dripping wet, he pulled on his pants, shirt, socks, and shoes, and then went hurrying around the edge of the robber baron's pool.

Grabbing Todd by the arm at the far end, Foster, in that gruff voice of his, said, "Let him go."

"No."

Not for an instant. Glaring at Rawlins's work partner, he pulled himself free, then hurried out of the pool room, through the exercise room, up that big staircase, and through that enormous hall of the *très riche*. As if it were some cheap screen door, Todd hurled open the oversized front door with its precious stained glass and dashed out into the cool night. Rawlins stood at the far end of the walk, his head bowed as he hung on to the thick black iron bars of the gate. As Todd approached, his pace began to slow and his heart began to shake.

"Rawlins, I'm . . . I'm sorry."

Without looking up, Rawlins said, "An appointment, an interview . . . or a date? What the hell was that, Todd?"

"Nothing, that's what it was."

"Oh, really? Is that what you call doing tub tricks?"

"Listen, Rawlins, I wasn't looking for it. And besides, it's not like anything really happened."

"At least not yet, right? Gee, that makes me feel so much better."

"Do you know who that is? That's Tim Chase, for God's sake, and he—"

"So you couldn't pass up the opportunity, right?"

"No, but—"

"You're just a star fucker, aren't you? That's all you are, a media whore desperately climbing some ladder."

Todd stared right at him and said it as deeply and thoughtfully as he could: "Fuck you, Rawlins."

"Yeah, well, fuck you too, you asshole!"

The remorse was gone, vanished. Todd turned to the side, looked across the gazillion-dollar lawn. The oaks, dark and massive, loomed overhead in judgment. No, he wasn't going to take this. No way in hell. And so he pulled out his own vial of poisoned knowledge.

"You know what, Rawlins, I'll tell you every little detail about Tim Chase. Everything. I'll be completely honest with you because, after all, that was our agreement, right? That was the ground rule of our relationship, correct?"

Rawlins turned to him, his eyes smoldering with hate.

"I'll tell you all about what happened between me and Tim Chase . . . if you tell me all about you and Andrew Lyman. Deal?"

"What? How the hell do you—"

"I know everything. Jordy told me. Remember him? Jordy, Andrew's previous boyfriend? He was really upset by you stealing Andrew. I know that Andrew was in love with you, that you two were quite intimate, and that—"

"You don't know shit!"

"What don't I know? That Andrew Lyman was a minor? That you could be charged with criminal sexual conduct? Or what? That you didn't mean for it to happen? What did you do, suck him? Fuck him?

Just what in the hell were you thinking? For Christ's sake, he was only seventeen!"

"Stop it!" Rawlins covered his eyes with his left hand and turned back to the gate, shaking his head and saying, "Oh, God." He took a deep breath and exhaled. "It's just so complicated."

"No shit."

"Todd, you've got to believe me, you don't know what this has been like, what . . ." His back to Todd, he leaned on the gate with both hands. "I went to his apartment that afternoon, just a few hours before he was killed. And something did happen, but not what you think. I wanted to tell you too, but when? I mean, I went over there about one-thirty, then I went on duty at three, and then . . . then he was killed and I was assigned to the case. There just hasn't been the right time for us to sit down and talk!"

Sensing that the truth, whatever it was, had indeed been torturing him, Todd said, "Rawlins, if something's hurting you, it's hurting me more. We're not going to last, we're not going to make it, if we have to choose when to hold back and when to give. Those are supposed to be automatic."

And now it was just that, automatic. Rawlins couldn't keep it bottled up, not a moment longer, that much was obvious.

"So . . . so I went over there, over to his apartment. Andrew was really upset. Someone had been over there—I'm still not sure who—and Andrew was crying. I mean, just bawling. So what was I supposed to do, just turn around and walk out on him like every other adult in his life had done? No, I couldn't. I just took him in my arms and held him and told him everything would be okay."

Todd kept his attention focused on the bull's-eye, asking, "Nothing sexual had happened before this?"

"God, no. Nothing. Nothing at all—and that afternoon it was the last thing on my mind. I was just trying to help him. I was just trying to be a good role model to him, that's all." His back still to Todd, he took a deep breath. "But it wasn't quite like that for him. I mean, I had crushes on older guys when I was a kid too. I wanted to sleep with my gym teacher in the worst way, so I should have seen it coming. I should have seen it in his eyes." Rawlins reached into his coat pocket and pulled out a small red spiral notebook. "It's all in here."

"What's that?"

"Andrew's diary—I stole it from his apartment after he was killed. He was writing in it just before I came over. He was writing how much he loved me and that he had seen it in my eyes, the lust. I mean, maybe I had looked at him admiringly." He paused. "What do I mean, maybe? Of course I did. How could any gay man not? Andrew was perfect. But I never wanted to seduce him and . . . and I never wanted him to fall in love with me." Rawlins sighed. "But . . . but he did, and that's what he last wrote in his diary. That he was in love with me, that I was coming over in just a few minutes, and that he was sure we were finally going to do it, have sex."

Todd stuffed his hands into his pockets and stood there staring at Rawlins. "So what happened?"

"I held him and then . . . then he started rubbing me, caressing my back. I mean, I knew in a second what was going on and . . ."

"Andrew, I . . . I . . ."

"God, you're so sexy."

"Don't," said Rawlins, *pushing him back. "We can't do that. I'm your mentor and I'm your friend."*

"Oh, come on. I won't tell."

"You're a great kid, but I'm much older than you. And nothing can happen between us."

"I want you," grinned Andrew, *flashing his white teeth as he reached out with his right hand. "I want to touch your hairy arms. I want to touch your hairy chest. Do you know how much you turn me on?"*

"Andrew, don't," said Rawlins, *gently pulling away.*

"What's the matter, don't you like me?"

"Of course I do—that's not the point."

Confused, Andrew stared into Rawlins's eyes, not at all sure what to do. The next moment he reached down and grabbed hold of his T-shirt, yanked it over his head, and whipped it off. Stunned, Rawlins stared at the most beautiful young man he'd ever seen, his shoulders thick and broad, his chest firm and ripe, and that stomach so lean and flat. Everything in Rawlins's mind screamed no, but everything in his crotch stirred and shouted yes.

"I'm not so bad, am I?" begged Andrew.

"No . . . no, you're beautiful."

His eyes bugging with excitement and want, Andrew then grabbed at the top of his jeans, unbuttoned them, and shoved them halfway down his thighs. Surrounded by glowing light brown pubic hair, his cock, already thick and strong and hard, sprang out.

Laughing, Andrew said, "Well, I'm ready."

A movie flashed through Rawlins's head. He saw himself pulling Andrew into his embrace, kissing him, rubbing his hands all over that Adonis of lust. Did it get any better? And so Rawlins did in fact reach out. He put his hand flat on Andrew's most perfect of chests.

But then he swallowed deep and pushed Andrew gently back, saying, "No, Andrew, we can't. It's not right. I've got to go."

"But!"

"I'll call you later. You're a wonderful kid and you're as sexy as hell, but we can't."

"No, don't go!" Andrew pleaded.

"Bye . . ."

"I was going to tell you right away," said Rawlins now, "but then I went on middle watch and then . . . then he was killed."

Todd stood there, staring down at the dark blades of grass as he tried to digest Rawlins's story. Did he believe him? He heard the pain and the earnestness seeping out of Rawlins, but . . . but he'd seen it so clearly the other way. Was Rawlins really that strong, could he actually have touched such naked temptation and turned away from it?

Footsteps coming from the house broke Todd's thoughts. He turned, saw Neal Foster, his gait stiff and awkward, coming their way. Both Todd and Rawlins fell into a kind of silence that was instinctual to any gay man when talking about sex and the exploits thereof.

"Rawlins, I hate to break up this little scene of domestic bliss," Foster said in his usual dry manner, "but you need to come inside. You gotta hear all this."

"Sure. I'll be right there."

Todd and Rawlins stood shrouded in silence as Foster made his way back to the house and disappeared inside.

Finally, Todd said, "I think my head's going to explode."

"Todd, you have to believe me—that's the truth. I didn't screw Andrew."

"But . . . but I'm not sure if . . ."

"Don't you see, don't you get it? That's my point exactly—if even you, the person I love more than anything else in this world, is having trouble believing me, what about everyone else? What about the police force? What about the media? If this ever got out there'd be a witch hunt. At the very least I'd be suspended and put under investigation, and then it'd come out somehow, some way, that I'm HIV-positive and then I'd be fired, I'm sure of it. And why? Because no one would believe my story. No one would believe that the gay cop wasn't a pervert—after all, everyone knows all gays are perverts, right?—and that he didn't screw the beautiful young farmboy. And they probably wouldn't even believe that I didn't murder him just to keep the truth from coming out."

"Yeah, maybe," agreed Todd, knowing the hysteria would feed precisely along those lines.

"Not maybe, definitely. You know damn well that's how it would go. Every fucking macho cop would want to shoot me on the spot, and every hungry person in the media would be trying to hang me. The charges alone would ruin my life."

Yes, they most surely would. There was, Todd pondered, no question about that.

Foster leaned out the front door of the house and called: "Rawlins, get your butt in here!"

"I'm coming!" he shouted back.

"Rawlins, I don't know what to think. I don't know if I need to apologize for that," Todd said, waving the back of his hand at the house and wondering just how big a fool he'd been. "Or . . . or . . . I mean, I thought you'd slept with Andrew, so that meant I could . . . well, you know . . ."

"We'll talk."

"Sure, but I gotta get some rest. And God only knows how late you'll be working tonight. So don't come over and don't call, not tonight. Let's just cool off and we'll talk tomorrow. Okay?"

"Sure."

Todd then simply stood there, watching as the broad-shouldered Rawlins slowly lumbered back to the huge house. Was this, Todd wondered, something from which they could ever recover . . . or was this simply the beginning of the end?

And which did he truly want, or rather who, the movie star or the cop?

Chapter 39

Seated on the big couch in the expansive living room, Rawlins stared at Tim Chase and saw no hero, not by any means. Instead, he saw some rich guy not only trying to save his own neck, but a bastard who'd done his best to shatter Rawlins's world.

"I can bring my lawyer into this if you like," said Chase, his tone calm and cool as he paced slowly in front of them, "but frankly I'd just as soon not. I'm afraid that would blow everything out of proportion, and obviously I'd like to avoid any and all publicity regarding this."

"I can understand and appreciate that," said Foster, who was seated next to Rawlins. "There is the matter, however, of a knife believed to be the weapon used to kill Andrew Lyman. That weapon has been linked to Victor Radzinsky, whom you employ."

"My bodyguard."

"Yes, your bodyguard."

Omitting the fact that it was an anonymous tip, Rawlins said, "We have a witness who saw Radzinsky throw the knife into Lake Harriet. Our witness also can identify Radzinsky's car, a white Saab."

Rawlins kept his eyes on Chase as the actor walked to the fireplace and leaned against the mantel. He stood there in thought for a few long moments, turned, and glanced to the hallway, perhaps wondering if Radzinsky, whom he'd told to wait in the kitchen, was doing just that.

"I'm going to tell you what you'll probably find out anyway," began

Chase after a careful moment of thought. "I'm just going to save you some time."

"We appreciate that," said Foster, sounding about as sincere as a burned-out cop could.

"I'm almost positive the knife you found is mine."

Rawlins, trying to conceal his surprise at so easy an admission, said, "You own a fishing knife?"

"That's right. And I have a rod and a reel. A brown plastic tackle box too. I bought them all here in town just last week because we've been shooting out at Lake Minnetonka. In between scenes I've been fishing a bit—anyone on the set can verify that."

"When did you last use the knife?"

"Actually, I never did. It was brand-new."

Foster asked, "Do you know when you last saw it?"

"Sure, exactly three nights ago."

Which was, Rawlins knew, the night Andrew was killed, and he pressed, "Where was it?"

"In the back of my Land Rover." Chase shook his head. "A little before ten that night I thought I heard something in back of the house. You see, Gwen has had troubles on and off with a stalker, some real twisted guy, and I was worried that maybe he'd shown up here in Minneapolis. So I went out back. I couldn't see anyone, but the side door leading from the patio to the garage was open, so I went in and looked around. Everything looked fine at first. It's a three-car garage, rather big, but at a glance nothing looked wrong. Just to be sure I looked in my car, wondering if someone had broken in and stolen my CD player. It was there, undisturbed. I checked in the back as well and saw my fishing pole and tackle box too. But then I saw something that I hadn't seen before, a plastic bag."

Foster cut in. "What color was it?"

"Dark green."

"Was your vehicle unlocked?" questioned Rawlins.

"Yes, completely. I mean, I never lock it in the garage. Why bother?"

"So what did you do? Where was the bag?"

"The bag was in the back by the rod. It looked like a shoe bag or something, and I wondered if I'd left something back there. So I opened up the rear hatch, reached for the bag, and looked inside. And there was my fishing knife, which I had never used, covered with blood."

"Were you worried?" asked Foster. "Concerned at all?"

"Very worried."

"Why?"

"Because I thought he was back, the guy stalking Gwen."

Rawlins studied him, and said, "What do you mean?"

"We still don't know who he is, but this guy is sick, real sick. Once he left a skinned rabbit on our doorstep in L.A., another time he butchered a cat and sent it in the mail to her. It's all true—you can ask the cops in L.A., they've been right on top of it. And then the last time, he wrote Gwen a love note in human blood. I mean, it was real human blood—the cops analyzed and tested the whole thing. So I saw the knife and assumed it was him again."

Sure this guy was an actor, but no one, thought Rawlins, could make up anything this quick. Or, for that matter, that disgustingly real. Rawlins would have to check with the cops in L.A., but he had no doubt they'd verify Chase's story, at least what they'd heard thus far.

"So what did you do?" Rawlins asked.

"Well, I didn't want to tell Gwen. She'd just gotten here and I didn't want to freak her out. She seemed so relaxed, so calm, so glad to be away from Hollywood, and here I thought this guy had already followed her all the way out here. Maybe that was dumb, maybe it was stupid. I don't know . . ." He shrugged, looked at the floor, and shook his head. "And then . . ."

"Then?"

"I went and talked to Gwen for a few minutes. And then I went and found Vic."

"What did you tell him?"

Storming into Vic's room, Chase said, "That fucking freak has fol-lowed us out here!"

"What do you mean?" said Vic, using the remote to flick off his TV.

"My fishing knife is covered with blood, that's what I mean. It's in a plastic bag in the back of my car. Shit, that asshole was in the garage! He was inside the house, Vic! Inside!"

Vic leapt to his feet. "I'll get him this time."

"Forget it, he's long gone, and we both know it."

"But . . ."

"Just get rid of the knife. I don't want Gwen to see it—it'll scare the hell out of her. I'm going to have to tell her soon enough, but just get rid of it."

"Certainly."

"Just throw it in one of these fucking lakes, I don't care. Just get it out of here."

"So that's what he did," continued Chase, looking right at Foster and Rawlins. "He went down and got the knife, then drove out to one of the lakes and threw the knife in the water. End of story."

No, thought Rawlins. Not quite. Whether all or even part of what Chase had just said was true or not remained to be proven. It did, however, open a host of other questions. Rawlins glanced at Foster and knew he was thinking exactly the same thing.

Foster said, "When did you last use your Land Rover that after-noon?"

"I don't know, five or six."

"And was the green bag back there then?"

"No, I'm positive it wasn't. I returned from the set with an extra set of clothes in the back and I would have noticed the bag if it had been there."

"How about the knife?"

"I don't know. The tackle box I had it stored in was back there, but I didn't look inside it."

"Did anyone use your vehicle after that?"

Tim Chase hesitated, then said, "Actually, Vic did. Sometimes he uses my car just to lead the photographers away from the house, and he went somewhere around seven."

"What about Andrew Lyman?" pressed Rawlins. "Did you ever meet or encounter in any way a young man, age seventeen, by the name of Andrew Lyman?"

Chase stared right at Rawlins, and said, "Please, all I'd like to say is that my private life is confidential. I can assure you, however, that I didn't kill anyone."

"Did you meet him or not?"

"Did I ever meet this kid, this Andrew Lyman? Well," he said, looking across the large room, "I wouldn't be surprised if I had."

"What's that mean?"

"It means I believe I met him once. If I'm not mistaken, he wanted my autograph, that's all."

Studying the face he'd seen and admired so many times on the silver screen, Rawlins wasn't sure at all what to believe. Did he, he wondered, dare trust this man who'd garnered so much fame and fortune by pretending to be other people, in other words, through his ability to lie and to do so beautifully?

On the other hand, Chase might lie but other things definitely wouldn't.

Rawlins said, "Mr. Chase, I just want to let you know that we've recovered a number of foreign hairs and semen samples from both Andrew's body as well as from his apartment. Those samples are now undergoing DNA testing, which I can assure you will tell us a great deal about who Andrew was with just prior to his death." Seeing the cloud of concern sweep across Chase's face, Rawlins added, "So, if we think it necessary, we'll get a search warrant for this house . . . and perhaps for a body search as well."

"What the hell's that mean?"

"It means you could be required to provide us with—"

"What? Hey, now wait a minute, wait just a single fucking minute."

"Oh, I'm very serious. A judge could require you not only to give us a blood sample, but to provide us with a number of cut, combed, and plucked pubic hairs. And I do mean plucked, so that we're sure to get the follicles." Pleased to see him squirm, Rawlins tossed in, "So, is there anything else you'd like to tell us?"

"Ah . . ." began Chase, clearing his throat. "No, not without my lawyer present."

Chapter 40

The following morning Todd realized what he'd known all along, that not only was it a gift to find someone to love, but that a relationship was an extraordinarily fragile thing.

He sat in his office at WLAK, the blinds turned shut and the glass door not only closed but locked. And now it was pushing ten o'clock and Rawlins and he still hadn't spoken since their confrontation outside Chase's mansion last night. Todd wanted to pick up the phone, he wanted nothing more than to call Rawlins, but what in the hell would he say? He simply didn't know, for he was, after all, even more confused than he had been last night. And the reason for that was simple: Tim Chase had called an hour ago not simply to say hi, but to ask Todd to stop by the house again tonight.

Holy shit, why? Why did megastar Tim Chase want to spend a third evening with Todd? And where the hell was this thing going? Todd had no idea, just as he had no idea where he wanted it to go.

Suddenly the phone on his desk started screaming, and Todd all but jumped. Hoping it wasn't a tip caller, he cleared his throat and picked up the receiver.

"WLAK, this is Todd Mills."

"Hey, it's me."

Todd could recognize that deep, easy voice anywhere, anytime. What he didn't recognize, however, was Rawlins's tone, which was all but despondent.

"I just wanted to call and . . . and . . . ," stumbled Rawlins.

"I'm glad you did. I was sitting here, wanting to call you but not knowing what to say."

"So where do we go from here?"

"I don't know."

Bluntly, Rawlins asked, "Are we over?"

"Oh, God," said Todd, pressing the phone flat against his ear and feeling that, perhaps, his heart just might break. "I hope not."

"Me too. I don't want that either."

"But . . ."

"But what?"

"I don't know . . . I'm sorry. Rawlins, I've just got to say that: I'm sorry. You're a wonderful person, the best thing that's ever happened to me, but . . . but suddenly I'm just so confused."

"Why? You don't have to be, you know. You really don't. Things just got a little muddy, but we can go on. We can just sort of learn from this, you know, and move on . . . can't we?"

"Rawlins," ventured Todd, determined to be honest and straight-forward, "Tim invited me over again. He wants me to come by tonight. I don't know if he's really doing research or . . . or—"

"Oh, shit."

"Well, I really don't know if he is in fact gay."

"Come on, Todd, you can't be that stupid."

"Maybe I am." Todd hesitated, then added, "On the other hand, maybe I just need to find out something. Maybe I need to be sure."

"Sure of what?"

Sure that there really wasn't such a thing as the one and only, that special person, *the* person, that prince on a horse, and that Tim Chase wasn't the man Todd was meant to be with for the rest of his life. Shit, all that Todd did know was that he couldn't wash Tim Chase from his mind and that, yes, a huge wave of infatuation had knocked Todd over and was not only on the verge of sweeping him away, but tugging him from the coast of Rawlins. Shouldn't he, didn't he need to, find out if Tim Chase was the one with whom he was supposed to live happily ever after?

Finally Todd, albeit weakly, replied, "Listen, Rawlins, I just don't want to have any regrets, that's all."

"Great, I don't want you to end up with me as your second prize either."

"Wait, I didn't mean that to sound so—"

"You realize, don't you, that we're about two inches from putting Chase under close investigation for the murder of Andrew Lyman? What do you think of that?"

"Rawlins, come on, cut it out. You know he didn't kill anyone."

"Right, and neither did a certain other celebrity kill—"

Out of nowhere, someone started pounding on his door. Todd rubbed his head with the heel of his hand, but couldn't think, didn't know what to do. The heavy knocking on his door went on, but instead of ignoring it, which he easily could have, Todd seized the opportunity.

"Rawlins, someone's here. I gotta go."

A voice outside his office called, "Todd, you got a Federal Express package!"

"Listen," pleaded Todd into the telephone receiver, "I'll call you back."

"When?"

"In an hour."

"Maybe I won't be here."

"Please, Rawlins. Let's just both calm down and clear our heads. I'll call you back in an hour and then we'll figure this out, okay?"

"Sure," replied Rawlins, who then slammed down the phone.

Todd lowered the receiver back into its cradle, and then just sat there. Could things be any muckier? No, not at all. He just didn't know what to do, what to think. Why in the hell would he even be tempted to jeopardize his relationship with Rawlins? On the other hand, why did he feel so deeply touched by Tim Chase? And how had Chase done that, gotten to Todd so easily, so quickly? And why?

A few moments later Todd rolled his chair over and cracked the door. A large express envelope fell halfway in, and Todd grabbed it, then shut the door again. At first it didn't make any sense, he wasn't expecting anything. Or was he? He glanced at the label, saw that it had been sent from New York. Looking more closely, he realized that Suzanne Levine at *The National Times* had fulfilled her promise. Ripping open the envelope, a note and a back issue of the weekly rag tumbled out.

> Dear Todd,
>   Fun talking with you today—hope life is great out there in Minnie-zohta. Here's the back issue. All best,
>   Suzanne Levine

Todd picked up the old issue of *The National Times* and the headline in big bold print jumped right out at him: "Mean Queen Chase Denies 7 Year Gay Romance & Buries Boyfriend in Poverty." Right beneath that was nothing less than the studliest photograph Todd had ever seen of Tim Chase, his hair whisked back, the eyes warm and dark and seductive, the smile flashing. Everything about him said cute, adorable, hunky, sexy, charming, friendly, disarming, engaging. And all of it, Todd knew in his heart of hearts, was absolutely true, and then some. He'd held Tim Chase against him, groped that gorgeous body, and bathed in his charm. He wondered what it would have been like, doing the act with Chase, and then he found himself wanting to do nothing more than just that. Chase had to be gay, didn't he? After all, Todd had felt the passion, seen it, heard it, right?

Rawlins drifted out of Todd's mind, Chase surged in, and Todd imagined seeing lots more of Tim Chase. He pictured himself going back to that big house, spending the night. Spending many nights. And then? How serious might it be? Could it be? But was that the life Todd wanted, a life with one of the most famous men in the world? Maybe not, but, dear Lord, he was just so handsome, so nice, so . . . so . . . Who in the world would be fool enough to turn him down?

Todd's eyes tore back through the article, reading yet one more time about Tim Chase's romance with Rob Scott. Yes, it had to be true, didn't it? Tim had to have been in a long-term relationship with this guy, whom the journalist Marla Glore described as a beauty of a blond. And if so, Todd didn't doubt that Tim Chase had thrown him out, either. But had Scott really been beaten up and bruised? Had Tim hit him . . . or could Rob Scott have been something like drunk or high? In which case, could he have fallen? And if they'd been together, why had they blown apart? What had prompted the fury that had consumed the relationship? There was a story behind the story, but the one that had surfaced and been served to the American public was by no means, Todd knew, the truth. No, America got what it wanted, a vindicated prince. The court of laws had made sure that the real story remained buried.

Flipping into the inside of the issue and the rest of the piece, Todd recalled the other articles he'd read on Lexis-Nexis, including of course the one about the photograph of Chase in the arms of another man. Todd hadn't seen it, but he now realized that it might not have been doctored, that it could in fact be real. All the other post-trial pieces about Chase winning those eight million bucks for slander could easily have been crap as well, products of Hollywood studios and PR firms.

The inside of the issue was a gallery of photographs of the world of Tim Chase, including pictures of his gorgeous wife, Gwen Owens, their son, Jack, their L.A. mansion, numerous photos of Tim and his horses, Tim flying a jet, and even Vic, the loyal bodyguard. Not to be missed, of course, were the photos of Tim's alleged former boyfriend, Rob Scott, and Todd's eyes caught there, on the face of the handsome blond. And handsome he was, his chin small, his smile sweet. The two must have made quite the beautiful couple.

Todd ran his right hand over *The National Times,* pressing the pages flat against his desk. Staring blankly at the photographs of Tim Chase and his world, Todd was wondering if a life with any star, particularly one so closeted, could actually work, when suddenly he saw the answer that had so far alluded not only Rawlins and him, but also the entire police force.

Yes, studying one photograph in particular, it was all too clear who had in fact slit young Andrew Lyman's throat.

Chapter 41

Thirty minutes ago Rawlins had run a criminal background check on their prime suspect, Victor Radzinsky. Rather than turn to the Bureau of Research, he'd simply headed over to the old, beat-up teletype machine parked in one corner of Homicide and contacted the NCIC, the National Crime Information Computer. And what had come back was none too surprising: Victor M. Radzinsky was a convicted felon who'd served time in California for promoting prostitution. Foster was now in the process of contacting the Los Angeles authorities for the specifics, yet both Rawlins and Foster were assuming that he had in fact been pimping not women, but young boys. Whether this was one of Radzinsky's secondary duties for Tim Chase remained to be proven, but it was most definitely a possibility.

And now . . .

Rawlins had spoken with Todd several more times, and instinctively he knew that Todd, whether by chance or simply through good research, had just discovered the key to Andrew Lyman's murder. And while all Rawlins wanted to do was sit there and obsess about Todd and their rapidly cooling relationship, he had a job to do. Right, this was no time to slack off, particularly if Todd's information was going to lead to an arrest, which it certainly might.

After Todd's first call, Rawlins had consulted with Foster and agreed what must be done next. Grabbing another officer, Rawlins had gone down to Lake Harriet and, according to their arrangement, left a marked unit. Now it was almost one, and he'd returned to City

Hall and his corporatelike cube in Homicide. As he attempted to un-cover a turkey sandwich that had been sheathed in an overabundance of plastic wrap, he saw how stupid he'd been and just how much it had cost him. Would that he could do it all over again—things would be entirely different.

The phone on his desk began to ring, and he snatched it up. "Homicide, this is Sergeant Rawlins."

"Hello, Sergeant, this is Martha Lyman, Andrew's mother."

"Yes, hello," he said, wondering what might have come up. "What can I do for you?"

"I just wanted to let you know that I have a new phone number. My daughters and I are moving in with my sister for the next few months."

"I see. Has there been a—"

"I've left my husband. We'll be divorcing."

Her bluntness surprised him, but didn't. The harsh realities of farming had surely dealt her a life of absolutes—drought, flood, frost, debt—and taught her to deal with such things matter-of-factly, even coldly.

"I'm sorry to hear that." Trying to pry more out of her, Rawlins said, "I didn't know you were having problems."

"Let's just say that I've learned that Andy wasn't so different from his father after all." She paused only briefly, then concluded, "Here's my phone number in case you need to reach me. John will be staying on the farm, of course. You can reach him there."

Rawlins wrote down the number, and then Martha quickly hung up. She had, he realized, just confirmed what Todd had earlier told him, and Rawlins was just starting to take some notes when his phone rang a second time. Hoping this time it was him, he immediately picked it back up.

"Homicide, this is Sergeant Rawlins."

"Hi."

Recognizing the voice, Rawlins was immediately pleased that this guy had kept his promise. "Hey there. It's you, right, my witness?"

"Yep. I saw the car. I just swung by the lake over lunch and checked and saw the empty cop car."

"Thanks. And thanks for calling so promptly," said Rawlins, who, with so much on his mind, was having trouble keeping everything straight. "I just wanted to let you know that I think we have our guy."

"Really? Wow, that's wonderful."

"Yeah, it is. And it's all because of you, because of the tips you provided."

"No kidding?" replied the witness, his voice happy, even proud-sounding. "What happened?"

"Well, all the information you gave us just sort of fell into place. Particularly the identification of the car—that was very helpful. I can't say too much, but we're tying up all the loose ends now."

"Wow."

"So I just wanted to say thanks, and I wanted to ask if you'd check in with me regularly. You don't have to give me your name, we won't try and identify you, but I'd like you to call me tomorrow and the next day just in case we have some more questions. Can you do that? Can you call me in the morning?"

"Sure. How about ten? Can I call about then?"

"Ten would be fine. I'll make sure I'm here at my desk." Rawlins paused, then added, "There's something else I wanted to ask. You mentioned that you were a photographer and that you're working on a project. I'm not really interested in what you're actually doing—that's your business, of course—but I would like to know if you have any photographs of the man you saw down at the lake. Any chance?"

"Of . . . of who?"

"The bald man you spotted is our primary suspect, of course, and I'd like to know if you have any pictures of him."

"Him? Well . . . well, no. At least I don't think so."

"Could you check? We'd all really appreciate it."

"Sure . . ."

"Good, check and then call me at ten tomorrow, okay? With any luck we'll be making our arrest within the next twenty-four hours."

Rawlins hung up, then sat at his desk, staring down at the turkey sandwich, which was finally uncovered and lying plainly in front of him. Was any of this really happening? Better yet, would their plan really work?

A few seconds later, Foster returned to their shared cubicle and saw Rawlins sitting there, staring at his sandwich.

"What are you looking so glum about, pal?" asked Foster. "Didn't your little witness fellow call?"

Rawlins shrugged. "He did. Everything's all set up."

"Excellent."

"I talked to Todd again too."

"Oh, so there's the problem."

"We talked everything through two or three times, and I really do think his theory about the murder is right." Rawlins could barely force himself to admit this one additional thing, barely force himself to say, "And Todd said he's going to go ahead and do it, he's going to go back to Tim Chase's tonight."

"No, shit, you're really going to let him?"

"Like I could stop him? It's his choice and he's determined."

Foster came over and squeezed him on the shoulder, and said, "Don't worry, pal. We're going to get the guy who killed that kid, and you're going to get your fellow back, you'll see."

"I sure as hell hope so."

In any case, Rawlins was going to do everything he could to make sure that was the case. Absolutely, because from the moment Todd stepped out of his condo and headed over to Tim Chase's tonight, Rawlins was going to be there. Yes, if Todd was determined to go fishing, then Rawlins was going to tail him, shadow him, and spy on him every second of every minute just to make sure, as they say, that Tim Chase didn't bite.

Chapter 42

Todd couldn't say that he wasn't glad to be back in the yellow brick mansion, but he certainly hadn't expected to be back here so soon.

It was just after eight, they sat again on the couch in the huge living room, and the thing that scared Todd about Tim Chase was how attentive he was. It was no wonder everyone fell in love with him, as Todd sensed he himself was now doing. And when Tim poured him a glass of cabernet, Todd felt like the most important person on the planet. But how was that possible? How could someone like Tim Chase give a rat's ass about him, Todd Mills, an investigative television reporter from fly-over land? After all, this guy swooning over him was a superstar.

"This is my favorite cab," said Tim as he put the bottle on the coffee table and moved closer to Todd.

Todd glanced at the bottle and knew from the label that it had cost over two hundred bucks. Perhaps that was pocket change to Tim, but . . .

So how, Todd couldn't help but wonder, was this going to go tonight? Would this be a simple continuation of last night's foray? Or?

Tim Chase reached over and squeezed Todd's shoulder. "You're a good guy, Todd Mills."

Todd was melting right there on the couch, of course, but proving true to his Midwestern roots, he held back, and simply asked, "Why do you say that?"

Chase laughed. "Because you're a nice guy, because—"

"You have people swarming over you all the time, surely some of them are decent."

"Yeah, but none of them are genuine, none of them are real. Actually, most of them are fools."

"Can I take that as a compliment?"

"Absolutely."

Staring straight into Tim Chase's eyes, Todd saw it again, that unbearable sense of loneliness. Todd knew only too well what it was like to be on display day after day, to be judged by your image, and to have any number of people ready at any moment to proclaim your fall. But Tim Chase's life had to be a million times worse. Todd reached over and patted Tim on the knee, a gesture that made the star smile almost sadly.

Tim ventured, "Like I said, I have very few safe harbors."

This was playing with fire, and it was right then that Todd knew he shouldn't have come. No, the cost was going to be too much, for his soul would be paying for this for months if not years.

Only the sound of voices from the hall roused Tim from a near sense of melancholy, and he said, "Come on."

Setting down their glasses of wine, they crossed the large living room to the entry hall, where they found the three other members of Tim Chase's small tribe. Gwen Owens and Maggie, holding little Jack by each hand, were just making their way to the front door.

"Daddy!" shouted the boy. "We're getting ice cream!"

"You are?"

"Yeah, and we're walking!"

"Well, you be good!"

Todd watched as Tim gave Gwen a light kiss on the cheek, then gently roughed his son's hair.

Gwen, wearing a light brown suede coat, turned to Todd and said, "I don't think Jack has actually walked anywhere before, certainly not from our house in L.A."

"Well, have fun."

"And you too," she said with a smirk.

Maggie looked at Todd with a kind, welcoming smile, and said, "Nice to see you again."

"Likewise."

Todd noticed that even though it was almost dark Gwen had a pair of large sunglasses perched atop her head. He presumed she never went anywhere without them, her makeshift disguise.

Like a doting husband and father, Tim ushered the little trio out the door, bid them well, then turned back to Todd, another huge grin on his face.

"Alone at last."

Todd's stomach flinched. "Really?"

"Yep. The cook, the trainer, and obviously Vic—they're all gone. Oh, my God, it's unbelievable. It's just us."

"Tim, what's that mean? What do you want from me?"

"So many questions."

"But—"

"Shh," said Tim, coming over and placing his right forefinger on Todd's lips.

The next moment Tim moved even closer, reaching out and pulling Todd into his embrace. Todd held back, determined not to fall, at least not so quickly, so easily.

Todd asked, "Are you going to call this research again?"

"Like I said, so many questions."

Somewhat reluctantly, Todd let himself be pulled and enfolded into Tim Chase's arms. But was it lust, was it want on Tim's part, or just some big game? Todd reached out, embraced Tim too, hugging him, feeling that powerful back. As if in reply, Tim started trembling, a deep, slow but steady vibration that came from a pained corner deep inside him.

"Hey, are you okay?" asked Todd, holding him tighter.

Tim's head, tucked against Todd's neck, went up and down. "I'm gay."

So there it was, the fog of deceit had lifted, exposing that very vulnerable truth, and he replied, "Of course."

Todd rubbed Tim's back, tried to pass from his flesh through Tim's some of the strength, some of the wisdom, and some of the pride that Todd was still discovering day after day. Yes, whatever label he chose to wear, Tim Chase, America's hunk and idol, and one of the top-grossing actors in the world, was by no means straight, his lips having just betrayed the secret that Hollywood moguls and public relations firms had worked so hard to conceal.

His words all but a whisper into Tim's ear, Todd asked, "Does your wife care?"

"Off the record?"

"Yes, you fool, of course."

Softly, easily, and without pretense, Tim said, "Gwen's gay too. Maggie's her partner, not our nanny. They've been together for nine years, longer than we've been married."

"No shit?"

"Yeah."

Stripped of his image, Tim fell completely into Todd's arms, just an ordinary person full of passion, desperate for touch, hungry for love. Todd tilted his head back as the firm lips came up his neck, over his chin, to his mouth. Yes, Todd realized, he very well might leap off a cliff for this guy.

"You know," whispered Tim in Todd's ear, "I've been looking for someone like you."

Most definitely, Todd could tumble real hard, real fast.

So there it was, Tim and Gwen, America's leading husband and wife actors, were nothing less than a queen and dyke. They obviously loved each other very much, just as they were devoted to their little boy. Tim was also obviously quite fond of Maggie, and this whole situation seemed to work quite well for all of them. It was, quite simply, a logical solution to a horribly complicated situation.

Unable to rein in his eternal curiosity, Todd asked, "What about your son? Are you his biological father?"

"Absolutely."

"So you've been to bed with her?"

"Gwen?" he laughed. "Oh, God no. She wouldn't have me, and I couldn't get it up for her. We love each other, but we just don't work like that. That's a turkey baster baby."

"Are you serious?"

"Of course. We had a doctor do it and everything, but . . ." He then took Todd's right hand and placed it on his own swollen crotch. "Enough of that stuff. Now, come on, let's go finish our wine on the patio and then . . . then see what happens."

Todd knew where this was going to lead, just as he knew there was no turning back, not now, not tonight, and so he waited while the actor fetched their glasses, then silently followed Tim through the grand hall and down the staircase. A few long and divinely tense moments later they entered the tiled pool room. Tonight Tim didn't turn on the brass sconces surrounding the pool, but instead lit three fat candles next to the whirlpool. And tonight he didn't pull shut the blinds covering the French doors that led outside, but rather threw open the doors. He next picked up his glass of wine, then turned to Todd and in the faint light smiled simply and easily. Taking three steps, he was next to Todd, kissing him on the neck and taking him by the hand.

"Come on, let's go outside."

"But aren't you worried, aren't you . . ."

"Shh. It's okay," said Tim kissing him one more time. "I mean, it's not okay, but I can only take it so much."

"On your scale it must be awful."

He shrugged. "It's a decision I made, and now I'm pretty much used to it, but every now and then I just got to get out and be myself. Come on."

When Todd felt Tim's lips nibbling his ear he realized that he could easily follow him anywhere. And do anything.

It was cool outside. And dark. The dry fall leaves rustled overhead in a gentle wind, and Todd peered up at the sky and saw a sprinkling of stars emerging as the evening faded into night. Standing on the slate patio that was surrounded by a low stone wall, Todd sipped his wine and looked out over the backyard, which fell away, cascading down a hill that was covered with a jungle of bushes.

"I spend so much of my time inside and behind closed windows just so people won't see me," said Tim in a giddy, almost nervous voice, "that sometimes it . . . it makes me go absolutely nuts!"

Todd turned around to see him frantically going after the buttons of his shirt and ripping them open. Seconds later he yanked off his shirt and threw it high overhead. The next instant he grabbed at his belt buckle and pulled it away, unfastened his pants and ripped down the zipper. He hopped around as he pulled off his pants and his socks, then stood there in white boxer shorts. Todd glanced across the yard, wondered if anyone was lurking out there.

"Tim, aren't you a little worried that—"

"Anyone out there?" he shouted with a whoop. "This is your chance to see Tim Chase buck naked!"

"But—"

"Don't worry," he said out of the corner of his mouth, "anybody snaps a picture of me and I'll sue 'em!"

With that he grabbed at his underwear, yanked it down, and kicked it away. Standing straight up, he clenched his fists and stretched them to the sky, then, as if he were running in place, did a little dance and whooped yet again. Stripped and exposed, the super-star then ran over to the low stone wall, jumped up, and ran along the top of it, laughing and yelping.

"Here I am, anyone wanna see? Come and get it, fresh Chase, fresh Tim Chase!"

Todd, holding his wineglass, stood there as Tim came charging along the stone wall and all but threw himself against Todd. With little choice, Todd tossed his nearly full glass over the wall and into the grass and grabbed Tim, who atop the wall stood a good foot and a half above him. Unable to stop himself, Todd wrapped his arms around the top of Tim's thighs and buried his face into the smooth, hard chest. How was he supposed to resist? Better yet, wouldn't he be a fool if he did?

"I'm glad we met," said Tim, bending forward and kissing Todd on the crown of his head. "You seem very real to me."

Rubbing his face deep into Tim's chest and running a hand up his ass, Todd mumbled, "Yeah, well, you don't." Seemingly out of nowhere, Todd asked, "Let me ask you this, what do you do for sex? I mean, how does someone so famous, so recognizable get . . . get . . ."

"Laid?"

"Well, yeah."

"That's Victor's department. He always finds me the best."

"Like Andrew?"

"Well, aren't you the nosy one?" He laughed, then lunged forward, smashing his crotch against Todd's clothed chest. "Enough of your questions, alright?"

"Sure."

Todd kissed him on the stomach, then stood back up and kissed him on one nipple, next the other.

"Come on," said Tim, pulling slightly away. "Let's go inside and finish what we started last night."

Thinking he heard something off in the bushes, Todd glanced around, then replied, "Sure."

Todd didn't put up the least bit of resistance as Tim, naked and taunting, took Todd by the hand and led him across the patio and through the open French doors. As they entered the candlelit pool room, Todd's heart began to beat in nervous anticipation. He reached out for Tim and pulled him right against him, and they kissed, long and hard and deep. Firmly and slowly, Todd ran his hand up and down Tim's muscular back, and Tim grabbed Todd's shirt, pulled at it, popping away three buttons, and then reaching inside and desperately waving his hand over the hair on Todd's chest.

"I want you," whispered Tim. "And I hope you want me too."

"Absolutely." Trying to express his last bit of hesitation, Todd said, "It's just . . ."

"Shh. You're with me now, so relax, just relax, and forget about that other guy, okay?"

The next instant Tim spun away, trotting across the tile decking and to a stack of towels. In the dim light, Todd watched as he reached into the subtle folds of terry cloth and pulled out something black.

Holding out a mask, Tim said, "Here, I want you to put this on."

"What?"

"Please? Just put it on and let me do everything. Let me undress you, let me take you all the way. . . ."

It wasn't a Halloween disguise, a black mask with slits cut for the eyes. No, it was a black blindfold with an elastic band.

"Are you sure?" said Todd.

"Absolutely. It'll heighten all your other senses, particularly your sense of touch. Here, let me do it."

"Well . . ."

Todd lowered his head slightly and let Tim slip it on, placing the mask over his eyes and the band around the back of his head. In an instant, the soft light disappeared and Todd tumbled into a world of darkness. Blindly reaching out, he groped for Tim's arm.

"Okay, now what?"

"Just let me do it all."

Vulnerable and helpless, Todd stood there as Tim started kissing his neck as lightly as a manic butterfly. An instant later he sensed one of Chase's meaty hands painfully flutter across his crotch. Blindfolded though he was, Todd saw it all in the darkness of his mind's eye, and he rode that vibrant image, that wild ride of lust, seeing but not seeing, witnessing but not, as Tim Chase, naked and stoked to the max, hovered all over and around him. It was more than Todd could bear, and he naturally reached up, begging to stroke the body and the tool lingering just inches before him.

Firmly pushing his hand away, Chase, his voice deep and dark, said, "You can't do anything—I'm in charge."

As unbearable as it was, Todd simply stood there as Tim slowly peeled the last of his shirt from his body, dropping it on the floor. And then he let himself be led along, followed deeper into this black charade.

"Where are—"

"Sh. Just do as I say—sit down."

Blindly complying, Todd let Tim lower him to the floor, where he sat on a long cushion. Tim then pushed him back, forcing him to lie, and started fumbling with Todd's belt. Todd reached down to help, to speed up this painfully slow process.

Batting away Todd's hand, Tim shouted, "I'm in charge!"

In an instant Todd understood just how terrified Chase was of how people would see him. Hence the blindfold—I can see you, you can't see me. Hence the control—I'll say when and where and why.

Oh, God . . .

He thought about Rawlins, where they were headed. Or weren't. Everything between them had been so perfect until a farm boy and an actor had come into their lives and thrown everything askew. And now this, his conscience pathetically moaned as his body beaded with silky sweat. What was he doing? Why the hell had he agreed to come here?

But then of course Tim rubbed that smooth, gorgeous face on the hair around and above Todd's navel, and Todd was right back there, right back in a whirlpool of lust. And before Todd knew it, Tim was pinning Todd's arms up and behind his head and mounting Todd.

Todd heard it first, the sound of footsteps on the patio. He flinched, struggled to get up, but Tim forced him down.

"I've got you!"

"But—"

"Don't move!"

And then a voice behind both of them loudly ordered, "That's right, don't move! Don't either one of you fucking move an inch!"

But Tim did just that, he rolled off Todd, grabbed a towel, clumsily wrapping it around his waist.

"I mean it, Tim, just stay right there or I'll blow your fucking brains out!"

Todd ripped off the blindfold and sat up. A dark unseen figure stood in the doorway, the gun in his hand perfectly obvious. Todd couldn't see the face, but of course it was him, of course he'd come spying on them.

"This time you're not going to get away with it, Tim. You're not going to pin it on someone like Vic."

"Don't be ridiculous!"

"You're not going to get away with it because when you fucked Andrew you left your sperm and your hair and your stupid fingerprints all over him and everything else in that rat hole of an apartment. I know how you work, Tim. I know very well."

"Fuck you!"

"You can't bring boys to your own house because someone might see. So Vic finds them, blindfolds them, and then you screw 'em and walk away."

Todd's eyes were trained on the figure as it moved into the pool room and as the dim light began to glow on the handsome face of Tim Chase's former lover, Rob Scott. Yes, it was exactly as Todd had surmised after seeing his picture in *The National Times.*

"I knew you'd do something like that, Tim, like screw Andrew Lyman," said Scott, amused by his own brilliance, "so I stole your knife and then I waited . . . and followed you and did the terrible little deed moments after you left."

"You bastard!"

"Actually, I thought it was kind of brilliant. Unfortunately the police are about to arrest the wrong guy, so I'm going to have to do it again—I'm going to have to kill your little fuck buddy here. Only this time I'm going to do it a little differently—I'm not only going to kill this guy you're about to screw, I'm going to kill you too. That way there'll be no questions at all, it'll be perfectly clear to the cops. And eventually they'll blame you for that kid's death too. Isn't that great? In the end of ends, the world's going to learn exactly what I learned—that their hero's not only a faggot, but a real son of a bitch. What do you think of that, hey?"

Todd didn't doubt him, not for an instant. He could hear the desperation in his voice, sense the determination in his stance. Oh, shit, why had he ever gotten involved with Tim Chase in the first place?

Taking another step into the pool room, Rob Scott trained his gun on Todd, and said, "You know, I'm going to like doing this. It's always been a fantasy of mine—granted a dark one—to walk in and find my lover screwing someone else. I always pictured myself going ballistic, which is exactly what I'm going to do. Ta-ta, Todd, you're first. It's been nice knowing you, however brief."

Todd's body flash-flooded with panic. No, this wasn't supposed to happen, no way. This wasn't part of the plan. They'd talked it through, worked out every detail, tried to anticipate how it might come down, and things definitely weren't supposed to go this far. Yet apparently they'd misjudged, horribly so, and rolling on his side, Todd curled into a ball. And the very next second there was indeed a blast of a gun, the sound of which exploded in the room. Todd shouted out, braced himself for the agonizing pain.

Instead, there was nothing.

As his pulse roared and sweat beaded on his forehead, Todd looked over at Tim, who stood paralyzed, the towel tight now around his waist. Todd then looked at the figure of Rob Scott, who stumbled back, grabbed for one of the French doors, and finally fell to the tile floor and lay there quite still.

Seeing two men rush from the patio into the room, Todd shouted, "Shit, Rawlins, I thought you were going to let him really do it!"

While Foster, his gun still drawn, stopped at the body, Rawlins rushed straight to Todd.

"You okay?" demanded Rawlins.

Nodding as he climbed to his feet, Todd replied, "Yeah, but . . . but that was hard, knowing that you were out there watching the whole time."

Grabbing Todd's forearm and giving it a good solid squeeze, he said, "Well, I have to tell you it wasn't easy watching. I'll have to say this much, you're not a bad actor."

Most of it was, of course, an act. A good part of it wasn't. But Todd would tell Rawlins that later, just as he knew Rawlins would understand. And he would, wouldn't he?

Turning around, Todd saw the lifeless body of Tim Chase's former lover, Rob Scott, sprawled on the floor. Foster, who was kneeling and pressing his hand against the man's neck, looked up and shook his head.

"He's gone."

"Oh, God," moaned Tim, turning away. "I didn't want it to end like this, I really didn't."

"Of course not," said Todd.

Tim covered his eyes with his right hand, and Todd broke away from Rawlins and went to the actor, putting his arms around him.

"I'm sorry."

"He . . . he just went crazy," mumbled Tim through his grief. "At first, you know, we were good. Really good. There was Rob and me, and Maggie and Gwen. I thought we had everything, that we had it all figured out. I don't know, I guess I was gone too much, spent too much time on the sets. I guess I was too involved in myself. Rob got into a fast crowd out there in L.A. He got into coke and then into some really hard stuff. I tried to help him . . . I did what I could, I really did."

"I'm sure."

"But he just spent everything on drugs. I told him he had to stop, that he had to get into a treatment program but . . . but . . . finally I had to throw him out. I just had to cut him off."

Which was when, Tim had told Todd and Rawlins earlier today, Rob Scott had gone to *The National Times* and sold his story. Not only was he desperate for money, he was desperate and determined to get revenge by outing Tim Chase and ruining him completely. And in a very real way, Tim Chase was ruined, for if he was fearful before, he was ultra-paranoid now, terrified of intimacy.

There'd been no witness, no paparazzi-style photographer who'd spied Vic's comings and goings—there'd only been Rob Scott posing as such and trying his best to manipulate the sequence of events. Yes, it was clear now that Rob Scott had stolen Tim's fishing knife, used it to kill Andrew Lyman, and then returned the bloodied thing to Tim's Land Rover. Watching what Tim would do, how he would handle the situation, Rob had then followed Vic down to Lake Harriet, where he'd seen the bodyguard throw the weapon in the lake. And then . . .

Holding Tim in his arms, Todd thought how it might very well have worked too. It most certainly would have if the WLAK camera hadn't caught one particular person on the banks of the lake when the sheriff's team had been diving for the knife. Todd had studied the videotape of that day, of course, and had searched the faces of the on-lookers, but he hadn't known who was who until he'd seen the photograph of Rob Scott in the back issue of *The National Times*. Realizing it was obviously more than a coincidence that Tim Chase's lover from California would be in Minneapolis, let alone down at Lake Harriet, Todd had called Rawlins. Surmising that Andrew Lyman's murder might very well be the work of a jealous man bent on destroying his former lover—which he'd already tried to do by cooperating with *The National Times* in the original story—Todd, Rawlins, Foster, and even Tim Chase had formulated a plan. Simply, they hoped to draw Rob Scott out by enraging him with the belief that the police were about to arrest Vic and not Tim Chase for the Lyman murder. Scott had come to Chase's mansion once to plant the knife, and they hoped he'd come back again, which he certainly had, meeting with the direst of consequences.

Tim broke away from Todd, wandering outside, where he sat on the low stone wall and buried his face in his hands. Was one of the most adored stars, wondered Todd, destined to be trapped in a bub-ble of loneliness, one from which he'd never be able to escape? Quite possibly.

Rawlins came up behind Todd and took him by the hand. "I checked on Jordy just a little while ago. He's awake now and he's going to be okay."

"What happened?"

"I got a statement this afternoon from the witness who tried to stop him from jumping. Evidently, Jordy thought the guy was chasing him."

"Oh, my God. So it was nothing? No one was after him?"

"Right." Rawlins looked down, then raised his eyes. "Are we okay, Todd?"

None of this was going to be easy, not by any means, but he had to trust in one simple thing, and he said, "I've always loved you . . . and I always will."

"Then can we start over?"

"No, Rawlins, I don't want to start over. I don't want to go back to the beginning. Besides, I don't think we can—we've learned too much. Let's just keep on going from here and eventually we'll get wherever we're supposed to. Deal?"

"You bet."

From there the night of course proceeded the way these things were wont to do. Foster and Rawlins rolled the Lyman case into this one, and they went about it all according to the book. First came the team from the Bureau of Investigation, who filmed and photographed, dusted and collected. And when they were done several hours later, the Medical Examiner came and removed the body of Rob Scott, all of which was caught on film by the throng of media folk smashed against the iron fence of the Mount Curve mansion leased to movie star Tim Chase.

By virtue of his promise to Tim, Todd gave up the story completely. In spite of that, WLAK management and every other reporter in town tried to get something out of Todd, some kind of inside scoop, some infinitesimal tidbit, but Todd was mum, completely so. In fact, he took the following week off and hid at Rawlins's duplex apartment, watching somewhat amusedly yet ultimately sadly as the truth was blotted out by a variation on the real story—cooked up by Tim Chase's publicity people of course—and spread across the country and around the world. Fearing a psychotic fan, the star's spokesperson claimed, actor Tim Chase proved himself a real-life hero, slipping his wife and son and nanny out of the house, then offering himself as bait for a police trap. The only quasi-mention of Todd was one journal, which stated that Chase had been warned of the danger by a local (and unnamed) television reporter.

Yes, with headlines like "A Real-Life Action Hero, Chase Protects Wife, Son, \& Home From Psycho Stalker," the disinformation was gobbled up by Tim Chase's legions of fans, leaving Todd to wonder who were the real heroes and the real victims in this strange world.